HEAVY SAND

ANATOLI RYBAKOV

HEAVY SAND

Translated from the Russian
by Harold Shukman

THE VIKING PRESS   NEW YORK

LIBRARY OF CONGRESS CATALOGING IN PUBLICATION DATA
Rybakov, Anatoliĭ Naumovich.
Heavy sand.
Translation of Tiazhelyĭ pesok.
1. Jews in Russia—Fiction. 2. World War,
1939–1945—Fiction. I. Title.
PG3476.R87T513   891.73′44   80-51773
ISBN 0-670-36499-1

Printed in the United States of America
Set in Plantin

Oh that my grief were throughly
weighed, and my calamity laid
in the balances together!
For now it would be heavier than the
sand of the sea: therefore my
words are swallowed up.

Job 6:2–3

1

And Jacob served seven years for Rachel;
and they seemed unto him but a few days,
for the love he had to her.

Genesis 29 : 20

Was there something special about my father? Not really.
True, he was born in Switzerland, in Basel, and there weren't
too many Swiss-born people in our little town. As a matter of
fact, he was the only one. Otherwise, he was just an ordinary
bootmaker, and not even a very good one. His father, my
grandfather, was a professor of medicine in Basel, and his
brothers were all doctors. My father was supposed to have
become a doctor, too, but he became a bootmaker instead.

My name, as you know, is Ivanovsky. My father was also
Ivanovsky, my Basel grandfather was Ivanovsky, my uncles
and cousins, who are still living in Basel, are all Ivanovskys.
Perhaps they have slightly changed it to look a bit more
German, say, Iwanowski, but, one way or the other, it is still
Ivanovsky. My great-grandfather was born in the village of
Ivanovka, and in those days it was the custom to take the
name of the town or village where you were born. Great-
grandfather was quite well off, so when his only son, my
grandfather, finished high-school, he sent him off to study in
Switzerland. Grandfather finished university in Basel and
there he married the daughter of a doctor who owned a large
clinic. The father-in-law died and the clinic went to grand-

father and after him to his two elder sons, my uncles. My father was also one of the heirs and had the right to part of the clinic, but he wasn't a doctor, he lived not in Basel but in Russia, he had done nothing for the clinic and he expected nothing.

My grandfather Ivanovsky had three sons – 'There was an old man with three sons, the eldest was a clever fellow, sturdy and tall, the middle one neither this nor that, and the youngest was a fool . . .' I don't know if my eldest uncle was cleverer than the middle one, I don't think so. They both finished university and became doctors of medicine and the owners of one of the best clinics in Europe, so they can't have been idiots. As for my father, he was no fool either, but he didn't have a university education, though he had the same opportunity as his elder brothers. My father was the baby of the family, the *mizinikel*, as we would say, meaning the little finger, and being the smallest he was also the favourite. Of the three, he was the only one who took after their mother, a very delicate German woman. The older boys were like grandfather Ivanovsky, strapping bulls. You can see from this old snapshot – the two in white caps and white bathing robes are the elder boys – don't you think they look like butchers? Just the same, they were famous all over Europe as surgeons, real masters of their craft. And this is a shot of my father, fair-haired, with pale blue eyes, slim, shy and very handsome, his mother's and father's little darling. Grandfather, Professor Ivanovsky, was a busy man, running the clinic with the two elder sons and seeing his patients, but he loved his wife and he also loved his youngest son, my father. My father's name was Jakob or, in Russian, Yakov, so my patronymic is Yakovlevich, and my full name is Boris Yakovlevich Ivanovsky.

As my father, Jakob, was the youngest and the favourite, his mother, my grandmother-to-be, tended to keep him close by her. On their walks in the streets of Basel, people would stop and ask her whose little angel he was. This pleased my grandmother, as it would any mother when her child is admired.

People say that at nineteen my father was a real Dorian Gray. What? You think I must have been a Dorian Gray myself? I don't think so. If I looked like Dorian Gray, it must have been when he ripped up his portrait. Still, out of all my brothers, and there were five of us, only Sasha, the youngest, and myself were like father. As you can see, I have fair hair and blue eyes, and am the same height as father, five foot ten. The others took after mother. She was a strong woman, and my brothers were tall, over six foot, big-boned and black-haired, like gipsies. How old do you think I am? Not more than sixty? You think so? Thanks very much! I really wasn't too bad as a young man. I wouldn't want to boast, but a fact is a fact. When I was still only a boy and worked as a bootmaker, the smartest young women would only have me to make their shoes, and when I used to measure their feet, I can tell you, it felt like an electric current flowing. But that's all gone, water under the bridge, evaporated. Let's go back to my father.

When father finished high-school and was preparing to enter the university, the idea cropped up of visiting Russia to see the ancestral sights. Quite why they had this idea I really can't say. I suppose they thought it would be a good thing for a boy who had just completed high-school and is about to start on his university education to see something of the world. And, then, grandfather had long dreamed of visiting the place of his birth and his forefathers' graves, his mother-land, in fact, and I suppose my grandmother also wanted to do something nice for her little darling. After all, her Jakob was not like his older brothers, who were men of affairs, practical, realists. Jakob was a dreamer, a romantic. Grand-mother wasn't even sure he ought to become a doctor, but as they all seemed to have been born doctors, at least let him not be a surgeon, but a physician, say, or better still a psychiatrist, like Freud.

So it was decided. Jakob's papers were submitted to the university, or perhaps he was simply registered, I don't know how these things are done in Switzerland, but it was all arranged, and they set off for Russia, my grandfather, Professor Ivanovsky, and my future father, the handsome, young, fair-haired Jakob from Basel, Switzerland. That was in 1909, nearly seventy years ago.

Try to imagine the feelings of a young man from Basel, travelling through Russia in 1909. I haven't been to Basel or Switzerland, but I've spent two years in Germany, during the war, in the army, and after the war with the occupation, and I think I've got a fairly good idea of what Basel and Switzerland are like. A beautiful country, the Alps, Lake Geneva. But we have mountains and lakes, too, just as beautiful. Not that I'm saying that Russia is the most beautiful country in the world. The song 'Bulgaria is a lovely country, but Russia's the best one of all' is obviously meant for Russians to sing, and I imagine that to a Bulgarian Bulgaria is as nice as anywhere else. Even so, you can imagine a boy of nineteen, daydreaming and impressionable, coming from Switzerland, travelling two or three days through Russia and looking out of the train window at the endless steppes, the tiny villages on the horizon, the whitewashed peasant cottages of the Ukraine, and the cherry orchards under the hot southern sun, the sky full of stars, the domes of churches, moustachioed Ukrainians, and the Ukrainian girls in their bright bead necklaces. This isn't your sedate, orderly Basel. Also, the young man knows that it was in these steppes that his father was born, and this was bound to make a big impression on him. Perhaps his heart wasn't gripped, as ours is when we return home to the motherland, and as no doubt grandfather's was when he saw Russia for the first time in nearly forty years, but even so, it made a very powerful impression on him, and later he told how he had been unable to turn away from the window, or tear himself away from our vast open spaces, or from the quiet little railway halts, the feather grass, the copses. Add to this that, apart from Switzerland, he had seen nothing. They had come via Austria, and I don't think Austria has anything special to offer by comparison with Switzerland.

In this state of mind, the young man arrived in our quiet, hot little southern town, and walked along the sunny, sandy street where his father was born, and where his grandfather and grandmother lived, a fairly wide street, as streets in steppe townships usually are, lined on both sides by little wooden houses with blue-painted shutters, wooden fences and strong gates, small front gardens, poplar trees, and not a soul in sight.

Naturally, everybody knew that the son of the late Ivanovsky had come to see his homeland and to show it to his son, so that the boy should not forget the family's origins, and, naturally, everyone wanted to have a look. But our folks are considerate, and nobody came out on to the street to crowd round and goggle at the middle-aged Ivanovsky and his young son, though they did open their curtains slightly and have a quiet look at them through their windows. After all, it was an event, people coming from Switzerland to look at the street and the house where their forefathers had lived.

However, one person did go out into the street, only one person went out to look at these Swiss, not through the window, but straight in the eye. You've guessed it, that person was my future mother, Rachel.

'Are they princes, or something?' she asked. 'Do I have to look at them through a window, as though I'm in prison?'

She went out and leaned on the little gate, and looked my grandfather and my future father straight in the eye. Imagine the scene. Here comes this handsome, fair-haired, immaculate young man in his foreign suit, wearing a tie and stylish boots, a young man from the neat city of Basel, where he was used to seeing immaculate German girls in white pinafores, here comes this young German, along the street in this hot southern town with its heavy sunbaked sand, and he sees, leaning over a gate, a bronzed girl, in a skimpy old dress that reaches to her knees, he sees her shapely bare legs, a waist he could encircle with two hands, he sees her lovely thick, black hair, her eyes that are bluer than blue, and her teeth that are white as sugar. And as for her, she gazes straight at him with her big blue eyes, without any modesty, even with a touch of brazenness, for she is a pert sixteen-year-old girl from a small southern Ukrainian town, the daughter of a bootmaker. No manners, she just didn't know any better, you see. She had never seen anything like this boy before. It wasn't only that he came from Switzerland, which didn't mean anything to her, anyway, but she had never seen a Jewish boy with fair hair and blue eyes and dressed like the son of a governor-general. She had only ever seen the boys on her street, tough, sunburnt bootmakers, leather-workers, tailors, wagon-drivers, loaders. And this was the first time she had ever seen such a pale young man with blue eyes, immaculate, neat and handsome like a young god.

What can one say? This was the Moment, with a capital M. It was love at first sight. This girl became my father's destiny, the wife to whom it was fated he should be bound. And he was bound to her for the rest of his life, just as our forefather Jacob was bound to his Rachel.

Many years later, father told us that when he saw mother standing at the gate, barefoot, in her short, torn dress, he fell in love with her the way the Prince fell in love with Cinderella, and he married her so that he could carry her off to Switzerland. But mother said that when she saw this pale handsome young man, dying of heat in his foreign clothes, with his waistcoat and white stand-up starched collar, she took pity on him, and that was the only reason she married him. They were joking, of course. They were joking, because they loved each other. Let's get back to events, however.

When grandfather and father came from Switzerland, there were no Ivanovskys left in the town. Grandfather's father had died long before, and both his sisters had died, too. But the sisters had left children and they in turn had children.

In those days, especially in a little township, a visiting foreigner was automatically taken for a millionaire, and in no time at all such a millionaire will acquire a whole tribe of relations. At least, that's what would happen if our story took place in some impoverished *shtetl* of the sort Sholom Aleichem wrote about, where the people lived on air. You couldn't say that about our town. Our town was different from the other *shtetls* in the Pale of Jewish Settlement, the only part of the old empire where the Jews had the right to live. In the north of Chernigov province, next door to the province of Mogilev, it is no longer the Ukraine proper, but rather Byelorussia, then you have Oryol and Bryansk and you're already in Russia. Also we had a big railway station, and although these were still Tsarist times when, as you know, the minorities – the Jews in particular – were being persecuted, the people of our town were anything but beggars. They practised trades and had status, working as tanners, wagon-drivers, loaders, and some were craftsmen, such as bootmakers, like Rakhlenko, my maternal grandfather.

Near the town was a pine forest, which was a healthy place for anybody, but especially so for people suffering from lung disease. The forest with its dry air from the steppes was simply a life-saver for such people. There was also a little river with a beautiful sandy beach. It was paradise! In the summer people came on holiday from Chernigov and Kiev, and even from Moscow and Petersburg. And people on holiday, as you know, need looking after. There's always plenty of work going where they are, especially for a bootmaker. The vacationer goes for a stroll, scrapes the sole off his shoe or knocks off a heel, and it has to be repaired quickly, urgently, instantly. But our bootmaking business wasn't built up only on repairs. By then the town already had its own tannery. The district was rich in cattle, and when the cattle were slaughtered the skins were sent to the tannery. Well, where there's leather you stitch boots, as they say. Even before the Revolution we had many bootmakers in our town making footwear for sale. After the Revolution a cooperative workshop started up, then a footwear factory. Of course, our town isn't Kimry and our factory isn't *Express Footwear*, but its products are not bad at all, and I say that as a specialist shoemaker.

Anyway, the people of the town were hard-working people, they made ends meet, owed nothing to anybody and valued their self-respect. And although the event I am talking about was exceptional – say what you like, a professor, a doctor of medicine, from Switzerland, a local, one of us who left this very street nearly forty years ago – still, it wasn't an earthquake. In one of Sholom Aleichem's *shtetls* it might have caused an earthquake, but in ours, no.

That's why nobody, apart from my mother, went out on to the street, and why nobody, apart from genuine relations, tried to impose themselves as kin. The closest relative turned out to be a niece of grandfather's, the daughter of his sister, a middle-aged woman who was married to a blacksmith, as a matter of fact a first-class, hereditary blacksmith – he was even called Kuznetsov (meaning the son of a blacksmith). At a certain time names were given according to trade, as well as where you came from. People would ask, who does he belong to ? Oh, he's the blacksmith's son, so he's Kuznetsov, and the son of the tanner is Kozhevnikov, and the turner's son, Slesarev, and so on. Our Swiss guests were on their way to the Kuznetsovs when my future father saw my future mother.

Naturally, they didn't go straight to the Kuznetsovs. On their arrival they stopped at the hotel. It was quite a clean hotel, owned by a widow, a Polish woman, Madame Yanzhvetska. Though it was summer and the height of the season, they gave grandfather the best room, not the sort of accommodation he was accustomed to in Basel, but tolerable. Grandfather settled into the hotel, made inquiries about his folks and found out that the wife of the blacksmith, Kuznetsov, really was his niece. As you can imagine, in such a small town there are no secrets, and next day, when grandfather and his son Jakob turned up at the Kuznetsovs, the whole family was waiting for them ceremoniously, the table laid with everything you'd expect on such an occasion. Sitting at the table, grandfather found out about other relations and, like a thorough and reliable German, he asked about each one in detail, how and from which side they were related. He weighed everything up, decided which ones he ought to see and which not, and those he chose to see were invited to the Kuznetsovs next day and grandfather gave them various gifts, and some he simply gave money.

The only relation grandfather had to go and see himself was a certain Khaim Yagudin. Khaim Yagudin was grandfather's brother-in-law, having married his eldest sister, who had already died. Khaim Yagudin said that if Ivanovsky had come to see his family, which only consisted of two deceased sisters, then he should have come first to the house of one of them and not to a niece, because everybody knew that a sister is much closer kin than a niece. And since Ivanovsky had crossed the whole of Europe to see his family, it wouldn't hurt him to walk the extra five hundred yards to his, Yagudin's, house. And if he didn't make the effort, Khaim Yagudin would be mortally offended.

With such pride, you can imagine what sort of man Khaim Yagudin was, what sort of character. By profession, he was a retired NCO. Jewish NCOs at that time were quite a rarity. But Khaim Yagudin had earned it, and had even won a medal. He was a dried-up little man and limped as a result of one of his war wounds. He was clean-shaven, apart from sergeant-major whiskers. He scented himself with strong eau-de-Cologne, smoked tobacco, spoke only in Russian, did not observe the Sabbath, did not believe in God and scoffed at those who did. He had to interfere in every scandal that happened in the town. Dishevelled and angry, he would stump off to the site of the event waving his stick, and he would push through the crowd and straight away start passing judgement and laying down the law. He would start off quietly but soon get so worked up his eyes would pop, and he would be beside himself because of 'the idiocy of these swine', and then he would start using his stick on both the innocent and the guilty parties. Though he was puny and decrepit, people feared him and kept out of his way. For his part, he despised everyone and ranted that he couldn't live with 'these idiots', and once he even announced that a *mullah* would soon arrive from Tiflis to baptize him into the Muhammadan faith. You can understand that in those days in a small town like that, such a thing was meant as an affront to everyone.

His wife, my grandfather's elder sister, had died, leaving him five children, and they worked to support him. Frankly, he was an idler who didn't want to work and thought of himself as cultivated. It seems to be a general rule about loafers that they have hard-working wives and hard-working children. A law of nature, almost. His wife had sold fruit and kept the family on it, managing as best she could. And the children began working at an early age, perhaps even as early as eleven, one dragging the other along behind it, and then after their mother died they began to support their father. The children were good workers, simple and modest and it was only the one girl, Sarah, who had no time for honest toil. Sarah was beautiful, the image of Vera Kholodny, star of the silent screen – we even called her Vera Kholodny. You'll never guess what she got into. Diamonds! It was even rumoured that she owned one of Tsar Nicholas's diamonds. Well, naturally, once a woman gets into that sort of business, it doesn't matter if she's gorgeous or even if she's Vera Kholodny herself, she's bound to end up in jail.

To return to Khaim Yagudin, however. It has to be said that he was a great man about town, an expert on elegant behaviour. He liked to drink and to relax in intellectual company and converse on intellectual topics. He would spend whole days sitting in the barber's shop in the company of idlers and gasbags, like himself. Our barber, Bernard Semyonovich, was also an expert on elegant behaviour and liked 'society' to congregate in his barber-shop, and while he would be snipping away with his scissors or lathering a beard, he liked to hear them chatting about current problems. The conversations did not always end peacefully. Once, Khaim Yagudin quarrelled with a pharmacist who made himself out to be a liberal. I've no idea what they were quarrelling about, but suddenly Khaim Yagudin stood up and declared that he had sworn allegiance to Tsar and fatherland and would not let anybody defame them, and therefore if, within ten days, the pharmacist did not depart Russia, the Russia for which he, Khaim Yagudin, had shed blood and given a leg, then he would kill him and not be responsible.

The pharmacist only laughed. But next day Khaim Yagudin didn't show up at the barber-shop, and that worried the pharmacist. Then Khaim didn't turn up the next day, or the next, and that worried everyone. In short, Khaim had taken an oath that he would go out of his house only on the eleventh day to see if that scoundrel of a pharmacist had got out of the country, and if he hadn't he would kill him.

The pharmacist ran to the local police officer, who said that as long as the pharmacist was still alive, or until Khaim actually killed him, there were no grounds for prosecution. Of course, if Khaim did go ahead and kill the pharmacist, they would have to arrest him. Some reassurance for the pharmacist! On the eleventh day, everyone crowded round

Khaim's house to see if he would kill the pharmacist, but they were unlucky. During the night, the pharmacist had gone to Odessa and taken a ship to America. Of course, I'm only reporting what others have said, maybe things weren't quite like that. Still, it does give you some idea of Khaim Yagudin. Grandfather Ivanovsky knew nothing about all this, of course, but the Kuznetsovs knew only too well what sort of person Khaim Yagudin was, and just what he meant about being mortally offended – he was capable of all kinds of hooliganism – so it was best to give in. Tactfully, they hinted to Professor Ivanovsky that his brother-in-law was an honourable NCO, that he was disabled and that it was hard for him to walk, and that it would be nice if the professor could visit him, especially as he was the widower of the professor's late sister and, after all, it was only five hundred yards to Khaim's house.

So our Swiss guests had to visit Khaim Yagudin. Of course, I wasn't there myself, but later I was often in the Yagudin house and I can visualize the whole scene clearly.

Imagine the old, dilapidated house of a widower, who is idle besides, and who has spent his life knocking other people's teeth out, but has never knocked a single nail into a wall. Imagine rickety front steps, broken banisters, loose floor-boards, holes in the roof, cracked plaster, a dark entrance-hall piled with junk. Imagine a 'drawing-room' – a crude table without oilcloth or tablecloth, a huge cracked sideboard with its glass broken, chairs with only three legs and torn upholstery. In the midst of this grandeur stood Khaim Yagudin, small, red-whiskered, with the grey, cropped hair of an NCO, and smiling his arrogant, however gallant, smile, as though to say, we are not from Basel, we are not doctors of medicine, but even so we do count for something.

As a matter of fact, they might well have had a conversation. For those times, and for our little town, Khaim was quite an educated man, even if he was self-educated. He even knew some English. What do I mean, he knew? Well, he could write an address in English on a letter. When anyone with family in America or Australia wanted to send a letter, they went to Khaim Yagudin. In other words, it was possible to have a conversation with him, and he liked conversation. But it always began with an incident, and it always ended with an incident.

It was a hot day, and grandfather and father were dressed for visiting, in three-piece suits, ties and starched collars. They were wilting in the heat, and the sweat was pouring off them, especially off the old man. But our gallant sergeant knew what to do: he would refresh his guests with eau-de-Cologne. Placing one of his tattered chairs in the centre of the room, he sat the professor down and proceeded to spray his face with triple strength eau-de-Cologne from an atomizer, one end of the tube immersed in the flacon, the other in Khaim's mouth. Note that he had no teeth. He puffed out his cheeks and blew with all his might, spewing over the professor the foul-smelling cologne together with a fair amount of saliva. When he interrupted the proceedings to take another breath, the professor stood up, took his handkerchief out of his pocket, wiped his face and pushed away the chair to demonstrate that the show was over.

The persistent Khaim, however, retrieved the chair and invited Jakob to refresh himself the same way, but the professor forbade it, and Jakob himself wanted none of it. Instead of reconciling himself and not inflicting any more of his perfumery on his guests, Khaim Yagudin began to insist and demand, and aimed the atomizer at Jakob, at which grandfather put on his hat, bowed and left the house with his son, thus acquiring a mortal enemy in the person of Khaim Yagudin.

Professor Ivanovsky, of course, couldn't have cared less

about making an enemy of Khaim. He didn't want to know any Khaim Yagudin, in fact he didn't want to know anybody here, apart from the Kuznetsovs.

The Kuznetsov family consisted of the father, who was the blacksmith, the mother, who was grandfather's niece, and three beautiful daughters. And these beautiful daughters had beautiful friends, including, as you have probably guessed, their best friend Rachel Rakhlenko, my future mother. And naturally Rachel arranged to be at the Kuznetsovs next time the Ivanovskys visited. Nothing surprising in that. The Kuznetsov girls invited their best friend, Rachel Rakhlenko, to come and meet Jakob Ivanovsky, who, even if he did come from Switzerland, was their relation, a third cousin or something like that. And there was nothing shameful in their friend wanting to have a closer look at this foreign object, this boy made of porcelain, to touch him and turn him over and see how such beautiful dolls are made. My mother knew a little reading, writing, and arithmetic, and nothing else. In those days, girls were rarely given any higher education, especially in bootmakers' families. Apart from the sky, the pine forest and the river, she had seen nothing at all, and here, all of a sudden, was a little prince from Switzerland.

My mother loved my father very much, all her life she loved him and she gave her life to him entirely. And if father had met her on the street in Basel, he still would have fallen in love with her, and only her – she was his destiny. But if father had been one of the boys from our street, I'm not so sure that things would have turned out as they did. True, he was handsome, but he was quiet, modest, and shy, and mother might easily have fallen in love with one of the stronger, bolder, more aggressive boys.

For all her impudence and wild behaviour, mother was a practical woman, she knew what she wanted and what she didn't want, and whatever she didn't want she had no time for. Bear in mind that as a girl, my mother was reckoned to be the prettiest in town – officers from the regiment would ride down our street, just to get a look at Rachel Rakhlenko.

On this occasion, mother took action. She wanted to see the foreigners, so without any fuss she went out on to the street and looked. She wanted to meet the good-looking boy, who looked like the son of a governor-general, so she went to her friends' house and met him.

What happened then, how their relationship developed, I have no idea, as I wasn't there. Mother used to say, 'I couldn't get rid of him, he followed me around from morning till night.' Father would say, 'From morning till night she laid traps and snares for me.' That was how they joked about it later, but I suspect there was more than a grain of truth, all the same. Father was in love, and mother was playing with her amazing new toy, though it was clear she would never give it back. Who realized this? In the first place, they themselves knew it. But in those days, especially in traditional families, marriages were made not on the highest level, in heaven, but by the parents.

Could Rachel's parents have counted on such a marriage? Grandfather Rakhlenko, it's true, wasn't some starving little shoemaker. He was a master, had his own workshop, and although he was no rich man, he was not a beggar either. Also, as you will see further on, he was remarkable in many ways, I might even say outstanding. Still, he wasn't a professor, or doctor of medicine, and he didn't own the best clinic in Europe. And surely in Switzerland there were plenty of brides for a boy from such a family.

As for grandfather Ivanovsky, he wasn't thinking about any sort of marriage for Jakob. Jakob must first of all go through university, get his degree and become a doctor, and then he could start thinking about getting married. Besides, the old man considered Jakob a baby and he simply couldn't imagine that his Jakob, his shy little Jakob, his *mizinikel*, could suddenly take it into his head to get married.

Of course, if the old man had tumbled to it, as they say nowadays, he would have got straight on to the train and cleared off back to Switzerland. But he tumbled to nothing, and although he did clear off, it wasn't back to Switzerland, but to Nezhin to see his old high-school chums, and he went there alone, without Jakob. And since it wasn't suitable for Jakob to stay alone in the hotel and eat in the restaurant, grandfather arranged for him to move to the Kuznetsovs, where he was given the nicest room and where he was assured of good home cooking.

The old man could not have done a sillier thing – he left Jakob and Rachel alone together. He was away for a week, and it was during that week that mother said father wouldn't leave her alone, and father said she kept setting traps for him. I have no concrete facts about that week, but I have a pretty good idea. They went swimming. Men and women swam separately in those days and mixed beaches were unheard of. But what did 'separately' mean? It meant that Jakob would be on one side of a bush, and the Kuznetsov girls and Rachel on the other. He would hear their squeaks and squeals and giggles, but being a well-brought-up boy he wouldn't peep, though somehow or other he would happen to catch glimpses of their flashing bodies through the bushes, and though he would avert his eyes, when Rachel went into the water he would see her instinctively like a beautiful Aphrodite in the foam. And all around were the steppes and the fields, and the chirr of grasshoppers, and everything being scorched by the kind of sun Jakob had not seen in his Switzerland and never would.

But the main drama was acted out in the forest. I have already mentioned that our town stood in a magnificent, dry, pine forest, of the sort that are found only in the south and only in the steppes. I don't think you will find such clean, dry, resinous air anywhere else, and people on summer vacation, even from Moscow and Petersburg, had good reason to come and breathe it. They would take their hammocks and hampers of food, and set off for the forest in the morning and just lounge there all day long.

We had an enterprising chemist called Oryol who set up a stall in the forest and sold *kefir* as a medicine or a wholesome drink. You could buy buns to go with the bottle of *kefir*, and ice-cream in little bowls. I remember the chemist Oryol very well, with his wholesome *kefir*, and buns and ice-cream. He revived his little business during the twenties, when I was already a youth in the time of the New Economic Policy, when private trading was allowed again for a while. I remember the drums of ice-cream, coated with frost, in wide wooden tubs. As a matter of fact, the summer people used to come from Moscow and Leningrad in the twenties, too, to spend the day in the forest in their hammocks.

I can imagine how things were with mother and father. They would go into the forest, not alone of course, but with the Kuznetsov sisters – for a young man and girl to go off alone in those days was considered not nice. I don't know if all three sisters would have accompanied them. I doubt it, because girls in our sort of community had work to do. There was the orchard, the kitchen-garden, this one's cow to see to, that one's goat, father to help in the shop if he was a trades-man, work to deliver if he was an artisan, then there were younger brothers and sisters, snivellers and tomboys to be watched, or to go to the market with mother and help her in the kitchen. In other words, there was plenty to do at home, and the Kuznetsovs couldn't have let their daughters spend the whole day cooling themselves in the forest. But we are talking about Jakob, our dear guest from Switzerland, and a guest must be kept occupied, entertained, and what better entertainment than our forest, which was famous throughout Russia, you might say, and what could be better for such a delicate, fair-haired boy than the resinous air? So, naturally, the Kuznetsovs let their daughters go into the forest with

Jakob. How Rachel managed to wheedle her way out of the house I don't know; considering the stern character of her father, my grandfather Rakhlenko, I cannot even imagine how she did it. But she did.

So they would go into the forest and, as you might guess, they would settle themselves down somewhat out of the way, out of view of summer visitors. The Kuznetsov girls would swing in their hammocks, or pretend to be gathering wild strawberries, and father and mother would be sitting on a rug among the pines, gazing at each other.

It was July, a cloudless sky, the still air saturated with the sharp resinous scent of the pines and the ground hot from the sun and soft with yellow pine-needles. Rachel would be wearing a thin, short dress, with an open neck. Her black hair would be tumbling over her shoulders, he only had to stretch out his hand to touch it. He was nineteen, she was sixteen. What language did they speak to each other in? Father knew two, German and French, and mother also knew two, actually three – Yiddish, Russian and Ukrainian. There were five languages on offer, you might say, but not one of them was any use as a means of communication. Instead, they used a sixth language, one which they both found the most beautiful and the most easily understood.

Mother was a woman in the full meaning of the word, she knew how to attract and at the same time to keep her distance – the most bewitching of feminine qualities. Like a coiled spring, she contracts and you think you have nearly reached your goal, then the spring expands and you find yourself ten feet away from her. Mother used this skill to perfection, and this was what father meant when he talked about her traps and snares, years later.

When Professor Ivanovsky returned from Nezhin, Jakob announced to him that he was going to marry Rachel. I don't know if grandfather had a seizure or not – I think not. Perhaps he took some sedative drops, maybe not, as surgeons have to have strong nerves. It wasn't so much the unexpectedness of Jakob's declaration, you can expect anything from a boy of nineteen who has just fallen in love. It was Jakob's firmness that grandfather hadn't expected. This was the first time Jakob had shown character and grandfather might actually have been pleased to see it. I even suspect grandfather was not particularly against this marriage in principle. First of all, he had seen Rachel and, as I've already mentioned, she was a prime beauty. Secondly, she was a simple, hard-working girl who had no pretensions and wasn't pampered, she would make a good wife and mother. Finally, it must have impressed grandfather that his son wanted a wife from grandfather's own homeland, which was surely a sign of great respect to a parent. As for their material inequality, well, thank God, Jakob had enough money of his own to make up for that. And university? Well, who says that you have to be a bachelor to study? Why shouldn't a married man also study, as long as his livelihood is assured, and his father is living and not about to die, and his mother is living, and also not about to die, and he has brothers who are surgeons and living, and there is the clinic, which is not the worst one in Switzerland? Jakob's father probably thought about it that way, but there was still Jakob's mother, who could not be left out. You can never leave out the mother in these matters, especially when it concerns her darling boy, her dear Jakob, as it did.

Grandfather Ivanovsky said to his son, 'Jakob, I have nothing against Rachel, I think she is a wonderful girl. But such things cannot be done without a mother's blessing. We simply cannot leave your mother out of it.'

Jakob was a sensible boy and realized that he must have his mother's agreement. Besides which, he loved his mother and didn't want to hurt her. So he told Rachel he would go to Basel to get his mother's blessing, then come straight back and they would get married.

Two days later father and son were on their way back to

Switzerland. Before they left, Jakob asked Rachel to get a photograph of herself, and as soon as it was ready she should send it to him in Basel. When his mother saw what a beauty she was, she would give her blessing at once. With that, they departed.

2 🔲

Rachel remained behind. She was no longer plain Rachel Rakhlenko, daughter of Abraham Rakhlenko the bootmaker. Now, she was the fiancée of Jakob Ivanovsky from Basel, son of the well-known professor who owned the famous clinic. It was a ticklish situation, I can tell you. The whole street examined the problem from all angles, turning it over and over. Everyone agreed that Rachel had only a hundred to one chance. The only chance in her favour was her beauty, and as for the ninety-nine against, you can take your pick – she was simple, uneducated, not rich, and so on and so forth, whereas, on the other side, there were doctors, professors, clinics, Switzerland, Europe. And then, if the old man had wanted his son to marry her, he surely would have taken certain steps, like visiting the Rakhlenkos, to see what her parents were like, what the family they were about to unite with were like, and he would have got to know the girl better. Professor Ivanovsky did none of these things. He didn't call on the Rakhlenkos, didn't introduce himself or acquaint himself with them, he didn't utter a word. It's obvious he considered the whole thing a childish whim and hurried off back to Basel with his son, using the mother's blessing as an excuse. That was what the whole street thought, and it was only a short step from that thought to open ridicule – such an unlucky girl.

But even then, at the age of sixteen, my mother was not one to let herself become an object of ridicule. She soon had things tidy. What do I mean by 'tidy'? Every day letters began to arrive from Switzerland. Each and every day at exactly the same time, the postman, who up to then didn't even know the way to the house, turned up at the bootmaker's and handed over a letter from Basel. The sceptics had to keep silent, though they probably thought to themselves that the letters didn't mean a thing, as a lovesick boy might scribble all kinds of nonsense on paper. But a fact is a fact; the letters kept on arriving. Rachel answered them, walked to the post-office and dropped the envelopes into the post-box. In other words, something was being done, things were moving, though in what direction nobody knew. So the people thought, let's wait and see, time will show.

The letters have not survived. But I heard later on from my grandmother that during that year, when the correspondence between Russia and Switzerland was going on, my mother somehow managed to acquire a little education and to widen her horizons; she also learned Russian properly and even a smattering of German. Of course, she got help. There were educated girls on our street and even educated young men and women, high-school and university students home on vacation. And who would refuse to help such a beautiful girl, especially as she was going to conquer Switzerland!

Now let us transfer in our minds to Switzerland, to the city of Basel. The chief character in Basel was my grandmother, Elfrieda, and grandmother Elfrieda would simply have none of it, absolutely, decidedly, definitely not! That her Jakob should all of a sudden get married, and to the daughter of a bootmaker, was simply out of the question. Of course, she said nothing bad about my mother to father, nor had she any reason to; besides they were intelligent, well-brought-up people, but first there was the university, and then, one doesn't marry at nineteen, and it would kill her, it would be the end of her, she wouldn't get over it, and so on and so forth, the way mothers go on when they don't want their sons to get married. As I understand it, there was plenty of noise and uproar, though naturally noise and uproar in the European manner, *à la* Basel, so to speak, as it is done in well-ordered German families, but it was still a matter of life or death.

Jakob also saw the question as one of life or death. He insisted on having his own way and then fell silent. This silence was worse than any din. He fell silent and then went into a decline before their very eyes. They realized that there could be no talk of university while the boy was melting away like a candle. He didn't eat or drink, or come out of his room, he didn't want to see anyone, he didn't read or do anything, but just sat in his room whole days at a time, and on top of everything else, smoked one cigarette after the other.

How was his mother taking it all? It wasn't so long ago that she had taken her Jakob for walks along Basel's famous boulevards, where everyone had admired him and smiled and asked whose this beautiful, pale-faced little boy was. And now here is this self-same boy, lying alone in his room, dense with smoke, smoking cigarette after cigarette, he doesn't eat, he doesn't drink, he won't speak to anybody, he's got thin and yellow, and you can see at a glance that he's got tuberculosis and is going to die. A year went by in this way and it became clear that something must be done. If it was a choice between life and death, let it be life. And so exactly one year later, also in July, a delegation set off for our town, consisting of Professor Ivanovsky and his wife Elfrieda, their son Jakob, and their housekeeper, a woman who waited on grandmother Elfrieda, and who could be trusted, and whose job it was to find out and dig up, so to speak, all the ins and outs, which a woman like grandmother wouldn't expect to find out for herself. Grandmother wasn't going there to get Jakob married off, but to break the engagement.

Meanwhile, however, the other side was also preparing itself. By 'the other side' I don't mean Rachel's family, not at all. I should explain that my grandfather Rakhlenko, Rachel's father, was one of the most important men in the town, if not the most important, even though he was only a bootmaker.

And considering that we had well-to-do people in the town, rich tradesmen, even merchants of the second guild (who could live outside the Pale if they wished), and engine-drivers and professionals, then if, as I say, the most prominent man is a simple bootmaker, he must be an outstanding personality. My grandfather was just such an outstanding personality, as will emerge in due course. For the time being, I will say only that he was a straightforward and decisive man who had no time for deception and intrigue – you want to marry your son to my daughter, do it then, take her as she is, and you can see for yourself what she is. You don't want to, then don't, she won't change and nor will her family. Calmly Rachel's parents awaited the arrival of the Ivanovskys. It wasn't they who were getting ready for their arrival, but the town – students who had come home on vacation, high-school pupils, teachers and dentists, the whole of the intelligentsia, that is, and the ordinary working folk in the bootmaking workshop, and the neighbours. Everyone was on Rachel and Jakob's side and wished them happiness and joy, because they loved one another, and love conquers all.

Although neither Rachel nor her parents intended to do anything just for show, or to put up any façades, the whole town was in a state of agitation, so that as soon as it was known that the Ivanovskys would be coming in the summer, it was natural that Rachel should appear wearing stylish new shoes, with high heels – after all her father was a shoemaker – and a new dress, and a hat, made by the best milliner, as it had become the fashion to call the seamstress who made hats.

And so everybody got ready for the forthcoming events excitedly and in a spirit of generosity. There were some evil-minded people, like Khaim Yagudin, of course, who declared that all these good works were far from unselfish. If Rachel marries the son of Ivanovsky, a professor and the owner of the best clinic in the world, they said, then all these expenses and good deeds will be repaid with interest. But, then, you will find evil tongues everywhere. As for Khaim Yagudin, it was obvious that he was offended with old Ivanovsky because he had declined the offer of his perfumery. Judge for yourself, what could there be in it for students and high-school pupils to help Rachel with Russian and German, and geography and history, and help her learn some social manners? They knew they would get nothing out of it, they didn't want anything and they expected nothing.

The Swiss finally arrived and put up at the hotel, where they were greeted by Madame Yanzhvetska, who announced that she was delighted to welcome back such important guests to her hotel. She took them to their rooms on the upper floor and appointed the maid, Paraska, to look after them, as well as the waiter, Timofei, who had been decked out for the occasion in a black bow-tie, just like a waiter in the best Warsaw hotels, as she put it. Since grandfather Ivanovsky was a famous surgeon and a professor, the leading figures of the town came to call on him, including the local police chief, the barrister, the state rabbi and the ordinary rabbi, the retired Colonel Porubailo with his wife and daughter, the railway hospital doctor, Volyntsev, who was an excellent doctor and a social-democrat, even though he came from the nobility. In short, the town gave the guests red-carpet treatment, and the only thing that was missing was a public religious service for them, though public services were usually given only when the Emperor came, and, after all, it wasn't he who had come.

Such a reception could, of course, be explained by the distinction of the guests – everyone wanted to have a look at the most famous professor in Europe, perhaps even in the world. Nevertheless, behind it all was interest in the romance; nobody could be indifferent to the touching love-affair of such beautiful young people, the lovely Rachel, daughter of the bootmaker, and the tender, fragile youth, Jakob, from far-off Basel.

Then the visits started, the Ivanovskys to the Rakhlenkos, the Rakhlenkos to the Ivanovskys. The housekeeper scurried around the town trying to find things out, but what was there to find out? She always got the same answer – Rachel was the most virtuous of girls, and her father the most respected of men. Then, of course, there was the forest and hammocks, and the chemist Oryol made such *kefir* and ice-cream that grandmother Elfrieda was amazed and confessed she'd never tasted such *kefir* and such ice-cream in all her life, even though she had been to the best cities in Europe and had stayed at the best resorts. When she needed to have her hair done, Bernard Semyonovich appeared and, as you know, he was the most gallant coiffeur in the entire province, and grandmother Elfrieda said such a coiffeur would make not only Basel proud, but even Paris, and as you know Paris is the lawgiver on women's fashion and hairdos. Our town was not found wanting, and revealed itself in all its beauty and splendour, and as for the beauty and splendour of Rachel there is nothing more to be said, and only a blind man would not have noticed, though even a blind man would have realized it from her voice, which was beautiful too, quite exceptional and melodic. It should also be said, giving my mother credit for intelligence, that she behaved perfectly with the Ivanovskys and kept her rudeness and obstinacy well out of sight. Possibly she felt timid in front of such distinguished people and in front of the parade. The fact is that with grandmother Elfrieda she appeared as the quiet, modest beauty, Rachel. That she was not a pampered young miss, but a hard-working girl who knew her worth and her obligations, grandmother soon sorted out for herself, of course.

It looked as if grandmother's resistance had been broken and that the affair was moving towards its consummation, when suddenly and unexpectedly grandmother wheeled out her heavy artillery. It turned out that grandmother was not Jewish, but a Swiss of German origin, and when grandfather married her he converted to Protestantism – either the Lutheran or the Calvinist variety – and their sons were also Protestants of some sort, and my father, Jakob, was therefore half German and a Lutheran too, which makes me one quarter German.

Since Jakob was a Protestant, a Lutheran and a Calvinist, grandmother made it a condition that Rachel must accept Protestantism, Lutheranism and Calvinism, and that they should be married in Basel.

It was like a bolt from the blue. Protestant? Lutheran? Calvinist? We hadn't even heard of such things here. Russian Orthodox and Catholic we knew, but Calvinist, Protestant? I don't believe in any God, and never have. I've been raised by the Soviet system to be an internationalist. Russian, Jew, Byelorussian – they're all the same to me. My wife, Galina Nikolaevna, is a Russian. Thirty years we've been together. We have three sons, wonderful boys, and though they are registered as Jews, they don't speak Yiddish, only Russian, they were born in Russia, they're married to Russian girls, so my grandchildren are Russian, too, and for all of us our motherland is Russia. All the same, I think a man can either believe in God or not believe, he can get faith and he can lose it. But there is only one God for the true believer, and that is the one he carries in his heart. If you want to believe, then you should keep the faith you were born into. It's absurd to change your religion for the sake of personal interest, like changing a pair of gloves. And here was my mother, Rachel, who as a matter of fact had never believed in God, having to become a Lutheran out of self-interest. You say love is higher, and I agree. This is how mother dealt with it.

She said to Jakob, 'Since we have got to go through this, and since I am one hundred per cent Jewish and you are only fifty per cent, you can return to the faith of your forefathers.'

That was logical. One hundred per cent was more than

fifty. To which grandfather and grandmother Rakhlenko added, 'Not for anything will our daughter go over to Lutheranism or Protestantism, whatever they are! We won't have such disgrace on our heads.'

Remember that this took place before the Revolution, in 1910, when religious prejudice was strong, especially in a small town in the Ukraine. One can understand how the Rakhlenkos felt. They would have to go on living here, while their daughter, if you please, went over to Lutheranism, and not just simple Lutheranism, but some Swiss variety of it.

I blame grandfather Ivanovsky. During his first visit he hid his Lutheranism. It had surprised a lot of people that he didn't attend the synagogue, where a place of honour had been reserved for him by the east wall. It was surprising but it wasn't dwelt on, especially as the old man had made a handsome donation to the poor through the synagogue. But he ought to have been completely open and said they were Protestants, Lutherans, Calvinists, Reformists or whatever. No doubt he was ashamed to admit that he had forsworn his faith, so he'd kept quiet, and now it all came out, just as everything was moving towards its completion. The carriage was heading at full speed for the finish, and all of a sudden Protestantism and Lutheranism are lying across its path, like a log, and when a carriage hits a log at full speed, it overturns, which, as you know, is not very nice for the passengers.

Then grandmother fired her second salvo: after the wedding, the young couple would remain forever in Switzerland, where there was the house, the family nest, the university, and the clinic.

In all, Rachel was going to have to pull up her roots for good, go over to the German faith, leave her homeland, and part from her parents, as though shaming them were not enough. Rachel stood her ground. She wasn't going to go to any Switzerland, she liked it here. As for Lutheranism, there was no question, especially as she didn't even believe in God, and how, she asked, could she possibly believe in God after being taken care of for a whole year by students, high-school pupils, free-thinkers, Marxists, social-democrats, socialist revolutionaries and members of the Jewish workers' movement. And Jakob wasn't such a devout Protestant, for that matter; in fact to be precise he didn't give a damn about it. What he cared about was Rachel, that's what he cared about, and she could have been a Muhammadan, a Buddhist or a fire-worshipper, and he would have been delighted to become a Muhammadan, a Buddhist, or a fire-worshipper, as long as she became his wife.

How long the battle raged I don't know, but at any rate it ended in a compromise – they would get married here and then go and live in Switzerland. On this point Rachel conceded that it is the wife's place to follow her husband, not the reverse. This arrangement cost a lot of money, as my father turned out to be, if you will forgive me, uncircumcised and therefore the rabbi couldn't marry them. You could, however, obtain fake medical certificates and the like, if you knew which palms to grease. Everything was organized, the whole town came to the wedding, and then the young couple walked from the synagogue, surrounded by singing, dancing and merrymaking and, with the orchestra playing marches and dances, the town rejoiced. Soon after, Rachel and Jakob, together with the Ivanovsky parents and the housekeeper, left for Switzerland, leaving behind them sorrow, delight, rumour and gossip.

The question was naturally enough discussed in the barbershop, too, and, naturally enough, it was Khaim Yagudin who had most to say. He declared that all the fuss over this business was so much hot air, a storm in a teacup. Well, actually, the business itself was not a storm in a teacup at all, but not in the way it was being seen and argued about and discussed by ignoramuses who called themselves learned sages, but who in fact had never seen anything in their lives apart from the

Torah and had driven themselves crazy with all their interpretations of it.

'What's wrong with Jakob's mother being a German and a Lutheran?' Khaim inquired. Absolutely nothing at all, according to him, and if anybody objects he'll smash their face, and get a reward for doing it, too, because the wife of our happily reigning sovereign, Her Imperial Majesty Alexandra Fedorovna, is also a German, from Hesse, as is the mother of the Emperor, that is to say the wife of the late Emperor Alexander III, God rest his soul; the Dowager Empress Marya Fedorovna comes from Denmark, which is the same as saying she's a German, and Catherine the Great was a pure German. But these hick Talmudists don't know anything about all that, they haven't a clue about what's been going on for the last two thousand years. And if they've even heard of Catherine the Great, it's only because her august countenance is featured on hundred-rouble banknotes, not that they've ever seen a hundred-rouble note in their lives, they've only seen copper money, and that's all they'll ever see, the swine, the blockheads, the hicks! The Germans aren't worse than the Jews, in fact they're better. He, Khaim, had a regimental commander, his excellency Baron Tanchehausen, who was of German origin, and he was a hero, a great swordsman! In a nutshell, the fact that Jakob's mother was a German was only to his credit. And the fact that she was a Lutheran, even a Calvinist, was better still. Who could say which God was more important, the Lutheran one who helped Bismarck beat the French, or the Jewish one, who nobody's afraid of, except the Jews? All this talk about Jakob's mother has got to be stopped immediately. She is an intelligent, cultivated, tactful lady, and if anyone wants to argue about it he, Khaim Yagudin, will smash their face in, because it's his duty as an officer to stand up for a lady, even if she is a German, a Lutheran, middle-aged and comes from Basel.

So the question of Jakob's mother was dealt with, once and

for all and that was that. 'But . . . but,' and here Khaim Yagudin raised his stick, 'there is another question, and that is, who is Jakob's *father*? Who, as a matter of fact, is this so-called professor, damn his eyes? Who is he? Is he a Jew? On what grounds do you say he is? Ah, he's from here, he's a local! What, were you present at his birth? Did you go to *kheder* with him? Who delivered him, who circumcised him, who registered him? Show me the midwife, show me the rabbi. Oh, yes, he was born in Ivanovka and came here with his mother, all right. Sure. But who was *his* father, who has actually seen his father? I'm asking you in plain Russian, dammit! Ah, you have only seen his mother. We're not talking about his mother, I've seen his mother myself, in fact she was my mother-in-law, my own wife's mother, may both their dear souls rest in peace. And I think I would know my own mother-in-law better than some idiot I could think of. Who do I mean? Whoever you like! You, for instance! You're welcome! And you can go to hell! Close the door after the block-head! Anyway, I would tell you a lot of interesting tales about my late mother-in-law. But, as I was saying, we're not talking about my mother-in-law, not about the mother of this damned professor, but about his father, or, if I may say so, my father-in-law. What was that? When I married his daughter he had already died? How do you like that, we've got another know-all here. You listen to me, know-all, my wife knew her father, he died when she was a young girl and she told me something very unusual about him. He was no ordinary bootmaker, if you don't mind, he was an extremely clever and extremely educated man, and not a Talmudist, mind you, but a man of the world, a philosopher. You've heard of the philosopher Spinoza? Well, they were always writing to each other. Ivanovsky would write to Spinoza, and Spinoza would write to Ivanovsky. My wife had seen it all with her own eyes and heard it with her own ears. Don't you understand, how many more times have I got to drill it into your idiotic heads? But what nobody can ever prove is that Professor Ivanovsky had ever seen his father, that can never be proved. Never, and you can take it from me, Khaim Yagudin. The fact is, our professor was born after the old Ivanovsky had already departed to the hereafter. Our professor was born when his mother, that's to say my mother-in-law, was a widow of three years standing. This professor is a bastard, that's what he is! And his father wasn't Ivanovsky at all, he was some railway contractor who supplied materials for building the Libau-Romny line, a merchant and a Christian. When the professor was born, this contractor bribed the right people and the professor was registered as Ivanovsky's son, then straight away the contractor sent the widow here, where the Libau-Romny line was being built, with both her daughters, who were of course real Ivanovskys, plus the new-born professor, and if he's an Ivanovsky, I'm Kaiser Wilhelm. Now do you see how it all works, or have I got to chew it all over for you again?

'Even though he was an Old Believer and a crook, like all railway contractors, this one turned out to be a decent chap, gave the widow money, took an interest in the boy's education, which explains how the professor managed to pass through the Nezhin high-school – how many Jews do you know who've been through Nezhin high-school? Well, with the sort of money that contractor had, the boy could even have gone to a theological college, but he couldn't have got into the Cadet Corps, because in the army the penalty for bribery is the firing squad, plus the loss of all rights and property. Anyway, it was thanks to his father, the contractor, that the professor was able to go through high-school and then university in Switzerland. If this isn't so, then would you kindly explain to me – no, don't bother explaining it to me, I already know all about it, but kindly explain to everyone else – how it is that the professor was born ten years after his sisters? Why did the widow move from Ivanovka to this place, where she had neither house nor home, or relatives or even friends? Can you tell me what dividends this poor widow had to cover first the school fees and then the cost of university in Switzerland? It was the contractor, the contractor, and again the contractor! And though he showed himself to be quite a decent chap where the future of his son was concerned, in every other way he was an absolute rotter, and if he was to turn up here I'd give his mug such a bashing that none of the Old Believers would be able to recognize him. And for why? Can't you guess? It was right to be concerned about his son but, dammit, he should have realized that they were a family, that it wasn't right to keep the professor in clover and luxury and cash and let the girls go around in rags and tatters, it was wrong that the professor should eat rolls and butter, while the girls had to make do with potatoes and nothing else. You know, that swine wouldn't give the widow a penny to spend on the girls, everything went to the professor, only for the professor. His sisters grew up without any education whatever, and without dowries, and I, Khaim Yagudin, married one of them out of the goodness of my heart, just to see that justice was done. As for a dowry, what does that matter to Khaim Yagudin, ha? Money for a sergeant of the Russian Army, ha! A Russian sergeant can sit down at the card table and lose his wife's dowry, and his family fortune as well, because money means absolutely nothing to him! As a matter of fact, I had been searching not for money, but for a person to share my life, and I found her in my late wife, whom I respected as much as any woman could want. I took her away from the home where she had been bossed about and where everybody had to worship the professor and everything was for the professor. So in actual fact, the professor is illegitimate, the bastard son of a contractor who was an Old Believer, and it turns out that Jakob, the bridegroom of Rachel Rakhlenko, is the son of a bastard. And if he has any Jewish blood, it's no more than twenty-five per cent, and the rest is German and Russian.'

Actually, he, Khaim Yagudin, saw nothing special in this, and rather viewed it all as an enlightened man, but he couldn't stand the local swines who made themselves out to be such goody-goodies but lived with anyone they could get, and even grabbed eagerly at the German colonist girls, because they're nice and juicy and like that sort of thing, as everyone knows. 'Anyway, the professor wasn't to blame if his mother slept with a railway contractor, and nor was Jakob. But, I ask you, what sort of rabbis and elders have we got, if they are prepared to give a Jewish wedding to a man whose mother is a pure German, and whose father is half-Russian, which makes him only twenty-five per cent Jewish?!'

This was the version put out by Khaim Yagudin, you understand. Anyone else could have put it out and it still would have been believed. Why not believe a strange fact which only adds to the amazing story of Jakob's marriage to Rachel? If Jakob's mother suddenly turned out to be German, and he a Lutheran, why couldn't his grandfather be a rich railway contractor of Old Believer background? In such a situation, if someone had declared Jakob's father to be a Kabardin or a Chechen or some other tribe, he would have been believed, because the whole story was so unusual. And some of the old folks did confirm that old man Ivanovsky from Ivanovka was in fact a learned man, and when a husband is a learned man and spends the whole time looking at books, people always want to know what his wife is looking at. His wife can only look left or right, as they say. Well, the professor's mother, even while she was still living in Ivanovka, looked to the right and the left, too, and pretty often, as it happens, and when her husband died she became a complete merry widow, and wore a massive gold chain with a golden locket round her neck. Nobody knew what the locket contained, because she never opened it, but perhaps it had a portrait, who knows, perhaps even a portrait of the contractor? Also a lot of people could remember what had gone on here when they were building the Libau–Romny and Kiev–Voronezh railways and they crossed at Bakhmach. People flooded in – peasants, mechanics, engineers, contractors, merchants, suppliers, agents, cashiers, and all with money, chasing after women, drinking, singing and carousing. There were eating houses, rooming houses, and bars everywhere and, well, where there's a demand, there's a supply.

But all that was on the one hand. On the other hand, everyone knew Khaim Yagudin was a gasbag, a braggart and a liar, who was quite capable of making up any story whatever. They all knew that he had a grudge against the professor over the eau-de-Cologne, everyone knew that he envied old Rakhlenko, Rachel's father, and you know why. And everyone knew what sort of man he was – a real man wouldn't allow himself to speak as he had about his own mother-in-law and brother-in-law. And they all knew that his wife had come to him far from empty-handed – she brought him the house, which we have already heard about, and the fruit stall which had supported the family while the wife was alive, but which Khaim sold, because an ex-Russian-army sergeant doesn't sell fruit to local hicks and louts! There were other absurdities in Khaim's account, and there were some old folk who firmly insisted that the professor was none other than the son of Ivanovsky from Ivanovka, who was both a learned man and a businessman, in the timber trade, supplying among other things timber to the sleeper-soaking plant, and as he was connected with the building of the railway, he moved here and though he did indeed soon die, nevertheless when the Ivanovskys moved here, the little boy-professor was definitely with them, so there can be no talk of some Old Believer or other. And old man Ivanovsky was a wealthy man, so he was well able to give his son an education with his own money, and had no need of help from an Old Believer.

As for Spinoza, some of the old men said that there had been something in it. A certain Baruch Spinoza had been excluded from the synagogue for free-thinking, and the old Ivanovsky, being the educated man he was, had sent a telegram protesting. Where had he sent it? Obviously, to Vilna. The fact that Spinoza had lived two hundred years earlier than Ivanovsky, and not in Vilna, but Amsterdam, didn't worry anybody, our old men were not ones for splitting hairs. A telegram is a telegram. But surely it doesn't prove that Professor Ivanovsky is a bastard?

In short, all sorts of arguments were brought against Khaim Yagudin's version, and as everyone knew what sort of man he was, they took Rachel and Jakob's side.

There were, even so, some envious and malevolent people who picked up Khaim's story in order to make slanderous and damaging denunciations, which they sent to Chernigov and even to Petersburg, to the Senate, about the illegal marriage according to the Jewish rite of the Lutheran Jakob Ivanovsky and the Jewess Rachel Rakhlenko.

The Tsarist bureaucratic machine, however, moved slowly and while these denunciations were being written, and being sent and examined, and inquiries were made, and answers sent back, and new questions to these answers were being asked and all this was being tied up and untied, the time was passing, and as time flies it was soon the First World War, then the Revolution, and in the face of such great events nobody was interested in whether Jakob Ivanovsky had been circumcised or not. Great history overwhelms small history. Still, perhaps it's little stories like this one, maybe millions of them, that make up the history of mankind?

3

I have only been able to judge what sort of life my parents led in Switzerland from the stories they told, which were rather few and even contradictory. Isolated words and phrases and jokes. 'You didn't talk like that in Basel', 'You didn't want that in Basel, you wanted this.' But I have managed to patch together from these snatches of conversation some idea of what went on in Basel, and why they came back.

So, they were living in Basel. After a year the first child was born, my brother Lyova, and six months later the train stops at our railway station, the guard unloads a trunk, suitcases and a folding baby-carriage, and out steps a young woman carrying a baby. The woman was my mother, Rachel, the baby was six-month-old Lyova, and mother just turned up with him at her parents' house. What had happened? Nothing, she had just come to visit her parents. Nobody was deceived, they all knew immediately that things were not going right – she turns up for no reason, with no husband and a nursing infant in her arms. There was no escaping the people who came to grandfather Rakhlenko's house to see how Switzerland had changed Rachel, but mainly, of course, they all wanted to know why she had come back. This was quite natural, people were sincerely interested in her fate and felt closely involved in it, and now something had happened – perhaps it had all turned to dust?

Mother had of course not come home to see her family and show them their grandson. She had left Basel for good. She didn't want to live there any more. Why? Apparently because of Jakob's female cousins. Father, it seems, had started running after his cousins, cousins on his mother's side. This, of course, was only an excuse. My mother was a jealous woman, I wouldn't deny that, but not because father was unfaithful, that was the last thing that would ever enter his mind, he simply wasn't that kind of man, nothing existed for him apart from mother. Mother was jealous by nature, and overbearing and quick-tempered. No, as I have said, the cousins were just an excuse, and the real reasons went much deeper. Without doubt, homesickness played a part. She had nobody there, apart from Jakob, no family, no friends, and there were none of our cherry orchards, or the forest, or the market, or the scent of our rich soil, or any of the things she had grown up with and got used to and found it hard to live without.

She could have overcome that. People move from one country to another and settle down in their new environment, and mother could have settled down, too.

There was something else, the main trouble, in fact. In the starchy, professorial German household, alongside her aristocratic mother-in-law and sisters-in-law, the wives of her husband's brothers – also aristocrats – Rachel, the daughter of a bootmaker from the Ukraine, felt herself to be not only not the first, not even the equal, but the last in line. She might have stood even that. After all, they wouldn't have to live with the in-laws forever, they would find a place of their own. The straw that broke the camel's back was language! Mother spoke Russian and Ukrainian, and could have mastered German, except that Yiddish, her mother tongue, got in the way. Knowing Yiddish, she could generally understand German-speakers, but they couldn't understand her, and when she tried to talk, her German came out as Yiddish, and to a German, Yiddish is a joke, and as mother couldn't stand a joke at her own expense, it was this joke that was the last straw.

Only father and I knew the real reasons for mother's return

home. I found out later, and I didn't just find out, but rather figured it out for myself, as there is a story behind it. As far as other people were concerned, mother's return home was a mystery, and they all thought she had come back because she couldn't settle down with Jakob. Many people felt sorry that such a beautiful romantic story, you might say the most outstanding event in the life of the town, had come to nothing. All the effort and the struggle had been in vain, unnecessary, and it had brought happiness to nobody.

They were mistaken, however. Not two months later, who should turn up from Basel but Jakob in person, and it became clear to everyone that there was no rift, they were husband and wife, as before, they loved each other, and whether they loved each other in Russia or in Switzerland made no difference to them. I don't know what discussions took place between mother and father, but I know for certain that it was precisely at that time that I was programmed, so to speak.

There were the usual ups and downs of family life. Lyova caught the measles, then the mumps, then mother was again in an interesting condition and father, who by now was called by his Russian name of Yakov, was dashing backwards and forwards from Chernigov to Basel and from Basel to Chernigov, while mother stayed behind, first to give birth to me, then to feed me, then, already by 1914, to give birth to and feed her third child, Yefim. All this went on until August 1914 when, as you know, the First World War broke out, and there could be no talk of going back to Switzerland. Father was stuck in Russia and, thank God, he wasn't mistreated as an undesirable alien for, even though he was a Lutheran, he was not from Germany but neutral Switzerland.

But what was there for him to do? He was a handsome, well-brought-up, polite, good man, a paragon of a man, but totally unsuited for life here. He had no qualifications. You can understand what that means, a man with no qualifications?

Then you can understand what it means to be an intellectual without qualifications, an intellectual without a higher education. Useless. He wasn't used to physical work and he was no good at clerical work, because he hardly knew the language. But he had to work, he had his family to support and he couldn't let himself and his wife and children hang round grandfather Rakhlenko's neck.

So grandfather Rakhlenko decided to get him going in trade. I've already mentioned that my grandfather Rakhlenko, even though he was a bootmaker, was a very wise and important man. In fact, he was the most important and respected man. He was the head of the synagogue, the *gabbe*. Usually this job was reserved for a wealthy man, who would be able to give money to the synagogue and help the poor and deal with the authorities, all things you need money for. So the *gabbe* would normally be not only a worthy man, but a rich one, too. Yet here it was my grandfather the bootmaker they had elected, because his virtues and wisdom far outweighed any wealth. I will say more about grandfather in due course; for the time being I will mention that, being a wise and practical man he thought up a trade for my father, and it was this.

We had a neighbour called Plotkin, Kusiel Plotkin. If you had to describe him in one word, that word would be 'loser'. There are people who are hard-working and industrious but who are just unlucky, nothing goes right for them whatever they do. Kusiel had a butcher's business, a little shop, more of a stall. He travelled round the outlying villages buying animals, which he slaughtered himself and sold as meat in his little shop. But he was unlucky, small, lop-sided and ugly. His first wife died and his second wife took his shop assistant as her lover, installing him in the house; when Kusiel went off round the villages to buy meat, she would entertain herself at home. Now, when an assistant is also the boss's wife's lover, he looks on the boss's money as his own, too, and if Kusiel sent his assistant to buy the animals and stayed at home himself, his worthless wife gave the poor man a life no beast would have endured. So now grandfather Rakhlenko suggested to Kusiel that he get rid of the lout of an assistant and take on father instead. Let father work for a year, and if they get on all right together and like each other, and if the business goes well with both of them in it, father should stop being the assistant and become a partner in the firm, with a half share. After one year, if all went well, father would put in half the value of the shop and they would split future profits down the middle. Where would father get the money? Well, Kusiel's stall wasn't such a big company, not exactly General Motors, so not a lot of money was needed. Some of it father brought with him from Switzerland, some Abraham Rakhlenko gave him, and with his reputation and his name, if he had needed a loan it would have been easily found. I don't know how Kusiel felt about the idea of making father a partner, after all everyone likes to be sole boss in his own business, but he liked the idea of chucking out that crook of an assistant, that swindling thief, his wife's lover, and taking on in his place such an honest, decent man as father. He also knew that my grandfather Rakhlenko would never suggest anything that wasn't a good idea.

Things weren't that simple. Kusiel agreed, but he had no authority – if a wife can install her lover right in the husband's house, the husband is nothing better than a dish-rag. On the appointed day, grandfather and father turned up at the shop and could see that Kusiel was not himself, and the lout of an assistant was standing at the entrance with an insolent smirk on his face.

Grandfather pointed to my father and asked, 'Kusiel, who is this man?'

'That's my new assistant,' replied Kusiel, trembling with fear.

Grandfather nodded in the direction of the loutish assistant, 'Then who is that man?'

'That's my ex-assistant,' replied Kusiel with a stammer.

'Have you settled up with him?'

'Yes.'

'In full, everything fair and square?'

'Everything fair and square.'

Then grandfather asked the assistant, 'Have you got any complaint against the owner?'

'The mistress told me not to leave the entrance of the shop,' the lout replied.

'You haven't got a mistress,' grandfather retorted. 'You *used* to have a master, but he's not your master any more and you're not his employee.'

With these words, grandfather grabbed the assistant by the shirt-front, dragged him out of the entrance and threw him into the street.

Then to Kusiel's wife grandfather said, 'If you go on shaming your husband, we'll have to divorce you and give you to pock-faced Yankel.'

Pock-faced Yankel was a mentally defective boy with a huge head and short paralysed legs, who sat all day cross-legged on the front steps, smiling blissfully at everyone, and if anybody said anything to him he would bellow back something unintelligible. He had a screw loose, we used to say, he was abnormal. We were all used to him and nobody would ever hurt him, neither the children nor, still less, the adults. So that's how my father became Kusiel Plotkin's assistant in the butcher's shop.

The butcher's trade is not altogether a simple one. What did it mean to be a meat-trader in those days? He had to find the animals, butcher them and then sell them. It takes experience to buy animals, you have to be able to judge by eye what the animal has been fed on, how much valuable meat there is on it, and how much fat, you have to know how to feel the animal, you have to know what breed it was and where it was fattened up. The cattle in our area are known as Circassians, or more technically, Ukrainian Greys. They're good cattle, an ideal breed both for working and for beef. Have you ever seen a Ukrainian bull? A real beauty! Two thousand five hundred pounds in weight, more than one ton! And it'll pull a ton and a half. Eight years such a bull will work, and work like an ox – excuse the pun – and then it'll go to be fattened up for meat. In short, you have to be able to discriminate with cattle, otherwise you can get landed with rubbish, even a sick animal, so you need experience and more experience.

My father had no experience whatever, but Kusiel did, as he had spent all his life in the meat business. So it was Kusiel who went round the villages buying the animals, and father who stayed in the shop. But then selling meat is not so straightforward, either. Each part has a different price, whether it's, say, fillet or best end, or loin or rump. Every housewife is after the best, as well as the cheapest, the tenderest and tastiest, and she wants enough to make a soup, and cutlets, and for frying and for brawn. She picks her meat by its appearance, its smell and its colour. She wants first-class meat, not too soft, not too tough, not too dry, but not oozing, not pale, nor too bright in colour. Stand in a shop for a while at the meat counter and watch a real housewife choosing meat, and then add to that the fact that ours is a cattle-rearing district and that any of the women was as good at judging meat as any present-day meat-refrigeration engineer, and you will understand my father's situation – he had only ever seen it dished up at the table, boiled, fried, or stewed. And bear in mind how polite he was, not at all the nifty salesman who can cut an appetizing slice off a beautiful carcass, turn it over in front of you like showing off a diamond, and then at home what you find you've bought is all bone. Father wasn't up to that, and you have probably already decided that the whole venture was a failure and a fiasco. In fact, there was no fiasco and the enterprise turned out to justify itself.

Not right away; that is, there were mistakes and slip-ups

on the cash side. For the first month, Kusiel stood next to father, or rather father stood next to Kusiel, learning the business. He did learn and the business prospered, and I'll tell you why it did. First of all, father was capable, and was from a family of surgeons, and however you look at it, surgeons are in the end butchers, up to a point. Secondly, most of Kusiel's customers were from the depot, wives of engine-drivers and other workers, as the shop was at the Old Martet, near the railway station. There was another butcher's shop, in the New Market, at the other end of town. All the people from the depot bought their meat from Kusiel, on credit. They would select their meat, Kusiel or his assistant would make a note of the price on a piece of paper, and when the drivers got paid, their wives would settle up. Kusiel and the crook of an ex-assistant had made these notes, and the customers had seen them writing them and understood what they were doing, but would argue over the amounts, and kick up a fuss. Kusiel would shove the notes in their faces and say 'Look, it's written down!' A lot of customers stopped going to Kusiel and went to the shop on New Market instead because of these notes; after all, nobody likes to be shown up as a fool. So my father insisted there must be no more notes. Kusiel had to agree, especially as he saw that the business was doing fine without the notes. Everyone knew my father was completely honest and that he would never take a kopeck more than he should, so there were no more rows and arguments, and the customers who had stopped coming because of the notes came back.

Thirdly, father introduced such cleanliness and order into the little shop as had never been heard of before. You know what the Germans are like in that respect. Maybe father remembered the clean German butchers' shops, with rows of salami and legs of ham and garlands of sausages, all hanging up and looking so nice and appetizing that you felt you wanted to eat everything in sight.

Then, finally, the fourth reason. The fourth reason and the main one, well, that was father's good looks. He wore a thin moustache and small pointed beard, what was then called the 'espagnole', and he looked like a Frenchman, and as well as German he could speak French, so he became known in town as 'the Frenchman', even though he was fair-haired. As a matter of fact, it's a mistake to imagine all Frenchmen as dark-haired. Far from it, many Frenchmen, especially among the aristocracy, are fair. It was very pleasant for the wives of the engine-drivers and the other depot workers to be served by such a courteous man, who looked like a Frenchman, and those who would normally have come in only every two or three days, started popping in every day, and the rumour went round that the women were in love with father. It seems quite likely. There was one woman, Mrs Golubinsky, the wife of an engineer at the depot, who definitely fell in love with father. She used to speak to him in French, and every day she called in at the shop and was head over heels in love with him. Years later father told me about it himself. She apparently wanted him to leave mother and run off with her to her father's estate.

Well, there was a lot of talk, gossip, rumour and tittle-tattle, which Kusiel's wife did everything she could to blow up. Naturally, it wasn't long before this gossip reached mother's ears and she was not one to ignore it! She set off for the stall which she found packed with women, among them Mrs Golubinsky. The fact that Mrs Golubinsky was buying meat was of no matter. Mother was a woman in the full meaning of the word, and she only had to see the way Mrs Golubinsky looked at her, and to see father in the middle of such a pack of females, and what with all the rumours and gossip, it was enough for her to declare that father wouldn't work at Kusiel's one more day.

What was that? Father had settled down on the job, got into the swing of it, become skilled, and in another month or two he'd become a partner, and now, if you please, just chuck it up! It was all female nonsense! Even grandfather Rakhlenko, who was tough with his sons but had never laid a finger on Rachel, banged his fist on the table and made the crockery jump. 'Let's have some peace,' he said. 'This talk has got to stop!' He was right. Three children were no joke, and the welfare of the family could not be subject to feminine whims and silly jealousy. Father understood this all too well, though he didn't bang the table with his fist. Instead, he laughed it off and went on going to work at the shop.

However, no amount of argument or reasoning or persuasion could convince mother. She sulked and wouldn't speak to father, and every day she went to the shop and stood watching the customers like a she-wolf. They were even afraid she might suddenly give Mrs Golubinsky a good hiding. Nobody can work under such conditions.

Jealousy takes its own course, and so does reality. Mother was sufficiently practical to realize that the family had to be fed. At home she kicked up a fuss, but meanwhile outside she was looking for another job for father. It would have to be the sort of place where there was not a trace of the scent of females. And she found it. An assistant was needed in a store owned by a certain Aleshinsky, who sold ironmongery, paints and agricultural implements. Who would his customers be? Is a peasant likely to send his wife to buy a scythe, a ploughshare or an iron tyre for a cartwheel? No, he goes and looks for himself, he'll turn a sickle over a hundred times, testing it to the touch and listening to the way it rings and feeling its vibration. It was the ideal place for my father. True, he would have to learn another business but, as mother said, it didn't matter to a real salesman what he sold, just as long as he knew how to sell, and father knew that, all right.

Mother stood her ground and father went to work for Aleshinsky, where he stayed quite a while, at least two or three years. I can still recall the smell of the paints, and I can see the little trays and drawers full of nails, the barrels of linseed oil, the iron of all sorts, in bar and tyre form, I can remember the coils of wire, the scythes and sickles, horseshoes, whetstones, saws, hammers, ropes and bridle-bits. Aleshinsky didn't make father a partner in the firm, as he had no need of one, being a rich man, but he paid well. Father was a good worker, the peasants respected him, he never cheated or swindled anyone, never tried to pass off shoddy goods, and he treated all the clients alike, giving as much attention to the ordinary customers as to the landowners. Quite possibly, father would have remained in hardware for the rest of his life, but for the fire. However, it was not the shop that went up in flames, but father's ironmongery career.

We had in the town a voluntary fire-brigade. Whether such voluntary ones still exist, I'm not sure. I imagine they do, as it is hardly sensible to maintain a paid brigade in a small town. When fire breaks out in a small town, everyone sees it, anyone can sound the alarm or ring the bell, at which the members of the fire-brigade must drop whatever they're doing and get to the fire-depot, or fire-station, where there are barrels of water ready, and pumps, hoses, ropes and grappling-hooks, all the things you need for putting out a fire.

Ours was a first-class fire-brigade. Even His Honour the Governor had said that if every town, village and hamlet had such a wonderful fire-brigade, it would be a great joy for the whole population and especially for their property, because when there's a fire it is the property that goes up first, and then the people who have been trying to save it.

Being a member of the fire-brigade was considered a great honour. It included the pick of the men, the healthiest, strongest, hardiest, bravest and most quick-witted. And so the title 'member of the voluntary fire-brigade' was a testimonial itself, especially for the younger men. At the head of the fire-brigade stood its leader, experienced, decisive and efficient, chosen by the rest of the team, and our fire-brigade chose as its leader grandfather Rakhlenko, naturally. Grandfather's first job as leader was to get rid of Khaim Yagudin, who bustled about when there was a fire, bellowed at the top of his voice, waved his stick about and only got in the way. Grandfather gave orders that Khaim Yagudin was not to be allowed anywhere near a fire. Grandfather was a strict man and kept up a high level of discipline, and each member of the brigade knew his place and what he was supposed to do. Of course, all grandfather's sons, my uncles, were in the team, being strong and daring chaps, and my father, as a member of the family, was also put in the team and would turn up at his proper place in the event of a fire.

And a fire duly occurred, on market-day, when a number of small shops caught fire. Father, naturally, made haste to get to it, but his boss, Aleshinsky, didn't want to let him go, and instead told him to move out the stock in case the fire got to his store. However, civic duty came first with father and, not taking any notice of his boss, he dashed off to the fire, which he put out, with the brigade, and he was so carried away, that he failed to notice that Aleshinsky's had caught fire. The store did not burn down, as it was the tail-end of the fire, and anyway the shop was built of stone and was also insured, and the assistants managed to move out all the goods, so in the end Aleshinsky lost nothing. Still, he couldn't forgive father for putting civic duty above the interests of his employer, so he began picking on him, and father left.

Meanwhile, despite the war, letters continued to arrive from neutral Switzerland, going by a roundabout route through Sweden, which was also neutral. And, of course, as always, the letters kept raising the question about a move back to Switzerland. But how could there possibly be any talk of a move with the war going on? It was absurd. They had no idea in Switzerland of the meaning of war.

Then came the Revolution, the Tsar was overthrown, the Pale of Jewish Settlement was abolished and you could go wherever you liked. Then it was the October Revolution, the war came to an end, letters from Switzerland came by the direct route, the demands for a return to Switzerland became more insistent, and a move itself a more realistic possibility. As far as I understand, even grandfather Rakhlenko inclined to the idea of father going back to Switzerland with his family. Grandfather loved his daughter, Rachel, and he loved Yakov his son-in-law like his own son, and he loved his grandsons, especially the eldest, Lyova. But grandfather saw that his son-in-law was totally unsuited to the way of life here. Having no profession he could only be a shop-assistant – not a job for a man like him. Nor could he go on living on handouts from Switzerland; for a grown man and the head of a family it was degrading.

They had to go to Switzerland. I feel sure that father must have dreamed of it. But mother wouldn't go on any account. She said 'I might have accepted being treated as third class, but I won't put my children through the same thing. Also, I don't want to be a burden to my mother-in-law and sisters-in-law. If Yakov wants to, let him go back to his Basel, let him go through university, and when he's a doctor we can think again – either he can come back here with a profession, or he can marry one of his pimply cousins, one of those skinny Swiss trout, and he can send me a divorce. I'll manage somehow to build my own life and my children's.'

Such talk in those days! Although mother already had three children, people say that she had just come into the full bloom of her beauty. In 1917 she was only twenty-four, and what is twenty-four for a real beauty? Of course, producing three children made it hard for her to keep her waistline. On top of that, ours was a simple family and our food was simple; we ate whatever there was, and there wasn't much, especially during the war, and the Civil War. If we had a bit of bread, a potato and a salted herring, we thought we were lucky. So of course mother lost the waistline she had had as a girl.

As for the rest of her, when I used to go with her to the market, young as I was, I knew from the way peasants would click their tongues and wink at each other as they glanced at mother, that she was no ordinary woman. She would walk through the market tall and straight, like a queen, and the people would open a way for her.

I mean by this that, as a woman, mother was sure of herself. Perhaps even a little too sure. As a beauty, she was without equal; as a housewife you wouldn't find a better one, practical, clever, authoritative, but she had three children and that was a bonus not every man will chase after. It's the first thing he'd think about. If a man was prepared to take her with her three children, he would be some widower who would throw in his own four orphans. Mother understood this perfectly, but of course she wasn't reckoning on another marriage, she knew things would never get that far, she knew that her Yakov would never get away from her, because he was joined to her by the heart for the rest of his life. And it sometimes occurs to me that father loved her all the more for her quarrelsome and wild character, and that he felt pity and realized that she wouldn't be able to settle down with anybody, but needed just such a man as he was, steady, considerate, and loving.

Because he was precisely that sort of man, that kind of husband, he began working in his father-in-law's bootmaking workshop. There was no alternative. When your brothers are both doctors and your father has a clinic in Basel, a boot-maker's workshop is no pleasure. Still, Kusiel Plotkin's butcher's shop, and Aleshinsky's hardware store, what pleasure were they?

Even so, when he was working at Kusiel's and then at the hardware store, at least he was leaving the house every day to go to work, and he brought home wages, and this helped him preserve a certain show of independence. I say a certain 'show' because, after all, we were dependent on grandfather, we lived in his house, enjoyed his hospitality and, as you can imagine, there was not a lot a family of five could do on father's wages. Even though he stood behind the counter at work, he was only an employee and didn't get a penny above his wages. Nevertheless, as I say, there was an appearance of independence, even in the fact that he came home in the evening after we had all finished supper, and he would eat alone, so it seemed at least as though it was his own supper he was eating.

Now that he was working for grandfather, he was completely under the old man's thumb. He was in grandfather's house all round the clock, he ate his meals with the rest of us, and in every way became a full member of grandfather's family. It was not a simple family either, and grandfather was anything but a simple man. On the one hand, he was the most respected man in the community, and on the other, he was capable of throwing Kusiel's assistant out on to the street without any argument. On the one hand, he was the honoured head of the synagogue, and on the other, he was the head of the fire-brigade, and if you could have seen him whipping up the horses when they were dashing to a fire, whooping and whistling like a Cossack, and cursing in foul language, and clambering into the fire, then I think you would understand that he had the most complicated and contradictory character, and it was no simple matter for my father to get along with him.

4

Grandfather Rakhlenko was broad-shouldered and black-bearded. He had grown up on the rich Ukrainian land and in a village backwater where his father, my great-grandfather, kept some sort of wayside inn and traded in vodka, and probably something illicit besides, and had dealings with people no respectable man ought to have dealings with. From an early age, grandfather was courageous, honest and fair. He didn't like the inn, and when he was still only a boy of fourteen or so, he left home to go and work on the construction of the Libau–Romny railway, lugging sleepers, work that suited him, as he was unusually strong physically. He did well to leave home, as where there's an inn, there's vodka, and where there's vodka, there's fighting, and fighting leads to killing, and in fact my great-grandfather did hit a man in a fight and the man died a few days later. Possibly it wasn't the blow that killed him, but his death was connected with the fight in the eyes of the villagers, and great-grandfather had to clear out, which is why his nickname in our town was 'the runaway'. Grandfather wasn't there at the time, being at work already on the railway, lugging sleepers, and already leading an independent life, at the age of fourteen.

I have mentioned several times that my parents, Yakov and Rachel, were very good-looking. Very. Yet their good looks simply didn't compare with my grandfather's. Such good-looking people, I'm sure, are only born once in a hundred years. He had a startlingly white face with wide cheek-bones, a black gipsy beard, a high white forehead, even white teeth, and beautiful blue, slightly slanting 'Japanese' eyes. Before the war, we went to Leningrad together when he was already well over seventy, and as we walked along the Nevsky Boulevard people turned round to look at us. My mother Rachel had someone to take after in her beauty.

The railway building was completed and grandfather left for Odessa, where he entered a bootmaking business and became an expert at it. He was practical, hard-working, a man of his word who disliked blather and he would probably have done well in Odessa. But Odessa! Today a pogrom, tomorrow a pogrom, and grandfather was not a man to let himself be beaten up and disfigured. He could do his own disfiguring, thank you very much! But what could he do? In the end he got fed up and went to Argentina. A year went by, but he didn't like it there. First of all, like his daughter Rachel, he was homesick, as he was very much attached to the places of his youth. Secondly, though he was reputed to have a flair for business, he was not really a businessman; he trusted people and expected them to trust him, he was no good at wheeling and dealing, he was straight, plain-speaking and open. How could he be plain-speaking and open in Argentina when he didn't know the language or the people or their customs? To cut a long story short, he went back to his home-town and took up bootmaking, the trade he had learned when he was living in Odessa. He knew his trade and our district was rich in cattle. There were tanners around and a tannery was built in due course; grandfather immediately saw the possibilities and his business flourished. As his sons grew up and began to help, he built up a good bootmaking workshop.

What sort of trade is footwear? I'll tell you. Footwear, if you really want to know, is the most responsible part of clothing. And how do people regard it? What do they think of the shoemaker? The lowest of the low, that's what a shoemaker is. Now, a tailor, that sounds like something, to make a suit is an art, but shoes? Shoes we buy ready-made, whereas we like to have our suits made to measure. But it should really be the other way round. Suits should be made up in standard designs to various combinations of height, chest and so on, or even better, they should be cut out and half-finished, and then run up for each customer in an hour or two. They do this, as a matter of fact, in many countries. After all, if a suit looks a bit baggy on you, it's only an aesthetic defect and you simply don't look the Apollo you imagined yourself; your vanity is injured, but not your health. Shoes, now, are a completely different matter. I have many years' experience, and I can tell you that there is no part of the human body as sensitive to clothing as feet are to shoes. Anybody who has been in the army knows that boots are the most important thing. When his greatcoat fits well, a soldier looks a fine fellow, but even if he doesn't look the manly campaigner, it doesn't matter, as long as he can still fight. But if his boots pinch, he isn't a soldier at all! Military leaders all the way back to Julius Caesar have paid more attention to boots than to anything else. I tell you as an expert, our feet have been so deformed by footwear, that you will only find a normal, healthy, straight foot on a new-born baby. As soon as an infant puts on its first boot or shoe, it's all over. From that moment he begins to deform his foot to fit standard or fashionable footwear. Over the centuries, it isn't shoes that have been adapted to the human foot, but the other way round. And what's the result? What does the average shoe-maker see when he looks at feet? Toes that are twisted, bunched up, crossed over each other, the big toe bent instead of straight, the little toe utterly deformed, flattened against the fourth, the line and arch of the instep destroyed and all its elasticity gone, so that it's afraid of walking. The shoe-maker sees corns, inflammations, abscesses, sores, ingrowing toenails, bunions, blistered heels, flat feet. A very ugly picture, and all as a result of bad, ill-fitting, too standard or too fashionable footwear.

I'm sorry for going on about it but, then, everyone likes to talk about their profession, or as the saying goes, you talk about what ails you, though maybe your problems are not so interesting to anyone else. I would just like to say one more thing, and that is that shoes should maintain the natural shape of the foot. Ideally everyone should have their own last, but you can't flout progress, and progress means mass production. Nor can you ignore fashion, and people simply have to have what's in fashion. Still, whether it's mass produced or hand-made, footwear should always take account of the most important thing, and that's the foot.

At the time that I'm talking about, mass production was not so well developed and many people preferred to have their shoes made to measure, and according to the latest fashion of course, though fashions didn't change as fast as they do now. Grandfather ran his business with careful consideration, making sure he had every kind of leather to hand, and he made both men's and women's shoes from beginning to end himself, from the measuring to the finishing. He was a master-craftsman and he employed good workmen, including his sons and grandsons, though not all of them went into bootmaking. My eldest brother, Lyova, and myself both began working for grandfather when we were thirteen; after all we were a big family, and father was unqualified. At that time, already the time of the Soviet regime, youths were allowed to work from the age of fourteen, but as grandfather was an artisan, and father counted as an artisan, Lyova and I helped as 'members of the family'.

You see the situation? In the workshop father was on exactly the same level as we were, in secondary roles doing secondary work, like hammering on heels and soles, sewing on buttons, writing down measurements as grandfather took them. Not very impressive work, in fact, and not very impressive workmates – his own little kids. But there was nothing to be done about it. Although we lived under the same roof with grandfather, as one family, a roof is a roof, a family is a family, but business is business. And as far as grandfather was concerned, the business came first, it supported his family and the family of his children and the families of his workmen. Grandfather himself worked without let-up and he demanded the same of the others. He made no allowances for anybody, neither his sons and grandsons, nor his workmen, nor his son-in-law, and if his son-in-law put a heel on badly, grandfather would fling the boot down and father would have to pick it up, which was very degrading, especially as father was no good anyway as a bootmaker and his work was constantly being flung into the corner, in any case. Father knew that grandfather did not do this out of anger, but because he demanded proper work, and there was nothing for it but to work and be patient. So father worked and was patient.

Things were more complicated in the other half of the household, the first half being the workshop, and the second half being the living accommodation. Things were much more complicated here, as two families were living together, grandfather's and ours. In grandfather's there were eight in all, and in ours five, so far. A devil's dozen! And every one of us with a personality of his own, often not a very polished personality, as this wasn't the well-ordered home of a German professor but a bootmaker's in a little town in the Ukraine with the whole world contained in it. Father had to adapt himself to this situation, and it was not an easy thing to do.

Grandfather's wife came from Gomel. He had travelled a lot. If he could get himself to Argentina and back, getting himself to Gomel was hardly an achievement. Grandmother had worked in Gomel as a wigmaker in a hairdresser's. In those days, religious Jewish women wore wigs after marriage. They cut their own hair short – not right off, of course, as they didn't want to look bald when they went to bed with their husbands without their wigs on. I've no idea where this custom came from, only that it was dictated by Jewish religious tradition.

Well, grandmother was a girl in Gomel, working at the hairdresser's, when somehow she met grandfather, they fell in love and decided to get married. For grandfather this was no simple matter – he was a very handsome man, who had travelled a lot and become accustomed to the bachelor life, and what a bachelor life! He'd had no end of women, and he found it hard to call it a day, hard to get hitched. Still, he decided to do it. But it wasn't so straightforward for grandmother to get married either, though for quite a different reason. Her father was a wagon-driver, and in those days the ties between tradesmen were very strong; artisans who lived on the same street often married their sons and daughters off to each other, so as to combine and strengthen their businesses. As the daughter of a wagon-driver, grandmother was being courted by the son of another wagon-driver, who was himself a wagon-driver, and this suitor persuaded his workmates that they should beat up grandfather to teach him to leave other people's intended brides alone, especially as he was from another town and a different trade.

One day grandfather arrived in Gomel to visit grandmother, and after they had been sitting together for a while, grandmother went to see him off at the station. And it was there that grandfather was set upon by the wagon-drivers.

Have you ever seen wagon-drivers fight? They fight to the death, with the crowbars they use for tightening up the ropes on their wagons. You will agree that it's one thing to be punched in the head by a fist or even with a bottle, but an iron crowbar is another matter. But grandfather managed to grab one from one of his assailants and, using it to beat off the others, he ran into the station, with his attackers in hot pursuit. Women shrieked, children howled, the station authorities hid. Station authorities are very brave people when they are confronted by a passenger without a ticket, but when they are faced by a mob of enraged wagon-drivers brandishing iron crowbars, their hearts sink into their boots and they hide. And there are no authorities in the world who can hide like the railway authorities. When there are no tickets left at the ticket-office and you have a train to catch, just try and find the station-master, let alone the official on duty! Grandfather was alone against ten infuriated wagon-drivers who intended to use their crowbars to turn him into mincemeat. But grandfather was not a man to be made mincemeat of. With the crowbar in his hand he fought his way back outside the station, grabbed his girl, ran all the way round the station with her, jumped on the train and went back to his own town, where they got married.

Although grandfather had won his bride, so to speak, on the field of battle and at the risk of his life, and had carried her off the field of battle in his arms, at home he didn't carry her in his arms, and in fact her life with him was not at all sweet. He was a stern, demanding man, very thorough and economical in his way of life. For her part, grandmother had made wigs at the hairdresser's ever since she was a girl, and had never learnt to do domestic work, and unfortunately she was not at all practical, nor even especially neat and tidy. Not that she was slovenly or anything like that, but she wasn't obsessed with cleanliness like the rest of the Rakhlenkos including, incidentally, my mother.

Grandmother was a quiet, reserved, very religious woman and, on getting married, she was completely at a loss. Grandfather demanded that the house be kept clean and everything done on time, according to the clock. There were a lot of people in the household as children started arriving. In time, of course, grandmother got used to it, but at the beginning there were blunders and misunderstandings, she didn't know what to do with herself at first, didn't know her proper place in the household, or what her role was. Grandfather was Number One, for her and for the children and the grandchildren and the neighbours, in fact for everybody, and although in time she learned to cope with the house and the family, she always played a supporting role. The star was always grandfather. Next to him came my mother, the slogger, powerful, thrifty, thorough – having attached her own family to grandfather, she felt herself obliged to do the work of two people, cooking for everyone, cleaning up after everyone, looking after the cow, running the entire household in fact. But given her character, she couldn't do it as if she were helping her mother, my grandmother, but only by pushing grandmother out of her position as mistress of the house and still further lowering her status in the household. Grandfather accepted this, because to him the most important thing was that there should be order in the home, and domestic arrangements must help and not hinder the bootmaking concern, and he cared least of all about any so-called hierarchy of power in the house, since the only real power he recognized was himself.

There was of course nothing father could do to change anything. He had come into grandfather's house as an in-law and he would not interfere with the way other people arranged their lives. From the first day, however, he showed concern and respect for grandmother, which nobody else was used to doing, and this attitude was something of a protest in itself. Not only that, father also compelled my mother to show respect to grandmother and, although she would not let go of the reins, so to speak, she was influenced by father and, feeling somewhat guilty in his eyes and not wanting to offend him, she didn't dare to treat grandmother roughly, but showed her what consideration she could and at least didn't quarrel or bicker with her.

The weekdays were all bustle and activity, clients and customers, suppliers, work and rush. Market-days, when the peasants from the surrounding district came into town, were especially noisy. Friday night and Saturday were quiet. The table would be laid with a snow-white cloth and flickering candles, there would be the smell of *gelfilte* fish and fresh *khala*, and grandfather, looking broad-shouldered and handsome, would walk back and forth muttering the evening prayer. Then on Saturday, wearing a new frock-coat and hat, he would proceed to the synagogue, slowly and gravely, with his hands folded behind his back. I used to follow behind, carrying his prayer-book and velvet bag containing his *talis*. I wasn't yet thirteen, the age of manhood, and I would run along behind grandfather, kicking stones and jumping on and off the wobbly planks of the wooden sidewalk.

As I have already said, grandfather was the head of the synagogue, the most important figure in the community, but whether he was a sincere and deep believer, in the way grandmother was, I couldn't say. There was something religious in grandmother's face, not in any sanctimoniously devout or ecstatic sense, but a look full of religious feeling, serenity, and resignation. Quiet and dignified in a dark blouse and skirt, with a wide belt and a black knitted shawl, she would walk to the synagogue, without a prayer-book, as she always kept one there, in a little drawer under her seat – she kept another one at home, next to her bed. Grandfather wasn't so religious or devout. Religion for him was more the style of his national way of life, a holiday and rest from his labours and troubles, the basic order by which he lived.

He was above all a man of concrete action and concrete decision. Certainly, there are bootmakers who love to discuss the world's problems, as they sit on their work-stools waxing twine or hammering in nails. Grandfather never discussed the world's problems. As a matter of fact, he didn't discuss anything at all, in the true sense. He would listen to others in silence, think things over, and then announce his decision. If he advised a client to do such and such, to have something made this way and not that, the client always took his advice, because it was known that Abraham Rakhlenko never put his personal interest above that of the client. He was active in the community not out of vanity, but because in community affairs he could demonstrate his sense of justice.

We had a rich man in the town called Freidkin, who owned a flour mill. He liked to live on a grand scale. At his son's wedding the first automobile in town made its appearance, specially ordered from Chernigov, or Gomel, I'm not sure which – anyway, he loved to show off. But like all rich men, he was tightfisted. Poor people bought flour from him to make bread, *khala*, and pies, which they sold at the market. What could they make from this? Pennies. And if the profit is in pennies, how can a business ever accumulate turnover capital? And if you don't have turnover capital, you have to get your flour on credit, as a loan, and like any kulak, Freidkin charged interest. There was nothing the poor people could do, but in hard times they couldn't pay back the loan, more flour would be needed, so interest would be added to the interest and they would become debt-slaves. At the Old Market, there was a widow called Gorodetsky, a beggar woman, filthy and ragged. She had what all widows have, a pile of kids, as filthy and ragged as herself. She baked rolls which she sold at the market and, as I said, earned pennies on which she had to feed, clothe and shoe her kids. She got so far in debt to Freidkin that he stopped supplying her with flour. It was like telling her to die, and her kids, too. Who did she run to? Naturally, to Rakhlenko.

Grandfather rose from his work-stool, took off his apron, went to Freidkin, who was at his warehouse, and said, 'You will let her off the interest, I will pay off her debt, and you will give her a hundredweight of flour, free. If you don't agree, I'll take hold of you with this hand, and with the other one I'll knock every single tooth out of your head.'

So Freidkin let the woman off the interest, and gave her the hundredweight of flour, and she started trading her rolls and pies again in the Old Market; and of course the whole market-place praised grandfather to the skies because, like all unfortunate widows, she had to tell everybody everything.

I remember another incident very clearly, even though I was only a small child. Living next door to us was a saddler called Afanasi Prokopyevich Stashenok, a Byelorussian. He made everything a saddler makes – carriage-harness, riding-harness, collars, traces, breechings, reins and saddles, and he even trimmed carriages in leather and upholstery. Saddlery is related to bootmaking, only the needle is different, as the bootmaker's stitch must be compact so as not to let in dust or water, and it must completely fill the hole made by the needle, whereas the saddler is not worried by that, so he uses an awl. They both use the same material, leather, so a certain amount of cooperation developed between grandfather and the saddler, and whatever one of them had no use for he would pass on to the other, all the more so as they were neighbours. Grandfather had a big yard and big sheds, where Stashenok stored the large quantities of leather which he kept, as he trusted grandfather completely. Thirty years they lived side by side, and in all those thirty years they never spoke thirty cross words to each other.

Well, one day two gipsies turned up; one of them, called Nikifor, was known to grandfather, the other wasn't. They drove into the yard and tied up their cart. Nikifor ordered some boots from grandfather, collected some goods from Stashenok, loaded up the cart and drove off. Soon after Stashenok's sons came running in to say that the gipsies had stolen something from them. Grandfather went out into the street, stopped the cart, and found the stolen goods under some hay. A crowd gathered, someone wanted to send for the police, but grandfather said, 'No, no police.' He ordered the stolen goods to be taken back where they belonged.

Then he asked Nikifor, 'How shall we settle this, Nikifor?'

The gipsy was silent, what could he say? Then grandfather gave him a punch that sent him flying to the ground with blood coming out of his nose and mouth. Grandfather didn't touch the other one, the one he didn't know. The punch was not for thieving, but for betrayal. That was the kind of man grandfather Rakhlenko was.

It was actually through grandfather's efforts that a new synagogue was built, when the old one became dilapidated and too small and cramped, and that's why they chose him as *gabbe*, the head man, on the first day of Purim. You know what Purim is? It's the happiest of all the holidays. According to biblical tradition, the Persian king, Ahasueras, or Xerxes as he's known today, had a minister called Haman, who persuaded the king to order the total destruction of all the Jews. But the king's wife, the beautiful Esther, got the king to change his mind and punish the scoundrel Haman instead. In honour of this even the joyful holiday of Purim is celebrated, when there is drinking and dancing, and rattles are shaken. So, on the first Purim after the building of the new synagogue, an armchair was taken there and grandfather was sat in it and carried home, with the people running along in front, singing and dancing and rattling their rattles, and doing honour to grandfather.

The population of our town was mixed, but friendly. Russians, Ukrainians, Byelorussians, and Jews lived together peacefully. Not far off, there were six German villages; their ancestors had come from Frankfurt-on-Main and were settled here by Catherine the Great. Before that, in the seventeenth century, schismatics, or the Priestless Old Believers, settled here in the forest. And in the railway depot there were Poles who had been exiled here after the 1863 rebellion. In general, it was a highly mixed population, yet there was no enmity or national group animosity whatever! It's proof enough to mention the fact that not a single pogrom ever took place in our town. After the 1905 Revolution, when the reaction set in, some pogromists did arrive, but grandfather and his sons went out to meet them, and you can see from these photographs what sort of men grandfather and his sons were, not just bootmakers, but real fighters! They were joined by the tanners and butchers, the joiners and wagon-drivers, and loaders from the railway station, all first-class, tough men, some with sticks, others with axes and clubs or shafts, and out came the workers from the depot, too, not empty-handed, either, and the pogromists took to their heels.

Now, there was no church in our town. Can you imagine! If the town had grown up out of some tiny village, it would have had a church for sure, because every village has its church. But our town had started life as a hamlet; then, when they brought the railway and built the depot, it became a little railway settlement, and from a little railway settlement it became a town, but without a church. The people used to go to church in the neighbouring village of Nosovka. Of course, there was a collection going on to build a church, but they could have gone on collecting for another twenty years if it hadn't been for grandfather. What he did was to make Tsimmerman, a rich builders' merchant, and Aleshinsky, the owner of the hardware store, and a number of other merchants, supply materials to build the church as though on credit, but not to ask for the money to be paid. And so the church was built. When the service for its dedication took place, the priest mentioned the name of the townsman Rakhlenko, whose works pleased God, though he was a Hebrew.

5

As I've already said, grandfather had a complicated and contradictory character. Let me give you an example of the way he treated his own children.

My mother had a remarkable voice. In fact, all the Rakhlenkos sang beautifully, but when mother sang, a crowd would gather outside the house – they even broke the fence down on one occasion. Once, when she was still a girl, and was in the forest with her friends, she started singing. The forest was full of summer visitors, as I've already described, and among them was a professor from the Petersburg Conservatory. The professor heard someone singing and producing trills he had never heard sung before, even at the Conservatory, so he got out of his hammock, followed the voice, and found the group of young people. But mother stayed silent when there was a stranger around.

'Which one of you was singing?' the professor asked.

They all kept quiet, because mother kept quiet. As long as she stayed silent it meant she didn't want to own up, and her friends wouldn't give her away. So the professor spoke to each of them in turn, and when he got to mother he recognized from her voice that she was the one who had been singing – after all he wouldn't have been a professor if he couldn't guess that.

'You have an exceptional voice,' he said. 'There are very few voices like yours, if any. You must come to Petersburg to study at the Conservatory. I will do everything for you.'

In short, he promised her mountains of gold. He took her

over to his wife and daughter, who also admired her voice, and also tried to persuade her that she must come to Petersburg, and also promised her mountains of gold, and insisted that she would live with them and want for nothing, and become a famous singer.

I don't know if mother really meant to go to Petersburg, but she told grandfather that she wanted to.

He answered, 'You can go. But if you come back here, I'll . . . do you see this axe? I'll chop your head off with it!'

Sometimes grandfather beat his sons till they were nearly half-dead, but he had never so much as laid a finger on his daughter, as I have already mentioned. And now such a threat! The moment he said it, mother made up her mind to go, even though, as you know, she didn't like moving from place to place, just as later on she wouldn't like Switzerland. But to give in? It was not in her character. Quite possibly, she would have gone. But soon after this event, another professor appeared, Professor Ivanovsky, and his son Jakob, and you know what happened then. From the moment mother saw my future father, the Conservatory didn't even exist any more.

Mother kept her voice into her maturity, not that it was trained, of course, or polished, but it was outstanding. I can remember a woman professor, this time from the Moscow Conservatory, coming to the town, and when she heard mother sing, she came to our house and said, 'I will make you a better singer than Katulsky. It won't be you who'll listen to Katulsky, but Katulsky who will listen to you.'

Mother just laughed. She hadn't a clue who on earth Katulsky was, and anyway there could be no talk of any singing as she already had grown-up children.

That gives you some idea of the way grandfather regarded her talent.

Grandfather's eldest son was Yosif. He was the first-born and much loved by grandfather. Yet grandfather never beat his other sons as much as he did Yosif. He used to beat the living daylights out of him, and for good reason. First of all, Yosif didn't want to learn. A teacher called Kuras, a very good teacher in all subjects, used to come to the house to teach Yosif, and grandfather used to take lessons together with his son, just like another schoolboy. Yes, I mean it. When Kuras came, grandfather would take a seat as though out of curiosity, and work out sums, also as though out of curiosity, and write essays and summaries, and in this way he himself learned to read and write in Russian and acquired some elements of an education. You must admit that for a grown-up, active and busy man this was quite an unselfish act.

So, the teacher would come to the house. Yosif was capable and picked things up quickly, and you would think he'd study to his heart's content. Not a bit of it. The fact is, he was obsessed with pigeons. He didn't want to know about anything, except his pigeons, which he spent whole days trapping. Though he was only a boy, he was the best pigeon-catcher in town, he ran it as a business. He had always done business, since he was a small boy, but pigeons were his main concern – he swapped them, sold them, claimed ransom for pigeons he'd caught, and that was his whole life. He grew up to be a regular crook, doing things you simply couldn't imagine, like stealing leather and finished goods from grandfather and from our neighbour, Afanasi Prokopyevich Stashenok, the saddler, and lying to everyone and gambling – in a word, a crook.

Physically he looked like grandfather, except that grandfather had a noble look in his face, whereas Yosif's reminded you of a bandit. It was pleasant to look at grandfather, and unpleasant to look at Yosif. Grandfather was clever, Yosif was cunning and treacherous. To some he behaved like a boor, to others he cringed and toadied. His motto was, 'An affectionate calf can suck two teats.' He knew how to smile, and when he did he could look like an angel and he would worm his way into your confidence, and then stab you in the back. He had a pal called Khonka Bruk, a swindler like himself, who worked at a firewood yard, where there was a watchman who had an iron stove. All their cronies congregated there at night to play cards, mess around with girls, and drink vodka. I think in time they would have turned into a professional gang, but for the First World War. Yosif was called up for army service, but even in the army he managed to set himself up. The band-master's wife fell in love with him and made her husband get him into the band and teach him to play the flute, and he fluted his way right through the war.

He was good-looking and daring and he knew how to dress. Women really went for him, even though he treated them like dirt. A lot of scandals and fights took place because of this.

Grandfather was great friends with our neighbour, the saddler Stashenok, though Stashenok was ten years younger. The Stashenoks were good, decent people, and I shall have more to say about them later on. For the moment, let me just say that the eldest Stashenok boy, Andrey, was called up in August 1914, leaving his wife, Ksana, on her own with a small baby to look after for quite a long time, as Andrey only got back from German prisoner-of-war camp in 1918. Now, Yosif came back from the army in 1917, and there, living right next door, was a soldier's pretty young wife, minus a husband. Naturally, Yosif had his eye on her. He would pop into the Stashenoks for this and that, stop Ksana on the street or chat to her over the fence, and it was soon quite clear to everyone what he was after. Ksana didn't respond to his passes, but it was a small town in the south, where everything is out in the open, everyone could see that Yosif was trying to get involved with her, he was com-promising her, and giving ammunition for gossips and rumour-mongers, who are always plentiful in the provinces.

A conversation took place between my mother and Uncle Yosif which I overheard. Mother thought I wouldn't understand anything, as I was only five or six, but children at that age understand quite a bit, they are very sharp and they remember a lot. I remember Uncle Yosif in front of the mirror, brushing his gleaming, brilliantined hair.

'You've started leaning on the Stashenoks' fence too much,' mother said to him.

'Mind your own business,' he replied, without turning round.

'You're going to disgrace a married woman!'

'Got anything else to say?'

'You're a loathsome swine!'

'Don't push me too far,' Yosif warned her.

That day or the next, Yosif was standing at the fence again, chatting with Ksana, when mother approached.

'Ksana! Are you blind? Get a big stick and give this beast the hiding he deserves, it'll teach him to stay away from you.'

There were other Stashenok women working in the garden and when they heard what mother was saying, they came up to the fence, too. I think that at that moment Yosif was ready to kill my mother, but there were women and children around and he had enough sense not to create a worse scandal. He just called my mother a 'silly fool' and cleared off. I clearly remember Ksana saying, 'Thank you, Rachel Abramovna.'

Yosif stopped popping into the Stashenoks and pestering Ksana after that, but I'm afraid he learned nothing from the incident.

There was a refugee from Bessarabia in the town, an unhappy, lonely girl. Yosif started living with her, and when she became pregnant he sent her off to Gomel, with a lot of talk and promises, which she believed. Later, he sent his pal Khonka Bruk to Gomel with money for her and instructions 'to give this idiot the money and tell her I'll never marry her, she's not the first and she won't be the last'. Khonka, being the swine he was, was glad to pass this on, word for word. Imagine what it was like in those days to be an unmarried woman, pregnant and alone, a refugee in a strange town among strangers. To be quite frank, we men are not exactly saints, especially when we are young and lucky with women. Even so, there are limits that should not be crossed. He liked her, they got together and had fun, fine, but to make promises and then to betray her, that's no way for a man to behave. Why promise? If she loves you, she's yours without making any vows.

Apart from that, to take advantage of the fact that the girl was alone and defenceless, a refugee, and then to abandon her to her fate, you must agree only a scoundrel would behave like that. Well, Yosif was a scoundrel, he thought only of himself, of his own pleasure and his own advantage.

I remember the story about the refugee girl perfectly, so it must have happened after the Revolution, perhaps in 1918 or 1919. I know the story not from what others have told me, but because I was a witness to it myself, and to everything that went on in connection with it.

A conflict took place between my father and the Rakhlenko family, it was their only conflict, the first and the last, and it was after it occurred, as far as I can work out, that we moved to another house.

Yosif and my father were the same age, so at the time this incident took place they were both around twenty-seven or twenty-eight, anyway, not over thirty. By that time father already had four children: Lyuba had arrived after Lyova, myself, and Yefim. Yosif, however, was still a bachelor and a dealer of some sort, he had packed up as a bootmaker and gone into commerce, speculation, no doubt, doing all kinds of shady deals, especially under the New Economic Policy with its free market, living a dissolute life and satisfying a big appetite for women. So, naturally, he and my father had absolutely nothing in common. They despised each other, but father, being the polite and considerate man he was, didn't show it, whereas Yosif, being a boor, didn't hide it. However, he wouldn't dare insult father, because there was still mother to contend with, and she was ready at any moment to leap to father's defence, like a brood-hen with her chick. Except that mother was no hen, rather a hawk, feared by everyone in the family, Yosif included. Between Yosif and father, then, stood mother, waiting to stifle any tiff and stamp out any spark. At the same time, she didn't want there to be friendship between them, as she was afraid that Yosif might drag father into his amorous exploits and, since for Yosif nothing was sacred, he would gladly have hurt his own sister by making father one of his cronies. So mother had to keep watch on two fronts, one where they might fight, and the other where they might become friends. She need not have worried about them becoming friends, as father found Yosif deeply repellent, nor could there be any idea of father running after women; he had a family to keep and no profession, so how could women come into it! Even so, mother failed to save him from a clash, and this refugee girl was the cause of it.

Nobody approved of what Yosif had done, of course. There was a difference, however, in the way father condemned him and the way the Rakhlenkos condemned him. Father thought Yosif ought to marry the girl: how could he abandon his own child to the mercy of fate? Responsibility came first where father was concerned. It had been from a sense of responsibility that he had sacrificed himself, and expected Yosif to do the same. Perhaps he was also moved by a feeling of solidarity with the girl – after all, she was a stranger here, like himself, alone, without family or friends, and he pitied her. The Rakhlenkos also condemned Yosif, though not for abandoning the girl in that condition, but for taking up with her in the first place. I overheard a conversation between mother and father on this subject, when they thought I was asleep, but I wasn't and I heard every word. Mother reasoned more or less like this: 'Are there no nice young girls from good families he could marry? Where were his eyes, where was his common sense, I ask you! He's not a child, he's nearly thirty, thank God. But no, he had to have this pathetic refugee. And she must really be bright! No doubt she thought she had hooked herself a good husband, except that she didn't know who she was dealing with, so the silly fool fell for him. Of course, I feel sorry for the child she's carrying, but what can be done about it now? Marry her? What sort of life would it be? As if he could respect a girl like that! Is she the wife for him? He'd beat her by day, and at night he'd be sleeping with other women. Is that a life? No, marriage wouldn't put wrongs to right.'

That was how mother saw it, and how the other Rakhlenkos saw it, too, probably with some variations: Yosif is of course a swine, but marriage? Marriage is no way out of the situation.

I think you can see from this disagreement the difference between my father and the Rakhlenkos. He put duty first, but he was a romantic, up in the clouds, while they had their feet planted firmly on the ground and reasoned realistically – the more so as it was perfectly plain that, whatever they thought and however they argued it, Yosif would act as he chose, and only as he chose, and no force on earth would make him do what he didn't want to do. Grandfather knew that Yosif would submit to no will but his own, so he kept quiet. And you know what grandfather was like as a young man himself. I think quite a few boys and girls with grandfather's slanting eyes could be seen wandering around in the outlying villages! It was a definite fact that he had a son by a peasant girl in the neighbouring village of Petrovka, a son he acknowledged as his own. I'm sure this was so. I remember vague conversations when I was still only in my infancy, I remember grandfather making trips to Petrovka and spending nights there, and grandmother being upset, and then some business with money, grandfather helping his village mistress and his illegitimate son. And so in similar cases he was quite lenient and detached. He was sorry for the unlucky refugee girl, but he knew it was no good trying to force Yosif to marry her, nor was it right, as no good would come of such a marriage, either for her or for Yosif.

I might not have remembered that story – I was very small at the time and there have been no end of stories about Uncle Yosif – but for the fact that I was an eye-witness to the scene involving father and Yosif, and it was something that engraved itself deep in my mind. I don't know what father said to Yosif, or how it all started, though even if he did say something, he would certainly have put it tactfully, but, as I say, I don't remember just what it was. I remember all too clearly, however, the enraged look on Yosif's face, and when he was enraged he was terrifying, he forgot himself and was capable of murder.

He shouted at father, 'You mongrel kraut! You dare lecture me! Who the hell do you think you are! Hanger-on, sponger, you sit on our backs with your horde, you can't do anything except produce kids, a cobbler's stooge, goddam kraut! You're not ashamed to eat our food, yet you've got the nerve to throw some cheap whore in my face, you came here to teach us, well, now you can clear off back to Switzerland, you mongrel kraut!'

He leapt at father, but, like a cat, mother leapt at him, because Yosif could quite easily have killed father, as he was a fighter, like all the Rakhlenkos, whereas father wasn't one to fight, he never laid a finger on anyone in his life. We children howled and also tried to shield father, and the noise brought grandfather and the others from the workshop, and when he heard 'mongrel kraut', grandfather gave Yosif a great smack in the face. Then that swine Yosif threw himself at his own father, an old man, at which the other uncles moved in and twisted Yosif's arms behind him while grandfather gave him a few more good smacks across the face on his own behalf, not father's.

That ugly scene was etched in my memory as the only time my father was ever insulted in grandfather's house. After that incident, our family moved to another house. Maybe we didn't move immediately, and maybe it wasn't because of this incident, maybe it was because, from grandfather's point of view, a family of six round your neck is, after all, a bit too much, and it was time they had a house of their own. I was only a child at the time and I have remembered only the most important incidents, which have become compressed with time, and so the affair with the refugee girl, the scene with Uncle Yosif, and the move to our new home come straight after one another, whereas in fact they might have been quite far apart.

We bought a little house on the neighbouring street. It was during the Civil War and everything was on the move. People were scattering and coming together, running away and settling in new places, and we got the little house quite cheap. It was only a living-room, two bedrooms, kitchen and store-room, and we were lucky to get it, as our backyard almost adjoined grandfather's. I say almost, because next door to us stood a two-storey detached house belonging to an engineer from the railway depot called Ivan Karlovich, an ethnic German and a very grand and austere gentleman. Ivan Karlovich had a big orchard, and we used to climb over the fence, run through his orchard, then over the other fence and into grandfather's yard. Ivan Karlovich was not pleased at this, and he told our parents off about it, and mother gave us all a clip round the back of the head, which was her speciality, but father didn't lay a finger on us, ever, as I have already mentioned. Ivan Karlovich was very angry with us children, as we were noisy and always making a racket and disturbing his peace. He also suspected us of stealing his apples off the trees, a suspicion that was not unfounded. He was, however, extremely respectful towards our parents, as was everyone else. In addition, father turned out to be an interesting man for

Ivan Karlovich to talk to, being in effect a German like himself. They spoke to each other only in German, which was good practice for Ivan Karlovich, especially as there was nobody else around with such pure German pronunciation as father's. He used to lend father books from his collection and was a great reader himself; it was through him that my brother Lyova and I became avid readers, too.

I'm sorry, I have lost the thread. This has been happening to me a lot lately, old reminiscences getting mixed up with new thoughts. The more the old reminiscences, the more the new thoughts. You think that that was the way you thought then, but really it's the way you think now.

Anyway, what was I talking about? Ah, yes, Uncle Yosif. Grandmother said, 'It'll be an unhappy woman that Yosif marries.' Yet, can you imagine, he actually married very well, he picked out a wife who really suited him, and even better than that, his wife was a dentist. But what was Yosif? Nothing, a womanizer, though the women loved him. The dentist, however, had some character, and she promptly took Yosif in hand and put him to work, learning to make false teeth. Like all the Rakhlenkos, Yosif had gifted fingers and mastered the skill, turning out crowns, bridges and false teeth and everything his wife needed for her patients. The business was pure gold, in the literal and figurative sense. There were two other dentists in the town, but Yosif's wife was the best, and Yosif was not only a good dental mechanic, but was also smart, cunning, and prepared to take risks, and even though he was dealing with gold, he wasn't afraid, especially as it was during the New Economic Policy or NEP. He expanded the business and made it flourish. When NEP came to an end, they closed down the practice and went to work in a clinic, keeping the surgery at home only for friends, and relatives, as it were, though in a small town like ours, practically everyone is either a friend or a relative, and then the district authorities have teeth, like anyone else – when it's a question of toothache, you have to shut your eyes to certain things, especially when everything is done for you quickly, efficiently and to the highest standard. There was always a queue at the clinic, so if the chairman of the district executive committee or the chief of the militia turned up, she would put him in the chair, give him some treatment, then say 'Come and see me at home tomorrow evening.'

She would give him more treatment at home, but she would take no money, God forbid, this was an official patient from the clinic, and anyway she had no private practice whatever, she was just doing a favour, showing respect, making it unnecessary to wait in line or to jump the queue, which is itself not a very proper thing to do, you would agree. And if she showed the same respect to their wives, there was nothing wrong in that, as they were her friends anyway, a doctor, a teacher, the librarian – they were the local intelligentsia, you might say, all her colleagues and friends, and she was in her own home and not taking money for it. If they liked to bring her a little something, a cake or a box of chocolates or something to wear from Kiev, there was nothing wrong in that. As a matter of fact, her surgery at home was a sort of annexe of the clinic, with a cosy, family atmosphere, where there was no bureaucratic red-tape or formality. Behind this front, however, there was concealed a real business, where everything was done for private patients who paid cash, and if they had no gold of their own for their crowns and bridges and false teeth, Yosif could always supply it.

Everyone could guess the kind of money Yosif and his wife were raking in, but Yosif ran the business shrewdly, giving nobody cause to criticize them, and nobody did. Though Yosif was bold and reckless, and greedy for money, his wife was a cautious woman, very diplomatic, and she taught him to be careful. Yosif used to travel to Kharkov, Kiev, and Moscow to get the gold, even to Central Asia; he was never caught, everything was kept hush-hush. They had gold and other valuables, all carefully tucked away, and they had a beautiful house of their own with good furniture. Every summer, they went either to the Crimea or to the Caucasus. Yosif loved the good life, and still liked to dress well, and to have his wife dress well, too. He had good taste, you can't deny that, and he was practical and energetic, you can't deny that, either, and he even became an exemplary family man. But never once in his life did he ever do anything good for anyone else, everything he did was for himself.

As for the refugee girl, I heard many years later that grandfather went to Gomel to find her and give her money, and she got married; in fact, grandfather put her life in order.

Grandfather's second son was Lazar, the complete opposite of Yosif. A dreamer, impractical, a philosopher, he was the only Rakhlenko with short sight, which was no doubt from all the reading he did as a child, even at night. He used to climb on to the stove, light the kerosene lamp and read all night. As a result, he wore pince-nez and passed as an educated man, though he was widely read, rather than educated, and widely read in an unsystematic way, reading anything that came into his hands. Seeing that he had this passion for reading, grandfather sent him to Ratner's high school in Gomel, a private high-school recognized by the state. But it turned out that Lazar had no real ability, though he did have a defect that was most unusual for a Rakhlenko, and that was laziness. His own mother would be chopping wood, and he would sit and read the newspaper, as though that was what he should be doing. He was decent, not an egoist, but his laziness simply overwhelmed him, so he was a dreamer, a romancer and a failure. He was an indifferent bootmaker, who could only learn the trade under grandfather's threats, but he liked to chat with the customers, make conversation and blather on all kinds of subjects. Later he worked in the cooperative and the factory, at first on the shopfloor, then as a technical inspector. The death of his wife broke his spirit. His wife, Tema, was a sweet, kind woman, she loved Lazar, forgave him his ineffectiveness, asked for nothing, and made do with what there was. She was the right kind of wife for Lazar, because he could work a little and philosophize a lot. But Tema died giving birth to their child. How Lazar didn't commit suicide I don't know. He couldn't bear to look at his son and it was grandfather who cared for little Daniel. He put the child in the hands of a wet-nurse in a village, incidentally it was the village of Petrovka, where his own illegitimate son lived, now a grown man and with his own family. Grandfather went there nearly every day to look at his grandson, to see how he was and that everything was all right. He nursed him and brought him up. As for Lazar, he completely went to pieces and started drinking, and even grandfather, who wouldn't tolerate drunkards, shut his eyes to it, as he knew Lazar's life was a failure.

Grandfather's third son was Grisha. I can't say anything in particular about him, as he was nothing in particular. He was robust, like all the Rakhlenkos, and he was the best fighter on the street, but he fought for justice, he defended the weak. Defending the weak means fighting the strong, and he handed out bruises right and left. When a boy comes home with bruises, the first thing they ask is, who did it? The boy answers, 'Grisha Rakhlenko'. Who do the parents complain to? Grandfather. Grandfather made no distinctions in such cases as to who was in the right and who was in the wrong. They've complained about you, so you must be guilty. Naturally, he couldn't punish someone else's son, but he could punish his own. The discussion would be brief, and then it was the strap. Both Yosif and Lazar had got the strap, and they used to clear out of the house and hide for days, sometimes. Grisha never ran away, and he had more than a taste of grandfather's strap, but he never cried or asked forgiveness. As a matter of fact, he soon settled down and became a good worker, in the bootmaking workshop, though he could turn his hand to any trade.

I remember when my uncles built a may-pole in the back-yard – there was a craze for it at that time. It was the real thing, just like the ones in the parks, and the kids came from all over the town. And what did Uncle Yosif do? He made a business out of it, and took one kopek from each kid. Uncle Grisha was standing next to him, quietly watching Yosif collecting the kopeks, and then he asked him, very calmly, 'Show me how much you've collected.' He took the money out of Yosif's hand, counted it up, then handed it to me and said 'Go and buy sweets with this, and bring them back here.'

I brought the sweets, Grisha shared them out among the kids, and Yosif didn't dare open his mouth. Even though Grisha was younger than Yosif, he was stronger, and as you know, it wasn't Yosif's habit to tangle with the strong.

Uncle Grisha was mobilized in 1915 and spent the entire war at the front, not in a military band like Uncle Yosif, but in the infantry, in the trenches; a real soldier, he was wounded and concussed, and after the war he went back to working in the bootmaking business. In time, he became a highly skilled master, quiet, hard-working, a man of few words, but extremely gifted in technical matters. First in the cooperative and later in the factory, he was always among the most productive workers, but he never let it go to his head, and preferred to stick to his work. When the factory was expanding and mechanizing, he introduced many valuable ideas for rationalization. There were always some smart operators trying to get in with him, but he paid no attention to them, as he was a plain, unambitious man, who put the interests of production first, a genuine master of his craft, a model worker in the original meaning of the word. I owe him a lot myself. When Lyova and I started working with father and grand-father, it was Uncle Grisha who taught us. If I said that he was simple and in no way outstanding, maybe it was just that

that was significant about him. He was a man of work, he saw work as a duty, and such people are the salt of the earth.

With all their faults, and some of them were quite serious ones, grandfather's children all took after him in some way or other, Yosif in his efficiency, Lazar in his decency, Grisha in his hard work, my mother Rachel in her authority, her self-will and determination. Yet not one of them had grandfather's character altogether. Perhaps only one son managed to reach his level, maybe even surpassing him, because he found himself in the thick of great historic events and took part in them. That was Misha, the youngest of grandfather's sons, and the youngest of my uncles.

I am already over sixty and Uncle Misha is long gone. He perished when I was still only a boy, but he illuminated my childhood with an unforgettable light and gave me something I have carried with me right through life. I can see him now, broad-shouldered, fearless, with his expressive, sunburnt Tatar face and kind, slightly slanting eyes.

There was something Tatar about all the Rakhlenkos, and about Uncle Misha in particular. Where did it come from? One thing is sure: the idea that each nation is racially pure is a myth, especially a nation with a history of four thousand years.

Uncle Yosif was mad about pigeons, Uncle Lazar was mad about books, and Uncle Misha was mad about horses. He would give his soul for the chance to gallop a horse with a Cossack saddle or a cavalry saddle, or bareback. During the war, when cavalry units passed through the town and stopped to rest, Uncle Misha would pal up with the troopers and he learned to ride as well as the best of them.

It was horses that started Uncle Misha off on his military career. In 1917 he went to the front with a cavalry squadron. He enlisted as a volunteer, they gave him a horse and he fought right through the Civil War. The front stretched over the whole of Russia, Uncle Misha disappeared from view and became a legend. We received a few, very short letters from him, you can imagine the state of the postal service at that time. The letters have been lost, but I can remember one phrase from one of them, 'Don't expect me at home till we've taken Warsaw.' He served with Gai's cavalry corps, which was advancing on Warsaw. Once, Uncle Misha turned up unexpectedly in his cavalry-man's cloak, Cossack fur cap, spurs, crossed belts, and a sword at his side, a real Civil War hero, decorated with the Order of the Red Banner, which really meant something.

He was decked out like a picture, or maybe it seemed like that to me, though he might well have been. The sword, the Cossack cap, crossed belts and spurs, his horses and the whole turn-out, to someone like me, who has been through the bleakness of the Patriotic War, it all seems perhaps a little naïve. But it was the style then, the norm, and they enjoyed strutting about and showing off, especially in the south, and especially fine swordsmen and partisans, like Uncle Misha.

I needn't tell you that every one of us, from grandfather down to us grandchildren, was proud of Uncle Misha, to say nothing of grandmother, who doted on him. The son of Rakhlenko the bootmaker from a little town in the province of Chernigov, and now, if you please, such a hero, not just a sergeant like Khaim Yagudin, but what you might call a Red general, and a house full of weapons, and horses out in the stable such as you've never seen anywhere, and our neighbour, Stashenok, making special harness for them. We trailed after Uncle Misha everywhere, wherever he went, we were right behind him. Quite a few important political figures were from our town, but we didn't know anything about them, they were miles away, in Moscow and Petrograd, whereas Uncle Misha was right here before our eyes.

He went on serving in the army, though he lived in Chernigov. What he was there I'm not sure, whether he commanded an army unit or was a member of the military tribunal or both.

Anyway, he was an important figure in Chernigov. And then, once, he came to see the family for a couple of days. Poor devil, why did he come? He came to his death.

The economy was in ruins, there was no hard currency, money was reckoned in millions, but who would take them, these worthless millions? Just paper! The peasants wouldn't touch them. Our district, as you know, raised cattle, but how do you buy cattle if the peasant won't touch your millions? The butchers bought cattle with old Tsarist gold currency, but this was prohibited as speculation in gold, and three men had been caught and were sitting in Chernigov prison, under sentence of death. So who did their families run to? To grandmother Rakhlenko, of course. After all, her son was the big chief in Chernigov, surely he would save his own people, fathers of families, surely he wouldn't leave their children as orphans? Then, as fate would have it, as if on purpose, Uncle Misha came home.

Grandmother said to him, 'Free those men.' He replied 'I can't do that.' She begged and pleaded with him, being a good woman and not realizing what she was trying to push him into, not knowing that it would threaten him.

'If they're shot, we'll have to leave this place,' grandmother said. 'We couldn't stay here, we'd have to go, leave our own home and wander God knows where. I wouldn't be able to look people in the eye here.'

When Uncle Misha said, 'If I did this, I would be shot myself,' she didn't believe him, she thought he was trying to get out of doing it, so she wept and insisted. The wives of the men under sentence pitied her, as she had promised to help them and, always being in second place in the family, she wanted to be able to show the world that her word counted for something and that her beloved son would do anything she asked.

If grandfather, or the uncles, or my mother and father had known about these discussions, they could have explained to grandmother that she was asking Misha to do the impossible. Unfortunately, she kept quiet about it all, and made Misha swear not to tell the others a word.

Uncle Misha gave in, he couldn't refuse his own mother, he released the prisoners, he took pity on them, as he knew them and their families, and he knew they had children, and perhaps he didn't think their crime deserved the death sentence. Don't forget, he was only twenty-two, a boy! He had seen death, but on the battlefield. He was a soldier, not a judge, a real fighter, reckless, daring, but decent, just, unselfish. Up to a point, he was a seeker after adventure, in the best sense of the word, the adventurousness of a brave and sensitive spirit. He could shoot, but not execute. He put his own decency above the iron laws of revolution and he had to pay the price.

Obviously, he wasn't such a fool as to let the men out of prison just like that. They appealed for mercy and Misha, as a member of the tribunal – before a decision was taken by the central executive committee – released them on bail, which he had no right to do on his own authority. The minute they got out of prison, they disappeared – a dirty trick, of course, but a man will do anything to save his own life. The fact remained that Uncle Misha had illegally let three men out of prison and allowed them to escape punishment. For this he was court-martialled and sentenced to be shot himself.

I think it wasn't easy for them to sentence him. They were all his own men, his friends and comrades, and they all loved him, and the chairman of the tribunal, Pikson, a Latvian, doted on him and would gladly have given ten men for one like Misha Rakhlenko. But they were men of iron, their revolutionary duty came before everything else, and they sentenced Uncle Misha to be shot.

After the sentence was pronounced, Pikson went to see Misha in his cell. Misha behaved very well in prison, joking and singing, he had a good voice, like all the Rakhlenkos.

Anyway, the Latvian, Pikson, the chairman of the tribunal, went to see him and said, 'Tell me, Rakhlenko, what would you like?'

'I have some debts, with the bootmaker, the tailor and a few others,' answered Uncle Misha, 'and I'd like to settle up with them.'

This was the truth, as Uncle Misha was a dandy and had his clothes and boots made by the best tailors and bootmakers, and he kept his horses better than anyone.

'Will three days be enough?'

'I can manage with one.'

'Fine, I'll give you a horse, go and settle your debts, and if you can't do it in one day, come back in three.'

Misha went home to his apartment, where grandfather was waiting, and they went round Chernigov together, paying off all the people he owed money, and then grandfather said to him, 'There are horses ready for you at a friend of mine's here. I'll give you money and you can get away. Pikson let you out, he must have had it in mind.'

'No,' Uncle Misha replied, 'I can't do that. I trusted those men and they let me down. I won't let anyone down myself.'

They said good-bye, and Misha went back to prison. Two days later a telegram came from Petrovsky, the chairman of the central executive committee, ordering a stay of execution. They reprieved Misha, but reduced him to the ranks, and he perished during an operation against some band or other.

Many people wouldn't believe it; the death of a man like that has to be something more visible if it's to be believed. He had risked his life so often that it seemed death couldn't claim him. There were rumours that he'd been seen in the Crimea and in Vladivostok, that he'd been sent to China as an advisor to the Kuomintang revolutionary army.

I don't believe these rumours. Uncle Misha did die, of course. He wasn't cunning, he was innocent, like the times he lived in.

6

During the Civil War, home took second place as far as I was concerned. I spent the whole time on the street, hanging around the station, among the army detachments, the soldiers and sailors, and the little world of the family was pushed into the background. At the same time, I think I resented the fact, perhaps subconsciously, that my father wasn't involved in this world of men hung with ammunition-belts, galloping around on horses, waving swords. Even crazy old Khaim Yagudin took part in drilling the civil defence units, carrying out inspections, just like some general. He would give the order 'Right turn! Left turn! About turn!' and they would follow his orders because, say what you like, he was an old soldier, an honourable old sergeant, with the red side-whiskers of a field marshal, grey cropped hair, and shaven red face. But when he tried to beat a lad with a stick for not carrying out a command fast enough, they stopped him. After all, these were not Tsarist times any more, you weren't allowed to beat a soldier. I mention this to show that everyone, including the useless old Khaim Yagudin, had found a place for themselves in the new world, yet my father remained exactly what he had always been, domestic, badly organized, without a profession or any real occupation, tied down by five children. Yes, five! During the First World War, when things had been reasonably peaceful for us, mother had had no more children, and everyone thought that she had come to a halt with the three of us, Lyova, myself, and Yefim. But then in 1917 came Lyuba, a child of the October Revolution, then in

1919 Genrikh arrived, making five of us in all. Father couldn't budge with such a load round his neck, not that there was a need to go anywhere now – a new life had begun, the old regime had vanished, everybody was equal, we were all Soviet citizens, so what was the point of any talk about Switzerland when we were at home where we were?

Whatever father wrote in his letters to Switzerland, there they knew that things were in a bad way with him, and they started telling him he should come back, especially as he still had his Swiss passport and was able to go, but again mother wouldn't hear of it. Why should they have to keep her? They would feed her and the children out of charity! She wouldn't allow such humiliation! It's one thing to be poor at home in your own country, it's another thing to be a beggar among rich relations. I don't know if father agreed with her or not, but at any rate he was resigned to his fate, got himself some sort of job with not much in the way of wages, plus a measly food ration, which was doled out irregularly, and sometimes not at all. By now, father spoke good Russian and could read and write it as well. He read a lot and wrote correctly. It wasn't that he had no abilities, and he was an honest man, but in the place where he worked, he wasn't in a very important job, in fact he was just a clerk bringing home a little something – on good days it would be a food ration, on bad days paper money with which you could buy nothing.

Then came the New Economic Policy, and fierce competition between the state and the private operator; 'who whom?' was the cry – would the state overcome the private operator, or vice versa? And if the state intended to overcome the private operator, then its goods had to be cheaper than his, as well as better. What did 'cheaper' mean? It meant cutting down the state apparatus, getting rid of surplus labour, after all the private producer didn't employ surplus labour, he squeezed the last drop out of himself, and out of his family and his workers. So the New Economic Policy brought massive cuts in staffs, the abolition of superfluous establishments, even if it meant unemployment, and many who suddenly found themselves out of work asked 'What did we struggle for?'

My father was also out of work. The question was, what could he do for a living? How could he earn his daily bread? It's true that at that moment I started work, right after Lyova, but even so, father was a man in his prime, yet he couldn't feed his own family and felt like the seventh member of it.

In the end, father got a licence and started up again as an artisan bootmaker. It wasn't easy, but he didn't let it get him down, and his sense of humour, a rare quality in a German, saved him. Perhaps he had acquired it living with mother, you certainly needed a very good sense of humour to get along with her, both as a defence and an escape.

If we were all indebted to mother, so to speak, physically, because she nursed us, it was father who shaped us spiritually, gave us our taste for reading, was concerned about our education, told us stories he had heard in his own childhood, Grimm's fairy-tales and Hans Andersen, and told us about all the films he'd seen in Switzerland, when we got a cinema ourselves, called the Corso.

With his gentle voice and tender hand, he found a common language with us. It's enough to tell you that it wasn't mother who put us to bed, but father. Of course, when you've been working hard, and knocked yourself out running around all day, you fall asleep as soon as your head hits the pillow. You couldn't play up with mother, if she said 'Quiet!' you were quiet, but children are children, and when there are five of them sleeping in one room, in two beds, and the first one pushes the second one, the second one shoves the third, the fourth pulls the blankets off the fifth, the fifth throws a pillow at the fourth, it's not easy to restore order, and sometimes mother was powerless and her clips round the head didn't work any more. Only father could calm us down. And when we were sick as small children, it was father who looked after us, made sure we took our medicine and got up in the night to see to us. Mother wouldn't get up, she had never been ill and didn't believe very much in other people's illnesses. I remember once Yefim had toothache and couldn't get to sleep, and when father got up to give him a mouthwash, mother called out, 'Why do you take notice of him? How can a tooth hurt? It's a bone, isn't it?'

However, fate soon smiled on father. A bootmaking co-operative was set up, initiated by my elder brother Lyova, even though he was then only fourteen or fifteen. Can you imagine, craftsmen and artisan bootmakers, grown men, masters themselves, following the lead of a lad of fourteen, a Young Communist, such was his power of persuasion. I won't hide the fact that some part was played in this by the pressure of taxation on the artisans, as the course was set for collectivization and the liquidation of the private producer, but our cooperative was one of the first, and it proved to be father's salvation. Father had four jobs in the cooperative, he took the orders, handled the cash, kept the books, and was the storeman. And he managed them all. Today, four jobs are done by four men, but in those days one had to do, because the first priority was profitability.

By the mid twenties, the family was on its feet, living decently, and the time came for my parents to reap the fruits of their labour and their troubles. Their life had been devoted to rearing and bringing up children, and making people of them. They were simple toilers, who didn't try to solve the world's problems, but lived for the sake of each other, the children were the fruit of their love, and they were happy. Though, of course, as you know, happiness is always relative – no, don't worry, nothing terrible was going to happen, we were all alive and well, but we were growing up, each one of us developed his own character, his own views, and some conflict was inevitable.

The pride of the family, of course, was Lyova, secretary of the district Young Communist or Komsomol committee, widely read, politically aware, an excellent public speaker, with the mind of a statesman, an unselfish man of principle, who needed nothing more than a leather jacket, a shirt, and patched-up trousers. Was he like Uncle Misha? Not to look at. He was tall and dark, too, but lean, and with little of the Tatar look. As for his character, I find it hard to say. Better just say, Misha was what he was, and Lyova was what he was. Uncle Misha was reckless, brave and open-hearted. Lyova himself was not timid, but he was of a different era, a different stage of development, it was no longer a time of chaos, but of iron discipline. Uncle Misha could carry out the most unexpected and even unplanned act. Lyova didn't carry out unplanned acts, his decisions were precisely thought out, and he executed them unflinchingly, quietly, judiciously and with indestructible logic. Uncle Misha was something of an anarchist, a partisan who decked himself out like a picture, with his belts and swords and fur cap, his horses and his whole turn-out, while all Lyova needed was his leather jacket, peasant shirt and a pair of breeches. Whereas Uncle Misha was capable of leaving his head – and his gorgeous fur cap – on the battlefield, without a moment's thought and even for the moment's sheer effect, Lyova would not give up his head without careful thought, or for effect, as he knew its worth. He was capable of sacrificing himself, but only if there was a point in it and if it was for the good of the Revolution. I am no psychologist and I will not try to compare them. Both were important in their own way. In any case, Lyova had a big influence on all of us, we were all confirmed Komsomols. I had absolute faith in Lyova and listened to everything he said.

The same thing was true of Olesya Stashenok. You remember, of course, grandfather's neighbour, Afanasi Prokopyevich Stashenok, the saddler. I have already said what good, decent people they were, the old man himself, and his wife, two sons Andrey and Petrus, and daughter Olesya. They were all pale-skinned, fair-haired, grey-eyed and of medium height. They had a frail look, but in fact they were all physically strong. The young wives of the Stashenoks, Ksana and Irina, were also pale-faced and fair-haired, and their children, old Stashenok's grandchildren, were pale little things, who ran around in white shirts and white pants.

Other Byelorussians in the town spoke Russian and dressed in city clothes. The Stashenoks spoke Byelorussian, pronouncing their o's like a's and their d's like z's, though we could understand them perfectly, having lived with them all our lives. There was an element of Byelorussian in the way they dressed, as well. Under a jacket and over their trousers, they would wear a shirt with a side opening, a short stand-up collar, and braid trimming, while their women wore a tightly laced jacket, a blue or red skirt and apron, and headscarf. The women in the Stashenok house were very beautiful, and the house itself was quite special, with embroidered cloths, birch-bark jugs, bast baskets, wooden spoons, and a sprig of grass or heather behind the icon. Their way of life was quite different from grandfather's, which was noisy, active and sometimes scandalous, whereas they lived quietly, in tranquillity, they were reserved in their speech and very dignified.

At table, the old man sat at one end, with his sons along one side, in order of age, the women along the other side and his wife at the opposite end. They had great respect for bread, and considered it a sin to waste even the smallest crumb. The face-slaps that grandfather Rakhlenko dished out so generously to his sons were simply unknown in the Stashenok household. They were good employers, though they lived meagrely, worked slowly and without rush, and produced work of high quality and good taste. As I said earlier, Stashenok trimmed carriages in leather and upholstery, before the Revolution. After the Revolution, nobody went round in carriages any more, so the Stashenoks made and repaired harness for cart-horses instead, halters, traces and breech-straps, the kind of thing a peasant can often repair for himself. You can imagine how much money they were making. The business went down, the eldest son, Andrey, went to work at the depot, repairing transmission belts, and making seats for railway carriages, the second son, Petrus, went to work at the leather factory, and the old man went on, on his own, making horse-collars. But they still lived together as one happy, warm and hospitable family. They used to greet us in a Byelorussian phrase that is hard to translate, something like 'Welcome!', 'Make yourself at home', or 'Make us happy with a visit!' They would always make us sit down at the table, and though their staple food was potatoes, they made them into the most delicious dishes, like potatoes with crackling, potatoes with mushrooms, potatoes with sour milk, and as for their potato fritters with honey, or sour cream, or mushrooms, we used to drool over them!

As a child I used to go and see them in their workshop. It always smelt of leather from the tannery, turpentine, lacquer, vinegar, vitriol, joiner's glue, and fish-glue; the Stashenoks would be sitting astride benches, fitted with vices for clamping their work.

When I came in, Andrey and Petrus would exchange cunning glances and one of them would start talking about the evil spirits that inhabited the forests and rivers and lakes. The forest demon was a disgusting, hairy creature with a booming voice and terrifying eyes that blazed fire, and the devils that lived in the marshes were always playing all kinds of tricks. The Stashenoks told these fairy-tales as though they were true, with lots of detail, and they made a powerful impression on me as a small boy, and became linked in my imagination with the magical world of mystery and fantasy. The Stashenok house is one of the most touching and poetic memories of my childhood.

They also liked to sing. None of them had a voice like my mother's, it's true, but the Stashenoks sang well, especially when they sang together. Byelorussian songs, if you've ever heard them, are slightly monotonous, even mournful, yet they do have a certain melancholy charm and compassion about them.

I've heard a lot of their songs, not only sad ones, but lively and even bawdy ones, too. I particularly remember one, perhaps because Olesya used to sing it, and I thought it was a strange song for her to sing, as it is about a girl who can't find the right lover. Olesya was an afterthought in the Stashenok family, coming ten years after Petrus; in fact she was the same age as Lyova and a year older than me. She was delicate and pale, supple as a twig, a mermaid with flaxen hair. You know, when a girl like that is growing up in the house next door, in the next backyard, and you see her over the fence, sitting under the apple tree making daisy-chains and singing a sad Byelorussian song in her little girl's voice, you don't pay any attention while you're still only a boy. Then as you get older and you suddenly discover that she is no longer a little kid, but a girl with strong, straight legs and young breasts, it causes a revolution in your life. As far as she cares, you're still just the boy next door and she treats you like it, she calls you 'nice lad', quite pleasantly but patronizingly, though as far as you yourself are concerned, you're not a lad at all and at night your mind is full of all kinds of thoughts about that girl. But it all stays inside your head, first as a secret, then only as a memory.

All right, fine. Olesya was a Komsomol with the job of running literacy courses in the neighbouring village of Terekhovka, an eight-mile walk for us in both directions. Although in those days we were not getting enough to eat, we had amazing stamina and would march twelve or even twenty miles, though not in the summer, when the peasant was busy in the fields, but in the autumn, through thick mud, and in the winter, through ice and snow. We would set out for Terekhovka together, Olesya and I, she to run the literacy course, and me to stick up wall-newspapers, but really to protect Olesya, who was only a girl, while I was, after all, a youth, and even though I was younger, I was fit and tough, and this responsibility made me feel like a knight in armour and able to take on any challenge to protect her. As it happened, there were no challenges to repel, as the gangs had been liquidated, so Olesya and I tramped along the cart-track, barefoot in the autumn mud, our boots tied together and slung over our shoulders. Olesya had only the one pair, and even though I was the son of a bootmaker, and the grandson of a bootmaker, and actually a bootmaker myself, I also had only the one pair, as I had given away my others to lads who had none. We would put our boots on before entering the village, as a barefoot town dweller had no authority in a village.

We would return the same way, sometimes, in the autumn, in a horse and cart, often, in winter, packed round with hay in a low, wide, village-sledge. Evening, the edge of the forest, the moon lighting up the snow on the fields, and the white snow on the trees illuminating Olesya's lovely face, her head and her bosom wrapped round with her shawl, and her beautiful, kind, cheerful eyes shining. The hay would rustle intimately and we would be warm in the sledge, yet I seemed to feel the warmth from her. What you won't imagine at the age of fifteen when you have a girl like that next to you!

I was then in love with Olesya, in love like a boy who is stirred by his young blood and his age, yet is also made by his age to feel ashamed of these feelings. I thought everyone was in love with her. Perhaps they were, but what we all knew, and what we all saw, was that Olesya liked my elder brother, Lyova.

Our second home at that time was the club. It met in a house which had been requisitioned from Aleshinsky, the rich merchant in whose hardware store my father had once worked. We spent whole evenings at the club, and sometimes even whole nights, rehearsing plays, painting scenery, writing texts for wall-newspapers – 'the live press' – reacting to recent events, whether it was the introduction of the metric system of measurement, or the recognition of us by England, Italy and Greece, collecting donations for the construction of the *Ultimatum* destroyer squadron by going from house to house with collecting boxes and hurrying through the railway carriages when trains were stopped at the station. We weren't thinking about organizing our own lives, we were thinking about organizing the world; we had destroyed the old style of life, and we were building a new one according to our experience. And what was our experience? Lyova, our leader, was all of sixteen or seventeen.

I remember Lyova's lecture on the Esenin craze. You know, I used to love Esenin in those days, in fact I still do, though I haven't the time to read his poetry any more, but when I hear it read it grips my heart the way it did then. Sometimes when you're young, you happen on a particular book, you fall in love with it and it stays in your heart for the rest of your life. Olesya gave me Esenin's poems, and it was my good luck that it was Esenin, because at that age I could just as easily have become hooked on a bad poet. Anyway, though Lyova's lecture was probably correct, from the point of view that was current then, still, I'm not sure. Lyova said that Esenin had lost his ties with the countryside, that he hadn't understood the Revolution, and had been alien to our great cause. That was being disrespectful and rude about the dead poet, about Esenin! 'Oh, Russia, to the point of pain and joy I love your lakeland melancholy, your crimson field, your blue river . . .' That was what we fought and died for in the Second World War.

At home I told Lyova that his lecture had not been objective. Esenin was a great poet, the young people loved him, and you couldn't dismiss him so easily and so rudely. Did he give me what for! Without raising his voice – he never raised his voice – he sat down opposite me and said that poetry was good if it served the proletarian cause, and if it did not do that, then it was harmful. The young people love Esenin? That's not true. Only a part of them are crazy about him, and they are the unstable part, that have not been tempered in the class struggle and have not understood the New Economic Policy and have lost all revolutionary perspective. It seemed I belonged to that part of the youth. Not only that, I had behaved dishonestly. I ought to have told the meeting sincerely about my misgivings, but I hid them, and if I continued with these views, my comrades would have to discuss me.

I'm ashamed to recall that at that moment I was chicken-hearted. I was terrified at the thought of standing up in front of the meeting, mumbling something incoherent, and what did I know about poetry, anyway? So, being afraid to appear stupid, I submitted to Lyova's authority, I didn't dare to defend my own views, and I'm ashamed when I think of it now. As the years go by, we learn to accept all kinds of things, we resign ourselves – that's life – but at the age of fifteen!

During Lyova's lecture, Olesya was also silent, even though she loved Esenin, read him over and over again, and knew many of his poems by heart. Like me, she looked up to Lyova. She had grown up in a simple family, with her mother who ran the house, and her grandmother and sisters-in-law, and she tried to keep up with Lyova, she wanted, so to speak, to meet his requirements, she wanted to study, to work, to be independent.

But what work was there, where could anyone go? It was the twenties, NEP, there was still unemployment, and in our little town it was no better. Like everywhere else, of course, there was some recruiting of young people into enterprises, but what sort of enterprises? The railway depot, the leather factory, the bootmaking cooperative. Even so, Olesya managed to get herself a job as a cleaner at the offices of the district executive committee. At that time, the district executive committee, the district party committee and the district Komsomol committee, and in fact all the other district institutions, were housed in one building, requisitioned at some point from the ex-flour-merchant Freidkin. So Olesya, in her blue overall and red headscarf, became an adornment of the district authorities.

Did Lyova like her? With a man like Lyova, you can never tell, as he never gave way to his feelings. Even so, I am sure he liked Olesya. Everyone liked her, everyone loved her, my mother, my father, my grandfather, my grandmother. When Lyova and Olesya stood side by side, you couldn't take your eyes off them, Lyova tall, slim, dark, like a gipsy, and Olesya, coming up to his shoulder, a pale mermaid with flaxen hair.

But nothing happened between them.

There was this character, Zyama Gorodetsky, the youngest son of the widow Gorodetsky from the Old Market – you remember, grandfather made Freidkin the flour-merchant let her off her debt to him and give her flour on credit? I should tell you that although she really was impoverished, after the Revolution her children found their feet, the sons worked at the railway depot, one as a mechanic, the other as an electrician, both skilled craftsmen, and her daughters married friends of their brothers who also worked at the depot. They owed their success to their own efforts, but their old mother always said that if it hadn't been for grandfather Rakhlenko, who was a noble man, none of them would be alive. But I want to talk about her son, Zyama, not her.

Unlike his elder brothers, Zyama didn't work at the depot, but went off somewhere and came back as a Komsomol and member of a SOU, you know, a Special Operations Unit, responsible for liquidating gangs in the villages, which meant that, unlike the rest of us, Zyama had been under fire, a real fighter. He turned up wearing wide breeches, a peaked cap, an old army greatcoat thrown over his shoulders, a typical member of the Civil War 'fraternity', except that the Civil War had long been over and done with, and Zyama didn't look at all like a sailor or a reckless young tough. He was skinny and stooped, wore spectacles and suffered from the disease of paupers, tuberculosis, which in fact killed him off in due course. However, he was not one to hide behind his illness and he shirked nothing, but he was illiterate and didn't want to study, and although his stoop and his short sight gave him the appearance of an educated man, in fact he was an ignoramus. If there was a conversation going on about litera-ture or something else he knew nothing about, he used to put on an offended look and say scornfully 'Cut the cackle!' or call us 'decadent intellectuals'. He declared the main enemy of the Komsomol and of the Soviet system to be the lower middle classes. 'When we were fighting the gangs, we didn't have any spittoons,' he told us, as he spat wherever he felt like it, and threw his cigarette-ends into the corner of the room. After all, we weren't nobility, we were all on an equal footing, all comrades, and comrades deal with each other on familiar terms. He was against everything lower middle class – decent clothes, neckties, window-curtains, shoes. When Zyama chatted with a girl or was walking alongside one, he would put his hand on her shoulder or round her waist, after all we were equal! Some of the girls didn't object, as they were afraid of being called lower middle class, but very few of them liked it. When he put his arm round Olesya in his 'comradely' way, she pushed it away. Zyama told her 'not to try to be a lady', and Olesya gave him a slap in the face you could hear all over the club. He should have swallowed it, the idiot, as she was a girl, after all, but he got on his high horse and laid a complaint with the district committee to the effect that Stashenok was behaving like an aristocrat from a finishing school for young ladies.

If I'd been in Lyova's place, as secretary of the district committee, I would have told Zyama that he shouldn't paw the girls, and that if he stopped doing it he wouldn't get any more slaps in the face. Lyova had been waiting to take Zyama down a peg for a long time, however, and this was his chance.

The case was dealt with at the club at a meeting of the town Komsomol cell. I can remember Lyova on the platform perfectly, as he gave the wretched Zyama a going-over, and when Lyova really laid it on, he could be devastating. Gorodetsky trampled on other people's dignity, Lyova said, he cheapened the lofty emotion of love. His struggle with the so-called lower middle classes was really a cloak for his own decadence, slovenliness, and ignorance, and he was making a cult out of what had been a dire necessity in the years of the Civil War, when our young people fought heroically at the front under the most difficult conditions.

The war had ended and a period of recovery had arrived, and other tasks confronted the Komsomol, who must now study and work, but Gorodetsky doesn't want to study, nor does he want to do real work, his flowery phrases are the clap-trap of an ignoramus. The district committee had, therefore, decided to send Gorodetsky to a village to work as an assistant in the Rural Cooperative Stores, where he could demonstrate that he was in tune with the current moment. As a sales assistant he would be working for the party, on the leading edge of the competition with the private producer, as there was a private shop right next door to the Rural Cooperative Stores.

At that moment it seemed a good decision to us, as we tended to be severe and categorical at that age – if it had to be, then it had to be.

Looking back on it, now, I think Lyova was too rough on

Gorodetsky. Of course, the work at the Cooperative was honourable, but was Gorodetsky the right person for it? The private trader he would be competing with had years of experience, he knew the peasants' needs, being a peasant himself, whereas Zyama had no experience whatever, whether in commerce or among the peasantry, and the private trader would run rings round him. This was a job for a tough, sharp lad, and there were plenty of them to choose from among us. But Lyova saw Gorodetsky as an incident, an incident to be dealt with decisively, severely and pitilessly.

On the other hand, Lyova didn't condone Olesya's behaviour; a slap in the face was not the way to resolve a conflict.

If Lyova had stopped there, in his remarks about Olesya, there would have been nothing more to say, but he didn't. He said that her un-Komsomol behaviour was no accident, but was the effect of the social milieu in which she lived, namely, the petty bourgeoisie.

The point was that Olesya's father, Afanasi Prokopyevich Stashenok, had remained an artisan. All the artisans had combined in a cooperative, except him. You could see why, as the only saddler in the town, what was he supposed to do? Which cooperative should he join? They shoved him into a bootmaking cooperative, but a saddler's work is not the same as a bootmaker's. As a matter of fact, quite a few one-man businesses hung back, like Bernard Semyonovich, the hairdresser, and the watchmaker, the milliner, the blacksmith. Everything was sorted out later on, when they set up *Multiprise*, a state agency to combine various trades, but in the early days, there were misunderstandings. Afanasi Prokopyevich dug his heels in and left the cooperative. Looking back on it now, it all seems such silly nonsense, but it was felt to be important at the time, and Stashenok was labelled a private producer. A dyed-in-the-wool private producer and ingrained individualist, that's what Lyova said he was, and he also said that Olesya had had no influence on her father, on the contrary the individualistic element in her family had overwhelmed her, too.

It was a painful meeting. True, old Stashenok had left the cooperative, but what had that to do with Olesya? She earned her own living, she was a Komsomol and carried out her assignments properly, she was committed to the new life, she had applied to enter the workers' school, and the authorization had just been received. As for the swipe she had given Zyama, she had done the right thing, and it might teach him to keep his hands to himself. Anyway, Lyova had condemned Zyama himself, what was the point of picking on Olesya, especially over such trivialities?

Trivialities didn't exist, as far as Lyova was concerned; also, as it was no secret that he liked Olesya and Olesya liked him, he felt he must blame her as well, otherwise everyone would think that he had given Gorodetsky a going-over just because it was Olesya he had put his arm around. In conclusion, Lyova announced, the district committee had decided not to send Olesya to the workers' school, but to send Kovalev, a lad from the depot, instead, as he was the son of a worker and a worker himself, and Olesya would have to wait until she had proved herself in her job.

Zyama and Olesya were sitting in the front row, the cause, so to speak, of all the celebrations. The rest of us sat further to the back. When Lyova pronounced his last words, Olesya got up and began to move towards the exit. 'Stashenok!' Lyova called out to her, 'The meeting isn't over.'

'I have to go to the village,' she said. 'It's getting late.'

I got up and followed her out. 'Ivanovsky, where do you think you're going?' 'I'm going there, too,' I replied. Everyone knew that Olesya and I went to Terekhovka together. In fact, it was still two days until we would be going, but I wanted to support Olesya's word, and I felt I must follow her, even though it was a breach of Komsomol discipline.

When we were outside, I said to her, 'Cheer up! Lyova often gets carried away.' I thought she would burst into tears, but not a bit of it – she started laughing. That's right, she started laughing. It turned out she had a strong character. The Stashenoks turned out in general to be people with character, as you will be able to judge for yourself.

She looked at me and smiled, and softly sang a verse from the song about the girl who can't find the right lover, except that in this verse, it's the man who rejects the girl.

Again she laughed and pulled me by the shoulder, 'You're a sweet lad, Borya,' she said, and went home. A couple of weeks later she left for Tomsk.

My parents never interfered in Lyova's affairs. Lyova took after mother, both in appearance and in character. He was decisive and masterful, and if there was a man in the world mother took notice of, that man was Lyova. She was proud of him, he was an outstanding person, the embodiment of the new order that had given us a life of dignity, with no Pale of Jewish Settlement or any of the other humiliating restrictions that Jews suffered under Tsarism.

But mother was also fair. She said to Lyova, 'You'll be sorry about that girl, mark my words. But did you have to pick on the old man? What does it matter to you, if Stashenok is in the cooperative or not? Haven't you got enough on your mind? I reckon Afanasi Prokopyevich has earned a hundred times more in his life than you have with your speeches.'

Gently Lyova replied, 'Don't let it worry you. The Stashenoks and I will settle our own affairs.'

Lyova had no intention of settling anything, there was nothing to be settled, he had disposed of the matter, the case was closed.

It was grandfather who settled things with the Stashenoks. He went to them and explained everything bluntly. The Stashenoks knew that grandfather and grandmother, and my parents, had nothing to feel guilty about.

Soon, Lyova was recruited to the circuit Komsomol – there were circuits in those days – and later he was sent to study in Moscow, at the Sverdlov Communist University.

As for Olesya, she entered Tomsk University, became a chemical engineer, worked in the oil industry in Bashkiria, on the Volga, and is now a Doctor of Science in Tyumen, with children and grandchildren. I met her when she came to visit, before the war and after. But she has always remained in my memory as she was then, in our far-off youth, when we used to ride together in the sledge.

7

In 1926, or perhaps it was a little later, grandmother and grandfather Ivanovsky came to visit us from Switzerland. The First Five Year Plan was in preparation, and many foreign tourists and specialists were coming to the USSR. Also, because the country needed hard currency, tourism was being encouraged, and it was as tourists that our Ivanovsky grandparents came.

Grandfather Ivanovsky was a portly, smooth-shaven old gentleman with a cigar stuck in his mouth. We hardly ever saw a cigar. Before the war, people smoked *papirosy*, then after the war a lot switched to cigarettes, though not everyone did, I didn't, for instance. But cigars have never caught on, and whenever I get a whiff of some eccentric's cigar, I immediately think of grandfather Ivanovsky. And I always think of grandmother when I see an old lady with too much make-up on, as she was a great one for that.

This visit of theirs didn't cause so much excitement. Times had changed, the town had changed, and so had the people, it would take more than some Swiss tourists to surprise them, now. Even the family relations weren't so interested, as they realized that the Ivanovskys had simply come to see their son.

My mother wasn't eager to put on a show. As usual, the house was spotlessly clean and shining, and for the sake of the guests she made a special effort with the cooking, which she really knew how to do.

They brought us gifts and souvenirs, but still they felt like strangers and, whatever you say, we lived in two different worlds, they couldn't understand our way of life and we didn't know theirs. Grandmother couldn't even understand what it was father did for a living, some sort of minor office job in a shoemaking business. Though she didn't say so in so many words, it was plain she blamed my mother for everything, for taking him away from Basel, and she blamed us children for being a millstone round his neck. I sometimes caught the puzzled look she gave us, as if she were wondering what we could possibly be to her, and what she was to us. Not once did she so much as touch us, never mind kiss us. She couldn't even remember our names, though she did manage to sort out the girls, as there were only two of them, but she got us boys mixed up. When she gave out the presents, she decided at a glance as she took them out of a box, who should have what according to our size, and that was all she would have to do with us.

Obviously, mother was offended by grandmother's attitude to the grandchildren, what mother wouldn't be! She was particularly hurt by grandmother's indifference to little Dina. I forgot to mention that, shortly before the Ivanovskys arrived, a year or eighteen months, our little sister Dina was born. For five years no babies, everyone thought that was it, and then, if you please, in 1925, Dina was born. That means I was wrong, it wasn't 1926 when they came, it was 1927, definitely.

Have you got children? You know how it is with a new-born baby, a tiny little wrinkled bundle of life. Dina was born with thick black hair and eyes as blue as the bluest sky. Imagine the situation. A big family with grown-up children and along comes a baby girl like that, a tiny miracle, running around, falling over and picking herself up, babbling all kinds of baby words – everyone doted on her, grandfather Rakhlenko wouldn't let her get off his knee, and she would pull at his beard, and everyone said she was the image of her mother, a perfect copy of Rachel as a child. Grandfather Ivanovsky was in ecstasy over her, too, but grandmother Ivanovsky wouldn't so much as look at her.

Mother had a fiery temper, but when she had to she knew how to control herself, and she behaved with dignity. Her husband's family had come to visit and she would pay them proper attention, but no more than that.

You think it was tactics? Well, up to a point. But she was also being sensible. She was showing her in-laws that although their son Jakob was not a professor or a doctor, still he was not a failure, he was respected in the town, he was a person, the head of a household, the head of a family, and what a family! Try and find such a healthy lot of children in Switzerland! He's the boss and everyone listens to him, and should he decide to go to Switzerland, then that's what would happen, but he doesn't want to.

The fact is, mother showed more and more respect to father, which was an example for us to do the same. As a young woman, mother had been wilful, had never watched her words and was capable of saying some very sharp things. As she became more mature she realized that if father had no authority, he couldn't be head of the family, and without a family head, there could be no home. When I try to analyse their characters now, it seems to me that they were both very much like each other. At first glance, it seems they were as different as chalk and cheese, fire and water, but I think the differences were smoothed out by love. Mother seemed to have the stronger personality, she was the one in charge, authoritative, assertive, unyielding, yet their character as a couple was not mother's, but father's. It seemed that he gave way to her in everything, and yet as the years went by, she became more and more like him. Father didn't change, mother did. Mother filled the whole house, she was, I must say, rather a noisy woman, but it was father who influenced the spiritual atmosphere.

During the visit by the Ivanovsky grandparents, father was

the only one who was capable of rising above all the resentment and grudges. He spoke to his parents in German, but if one of us or the Rakhlenkos was present, to say nothing of mother, or even if there was an outsider there, he was sure to translate every word into Russian, even if they were talking about something that was not meant for other people to hear. In exactly the same way, he would translate into German for his parents every word spoken in Russian, Ukrainian or Yiddish. In this way, he kept everyone together and showed that there were no secrets in his house. It may have been a small thing, but it helped to soften the bad feeling.

In fact, this was the cause of some amusement. Grandmother asked father about something, and he translated it, stumbling somewhat, as 'She wants to know if we have any savings.' Mother, never lost for a word, replied 'Yes, two alarm clocks!'

No doubt father would have softened mother's reply, but when she mentioned the alarm clocks, grandfather Ivanovsky, who had not forgotten his Russian, burst out laughing and explained to grandmother, who gave him a puzzled look, that Jakob and Rachel were spending everything on the children's education, which they must have, but that their financial position would be fine in the future. Without hesitation, father translated this reply into Russian.

Grandfather behaved altogether differently from grandmother. It's true that for a while at the beginning he was at a loss, puffing away at his cigar, and no doubt grandmother nagged him from morning till night: you brought Jakob to this God-forsaken little town, you didn't keep an eye on him, you let him out of your sight, and now look at the result, we've lost our beloved son.

A bit later on, however, when he'd got his bearings and felt a bit more at home, I think he began to realize that they hadn't lost their son at all, because even if their son was living in another country, in his own way, that didn't mean he was lost to them. Grandfather had been born here, he remembered the old Russia, he could make comparisons, and he took a good look at everything that was going on here. I think he realized that, if his grandson Lyova, who was still only a young man, could be a political figure, and his other grandsons were preparing for a higher education, then possibly his son, Jakob, had something that could be considered a real investment, even though it was not in a Swiss bank. When I think of grandfather Ivanovsky, the stout old professor with his cigar and his short breath, and I remember his attentive look, his curiosity and even excitement, it seems to me now that he understood what had happened to his son in quite a different way, that he assessed quite differently what in Basel they regarded as recklessness and a catastrophe. If you have to be young to commit an act of extreme folly for the sake of love, then perhaps you have to be getting on in years to be able to understand such an act, and maybe to regret that nothing like it had happened in your own life. I think grandfather approved of his son Jakob, and maybe he also envied him.

After a week, the old Ivanovskys left. Father went with them as far as Bakhmach, where they could catch the train to Moscow. Though they were foreign tourists, carrying their tickets which needed only to be punched, still they were in a foreign country, at a strange station, and even a doctor was capable of getting lost. Father did everything properly and said good-bye to his parents, this time for good. It must have been a very sad parting. Nobody else knows what they said to each other, but they must have spoken many words and shed many tears. When father returned, you could tell nothing from his face, and he never said a word of what had passed at Bakhmach, even to mother, as I could guess from her silence. When mother was angry with us kids, she would tremble and shake, but she certainly didn't go silent. When she was displeased with father, she fell silent. In the early days this must have tormented him, but he got used to it in time and he knew that she would stay silent for only a day or two, never more.

That's how it was this time. For two days she sulked, then she started talking, after all, life must go on, and you can't answer the questions life poses with a closed mouth. The Ivanovskys' visit was pushed into the background by other problems. The presents they had brought got worn out, the knick-knacks broken, and the visit itself, the scent of grandfather's cigar and of grandmother's face-powder, dwindled into the depths of time, sank into oblivion, as they say, especially as soon after they left, or at any rate within six months, mother almost died.

I've already said that for five years before she had Dina, mother had no babies, and when she had Dina everyone thought that at last there would absolutely be no more children, she simply couldn't. It turned out she could. In 1928 she gave birth to my youngest brother, Sasha, her seventh and this time definitely her last child, born prematurely in the seventh month.

How or why this happened I cannot say, I'm no doctor, and anyway in 1928 I was sixteen, so what would I know? I only remember the horror of the situation, the fear. I remember mother was taken to the railway hospital, where father and the rest of us waited in the vestibule. She was put straight on to the operating table and Doctor Volyntsev – I think I've mentioned him – performed a Caesarean section, and an hour or two later came out and told us that mother and the baby were both alive and would be all right. Sasha was born premature and weighed only four and a half pounds. Mother's life hung on a thread, we could think only of her, and whether she gave birth to a live or a dead baby didn't matter to us at all, to be quite honest, but in the end Dr Volyntsev saved them both.

Mother stayed in the hospital for ten days or maybe three

weeks, and then we took her home, together with Sasha. As long as she had been in hospital, we had thought only of her, but now she was home again everyone's attention turned to Sasha. Can you imagine, only four and a half pounds! He was as weak as could be, he didn't cry and could barely give a squeak, first he would be too hot, then too cold, he mustn't be too tightly swaddled, he had to be fed every three hours day and night, but he sucked badly and couldn't swallow, and what illnesses didn't that poor little mite catch – flu, bronchitis, diarrhoea, boils – and he should have died from any one of them, but he didn't, he stayed alive. God had given him a healthy mother and a caring father, and after a year or so, he was already a normal child. Not in the pink of health, like the others, still on the weak side, but a child all the same, a boy all the same, and more than that, at the age of two he was a perfect angel. It's a pity we haven't got any pictures of father as a child, they are all in Basel, but I'm sure they are just like photographs of Sasha.

The care and trouble lavished on that child! If only he survives, if only he survives! He survived all right, a cherub, a quiet, graceful, wistful, pale little fragile boy, with blue eyes, the image of father, and the *mizinikel*, the baby of the family like him. Mother kept him close by her, just as grand-mother Elfrieda had done with father, so Sasha didn't grow up on the street, like the rest of us, he was an indoor child, hardly played with other children, read a lot, then started writing poetry, a little poet, a dreamer. All us older ones were mechanical, practical people; if Lyova hadn't gone into politics, he would have been in some sort of engineering, too, as we were all mechanically inclined. The two youngest, Dina and Sasha, weren't at all mechanical, and had talents in completely different areas. With Dina it was music and her voice, and with Sasha it was his dreaminess, his poetic, spiritual loftiness, which is how I would define his nature. I'll be saying more about that later on. Meanwhile, in 1930 he was two years old, he had survived, he was healthy, he was the image of father, and he was his mother's favourite, in fact he was the favourite of all of us.

In the thirties, a state shoe factory was established on the basis of our cooperative, and as he could be relied on, father was appointed by our manager, Ivan Antonovich Sidorov, to run the raw material and accessories store, which he coped with very well, keeping everything in perfect order.

I'd like to say something, as an expert. In a shoe factory, the finished goods store and the raw material store are as different as day and night. If the manager of a finished goods store is a thief, he can steal a pair of boots or a case of boots, but he's bound to get caught, because you can't write off a case of boots just like that. The raw material store is another matter. The raw material is hide, kid, box-calf, Russian leather, calf, shagreen. No hide is like another, here a hole, there a cut or a blemish, and a different yield from each one. One craftsman might get two pairs of boots out of a hide, and another will only manage one from the same hide, in other words, you can use your wits with the hides. A crook can feed himself, his boss, the engineer, and the craftsmen, all from the hides, as long as they are all crooks, of course. Sidorov, the manager, was an honest man, however, a worker up from the shop floor, who wanted nothing for himself, not even a separate office. 'We have a housing crisis on our hands,' he would say, 'I can't have my office in a room big enough for a whole family.' He sat instead in the general office and it didn't prevent him talking to people and running the factory. Also he earned less than his deputies, because there was at that time a maximum wage for party members, one hundred and seventy-five or two hundred and twenty-five roubles, I can't recall. Sidorov said 'The hides must be in reliable hands.' So he appointed father to look after the raw materials and accessories store.

Where responsibility for goods is concerned, it's not enough just to be an honest man. I've known many an honest man who had responsibility for state property and who still came to a bad end. And I've known crooks who built themselves country cottages and bought cars for themselves, who didn't come to a bad end. A crook trusts nobody, he doesn't let anyone con him, he does the conning, he's always on his toes, and he gives the Speculation and Embezzlement Squad a wide berth. But if an honest scatterbrain shows one shortage, he's had it, the accountant's had it, the manager's had it, all of them absolutely honest and none of them with his hand in the state's purse.

Father wasn't just honest and decent, he also had a good head on his shoulders, in the sense that he was orderly, punctual and precise, a real German. Sidorov doted on him, and though some people tried to trip father up by throwing his Swiss nationality in Sidorov's face, Sidorov took no notice, he stood by father, and everything was fine.

What's the matter with our shoe industry? The fact is, the consumers all want to buy foreign shoes. Is our leather worse? No, it's better! Our dyes are a bit out of date, it's true, but nobody could ask for better leather. But our shoes are always out of fashion. Our factories find it hard to change over to new production. You design a new model and you have to get it approved by ten different departments. Nobody can cope with that. New models need new lasts, new tools, new presses, new accessories, and these things are all in different hands, made in different factories, which can't be bothered with new models when they feel perfectly happy with the old range. The result of all this is that, while preparations are being made for new models several years go by, and by the time they get on to the market, they are already out of date. Our factories need more freedom so they can change round more rapidly and satisfy the consumers.

Sidorov was a fine boss who knew all about production, had a feel for the market and wasn't afraid of taking responsibility; when he saw a good shoe or sensed a new fashion, he wouldn't wait for the green light before changing over, though he obeyed every letter of the law and would nip any attempt at deception in the bud. The factory flourished under him, its goods were in demand and never stood for any length of time on the shelf. Everyone was happy, the consumers and producers alike. When a factory is working well, the workers earn good wages and feel good, too.

Not that father got what you could call a top salary, after all, a store manager is not exactly an academician. Still it was enough of a living, especially as Lyova and I were both working. Lyova was completely taken up with his work, which was, as a matter of fact, to do with the collectivization and dispossession of the kulaks. At the beginning of the thirties, there was a famine in the Ukraine that was worse than the one on the Volga in the twenties. The newspapers had all carried news of the famine on the Volga and the whole country had come to the aid of the starving, but nothing was said about the famine in the early thirties. A certain amount of food was doled out on ration cards in the cities, but there were no ration cards in the villages, so the people began to pour into the cities, for which they had no permits. It was a tough time.

On the other hand, industrialization was taking place. New factories and mills and power-stations were going up and the country was becoming a powerful state, and all this created enthusiasm, with the young people doing their utmost for the First Five Year Plan, at Magnitogorsk, Kuznetsk, Chelyabinsk, Stalingrad and other cities. My brother Yefim, who was two years younger than me, went off to Kharkov to help build the Kharkov Tractor Factory. He went there as a simple bricklayer, acquired industrial skill, studied and became an engineer, and a good one at that. During the war he was the manager of a large plant, which he had to build on the bare steppes, using evacuated equipment, and there he produced tanks and other armaments, and was decorated with medals for his valuable work.

When Yefim went off to Kharkov, I was called up for military service, and I ended up in the artillery. There was a saying, going back to Tsarist times, 'Put the handsome in the cavalry and the healthy in the artillery.' I did my stint and then went home. Everyone was studying, there were new universities and polytechnics and technical schools, which was perfectly understandable, because you can't industrialize without engineers: you want to study? Then go ahead, study to your heart's content!

Lads from the depot who had had only five or six years of school, went through accelerated courses and got into the universities, and all these paths were open to me, too. I had been a worker from an early age, on top of which I was now a demobilized Red Army man, so I, too, could take courses and enter university in Kharkov, which was then the capital of the Ukraine. But, you see, I was now the eldest in the family. Lyova was the eldest by age, but he was the deputy chief of the political section of the railway, with responsibility for Komsomol affairs, a man with the mind of a statesman, a man for whom family problems are a burden, so our parents always tried not to bother him, and anyway he had lived apart from us for some time. So I was regarded as the eldest and on me fell the responsibility of helping the family and pushing the younger ones along, as our parents wanted them to have an education, especially Lyuba, who had finished school and had never had any other mark than 'Excellent'. Lyova and Lyuba were considered to be the brainy ones of the family, while my brothers and I were regarded as just ordinary, even Yefim, who was working as a bricklayer at the Kharkov Tractor Factory, though nobody could guess that he would turn out to be so important in the war.

First of all, together with mother and father, I had to help bring the rest along, above all Lyuba, who would get a grant for the university. Then we'd only have Genrikh, Dina and Sasha. Nothing much was expected of Genrikh, who would finish primary school and start work. Then there was little Dina, who was about to enter first grade, and little Sasha who would be looked after by our parents, and finally, at long last, I would be free and could start to organize my life.

8

I understood my parents' position and stayed at home, working at the shoe factory as a craftsman. I was earning good
money and could afford to dress well. At twenty-one I
wasn't bad looking, I had been in the army and was no milk-
sop, I had read a bit and knew how to talk to girls, I could
dance anything you liked, Western or traditional ballroom,
in fact I was pretty good on the dance floor. I wasn't even
thinking about getting married as things were fine just as
they were, and mother kept telling me 'You've got plenty of
time!' Our little town wasn't exactly the sticks, as you know,
there were the summer vacationers, who often brought
interesting people with them, sometimes famous people.

In fact we had a national celebrity, a conductor who is still
alive, an Honoured Artist of the USSR. He used to visit
his parents occasionally and relax for a week or two.

On one occasion he brought with him a painter called Gaik,
who was doing his portrait, an Armenian, who is also famous
by now. Gaik would work on the portrait in the mornings and
for the rest of the day he would sit at his easel on the bank of
the river or in a glade, or wander round the town with a pad,
sketching people or houses, or collective farmers at the
market. He was no youngster, around fifty or so, but he was
a good-looking man, I must say. He had thick, wavy, grey
hair, a black moustache, an aquiline nose, thick eyebrows and
a piercing gaze. When a man turns up with looks like that,
and with his unusual occupation of wandering around all day
sketching, the whole town gets to hear about it in two days,

especially as he was sociable, despite his stern appearance, and spoke with a charming Caucasian accent, gave sweets to the children, and didn't chase people away when they stood by his easel while he was painting.

Well, one day at the market, Gaik caught sight of my mother; I heard about it from Lyuba, who was with her at the time. Gaik saw mother, stopped and stared.

'What's the Caucasian staring at us for?' mother asked in surprise.

'It's you he's staring at,' Lyuba replied.

'Well, there's a thing!' said mother.

As they were leaving the market, Lyuba looked back and saw Gaik was still staring, and she told mother, who didn't say anything.

That evening, Gaik and the famous conductor came to our house. Such honoured guests! Naturally, we invited them to sit at the table and offered them tea, but mother was very restrained, which wasn't like her, as she was always strict about being hospitable. Then the conductor announced that his friend wanted to paint mother's portrait in oils, and that she would have to sit for several days, two hours at a time. Mother looked amazed.

'Two hours? My family will also sit – and starve!'

'My dear Rachel Abramovna, I assure you,' the conductor said, 'throughout history the most outstanding personalities found the time to sit for artists so as to leave their portraits to their descendants.'

'I'm not a commissar, they'll manage without my portrait,' mother replied.

Gaik declared, in his Caucasian accent, 'A beautiful woman is also an outstanding personality.'

We weren't used to such compliments, especially when said to a married woman, right to her face and with her husband and children there, too, but it sounded proper, coming from Gaik. Maybe it was his Caucasian accent or his oriental charm. Also, being an artist he had the right to make such judgements.

However, mother wasn't embarrassed and didn't blush, and replied with dignity, 'There are women who are more beautiful and younger than me.' To which the conductor objected that it was not a question of beauty or age, but of nature. There were some people whose faces simply had to be got down on canvas. It was mother's duty to art to pose for Gaik.

The conductor wasn't just our pride, he was also our glory. Who'd ever heard of our town? Nobody, apart from its inhabitants, the people in the surrounding villages, the summer visitors, and the regional authorities. But our conductor was known over the whole of the Soviet Union. Practically every day on the radio they were broadcasting symphony concerts conducted by none other than our local boy. Any one of us would have considered it a pleasure to do anything he asked, but mother didn't want that pleasure.

'My descendants will manage without my portrait,' she smiled. 'Anyway, they'll have plenty of photographs of me.'

To this our famous conductor replied that a photograph only gives the outward appearance of the person, whereas a painting reveals the inner world. So if mother wanted her children and grandchildren and great-grandchildren to see her as if she were alive, she must agree to sit.

Mother was about to object again, when father said, with his usual tact, 'Your proposal is a great honour for us. Please give my wife time to think it over, and maybe she'll be able to find the time.'

The painter and the conductor left, we went on sitting round the table, and mother asked father, 'Why did you encourage them?'

Father replied, 'Look, maybe Gaik feels that your portrait could be a success, and often everything depends on one success for an artist. After all, you really are beautiful.'

Mother took no notice of what he said. She looked hard at father, I can still recall the way she looked at him, and asked, 'You want me to do this?'

'Why not help the man out? And anyway, why shouldn't we have a portrait of you?'

She looked at him again. 'All right, it's as you like.'

Next day, Gaik came with his easel, stretcher and sketchpad; he had been sure that mother would agree.

Posing, as you well know, is not just a matter of sitting for a couple of hours and looking where the artist tells you to. The first thing to decide is what to wear. Gaik was a very courteous man, but when it came to work, he was very demanding – this dress is no good, that one won't do, let's try it with a shawl, without a shawl. So she would have to go into another room and change, then come back and let him inspect her, then go and change again, then come back, hold a bouquet, put it down.

God knows what mother had in the way of a wardrobe, but still she did have a few dresses, a very nice one in pale blue crêpe de Chine, for instance, but Gaik made her wear a dark woollen one, with a medium neckline, a white lace collar, a very close-fitting bodice and long sleeves. We were a bit surprised by this choice, as we thought the pale blue made mother look younger and brighter, but Gaik went for the dark woollen one. You would agree that to have to sit in a woollen dress in the heat of July is an exhausting thing to do. The only thing Gaik didn't change was mother's hair, which she wore smoothly brushed back in a large bun.

The real point of course was not what mother wore to pose in. You'll have guessed that I'm not describing this event just by chance, and that it was more than merely an incident in mother's life. Some of what happened I saw for myself, some of it I heard from Lyuba, who helped mother when she was changing. Lyuba was seventeen, then, and she was the most subtle and perhaps the cleverest member of the whole family. I am telling it as mother told me, later, in a moment of frankness.

So, first of all, mother had to concern herself with something she hadn't taken notice of for a long time, her appearance. She was beautiful, stately and naturally elegant, but she hadn't the time to sit in front of the mirror, nor did she have to, as she was sure enough of herself to manage without it. Now, at the age of forty, she had to exhibit herself to a strange man, to undress, not in front of him, of course, in the next room, but it was for him that she undressed and dressed and presented herself for his appraising glance. This was something quite new and unexpected in her life. She was used to being looked at by men, but she paid no attention to it, for twenty-four years her husband had been the only man in her life, and other men's glances simply didn't exist for her. And now, all of a sudden, this handsome man turns up, with his grey hair and eagle eye, and she has to undress for him, and dress again, and undress, and try different clothes on, for him to give his approval. Had she been from the big city and circulated, so to speak, in the art world, mother would have been able to separate the man from the artist, as women separate the man from the doctor, but she was not from the big city, she had never seen artists before, and she had only ever had the doctor once, and that was when she gave birth to Sasha.

At first, mother was confused, which wasn't like her. She was a decisive, straightforward sort of person, but at the beginning she was confused in front of this unusual and distinguished man, who was controlling her, not she him, who dominated her, and not the other way round.

It was in this state that mother posed for Gaik, completely alone with him, *tête à tête*, for two hours every day. Two hours, in a manner of speaking, that is. Gaik allowed her to stand up and walk about and stretch her legs, and go into the kitchen, after all the children were around, demanding this and that, and father and I would be coming home from work. Lyuba helped, of course, but she was busy with exams. Mother became distracted and Gaik stretched the sessions out to three hours, sometimes even four hours, as he worked at his own pace and didn't like to break off until he'd reached a certain point, being completely obsessed by his work, as he was.

They chatted during the sessions. Gaik wanted an animated face to paint, so he told her about himself, and she replied to his questions and, having now found this attentive listener and interesting company, she began to feel liberated from the monotony of the years of work and worry.

He told her about Turkey, where he had lived as a child with his parents until they fled to Baku during the Armenian–Turkish massacre. He told her about Paris, where he studied to become a painter, and about Vienna, Berlin and Switzerland, where he went from Paris. These stories took mother back to her younger days, when she lived in Basel, and they stirred memories in her. What impressed her most, however, was the way he looked at her as he painted, in total silence, the searching look an artist gives the object he is painting. Mother told us later that the moments when no words were spoken seemed all the more significant and full of meaning, a certain something in the air, as when a man and a woman begin to feel interest in each other, and perhaps attraction.

Did father have any idea what was happening? I'm absolutely sure he did. He knew mother as well as he knew himself, and anyway she could never hide anything or pretend. She became silent and distracted. She still loved her husband, he had always been the only man for her, but now all of a sudden this other man had turned up, strange, unwanted, but occupying her thoughts the whole time. A disturbance like that could not pass unnoticed but, as always, father was unruffled and calm, he made jokes and laughed as though nothing had happened. He never asked about Gaik, or how the portrait was coming along, not a word. Gaik came at noon and left at three or four o'clock, before we got back from work, never once staying for dinner, and always refusing with the excuse that he was expected at the conductor's, though in fact it was because he wanted to avoid any embarrassment that his presence might cause. Only his easel, leaning in a corner of the dining-room, the canvas turned back to front and a piece of cloth thrown over it, reminded us of him.

It was an unspoken romance, and the ending came un-expectedly. I came home from work one day to find mother different, now she was the woman she had been before, not distracted or pensive, but just as she used to be, decisive and busy. She cleared the table and washed the dishes, then she pointed to the easel and she said to me, 'Take that thing out of here.'

She had no need to explain anything, I understood right away. The portrait was covered up with the cloth and although I wanted to look at it, I didn't uncover it, but wrapped it in some clean sacking, tied some string round it, picked up the easel, which folded like a tripod, and set off for Gaik's.

The sound of a piano was coming from the conductor's house, and it was evidently him playing, so I felt uneasy about interrupting, but I couldn't very well leave the painting on the doorstep, and I certainly couldn't take it back home.

I went in. The conductor was playing the piano. Gaik was sitting in an armchair with his pad, sketching as usual. He got up when he saw me and understood at once. His stern face expressed anxiety, rather than surprise. We went out on to the porch.

I leant the easel and the portrait against the handrail. 'Mother asked me to bring this.'

He said nothing. You know, I felt sorry for him, and I waited, as he seemed to want to say something.

'Sad.' That's all he said, then he turned and went back into the house.

It was much later that I heard what had happened that day. During the session, mother had gone into the kitchen and when she came back to sit, she couldn't find the right pose. Gaik approached her and, holding her head in both hands, turned it to the angle he wanted. This first and only physical contact decided everything.

The first physical contact is often very decisive, it can either attract or repel, and for mother it felt like the touch of a stranger, it repelled. At that instant, she knew that she had Yakov, and that there would never be anyone but Yakov for her. It wasn't a matter of duty, for if mother had loved Gaik she would have followed him to the ends of the earth, regardless and in spite of everything. You don't think so? I do, judging her by her own standards. But when Gaik touched her, and she sensed his feelings for her at very close quarters, she realized very clearly that she didn't love him, that her feelings were simply confused, because an unusual man had intruded into her life unexpectedly. This confusion had to be overcome immediately, without delay, so she sent back the unfinished portrait. Everything returned to normal. Gaik made no attempt to continue the relationship, knowing that it was useless.

Did mother ever recall Gaik, the handsome man with grey hair who had been in love with her? Yes, and she had pleasant memories of him. Much later she told me about it with a smile, but her feelings during that experience, when her love for father was put to the test, were much deeper and more full of meaning than her light-hearted recollections would suggest. After all, what matters is not the situation people get themselves into, which may not depend on them, but the way they get themselves out of it, which depends on them entirely. In my opinion, mother, father, and Gaik got themselves out of the situation with dignity.

Life returned to normal. The conductor and Gaik left, and

we were, so to speak, back in our proper places, going on as usual.

I worked at the factory, went dancing occasionally, went out with girls, of course. On the quiet, I was preparing myself to get into an institute and didn't give up hope that I might continue my education. I read a bit, so as not to forget everything for good, and by this time I acquired a new interest.

We had a literary circle at the factory. A lot of people were becoming interested in literature at that time, and many even had the ridiculous idea of becoming writers. We had the example of Maxim Gorky as an inspiration. He had started as a tramp and ended up a famous writer. We read and re-read his stories, *Chelkash*, *The Old Woman Izergil*, *Makar Chudra*, as well as his other famous books. After the October Revolution, the idea was that everyone should be literate, and when a person becomes literate in adulthood, he very often feels he wants to try writing something himself, it seems such a simple thing to do. So, this literary circle started up at the factory and I used to go along with some of my observations of life in writing. A writer used to come to run the circle, paid by the factory, mind you, as there was some money for cultural activities. He wasn't paid very much, but he was pleased to have the money. His name was Rogozhin, he worked on the regional newspaper and came twice a month to add the finishing touches to the work of the literary circle. Nothing ever became of Rogozhin, his name has sunk without trace. Not that any of us became writers, for that matter, obviously the talent just wasn't there, and after a couple of winters, I dropped it. But I recall the literary circle with pleasure, as it somehow gave one a lift. After all, when you've spent the whole day looking at soles, heels, and uppers, you need something to nourish the spirit, and the dance-hall isn't enough.

In 1934, Lyuba went off to Leningrad to study medicine.

She took after father, a slim, fragile, graceful blonde. Her appearance wasn't as striking as mother's, or Dina's – you could see from a mile away that they were beauties. You had to really look at Lyuba, but once you had, you couldn't take your eyes off her or get her out of your mind. As for her intelligence, she always got top marks, she was a consolation to her teachers and the salvation of the less bright, as she let them copy her schoolwork. All the boys in school were in love with her, but she always came home by nine o'clock at night. So, although she was on her own in Leningrad, we weren't worried about her, and we knew that nothing would happen to her, because she wouldn't let it.

But, believe it or not, it did happen, and she let it. You mustn't think she didn't know who the father was, everything was above board. She and her Volodya Antonov had got married, he was a good boy, a wonderful boy, in the last year of his studies, also in medicine, but Lyuba was only eighteen, still a child herself and, anyway what could they do with the baby, living in a student hostel, how could they afford to look after it, when they were both on student grants, and Lyuba still had four years of study to go? So little Igor appeared in our house, our parents' first grandchild, my first nephew. Naturally, Lyuba and Volodya spent every summer and winter vacation with us, making a fuss of their little boy; then they would go back to Leningrad, leaving Igor to be raised by my parents, and there was nothing to be done about it, as he was our own flesh and blood. Somebody once said that our job is to look after our grandchildren until they reach their pensions, and then we can relax. Anyway, if you count mother and father as the first generation, and me and my brothers and sisters as the second, little Igor had started off our third generation.

More about the third generation later on. Let's get back to the second, in fact back to 1935. I was twenty-three, earning good money, the famine was over, thank God, ration cards were a thing of the past, father had his job at the factory, where he had the solid backing of Sidorov, the manager, and at home there were only Genrikh, Dina, Sasha and little Igorek. Genrikh was already in the depot workshop training school and dreaming of entering flying school. I ought to say that our little family was just like the Rakhlenko family had been, nothing special in the academic line, but all fit and always ready for a fight. Genrikh, however, was the end, Genrikh was beyond a joke. You know how it is when there are five brothers backing each other up, everyone on the street is scared of them, and the more scared everyone is, the more insolent and cocky they get. Lyova and I hadn't had time for pranks and street fights, as we had been working since an early age. Yefim was a peaceable, even-tempered boy, but Genrikh, who felt he had the strength of his elder brothers behind him, was such a hooligan, that I don't know to this day how he didn't get his head knocked off. He used to fight with the kids from the depot, the ones from across the river, and the peasant kids from the outlying villages, he used to go into other people's orchards and kitchen-gardens, all his teachers and instructors moaned and groaned about him, not a day went by without a fight, a broken nose or a black eye. And he was a cunning devil; at home he was as quiet as a mouse, because he was afraid of mother, who had a heavy hand, and he was afraid of me, because though I didn't hit him often, when I did he felt it. At school and in the street, however, he was an absolute pest. They were always expelling him, and taking him back, then after the sixth grade there was no alternative but to send him out to work, at which everyone sighed with relief and the school virtually celebrated it as a holiday. Luckily, the depot opened a work-shop training school, so he started to train as a repair-mechanic, having no desire at all to become a shoemaker.

The hereditary Rakhlenko profession of shoemaker actually came to an end with me; I am, as you might say, the last shoemaker of the Rakhlenko and Ivanovsky clan. I can quite understand Genrikh. A shoemaker's wages are next to the bottom of the scale, or at most two steps from the bottom. How can he live on such wages? He has to do what he can, give a receipt for one job, but not for another, it's a constant juggling act. What does a young man want that for, when just across the road, working on the conveyor-belt, he can earn a hundred and fifty or a hundred and sixty roubles, and in addition he's got cultural and sports facilities and all kinds of other perks, and in a couple of years he can expect to get a new flat with all mod. cons. Anyway, in the thirties everyone was going into heavy industry and transport. To be a metalworker, a machine-operator or a coal-miner sounded good, but a shoemaker? So Genrikh went through the training school and became a fitter in the depot workshops, and dreamed of going to flying school.

By 1935 everyone was busy getting on with their lives, and only Dina, who was in third grade, and Sasha, who was starting the first, remained at home. Dina didn't indulge us with excellent school results, but she had inherited mother's musical nature – you remember that mother had a wonderful voice. Dina had perfect pitch and promised to become a famous singer. She used to sing Russian, Jewish, Ukrainian and Byelorussian songs. If you're familiar with Ukrainian songs, you'll agree that they are particularly melodious and intimate. Every nation has its own songs, which it loves, and which in a sense are the soul of the nation, but the Ukrainian language is better suited to singing than any other except, perhaps, Italian. I don't think this comment is offensive to anyone. For instance, I'm a great lover of gipsy and Byelorussian songs, but my mother used to sing Ukrainian songs to me when I was small, and the songs your mother sang to you in childhood cling to you forever. Singing had not been possible for mother, but Dina's life was being shaped differently. Singing lessons were the rule at school, and there were the music and dramatic circles at the factory club, and everywhere there were teachers who could pick out talent, and they grabbed hold of Dina. And, of course, there was Stanislava Frantsevna. Haven't I told you about Stanislava Frantsevna? Well, Stanislava Frantsevna was the wife of Ivan Karlovich, our neighbour, the one whose garden we used to run through to get to grandfather's, and who became friends with father and lent him books and conversed in German with him. Well, Stanislava Frantsevna taught music, as they had a piano in the house, and she and Ivan Karlovich virtually adopted Dina as their own daughter, having no children of their own, and they used to get her to sing in her bell-like voice. When it turned out that her voice was not just a bell but a real talent, Stanislava Frantsevna began to teach her to read music, as she believed that Dina must have not just vocal training but a proper musical education.

While she was still in the fourth grade, Dina was already the soloist of the town choir, performing at amateur concerts. The club at the factory cooperative was quite large, with a hall for two hundred people. Grandfather and grandmother Rakhlenko would come, grandfather already seventy-five, but still robust, broad-shouldered, with his thick black beard only just tinged with grey, and his high white forehead, and grandmother, plump, calm and good, and there would be Uncle Lazar with his son Danya, and Uncle Grisha with his wife and children, and of course me, with my younger brothers Genrikh and Sasha, and there in the front row, mother and father, all dressed up for the occasion, both of them still young, father forty-five, mother forty-two, which is nothing for such good-looking people. I'm over sixty myself, now, but I don't think of myself as an old man.

The amateur activities at our club were very well organized. They were run by a young man called Bogolyubov, who had just been through music school, and conducted the choir and the orchestra, and directed the drama group. He could play all the instruments and paint, too; in other words, he was highly talented, good at everything, extremely enthusiastic and able to get others involved. He was even good at inspiring whole families: the Stashenoks, for instance, who made up a Byelorussian choir on their own, including even the old parents. They would come out on stage and form two rows, according to age, Afanasi Prokopyevich and his wife, then their sons Andrey and Petrus, with their wives Ksana and Irina, and then their children, all of them fair-haired and in Byelorussian national dress. They sang beautifully, and they were just as good, in my opinion, as today's group, The Songsters, though without doubt The Songsters are one of the best groups going, but of course they're professional, whereas the Stashenoks were amateurs. Nevertheless they won a prize in a regional competition. There was, I remember, also the Doroshenko family of young Ukrainian boys and girls, who danced the *gopak*, the *kazachok* and other Ukrainian dances, and there was a balalaika ensemble, and poetry readers, and tap-dancers, and even acrobats. In fact, the club really went with a swing. But without any doubt at the top of the bill came the town choir. Bogolyubov's main interest was singing, and the choir he put together was really first-class.

Imagine the scene, there in the front row mother and father, on stage the choir, a semicircle of women in front and behind them a row of men, standing on benches to raise them up, every one of them with an excellent voice. They announce the next item, 'and the soloist will be Dina Ivanovsky', and out comes Dina to the front of the stage, a girl in a million, well developed, like all the girls in the south who develop early, tall and slim, with black hair, plaited into two thick braids, and blue eyes. When she begins to sing you can hear a pin drop, and even the roughs, who usually did nothing in the club but make a din, look as though they have been bewitched. Dina's wonderful voice brought tears to many an eye – hers was genuine art, and art, like love, conquers the world.

As for my parents, what is there to say? This was their crowning glory, the reward for all the troubles and misfortunes they had been through, it was the shining hour of their love. The audience's tears made a big impression on mother. Never mind, she thought, her children would turn out to be doctors, too, not in some Switzerland or other on the edge of the world, but in a great country, a country which occupied a sixth of the world. That was mother's victory, it had come late, but it was all the sweeter for that.

Of course, we had our sorrows, too, that's life. For instance, Lyova got married. Well, what's wrong with that? It was none too soon, he was twenty-five, working from morning till night, rushing all over the region, dealing with transport problems in the regional committee, but he was alone and without a home of his own, eating whenever and whatever he could, and if he were to get an ulcer he had no one to look after him, no one to do his washing and mending, or to cook for him and give him his medicine if he got ill – a typical bachelor, so it was high time he settled down with a wife and family in a home of his own. The fact that he got married was in itself a good thing, and the fact that he got married in Chernigov, where he was living, and that he hadn't brought his bride to present her to his parents, well, what could anyone expect from him, especially as such things were not considered important any more.

Arranged weddings were also not thought important in those days, when all you needed was to sign at the register office and that was that, though my parents didn't much like this way of doing things, as their own marriage had been so out of the ordinary, as you know. I'm sure they would have preferred it if their own children were married in a less humdrum, simple way, especially their eldest son, Lyova. Still, what could you do, that's how things were done in those days. There was also nothing to be done about the fact that

Lyova didn't even tell us about his marriage himself, and that we only heard about it from one of the many local people who were living in Chernigov, after all, Lyova was a special sort of person and lived according to his own rules. We also heard from other people that his wife was an important person, an instructor in political economy, who didn't like housework, so they ate in the regional committee restaurant, but that was his problem; if that was the way he wanted to live, let him. The trouble was something else. His wife, who was called Anna Moiseyevna, was five years older than him, which meant she was thirty, but the main thing was she had a child, a little girl of three, from her first husband, and Lyova, by the way, was her third.

Lyova was a man of sound common sense, with the mind of a statesman, so he must have thought the whole thing out, and anyway it was his business. Though we shouldn't forget, either, that with all his sound common sense, he had the hot blood of the Rakhlenkos in his veins, and we know the kind of unexpected tricks they could get up to, and even father, with his German coolheadedness, had taken the most unexpected decisions, like his own marriage, for instance.

Mother was beside herself. Couldn't he find himself a decent, honest, young girl? A man like Lyova! Wasn't he capable of producing children of his own? Does he have to bring up someone else's? To turn down Olesya and to take a woman who by the age of thirty has managed to have three husbands, and that's only officially! How many has she had unofficially? What did it all mean?

But Lyova was Lyova, we were here, he was in Chernigov, and even if he had been here, we wouldn't have been able to do anything as he wasn't one to take orders, and anyway mother wouldn't have dared to say a word, even though he was her son, because he was special, he was apart. Mother kicked up a din and then said no more. Everything went back to normal.

Everything was fine, and yet something was bothering mother, and when I asked her, 'What's the matter, everything's all right, isn't it?' she replied, 'Too good!' Then I knew what it was that troubled her: she had the feeling that something was going to happen.

9 ❈

Mother's foreboding proved to be justified. The thunderbolt struck in broad daylight, right out of the blue. An article appeared in the regional press entitled 'Intruders and Embezzlers at the Shoe Factory'. It was about our factory. My father was referred to as an intruder, 'a man of doubtful social origins', it also mentioned a number of former artisans who had at some time used hired labour, and of course, it mentioned our manager, Sidorov, as 'the protector of intruders and embezzlers', and it named as the embezzlers two workers who had at one time stolen a piece of hide. Sidorov had certainly not protected them, he had actually fired them and handed them over to the courts. As it turned out, during the trial they would appear as witnesses for the prosecution. The article also stated that nepotism flourished at the factory, that relatives were working there, which of course is unavoidable in a small town like ours with just the one shoe factory, where generations of shoemakers worked. You could say the same of any collective farm, for that matter. In short, Sidorov had rubbed someone up the wrong way, stepped on someone's corns, the case was cooked up, and the article written to defame decent people, ten in all, including my father.

Father said the whole thing was rubbish, untrue, and not worth wasting one's breath on. But father was naïve. Everyone, including mother, realized this was not rubbish at all, and that it was vital that the case should not get to court.

Who should we turn to? To Lyova, of course. He was an important party-worker, and here they were, saying that his father, in league with other 'intruders', had misappropriated the people's property. Lyova wouldn't leave it at that! He knew his father and Sidorov to be the most honest of men.

I took the train and arrived to find Lyova nervous, confused and agitated. Although he was a man of cast-iron stamina, it was clear that his nerves were starting to give way, he showed the signs of irritation and impatience of a man who is compelled to be merciless. Such were the times, and such was his job in transport – to get rid of those who were fixing work-loads according to outdated figures, and to purge the railways of 'intruders' and 'leeches', and now, out of the blue, his own father had turned out to be an 'intruder'. Although Lyova gave the appearance of calm and common sense, I could tell he was under terrible strain, and I should know my own brother.

The rumours that had reached us, that his marriage had had no effect on his way of life, were not true. This was my first visit to him since his marriage. He had a good three-room apartment in a new block, with all the conveniences, and at that time a modern, new block was quite an event, as they weren't being built by the thousand, like they are today. True, Lyova didn't show me over the whole apartment, he took me straight through to his study. Neither of us was interested in apartments at that moment.

The door had been opened by the domestic help, a plump, pleasant-looking middle-aged woman. The lobby was clean, and contained a coat-rack, a mirror, and a box for shoes. There was a runner on the floor of the passage, and in the study the parquet gleamed, there were bookshelves full of books, a comfortable divan and a large desk, on which there were papers and more books. In fact, it was a home with every comfort.

While Lyova and I were sitting in his study, his wife, Anna Moiseyevna, came in. She was a brunette, with her hair smoothly brushed, rather like the film actress Emma Tsesarsky – you know, she was Aksinya in *Quiet Flows the Don*. She was good-looking, if a little overweight, and she seemed to me too short-legged. But to each his own.

'I think you've never met,' said Lyova. 'My wife Anya, my brother Boris.'

I stood up, she gave me her hand, though it was more of a light brush than a handshake, she smiled a brief, official smile, which immediately vanished from her face, then she sat down in an armchair and, believe it or not, she didn't utter a word. On her face I could see no sign of sympathy for father and the rest of us, on the contrary, I sensed hostility, we were complicating her life. It was clear enough that she and Lyova had gone over the whole thing already, she knew all about it, she didn't ask a single question or make a single observation. This wasn't her affair, it was someone else's, and the only reason she was sitting there was to make sure I didn't drag Lyova into the story. If she had entered the discussion, I know exactly what she would have said: 'Don't you realize just who your brother is, and what responsibility that puts on you?' That's what she would have said, but she didn't say anything, she stayed completely silent. The only time she opened her mouth was when her little girl ran into the study wearing a coat and beret, ready to go out for a walk, and with her was the help, also dressed to go out in a coat and head-scarf.

'Olya, what do you say to uncle?' Anna Moiseyevna asked the little girl, like a schoolmarm. Notice she didn't say 'Uncle Borya', just 'uncle', as if I were any ordinary visitor.

'How do you do?' came Olya's response.

Lyova stroked her head and said, ' "Hello, Uncle Borya," that's what you must say.' He obviously loved the child.

She repeated obediently, 'Hello, Uncle Borya.'

Lyova had slightly improved the situation, and it was clear

he wasn't totally under Anna Moiseyevna's thumb, thank God.

'Anna Yegorovna, don't take her out for more than an hour,' she ordered.

'Very good,' the woman replied.

Lyova spoke about father's case calmly, but I knew he was anxious. The case itself worried him, as he loved father, and it worried him also because he knew it would cause trouble and complications for himself, as they were bound to take him off his job on the regional committee; after all, what authority could the chief party-worker have, when his own father was being charged with a criminal offence? In fact, he was soon moved to other work.

Lyova said he was convinced of father's innocence, and of Sidorov's innocence, but he conceded that 'intruders and embezzlers' could have used them and got them implicated, because father was so trusting and Sidorov was not all that intelligent. Lyova himself wouldn't intervene, as neither he nor even the party regional secretary himself had the right to interfere in legal proceedings, it was against the law. He was sure that it would all be sorted out by the court and that everything would be back to normal, but at the same time, we had to face the fact that, because of father, the case could acquire a political tinge, as he had been born and brought up in Switzerland, where he still had relations he corresponded with. It was vital to fight precisely on that point and to prove that father was not an intruder, but an honest Soviet citizen. That was the essence of the whole thing.

You can tell that Lyova really did have the mind of a politician and statesman.

'When are you going home?' he asked.

It was several hours from Chernigov to our town and, frankly, I would rather have waited till next morning, but if I had stayed, it would have meant waking them all up here very early. Sometimes the bigger the apartment, the harder it is to find room to put up an extra person for the night.

'I'll leave right away.'

'All right, but keep me informed of what happens.'

I would have liked to embrace him, as we said good-bye, but the surroundings felt wrong. We shook hands. Anna Moiseyevna held out her hand to me, too, and we made contact, as they say in football, and she gave me one of her brief, official smiles.

I spent the night hanging around the station, then took the train back home.

When I got back, I told mother that Lyova and Anna Moiseyevna lived very nicely, that they had treated me beautifully, that Anna Moiseyevna was an intelligent woman, that Olya was a delightful little girl, that she adored Lyova and called him 'papa', and that he doted on her.

Mother's face was like stone. She allowed that Anna Moiseyevna was an intelligent woman and that Olya was a delightful little girl, why shouldn't she be, at the age of three? She allowed that Lyova doted on her, but why should she want to know about this child, who was not her granddaughter? She didn't want to hear about any of them, they were not what was occupying her mind. It was father she was thinking about.

'What did he say about the case?'

'He said he hasn't got the right to interfere. The investigation will sort it all out and everything will be all right.'

You could understand him. If he tried to defend father, he would be indirectly confirming his guilt, because an innocent man has nothing to defend, the law protects the innocent, and Lyova had absolute faith in the law.

In his own way, Lyova was right, and this was something that father, grandfather Rakhlenko, and I all understood. Mother couldn't. What? A son not try to defend his own father? Who ever heard of such a thing? He's in a job like that, and he can't say one word against these bare-faced lies? And that's Lyova, her pride and joy! Had she really been wrong about him? Had she been wrong about all her children?

The regional auditors came and started sifting through the documents, and there can surely never be inspectors anywhere in the world who will report that everything is absolutely perfect, you'll never find a factory where there hasn't been some negligence or shortcoming. Then, as well as the auditors, we had a special commission, which began questioning people, and people vary. The dissatisfied are glad to have the chance to spread slander, those who feel offended have an opportunity to get their revenge, cowards are scared to speak the truth, and the cautious will give evasive replies.

Father, Sidorov and the others, all ten of them, in fact, were released from work, and the interrogations began. Father knew at once that things were going to be bad and came home depressed.

The audit and the investigation took six months, it was already 1936 and the investigator decided that they should all be tried; the decision was confirmed by the state prosecutor, and father, Sidorov, and the rest were all sent off to prison in Chernigov, as we had no prison of our own.

What can you say? What can you say when they suddenly come and search the house and take your father away, a harmless man, and when they turn everything in the house upside down in the search for the stolen goods and money and valuables, as if they don't realize that, had father really been a thief, he would have got everything out of the house during the six months of the investigation! Still, they searched everywhere and of course found nothing, except the letters from Switzerland, which they kept. It was to father's credit that he took it like a man and smiled to reassure us, though there was something guilty in that smile. I don't mean guilty in regard to them, but in regard to us, as though it was his fault that these people had come in the middle of the night and given the family so much anxiety.

Mother wasn't as polite and well brought up as father, however, and neither was Genrikh. At first he was timid, you know, like a kid in the street when he's faced by the police, but then when he realized that they had come for father, he started to be rude to the militia-men, he was cheeky and stood in the doorway and wouldn't let them through, jostled them and started up with his schoolboy tricks, and if I hadn't yelled at him to stop, things could have taken a turn for the worse.

As for mother, I can't tell you what it all did to her. I really thought she would go off her head that night. She was hysterical and father could do nothing to calm her down. Dina said, 'Mother, don't cry, mother, don't cry!' But mother just sat on a chair, rocking herself backwards and forwards and repeating loudly 'It's the end, it's the end, it's the end!' Sasha, who was only eight, sat in silence and watched everyone pensively. I think he must have remembered that night to the last day of his short life. Little Igor was sleeping, thank God, and heard nothing. When a militia-man said to mother, 'Citizeness Ivanovsky, calm yourself,' she screamed at him, 'What do you want here? Who asked you to come? Get out!'

The militia-men were people we knew, people from our own town. They gave each other meaningful looks and father said politely, 'Please forgive her, she's very nervous.' To mother he said, 'Rachel, if you want to help me, please be quiet.'

She stopped screaming, but went on clutching her head in her hands and rocking back and forth on the chair, like a mad woman. Even when they took father out, she didn't get up or say good-bye or hang on to him, the way women do when their husbands are being taken away. I put a few things together for father myself. He kissed us all and went to mother, who was sitting with her eyes closed, as if she were dead, and he obviously wanted to stroke her hair, but then he changed his mind and left the house with the militia-men. One door slammed, then the outer door, but mother didn't move, she just sat there with her eyes closed, seeing nothing and hearing nothing. I went to the window, it was getting light already, and I watched them taking father down the street, and all the neighbours were watching, too, nobody was sleeping, everyone knew they had come for him, and they watched as he was taken away.

I told the children to go back to bed and get some sleep, as Genrikh had to go to work later and Dina and Sasha had to go to school. Then I touched mother on the shoulder.

'Mother, lie down,' I said.

She opened her eyes and looked at me, but she seemed not to see me, closed her eyes again and went on sitting there, and it was then I realized that her mind had been affected. She sat like that till morning. The children got up, had breakfast and left, Genrikh to work and Dina and Sasha to school. Igor woke up, I dressed him and gave him his breakfast.

Mother heard his voice and only then did she open her eyes, look around and say 'It's finished.'

Then she got up, went to the bedroom, lay down in the clothes she was wearing, and slept right through the day, until evening.

Grandfather and grandmother Rakhlenko came, Uncle Lazar and Uncle Grisha came, the neighbours and others came, but mother slept right through it all, and so as not to wake her, I spoke to them all outside on the porch. I told them what had happened and they sympathized, the women cried and were sorry for father. Among them were mother's old friends, you remember, the Kuznetsov girls, now married women, and also the Stashenoks and others came, but I didn't let anyone go through to mother, though I often went to see her myself, as I was afraid she might do herself some harm, as she was obviously out of her mind. Dina and Sasha came home from school, then Genrikh came from work, and grandmother took them home to her place, with little Igor, to feed them all.

In the evening mother woke up at last. She washed and came into the dining-room, and at once I saw I had been wrong about her mental state. She was calm, severe, masterful as she had always been, and now she told me to go and get grandfather, Uncle Lazar, Uncle Grisha, and our neighbours Ivan Karlovich and Afanasi Prokopyevich Stashenok – without their wives, as what she wanted now was masculine advice. When they had come, we sat round the table and began to think what to do. Of course, everyone thought of the same thing, which was to get a lawyer, not just any lawyer, but the best in the business, as father's life was at stake.

The top lawyer in the Ukraine at that time was a certain Dolsky in Kiev, whose name was as famous in the republic as. say, Braude's or Kommodov's in the entire Soviet Union, Braude or Kommodov were not likely to take our case, but Dolsky might, as Kiev was nearer than Moscow. Also, as Ivan Karlovich noted sensibly, if the decision of the regional court was unfavourable, the case would go to the Supreme Court of the Ukraine in Kiev and Dolsky would be the ideal man, as he knew everyone in Kiev and everyone knew him. But, Ivan Karlovich added, Dolsky was a very expensive lawyer, his fees were beyond anything we could imagine.

Mother replied that the fees didn't matter, she would pay anything he asked, she would sell the house and everything she possessed, and everything the children had, too, we would go naked and barefoot, without a roof over our heads, if it would save father. Uncle Lazar and Uncle Grisha also said they would sell everything to save Yakov, and Afanasi Prokopyevich promised to give whatever he could.

It seemed clear enough that you couldn't get a better lawyer than Dolsky, who had authority throughout the Ukraine, even throughout the Union, and if he agreed to take the case, father would be saved.

Mother was waiting to hear what grandfather thought, however, as she valued his opinion highly. Though he was over seventy-five he still had a sharp mind, and in seventy-five years you build up quite a bit of experience.

Grandfather Rakhlenko was brief: 'We must get Tereshchenko.'

We couldn't have been more amazed if he had said we have to get King Solomon. Tereshchenko! You know about the Provisional Government, of course, the government that replaced the Tsar in February 1917 until the October Revolution, and that included ten capitalist ministers? One of them, the minister of finance, was Tereshchenko, who owned sugar mills in the Ukraine and was either a Constitutional Democrat or a monarchist, I'm not sure. The Tereshchenko grandfather had in mind was of course not that one, though this one had had enough troubles on account of the minister, as he'd had to prove that he was not related to the minister and that the minister was not related to him. That's how it was in those days, you had to prove you were not related, though how you could beats me! Especially as our Tereshchenko used to be a big boaster, and when the minister Tereshchenko was in power he used to brag that he was his favourite nephew and heir to all his sugar mills, even though everyone knew that if he was the minister's nephew, Kerensky was my grandmother! He was the son of a customs official and everyone knew them both inside out. He was an absolute bum as a young man, though he was a student and, can you imagine, he actually fancied my mother just at the time when she was engaged to my father. Everyone fancied her, but the others knew she wasn't free and easy, and they contented themselves with admiring her. But he had the nerve to come to us to have his boots repaired, when in fact it was really to pester Rachel. Grandfather saw through him right away and grabbed him by the scruff of the neck and threw him out into the street, together with his unrepaired boots.

Tereshchenko, the idiot, hadn't had enough, and obviously didn't realize who he was dealing with. He bragged that Rachel would be his, whatever happened, because there wasn't a girl in the world who could resist him. He said this at the station, where the young folk used to congregate and wander up and down the platform of an evening, waiting for the passenger-train to arrive. Uncle Grisha happened to hear his bragging, and though he was only fifteen, to Teresh-chenko's twenty, and Tereshchenko was with a group of his friends, Uncle Grisha went up to him and gave him a punch in the face as only Grisha knew how, and he really did know how. Tereshchenko's pals didn't budge an inch, as they saw the rest of the Rakhlenko brothers coming, and the whole town knew the family and knew that it was wise not to tangle with them. Anyway, the train was arriving and a gendarme was running towards them, trying not to trip over his sword, and while the train was coming in and the gendarme was running towards them, Grisha knocked the living daylights out of Tereshchenko, which was the right thing to do, because only scum would say the things he did, and Uncle Grisha was honour-bound to defend his sister's good name. He wasn't simply a good brother, he was the kind of brother who looks for the chance to have a fight, and what better reason could there be than when someone tries to blacken your sister's reputation, especially if she is engaged, and not just engaged, but in a difficult position, with her fiancé in Switzerland and the future so uncertain?

Nothing more happened. Tereshchenko, as they say, with-drew, covered up his bruises and took himself back to Petersburg, as the holidays were over. Then his father, dressed in his customs uniform, called on grandfather and apologized for his son's behaviour, to which grandfather replied, 'Young people get up to all sorts of things.' Grandfather said no more but, as I understand it, he liked what the elder Tereshchenko had done, he valued good acts. For a customs official, in full double-breasted uniform, to apologize for his son, who had first been thrown out into the street and then had the living daylights knocked out of him, and to apologize to a simple shoemaker, was really something, you will agree! I think the old man was prompted to apologize not only by his son's behaviour, but by the fact that the whole town sympathized with Rachel, my future mother, and probably old Tereshchenko sympathized with her, too.

Then came the war and the Revolution, and fifteen years later the young Tereshchenko turned up again, making his living as a respectable defence counsel in Chernigov. He came to our town to defend cases in our court, and he was so successful that our townsfolk always turned to him whenever they had any business with the law, after all, he knew his job and he was one of us. There were better lawyers than Tereshchenko in Chernigov, I'm quite sure, but people like to stick to what they know, especially as Tereshchenko was keen to take the cases, he never refused, and there were plenty of cases to take, what with NEP, taxes, and the finance inspectors – plenty.

Then he had some unpleasantness. He apparently split up with his wife and took to drink, left Chernigov, went back to Chernigov, was expelled from the Bar, then was reinstated, and meanwhile other lawyers had been coming here and people forgot about Tereshchenko, and now, all of a sudden, grandfather remembered him. And when? When we were discussing the question of father's survival. Who should he remember but the man who had once pestered his daughter in the most boorish way, and who he himself had thrown out into the street, and now this same man was to defend father, his lucky rival, so to speak!

Without doubt, grandfather Rakhlenko was a very wise man, he had a very good mind, but seventy-five is, after all, seventy-five. I don't mean to say that at that age a man becomes stupid, far from it! But he was a bit out of touch. He remembered that Tereshchenko had conducted cases here, that he had done well, and he didn't know any other defence lawyers, never having been involved in a court case himself, so he came out with Tereshchenko.

He saw we were puzzled, so he explained. 'No Kiev lawyer will take this case. If he's that famous, Yakov for him is nothing, less than nothing. Whereas Tereshchenko could make his name again here with this case.'

This argument had some sense, but we were trying to save father's life, not Tereshchenko's reputation. Wasn't it taking too much of a risk?

'You are quite right, my dear Abram Isakovich,' said Ivan Karlovich. 'Tereshchenko is a capable and knowledgeable lawyer. But he drinks, he has let himself go. Appearing in court drunk deprives a lawyer of his right to act, and that would mean the certain loss of the case.'

Grandfather stood his ground. 'We have to check to see if he hasn't already died of the DTs, if he's sane, and if, please God, he's stopped drinking, and if he has, then we won't need a better lawyer.'

Mother then announced her decision. 'Tomorrow, Borya and I will go to Chernigov to ask Lyova's advice,' she still had some hope of him, 'and we'll find out about Tereshchenko. If he's someone we can deal with, as a person, and Lyova also recommends him, we'll take him. If not, Boris will go to Kiev and talk to Dolsky. We'll pay him whatever he asks. Now, what about the children?'

She had Yefim and Lyuba in mind and whether we should tell them about father's arrest. Yefim was working in Kharkov, at the Tractor Factory, and Lyuba was in Leningrad in her second year of medicine.

Grandfather said, 'No need to worry them, there's plenty of time.'

Afanasi Prokopyevich, however, thought that, as adults they should be told the truth, and Ivan Karlovich sensibly pointed out that it could be worse for them if we left them in ignorance, as nobody would believe them if they said they didn't know their father had been arrested, and they could be accused of trying to hush up a very serious matter. So we decided to write to them, but not to worry them too much. We would tell them it was nothing too terrible, just some misunderstanding at the factory which would soon be cleared up and father would soon be released.

Mother and I travelled to Chernigov and went straight to Lyova's apartment. Anna Moiseyevna was not in and the door was opened by Anna Yegorovna, the domestic help, who looked very much put out by our arrival, and stood in the doorway without saying a word.

'Is Lev Yakovlevich at home?' I asked.

'No,' she replied. 'He's gone to Moscow. He was called to Moscow.'

'What about Anna Moiseyevna?'

'Anna Moiseyevna is at work.'

She went on standing in the doorway, and I realized that Anna Moiseyevna had given her orders never to let any of us into the house. But Anna Yegorovna found she couldn't send away Lev Yakovlevich's own brother, even less could she send away his mother. Even if she didn't know it was Lyova's mother standing there, she still couldn't have sent her away, mother wasn't the kind of woman you could dismiss just like that, because she inspired respect at the first glance, she was so striking in appearance. So Anna Yegorovna just went on standing there, confused and embarrassed and not knowing what to do. The best thing would have been for us to turn round and leave. But then what could I say to mother? Anna Yegorovna hadn't let us in because she is an idiot and ignorant and didn't know who we were, she had never seen mother and she obviously didn't remember who I was, so she was afraid to let us in. That's what I would have said. Then I would have taken her to one of our friends from home and left her with them, while I would have gone back and had a talk with Lyova's wife, face to face, and as I already had a good idea of how the conversation would go, I wanted to spare mother from it.

Anna Yegorovna was so confused, however, she didn't slam the door in our faces – anyway she was too decent a person to do a thing like that – so she let us in instead, taking us through to the kitchen, not the living-room.

I wasn't the only one who realized what was going on. Mother was no fool, and anyway you didn't have to be very bright to understand. The domestic help didn't know whether to let us in or not, so she took us to her own part of the flat, the kitchen, not the living-room, and didn't even offer us a glass of tea. She was so upset, she didn't call Olya to come and see her grandmother and uncle, though Olya was at home, as we could hear her in her room, talking either to her doll or to herself, and we could hear her running about. You agree this was no way to greet the mother and brother of the master of the house, not even distant relatives should be treated like that, if they are still regarded as relatives, that is.

So there we were sitting in the kitchen, mother and I, with mother staring at Anna Yegorovna, as only she knew how, which made the poor woman so uncomfortable, that she kept running backwards and forwards to Olya's room, until she finally found a way out.

'It's time for me to take Olya for her walk.' And the poor thing would like to have added, 'And you must go, too, as I have been told not to leave strange people alone in the house.'

She couldn't say it, but nor had she the right to say we should stay, either, as she was under instructions. To get her off the hook, I asked her where she and Olya were going to go for their walk.

'Just outside, in the little square,' she indicated through the window.

'That's fine,' I said. 'We'll come and sit on a bench with you till Anna Moiseyevna arrives. Come on, mother, let's have a little fresh air.'

Mother went on staring at Anna Yegorovna. She understood everything, of course, but said nothing, and the poor domestic help was getting more and more upset.

'There's no rush. Do sit, please, I still have to get Olya ready.'

I told her we would go and wait for her in the square. Mother and I went out and sat on a bench. It was a beautifully sunny September day, still summery, the shrubs and trees still lush and green, children were digging in a sandpit, people looked cheerful as they walked along the street, everything seemed so serene and pleasant and radiant, and old Chernigov was so beautiful, that it was impossible to connect all this with the thought that father had vanished from such a beautiful world.

'Well, what have you got to say?' mother asked, turning towards me.

'What do you want from her? She's only the help, an uneducated woman.'

'Fine!' she said, turning away. 'Then we'll wait for the educated one.'

'Perhaps we ought to go to the Rudakovs' – they were our friends from home – 'you can have a rest there, and I'll come back here and talk to her, find out where Lyova is?'

'No,' she replied. 'I want to have a look at this beauty of ours myself.'

Anna Yegorovna came along with Olya. She sat down next to us and Olya was going towards the sandpit when I stopped her.

'Hello, Olya!'

'Hello!'

'Do you remember me?'

She replied hesitantly, 'I remember you.'

'What's my name, then?'

'Uncle . . .' she hesitated again and looked at Anna Yegorovna.

'Uncle Borya,' I prompted her.

'Uncle Borya,' she repeated.

I pointed to mother, 'And this is Grandmother Rachel.'

I knew mother would not be pleased by this title, she was no grandmother to this child, nor was the child a granddaughter to her. But to call her by anything else would have been to act as Anna Moiseyevna had acted towards me, to wipe out any relationship whatever.

The little girl looked at mother from under her brow, mother's imposing looks made her shy. She dug her heel into the ground, then went off to play in the sand. Mother didn't take her eyes off the child, but it was an unkindly look, as she saw the child as a part of Anna Moiseyevna, whom she already hated with all her heart.

It wasn't much fun, sitting on the bench. Mother sat like a statue, and Anna Yegorovna was silent, too, though she obviously enjoyed chatting, what nanny doesn't, sitting for hours on a park bench with nothing to do? However, she could hardly talk about what was on our minds, as she had no right, but it also made her uneasy to prattle about trivialities, when she knew what we were thinking and that we were weighed down by it. She had been schooled by Anna Moiseyevna, she knew exactly what she was permitted to talk about and what she wasn't. Even so, her training hadn't made her servile, but rather dignified, as if she were saying, 'I'm here to look after the child and it's not for me to know about the rest. I am the domestic help, the nanny, my place is in the kitchen. I'll talk about the child, but I know you're not interested in her at this moment, you have serious business, which you want to talk about with the mistress.'

◆

We had been sitting there for two or three hours and it was getting towards evening, when Anna Moiseyevna appeared, walking along the street. She didn't see us. She looked heavy, pompous, broad-shouldered, and was wearing a long grey jacket, which made her look even heavier. With her smoothly brushed dark hair and angry frown, and her tightly stuffed briefcase, she looked very business-like, a real somebody. She crossed over towards the square, obviously knowing that Olya and the nanny would be there. She walked at a calm, assured and accustomed pace to the bench and saw Anna Yegorovna, though she didn't notice us, as she was only interested in Anna Yegorovna and Olya. She gave us a glance, without taking us in, turned away and suddenly realized that she knew who I was and guessed who was sitting there next to me, as mother was like Lyova. Her face changed immediately, and from the look of hostility and malice on it, I knew she had recognized us. Anna Yegorovna got up. I got up, too.

'Hello, Anna Moiseyevna. This is Lyova's mother.'

She didn't respond to my greeting, nor did she want to meet mother. She straightened Olya's beret.

'Lev Yakovlevich has been called to Moscow by the Department of Transport. He is being given a new job, and if he thinks it is necessary, he will let you know his address.'

She was precise, clear, and definite, as if she were chopping with an axe. 'If he thinks it necessary', eh, how do you like that? It was so alien and hostile, I was stunned by her boorishness, her rudeness and her heartlessness. I had been prepared for anything but that. If a man had spoken to us like that, I would have had an answer for him. But here was a woman, and however big a bitch she was, she was still a woman, and I wasn't about to get into a slanging match with her in front of the child and the nanny.

Instead, I said, appeasingly, 'We're in terrible trouble, Anna Moiseyevna. Father has been arrested.'

'Well, what do you expect?' she replied with indifference. 'He should have stayed out of intrigues and kept himself honest.'

Then mother said, 'We've got a double tragedy. One you know already, the other is that Lyova got himself mixed up with trash like you.'

Anna Moiseyevna didn't answer, as she wasn't interested in having a conversation, she wanted to cut us off as quickly as possible to show us that we were nothing to do with her.

They left. Anna Yegorovna lingered to collect Olya's little bucket and spade, and she said good-bye to us.

We spent the night at the Rudakovs, friends from our town, who of course knew the whole story. They were quite clear that Tereshchenko just wouldn't do, as he was only a petty lawyer, and a drunkard who wrote out applications for people at the market. There were some real advocates, like Petrov, Shulman, Velembitsky, and, of course, Dolsky! Dolsky was far and away the best. If only we could get Dolsky!

So, mother went home and I took the train to Kiev. I won't burden you with the details of how I managed to get through to Dolsky. Everyone wanted Dolsky, everyone needed Dolsky, and they were all waiting to see him, trying to catch him, looking for him. He was one of those lawyers who demonstrate the simple truth that, the harder they are to get, the more people will try to get them, and a man everyone wants is undoubtedly a valuable man, and a valuable man costs money. I tried for exactly a week to get to him and I finally made it. He listened while I told him about the factory, and the newspaper, and father, and Switzerland, and Lyova, about everything, in fact. I must say, once you had actually managed to get to him, he listened to you and went very thoroughly into the case; he was very attentive, I will say that. He was a well-groomed gentleman, dressed in a slightly old-fashioned way, with a beard and thick, long hair, like a singer. He had a solid appearance, an important consideration for any lawyer.

He refused to take the case, however. 'I would very much like to help you,' he said. He was the sort of man you felt you oughtn't to interrupt. He spoke in a beautiful and imposing voice, the kind of voice that would no doubt make an impression on both the judge and the public. 'I simply cannot leave Kiev at the moment. I'm tied up with other cases which I haven't the right to drop. Look, you can see for yourself.' He leafed through his diary. 'This month and next are completely booked up. Let's hope your father's case doesn't take a turn for the worse. I see nothing criminal in what you've told me. But if the court reaches an unfavourable decision, then I promise to take the case when it comes to Kiev on appeal.'

How could I object, when the man obviously couldn't take on another case, as I had seen for myself from his diary, which showed he hadn't a single day free? Besides, what was a little factory in some small provincial town to him, when he was famous throughout the Ukraine and the Union, and everyone was trying to reach him and not everyone even managed to talk to him?

'As soon as the case goes to Kiev, let me know,' he said, getting up to let me know the consultation was over.

I got the point, and was about to pay for the consultation, but as I took out my wallet, he pushed my hand away and said, 'There's nothing to pay, I haven't taken your case yet.'

I returned to Chernigov and went straight to the legal advice office. You know what a legal advice office is like, I'm sure. Two tiny rooms, in one the lawyers, and in the other the clients, or at least the clients who are getting close, the rest stretch out in a long line to the street. The room was minute, the line endless. I waited for a couple of hours, got in, paid the secretary the appropriate fee for a consultation, and asked for Petrov. Petrov was ill. I asked for Shulman, Shulman was in court. Only Velembitsky and, can you beat it, Tereshchenko were left. Naturally, I chose Velembitsky, but it turned out she was already defending three of the defendants in our case. Then I discovered that Petrov was defending Sidorov, and Shulman two others. Only Tereshchenko was left. While I had been running around Kiev after Dolsky, all the best lawyers had been grabbed. What could I do? Well, mother had said that if I couldn't get Dolsky, I should take Tereshchenko.

When I got into the lawyers' room, I saw a dried up old man sitting at a desk, a small man with a very loud voice. You know how you can get a dumpy little man with a voice like a trumpet, and a giant with a voice like a tin whistle. I sat down opposite Tereshchenko. He shuffled some papers around without looking up at me, and in a deep, hoarse voice, said 'I'm listening.'

I told him where I was from, gave him my name, but as I wasn't sure that he knew it, I told him I had come to him on the advice of my grandfather Rakhlenko.

When I pronounced the name Rakhlenko, he lifted his eyes and looked at me intently, then he grinned, openly and maliciously, as though to say he was glad to have the chance to meet that little family again, and that that little family had had to turn to him for help. I was sorry I hadn't managed to persuade Velembitsky to take father's case as well, and that I had ended up with Tereshchenko, who was clearly a petty and vengeful creature. Only such a person would grin maliciously and triumph over someone who had come to him with such a tragedy as ours, with such a situation as ours.

There was nothing for it, I couldn't possibly get up and say, 'I don't want you, I want another lawyer, because you looked at me in a way you shouldn't and you grinned in a way I don't like.'

You must agree that such a step on my part would have been stupid, as they were all for each other in that place, they had their professional solidarity, so if I had gone to another lawyer, without any cause whatever, he wouldn't have treated me any better.

I saw that there was nothing else to do but tell him everything. He listened to me, putting a question occasionally, and covering his mouth with his hand, the sure sign of a drunk, a drunk always covers his mouth to hide the smell of alcohol, and even if he isn't smelling of vodka, he still does it automatically, so that the person he's talking to shouldn't be able to tell whether or not he's drunk or sober, or hung over.

In short, I was looking at an alcoholic and I knew the situation was bad, grandfather had been wrong, Ivan Karlovich had been right, with an alcoholic like this one we would lose the case, we would be burying father. I had to get free of Tereshchenko, but only after careful thought, and with tact. To begin father's defence with a scandal would be an even bigger stupidity.

While I was telling Tereshchenko about the case, I emphasized the fact that father was from Switzerland, and that this was something apparently to keep in mind.

With his hand over his mouth, Tereshchenko replied, 'You don't think they're going to try him for being born in Switzerland? Switzerland has absolutely nothing to do with it.'

Yes, Tereshchenko couldn't see beyond his nose, he was a petty provincial lawyer who couldn't grasp the main point, and the main point was what Lyova had warned us about.

Suddenly he said, 'In her time your mother was a very beautiful girl.'

Again he gave me his malicious grin, as though to say, such a pretty girl could have had a happy life, but she had spurned him and married a failure and now through her own stupidity she had landed in this terrible mess. I thought I would explode, I wanted to smash his ugly mug so much, but in a situation like that, you can't give vent to your feelings, you must control yourself, so I controlled myself, said nothing about mother in reply, and only tried to think of ways of presenting the case so that he wouldn't want to take it.

As luck would have it, he asked, 'And what is your famous brother's opinion of the matter?'

Again a malicious question, but this time I made use of it. 'My brother is pessimistic.'

'Yes,' Tereshchenko agreed. 'There are good grounds for such an opinion. For a final judgement, of course, I need to know more about the case. Come and see me at the same time the day after tomorrow.'

A day passed. I was staying with people from our town, there were a lot of them in Chernigov, and others came to see me while I was there, all sympathizing and all wanting to help, and the talk was mainly about lawyers. Opinions varied. Some thought that the only real lawyer was Petrov and that Shulman was rubbish, others thought that Petrov was rubbish and Shulman a real lawyer, and still more thought they were all rubbish, Petrov, Shulman, Velembitsky, and Tereshchenko.

In any event, when I arrived at Tereshchenko's at the appointed time, he said, 'I have familiarized myself with this case and in my opinion it is complicated and probably hopeless.'

'Well, then,' I replied, 'if you regard it as hopeless, I ought to see someone else.'

'No,' he said. 'The duty of a lawyer is to defend the accused in even the most hopeless case. Anyway, as the investigation has been completed, the trial is likely to take place soon, even in the next few days, and you haven't time to find another lawyer. I will conduct the case. The secretary will arrange the proper documents for you.'

I hesitated. 'We have to agree . . . '

He interrupted me in an official voice. 'No special agreement will be necessary. See the secretary.'

I signed the papers, paid the bill and went home with a heavy heart. The case had got into the wrong hands, and nobody was to blame but myself. While I had been running around Kiev after Dolsky, all the best lawyers in Chernigov had been snapped up, and they would be defending the other defendants, while my father would be defended by an alcoholic, who of course hadn't forgotten how mother had rejected his advances and how grandfather had chucked him out into the street, together with his boots, and how Uncle Grisha had knocked the living daylights out of him, not in some tucked-away side street, but right out in the open, at the railway station, in front of the entire intelligentsia of the town.

◆

Back home, however, I told mother that everything was all right, that I had agreed with Dolsky that he would take the case, if it came to Kiev, and that I had also come to terms with Tereshchenko, who had made a very pleasant impression on me, and that our friends were quite wrong to paint such a negative picture of him.

Mother listened to what I had to say, and nodded silently. As a matter of fact, she didn't say much at all at that time. Her life came to a stop the moment they took father out of the house. Our lives carried on, I mean my life and the lives of my brothers and sisters, uncles and relations. You can't get away from it, life goes on, even when someone very close to you dies, life still goes on. But mother's life had stopped, father was her life, she knew no other, she had had no other. Don't think that for one instant I was reconciled to father's fate, not at all. I did everything I could to save him, but I was living in the real world, I was working in a factory, the whole family virtually rested on my shoulders, the thought of father never left my mind, but I also had room in my mind for other thoughts or it would have been impossible to live and work. Mother had no room for other thoughts. She could think only about father. I'm only grateful that nothing else happened to any of the rest of us at that terrible time, because I don't know how mother would have taken it, and I have the awful thought that, with father's frightful situation on her mind, she might have been indifferent or not attentive enough, if some other accident had happened, even if it had involved one of her children. She had seven children, but her husband, her Yakov, was her one and only.

A week went by, then another, and still no trial. Mother and I went in turn to Chernigov with parcels for father, then mother stayed in Chernigov to prepare his food for him and to take him in parcels, as even a healthy man would hardly have survived on prison food, and father was used to home cooking, not ordinary home cooking, either, but mother's. Father was our first priority. I gave all my wages, Yefim sent what he could, and Lyova, to give him his due, also sent money from Chelyabinsk. He wasn't working in Chelyabinsk, but at some other large station on the South Urals line, he didn't say which one. He only said that Anna Moiseyevna was also being transferred to Chelyabinsk, that they had given up the flat in Chernigov, and that they would soon have a proper address; meanwhile he wanted us to write to him poste restante.

◆

Lyuba and Volodya came from Leningrad to collect Igor, as they didn't want to burden mother with any more worries, as if she didn't have enough, and anyway she was spending so much time in Chernigov. But what could they do with Igor, when they were still living in a student hostel? Grandfather and grandmother took him to live with them – as it was they already had Uncle Grisha and his family living with them, and in a big family one more child is no problem. Then mother wanted us to sell some odds and ends so that father could have chicken soup in prison, and fresh butter from the market, and fruit. Incidentally, father told me later, in strict secrecy, that he received none of this stuff, as it was all stolen by racketeers. Mother didn't know this, she knew one thing only, and that was that we had to get father out of prison, and while he was there, we had to give him all the support we could, and everything else had to take second place.

It was at that time that I learned from mother much of what I have told you. She recalled their life from the moment of their first meeting on our dusty, sandy street, right up to the day they took father away. In those terrible times, those bitter moments, I realized just how much people can love each other, and how they can go on loving right through their lives. The poet Mayakovsky said, 'Our planet is badly equipped for gaiety.' Perhaps, I don't know. I do know our lives are badly equipped for love.

Meanwhile, Tereshchenko began coming to see us, as though on court business, but in fact to work on our case. He would go and see grandfather, too. What they talked about I don't know, grandfather was keeping things dark, which offended me, as I didn't think there should be any secrets kept from me concerning my own father. I pondered on it and reckoned that Tereshchenko was coming to terms with grandfather about his fee, maybe he was getting an advance, so that he could grease the right palm, after all, grandfather had grown up under the old regime when bribe-taking was widespread. I told grandfather he shouldn't give anything to Tereshchenko. Grandfather replied that he hadn't given him anything, that they were meeting as old friends – old friends, when one had chucked the other out into the street! — and remembering the old days and talking about father's case.

I didn't believe that. Tereshchenko would have done better to talk to me about father's case, after all I was a craftsman in the workshop and could tell him more about how the factory operated than grandfather. Obviously, Tereshchenko was squeezing money out of the old man, knowing he wouldn't get any from me. Giving money to Tereshchenko was like throwing it down the drain, we would get no sense out of him, and we needed the money, for the parcels, for the children, then there would be Dolsky, and that would take a lot of money. But grandfather admitted nothing, I had no proof, so I shut up about it.

We waited for the trial a month, then another month, soon it was a year, and then all of a sudden, like an avalanche, the trial was to take place in a week's time, not in Chernigov, but here, in our own town, and it was not to be a simple court-case, but a show-trial to be held in the club, and it wouldn't be our own People's Court, but a session of the regional court assizes! In other words, it was going to be done in a big way, and we could expect the very worst possible outcome.

The club was packed to the rafters. The trial lasted three days. They were the blackest of days. I have been face to face with death at the front, but nothing could be as bad as seeing your own father sitting in the dock, transparently honest, utterly innocent.

In that one year, eight months of which he had spent in prison, father had aged ten years, he looked pinched, thin, and stooped. He couldn't use cunning or extricate himself from tricky positions, he didn't give the answers they wanted, in the way they wanted. And, goddammit, he had that look on his face, as if he really was guilty of something! Only those who knew him well understood that his guilty expression came from the embarrassment and discomfort he felt at being the main cause, in his own eyes, of this terrible mess, bringing so many people here because of him. Also, he felt embarrassed at having to contradict the judge and the prosecutor, who were talking such nonsense, and having to show up their abysmal ignorance of our factory procedure. He felt awkward correcting them, as he never liked to make others look silly.

Incidentally, I had known the judge since the twenties, his name was Sheidlin. He was one of the lads, Semka Sheidlin, a wit and a clown, a bit of a bragger but harmless, he was friends with everyone, especially with Lyova. When Lyova was secretary of the district Komsomol, he became attached to Lyova, a kind of yes-man, but also capable of slipping in a clever word from time to time, which Lyova liked, so he protected Semka. He kicked his heels for a time in the furniture factory, I don't know what as, most likely getting in some factory service, especially as his father was an accountant, a white-collar employee. Apart from his clowning, Semka didn't excel at anything, with the possible exception of having been the most unsporty boy, just getting through Physical Efficiency, he was such a thick-lipped clod. When we played football, he used to sit at the edge of the field and shout jokes at us. He left quite soon to study, he finished law school, worked in the regional court but didn't visit us, especially as his parents had moved away somewhere, and then, after ten years, he turned up again as the president of the regional assizes, still the same, small and thick-lipped, in a soldier's blouse, wide belt, breeches and boots. He had filled out, gone bald, and his eyes bulged. I don't know if he was still the same wit and clown he had once been; as you can imagine, he cracked no jokes in court, but sat with a gloomy, jaundiced, distant expression, as though he was here for the first time, and as though he had no relations or friends here, and it was clear that he was going to condemn everyone, including the father of his old friend and protector.

It took them half a day to read the charges. Although to me and to everyone who worked at the factory it was obvious that the whole thing was a fabrication, to the public it wasn't so clear. Such a long charge sheet sounded convincing in itself. All kinds of facts and figures were listed, specialist terminology, data, witnesses' depositions, they were all piled up in a heap together, the truth and the lies. The real thief had confessed to stealing, and soon after his name, the list mentioned his fellow-employee, my father, so the ordinary member of the public, sitting in the gallery, was bound to believe that father was a thief, too, and that Sidorov was a thief, and that all the rest were thieves and crooks, because the charge tied them all up with one rope.

Sheidlin asked father why he had come to Russia. Father replied that mother had wanted him to. Sheidlin grinned, the other judges grinned, the prosecutor grinned, and there's no denying it, it did sound most unconvincing, and absurd, too. Who would believe that a husband had submitted to his wife, that he had been guided by love? Why bring love into it, when the case was about embezzlement, misappropriation and the execution of a wide-ranging plan? Spoken in the same breath with words like these, 'love' sounded like a mockery of the court.

Sidorov's record was clean, he was working-class from the Donbass, a Communist, he had taken part in the Civil War, he had never belonged to any of the oppositions, nor any of the deviations, in other words you couldn't get at him. Yet that was precisely what the prosecutor got at. Intruders and socially hostile elements had found him the perfect cover, behind which they could do their dirty deeds. Sidorov gave this gang his supposedly untarnished name, his supposedly spotless reputation. Therefore, of all ten of the accused, Sidorov was the most insidious, the most treacherous enemy. The others were only guilty of stealing, they were easy to see through, but Sidorov had disguised himself as an honest Communist to make it easier for these intruders to do their damage.

It was on this sort of rabble-rousing that the case was built.

Lyova had predicted it, and he had been right. That was precisely why Petrov, Shulman, and Velembitsky defended their clients on the political front, they knew it was the main danger. Petrov emphasized Sidorov's background, his honesty and unselfishness, and the fact that despite only four years of schooling, he had virtually created the factory, and it had absorbed all his attention, all his efforts, and therefore he had overlooked many things, he had trusted evil people, who took advantage of his lack of education, so that without knowing it, he became their tool. Subjectively, however, he was an honest man, he was not a thief, or a swindler, or an intruder, and the court should take this into account. Shulman, who was defending Romanyuk, the chief engineer, and incidentally a first-class one, pointed out that when he was still only fifteen his client had joined the Komsomol and had broken with his father, who had been a supporter of Petlyura, the Ukrainian anti-Communist.

Only one man in the court didn't realize what the case was really about. That man was our defence lawyer, Tereshchenko. Lyova had been right about that, too. Tereshchenko said nothing about Switzerland, and only mentioned in passing that father had come to Russia in 1911, requesting that this be entered in the record. As a matter of fact he asked for everything to be entered in the record, every triviality and nonsense, and this irritated Sheidlin and made the public laugh. All right, he could be forgiven for that, he was only a little provincial lawyer, a formalist, a pedant. The problem was elsewhere. Not only did he say nothing about the political side of the case, nor anything to prove father's honesty, like the fact that he had taken nothing and that nothing had been found in his home, but he actually built his case precisely on the trivialities, like an invoice number or a part number, the date of a delivery or a particular dispatch.

'Ah! so that type was sent instead of this type, is that allowed or not allowed? It is not allowed? Forgive me, but according to instruction number so and so issued by the Department of Light Industry, such and such a date . . . So, it *is* allowed! I request that the instruction be entered in the record. I also request that this circular, of such and such a date, be attached to the record. What is the rate allowed for clippings? What was that? Excuse me, I should like to read this extract from Circular number so and so, dated so and so, and I request it be attached to the record. Also the supplementary explanation to Circular number so and so, dated so and so, to be attached to the record. And I request that the plan output figures be attached to the record. Not only the annual figures, but the quarterly figures, too, if you will allow me, and also the balance commission's report for the current year and for the previous year. The report of the balance commission does not correspond with the report of the investigation? Then, I demand that it be attached to the record, as well.'

In brief, he bored the public out of their minds, dragged out the proceedings and stuffed trivialities down the court's throat, which Sheidlin, the judge, didn't like at all and as he was eager to pronounce the sentences, he interrupted Tereshchenko, at which Tereshchenko demanded that it be recorded in the proceedings that the judge had interrupted him, thereby infringing point number so and so of the legal code. Sheidlin retreated, as he didn't want to give Tereshchenko grounds for appeal.

I realized then that, of all the lawyers, only Tereshchenko had prepared himself properly for the trial, and I began to understand why he had been coming and what he had been talking to grandfather about and what sort of documents he had been looking at. I began to understand his tactics, and to see that it wasn't Lyova who had the mind of a politician, in this case, but the old boozer Tereshchenko, who, incidentally didn't touch a drop during the entire trial, and didn't even cover his mouth with his hand.

Tereshchenko also made the most long-winded and boring of all the defence speeches. He didn't say a word about what sort of man father was, or that he had a wife and family, or that the family were workers and Komsomols and Red Army men and students, he said nothing about any of that, he didn't play on the court's feelings and emotions, but stuck to the facts and figures and the documents, which, as you can imagine, the public wasn't interested in one bit. When Petrov, Shulman and Velembitsky made their defence speeches, they had the whole court near to tears, but there wasn't a tear in sight when Tereshchenko took the floor: invoice numbers, circulars and instructions don't have that effect. Tereshchenko wasn't bothered about the public, it wasn't the public who would pronounce sentence, it was the court. Actually, Tereshchenko wasn't even bothered about the court, either. What concerned him was the record of the proceedings and he made absolutely sure that everything was duly recorded, and after the verdict was given, and father and Sidorov and Romanyuk were all sentenced, Tereshchenko sat down in the court office and wrote out seventy pages of supplements to the record, the parts the clerk of the court had left out. I saw those seventy pages with my own eyes. The judge allowed them to be attached to the record, as they corresponded with the facts and, though once again they contained nothing but trivial details, the procedure was that you could add supplementary material or corrections to the record after a trial, as long as the court allowed it, of course.

Sidorov and Romanyuk got ten years, the rest ranged from eight to five, and father got five years for negligence in carrying out his duties as an employee. The sentences were fairly mild, I suppose. They had ten days in which to appeal.

Tereshchenko then sat down and wrote his thoroughly detailed, well-argued appeal to the Supreme Court of the Ukraine. He wrote that the court had infringed certain articles of the law, had ignored certain evidence given by witnesses, that it had blatantly distorted certain obvious facts, and totally refused to take notice of certain circulars, instructions and directives issued by higher authorities and institutions. Fact by fact and figure by figure, he took the whole case apart, leaving no stone unturned, and showed that there was no evidence for a criminal charge, and therefore it followed that there were no grounds for a political charge, either. At each point, he supported his argument with material from the record, quoting page numbers and document numbers; in other words, he made a cast-iron appeal.

It would be unfair to say that Tereshchenko alone saved father. It was a great advantage to have the case tried in an ordinary court, but Tereshchenko was the only one of the lawyers who got the proper scent and who managed to give the case a purely criminal character. I saw the dossier, it was in several volumes, and, believe me, ninety per cent of it was what Tereshchenko had collected, or said, or written, which meant it was solid fact, with no sentimentality. And the solid fact was that, once upon a time, there had been two thieves working at the factory, Sidorov had fired them and had them prosecuted, and the prosecutor had been stupid enough to bring them as witnesses for the prosecution, even though they had already been found guilty.

I can't hide the fact that I acted against my conscience in regard to Tereshchenko. As soon as the appeal was in, I went off to Kiev, to find Dolsky. A trial in our own town was one thing, I thought to myself, in Kiev it was something else. In Kiev, Tereshchenko was nobody, Dolsky was a figure. Tereshchenko had prepared a wonderful appeal, but they might not take notice of it if he presented it himself, whereas if Dolsky did, they were bound to.

Again it took me a week to get to Dolsky, and when I did he said, 'Tereshchenko conducted the case brilliantly, I have always considered him one of the greatest lawyers and I'm glad he's starting a new lease of life. I'll keep an eye on your appeal, and on the others as well.'

It was a case of having to wait, so we waited, until a telegram came from Dolsky, saying, 'Case returned regional court new review new court.'

Of course, we had no idea what the new court would decide, but the sentence was revoked and the case was going to be re-examined, and it surely wasn't in order to add to the previous sentence? We were excited and concerned again, as it would have been easier for them to have simply declared the case closed, but now, thank God, there was a chance to save father.

Mother and I went to Chernigov to see Tereshchenko, who knew all about what was going on and who told us there was nothing to do but wait until a new hearing was fixed for the case. Again, we had to wait and worry, wait and worry.

I won't burden you with all the details. The re-trial took place three months later, not in our town, but in Chernigov, and not a show-trial but an ordinary one, and it didn't last three days but only a few hours. Father was given one year, suspended, Sidorov one year in prison, but as he had already been in prison for more than a year, he was released from custody. As for the others, some got conditional sentences, some reduced sentences, and some lost their wages for the eighteen months they had been in prison.

10

So father was back home. At that time, it was about as likely as finding a palm tree at the North Pole! And we had found one!

Not everyone went back to work at the factory. Sidorov returned to his former trade, as a mechanic on a Machine and Tractor Station. Our neighbour, Ivan Karlovich, fixed father up as assistant manager of the depot stores. The work wasn't easy, handling locomotive parts is not the same as handling spares for pocket-watches. You can't just hand them through a window or across the counter, they have to be pushed along on trolleys and through gates, the trolleys have to be loaded and unloaded.

Father really had to move on that job, and the gates between the workshop and the stores were open all day. Of course, there was no thieving – what would anyone do with locomotive wheels or pistons and connecting-rods – but the workers were often in a great rush and hadn't the time to sign for the parts. They would say they'd do it later, then they'd forget and there'd be shortages and misunderstandings. Father had to keep his eyes open and watch everyone, especially as he was new to the job, though he soon got the hang of it, as he had with all his other jobs. After all, he was an experienced store manager, attentive, precise and conscientious, if someone took a part without signing for it, father would go to him later and remind him, without any bother or fuss, and he was very much liked for it.

He soon recovered physically. At the trial he had been a

stooped old man, now he was a handsome man of middle age again, and his greying hair made him look even more distinguished. He also seemed to have acquired more composure, more grip.

As for mother, well, it goes without saying! The terrifying nightmare was a thing of the past, her darling Yakov was home again. What's more, he had a good job – the depot, you know, wasn't the butcher's stall, or the hardware store, or the shoemaker's workshop, or the hide and accessories store. Even before the Revolution, a job with the railway was considered an honour and very desirable, and since the Revolution, many people had gone to work on the railway, as mechanics, lathe-workers, fitters. The depot was the chief enterprise in our town, and a job there was regarded as one of the best – you were the real working class.

◆

All in all, things were running smoothly, the shops were full, to say nothing of the markets, there had been a bumper harvest, the country was moving forward, as we could see from the example of our own town. Cars were no longer such a rarity, the bus went to the remotest villages, tractors and combine-harvesters had made their appearance, a meat-packing factory had been started, as well as a milk and butter dairy, there was a garment factory, a furniture factory was under construction, the shoe factory was expanding, and as for the depot, it became a major railway station, with sheds and elevators, as well as housing the State Grain, State Livestock, and State Flax Agencies, and not far off were the distillery and sugar refinery.

At home, everyone was settled, either working or studying. Genrikh's dream had come true and he had got into flying school, though he had been afraid they wouldn't take him because of father: you can understand how he must have felt. The family's position improved and I began to think again about my own education. It was time to make a decision, I was already twenty-five and in another year or two I'd be too old.

What was my parents' attitude? I can't complain. Still, as you must have realized, family life was such that mother had never had to think what it would be like without me. Dina would definitely go to the conservatory, and Sasha was sure to get into university. But what about me? I'd been a shoe-maker all my life, a working man, a craftsman, and my career, so to speak, was already established, so why, you might ask, should I suddenly go off to study? What for? That was how mother saw it, though she didn't say a word against it, not that she actually said she was in favour, either.

Father was quite a different matter. He loved me more than mother did, you know. You mustn't think that I resented this. I loved mother very much and had no ill feeling at all towards her, it's just that I knew her so well, and I understood that she had to give her attention to those who needed it most, and I didn't need it. It's just the way things turned out. I became independent at an early age and had to help with my brothers and sisters, and the house, and so from an early age I shared mother's concern for the others. I know that if anything had happened to me, mother would have moved heaven and earth, but as nothing did, she had no particular reason to show me love.

Unlike mother, father didn't need a special reason to show his love, with him there was no need for special circum-stances, and I was closer to him than my brothers anyway, as they lived their own lives, whereas I lived the life of my parents. Father always consulted me, always shared every-thing with me, I was like a friend to him and he was like one to me, he understood me and didn't think at all that I should stay at home forever.

It was my sister Lyuba who played the biggest part. We used to correspond – I would tell her what was going on, and send her Igor's scribblings and drawings, and through me she would let us know whatever she needed, or wanted done. She was a very sensitive girl, she understood everyone, including mother and me, and she begged and insisted that I should enter an institute and she even suggested which one, the Leningrad Institute of Cooperative Industry, which had an external department, so I could work and study at the same time, and where the entrance requirements had been specially lowered for people like me, working craftsmen. That was how Lyuba saw it, of course, but twenty-five isn't seventeen, I had left school ten years before, after only seven years of schooling, and I had forgotten absolutely everything I had ever learned. Lyuba suggested that, in addition to the leave I would get to take the examinations, I should also take my normal holiday, add a couple of weeks on my own account, and come to Leningrad for two months, where she and Volodya and their friends would prepare me for the exams. She had a great talent for helping others, as I saw from other examples, apart from my own. Without her I'm sure I wouldn't have got a higher education, even though the times were in my favour. It was exactly at that time, in the thirties, that the country was becoming technologically educated, millions of boys and girls were entering institutes and polytechnics, tens of millions were learning in factories, in classes, seminars and special courses, apart from the compulsory seven years of ordinary school, that is.

So, I took my normal holiday, plus two weeks on my own account, and the three weeks I was entitled to on being released to take an exam, and I left for Leningrad.

Naturally, I stayed at Lyuba's. After Volodya's final year, he had been transferred to the Army Medical Academy and they had been given a good room in the centre of town. It hadn't much in the way of furniture, but that didn't bother them, they weren't interested in such things. Like everyone else in those days, they worked hard and took on extra work to supplement their grants, Lyuba with night duty at the hospital, and Volodya with first-aid classes. They had very little money, yet they went to symphony concerts and recitals, and to the theatre and exhibitions. I liked all that, and I was glad that they tried to bring me, so to speak, into the world of the beautiful, as well. They had a collection of books on their subjects, as well as literature. Lyuba was prepared to deny herself everything and to live on a crust of bread so as to be able to buy the publications of the Academy of Sciences, and she also bought books for Igor. She pined for her little boy, though he couldn't have been in better hands; grandfather and grandmother doted on him, and were bringing him up in perfect conditions. Still, it was hard for her not to see her own child for half a year at a time. On their last visit they had wanted to take him back with them, but mother rose up like a stone wall.

'All day you're out of the house,' she said. 'Who would you leave him with? You'd take a nanny? How much do you think that would cost? Kindergarten? Grandfather and grandmother are better than a kindergarten, if you ask me. And Leningrad! Fog and damp! You can't breathe the air there, and you'd have to count the cost of every apple you gave him. Here he can eat as much fruit as he likes.'

Lyuba and Volodya were no match for mother, so they left Igor, they left their one and only beloved little boy to his death. Well, more about that later.

Sometimes they had friends in to drink tea and listen to records. It was at their place that I heard singers like Vertinsky, Leshchenko, Vadim Kozin, and Klaudia Shul-zhenko for the first time. Whenever I hear those tunes now, I think of Leningrad and our young days. Life's good wherever you are, when you're young. Even so, there was a special atmosphere at Lyuba and Volodya's. The young generation at the end of the thirties were something special. Of course, they didn't know everything, but they were sincere in their beliefs. Lyuba, Volodya and their friends went straight from their studies into the thick of battle, they performed operations in field hospitals by the light of candles and oil-lamps and pocket flashlights, and they saved many lives, for which they deserve eternal glory and gratitude.

At that time, however, they were still studying and working, studying seriously and working hard, occasionally meeting at Lyuba's to drink tea, listen to records, and talk about things I had hardly heard of, if at all – plays, exhibitions, concerts, international prizewinners, writers. They admired Hemingway, who was very much in vogue at that time, especially among the girls. Later on I read his *Fiesta*, *Farewell to Arms*, a book of short stories, I can't remember the title, but the hero was Nick Adams, who was Hemingway himself, I think. But at that time I didn't know Hemingway, or the painters they all admired, or the actors, and as for the international prizewinners, I'd only read about them in the papers. Lyuba and her friends were, of course, way ahead in all these things, and when they argued, I kept quiet and just sat and listened.

There were four exams I had facing me. Lyuba took me for Russian language and literature, I had Volodya for physics and chemistry, and for maths I had Valya Borisov, one of Lyuba's girl-friends, a student in mechanical mathematics at Leningrad University. I'm not an idiot or a blockhead, I knew what I had to do and I valued their help and did my best to give them no cause for complaint. After all, it meant work for them, too, as they had to dig back in their memories and they also had to make sure our work was up to date. All in all, I owe them a lot, especially Valya, because it wasn't as if I was family to her.

Volodya was very businesslike in his approach. We started on time and finished on time, and we had no superfluous chat. While I solved problems he either had his supper or read the newspaper or did work of his own, as his time was precious.

'Finished? Show me! That's right, but try to write more clearly. Now try this one.' And he would plunge into his book or newspaper.

'Done it? Wrong, where have you gone wrong? Can't you see? Look! Got it? Right! Now what have we got to do? Boyle's Law, Gay-Lussac, try to be concise, describe the application fully, but briefly.'

Volodya was very gifted with natural talent. It's enough just to say that today he's a professor of medicine. Even at the age of twenty-three he was exceptional. He was an orphan, the son of a peasant who had perished in the First World War. He started off as a shepherd boy in a remote village in Kostroma province, yet he'd got on and overcome every-thing, without the benefit of any workers' school or special courses, and against tough competition, ten candidates to each place, but even if the competition had been a hundred to one, Volodya would still have got in. Everyone said he was a future Pirogov, Lyuba knew this was true and did all she could to help him get where he is, though she had a lot of promise herself.

Lyuba also expected me to give concise explanations and clear answers. Still, you know how it is with literature, Pushkin, Lermontov, Griboyedov, she would get carried away, and I would get carried away with her.

As for Valya, that rosy-cheeked young girl had a brilliant mathematical mind, she used iron logic, and working with her demanded enormous concentration. If you missed a word or dropped the thread of her argument, you were lost. She was a big-boned, broad-faced girl, robust, but not sporty, the type of girl who is at her best when she's young and becomes heavy as she gets older. But you never think about what a girl is going to look like when she's middle-aged, you only see her as she is now, and she was a picture of health, as they say. It was a bit odd to see such a healthy, blooming young girl living in the middle of the city, especially a city like Leningrad, but she was a Leningrad girl all right, born and bred, from a Petersburg intellectual background. Valya didn't test me, as Volodya did, or explain things, as Lyuba did. Her way was to read the maths course to me, thoroughly and slowly, so that I understood it and had time to make notes. When I was working out problems, she didn't do something else, she watched while I worked, and she watched with a completely straight face, so I couldn't tell by looking at her whether I was going right or wrong. Then with the same straight face, she would take the exercise book, check my answer and if it was wrong she would point out my mistake and give me another question of the same kind to do.

This happened every Tuesday and Friday evening. Lyuba and Volodya used to go out and leave us alone for the whole evening without any interference. Afterwards I would walk Valya to Liteiny Boulevard, where she lived.

Have you ever noticed how, if a pretty girl has a brother, her girl-friends will quite often take special notice of him, show particular interest in him, and not regard him as an outsider? When Lyuba's girl-friends got together I sometimes noticed their interest in me. But to be quite honest, they didn't exist for me as women. Why was I here, I asked myself? People were giving up their time to help me prepare for my future life, and I should start having affairs?

Then one day Lyuba came home from the Institute, sat down as usual to change into her slippers, incidentally with the same unhurried movements as father, placed her hands on her knees and announced, 'Well, Boris, congratulations, Valya has fallen in love with you! Did you hear that, Volodya? Valya has fallen for Boris.'

'A well-known situation,' Volodya replied. 'An artist falls in love with his model, a teacher falls for her pupil.'

'Did she tell you herself?' I asked.

'What difference does that make? You can take it from me, she loves you.' They both laughed.

'Do you like her?' Lyuba asked.

I made some sort of joke in reply, but what did I really feel about Valya? It's hard to say. She was my teacher, I was her pupil, a full-grown hick from the country who had clean forgotten everything he'd learned in school except basic arithmetic. Every Tuesday and Friday she came to coach me, staying till late, frowning slightly as she explained things to me; she didn't smile or laugh, she was serious and very intense, sometimes she would push her light, downy hair back from her forehead, and when she did I noticed the scent of water and children's soap, a sudden whiff of clean freshness. Her hair and the way she threw it back and the scent of it were all part of my image of her as a teacher of maths, with her equations and proofs, but nothing more. As you know, mathematics is no laughing matter. I really had to struggle and work from morning till night, I was beginning to understand something of it, and I even felt a certain pleasure in it, I swear!

My relations with Valya went no further than our work together on my maths. She was a nice, clever, pretty girl, but unfortunately these things don't count, of course, when it's a matter of love. Maybe I was wrong, but at any rate, what I thought at the time was that we were on too many different levels, she wasn't right for me. Still, when I think about her, with her intelligent, tense, serious look, her soft, clean-scented hair, and the way she threw it back, I have a good feeling.

Well, in due course, I passed the exams and registered in the external department of the Leningrad Cooperative Industry Institute.

I still had three days left of my holiday and was feeling on top of the world, so I decided that on the way home I would drop in on Yefim in Kharkov. He was working at the Kharkov Tractor Factory, having been through the Kharkov Polytechnic without taking any time off from his work, and he lived with his young wife on a housing estate for tractor engineers. He had got married at the factory and had told us about it as though it was nothing special, just something he had done in the normal course of events; he announced it as an accomplished fact. In those days you just got married and that was that, no cars tied with coloured ribbons and dolls on the radiators!

I arrived in Kharkov and found Yefim's house, the door was opened by a young woman with black eyes, black hair and a dimple in her chin.

'It's good to meet you,' I said. 'You're part of the family.'

'Come in, make yourself at home, we're always delighted to see relatives.'

Her name was Natalya Ivanovna Ponomarenko. Like many women in those days she kept her own name, and she was known as Natasha. She also worked at the Tractor Factory and, like Yefim, she had her diploma as a tractor engineer, they had finished the same course together.

Naturally, I wanted to have a look at the factory, which was one of the giant projects of the First Five Year Plan. Yefim got hold of a pass for me, and Natasha took time off to come with me as a sort of tour-guide, she knew the whole factory like the back of her hand. Of course, it's impossible to see over the factory in half a day, even a whole day wouldn't be enough, it's giant in the full meaning of the word! I wonder if you can imagine the impression it made on me? They were producing one hundred and forty-four tractors a day, as many as the Stalingrad factory, and in the course of the Second Five Year Plan nearly sixty thousand tractors were produced. Forgive me for repeating well-known truths, but I watched with my own eyes as finished tractors drove off the conveyer under their own power and out on to the parking lot at the rate of one a minute, and there were already thousands of them there. It was a powerful spectacle!

The mood of celebration stayed with me all day. I was proud of the fact that we had built such a fantastic factory, proud that my brother Yefim, who had started as a simple bricklayer, was now working there as an engineer. Natasha also seemed to fit in there perfectly, she was full of life, energetic, sociable. I had got into the Institute, everything was wonderful, things were going right!

As it turned out, I hardly saw Yefim in those three days, I hadn't come at a good time, but just at the moment when they were changing over from wheeled tractors to tracked ones. They were making the change without interrupting production and everyone was spending whole days and nights at the factory. Natasha offered to take me to the theatre and show me the town, but she had enough to do already and was working all day at the factory, as it was, so I went round the town on my own. I saw the main streets, took in the view from the top of the university hill, I saw the famous State Industry House on Dzerzhinsky Square, the biggest square in the world according to the people of Kharkov, twenty-seven and a half acres. The city was being built anew, there were masses of new industrial enterprises, and new blocks of flats at a time when they were still a rarity. In short, I took in the city, even though I only had a quick look. As they say, you've hardly arrived before you've got to leave.

I said good-bye to my brother and Natasha, packed their gifts for father, mother, Dina, Sasha and Igor, got on the train and rolled up at home as a brand-new part-time student.

11 ❈

Dreadful news was waiting for me when I got home. Lyova and his wife Anna Moiseyevna had died under the wheels of a train at Miass, near Chelyabinsk. A week had passed before the news got to us, Lyova was new there, he hadn't yet made any friends, nobody knew our address, they'd given up the flat in Chernigov, Anna Moiseyevna had also moved to Chelyabinsk, and Olya had gone for the time being with her nanny to stay with the nanny's relations in the country. The news came via the railway authorities to the Ministry, then from the Ministry to Chernigov, to Lyova's old place of work, so it took a week to get to us. Lyova and Anna Moiseyevna had been buried in Miass, we were too late for the funeral, but we decided I would go there later on to set the stone and arrange for the maintenance of the grave.

Meanwhile, I wrote to the manager of the railway at Miass and to the party organization, and they wrote back that Lyova and Anna Moiseyevna died as they were crossing the line.

Our neighbour, Ivan Karlovich, who was an engineer at the depot, told us that statistics showed that most of the deaths on the railways were not of passengers involved in train crashes, or of people crossing the lines, but of railway workers and employees. The railways were officially designated a 'high danger zone', he said.

Ivan Karlovich's information did nothing to console anyone. There are jobs that are a lot more dangerous than the railways, yet people manage to spend their whole life in them without getting killed. I was very much affected by

Lyova's death. He was a hard man, in some ways even merciless, but a brother is a brother, I loved him very much, he was an outstanding personality, I was proud of him, and he had done a lot for me when I was young. I couldn't get the absurdity of his death out of my head, and it seemed to me that somehow the careless crossing of the line was Anna Moiseyevna's fault. She was pompous and ponderous, and she even walked along the street as though everyone else should get out of her way, probably that was how she had walked there, too. You can imagine how many lines criss-cross each other at a large junction like Miass: suddenly a train appeared, Anna Moiseyevna lost her head and froze, Lyova tried to pull her out of the way and fell under the wheels himself. Maybe it wasn't like that at all, but in my mind that was how they died.

It was the first death in our family, and we were numbed by it. I expected even more grief and despair from mother, after all I had seen her reaction to father's arrest. She didn't have such a reaction now. She locked herself in her room, but she didn't cry or wail. Why? Maybe she'd already used up all her spiritual resources on father's salvation. I don't know. She loved Lyova, and how she loved him! Such a son! And now he was dead, absurdly, accidentally. Still, he had been the only one to stay aloof from father's affair, not because he was indifferent or wicked, but because he lived according to his own laws, which were incomprehensible and alien to her. I think that's what it was. When I was thoughtless enough to suggest that Lyova had died trying to save Anna Moiseyevna, mother remarked bitterly, 'He tried to save *her*!' In other words, he had been prepared to risk his own life trying to save Anna Moiseyevna, but not to lift a finger to save his own father.

You know, it wasn't pleasant to hear her say that. In the face of such sorrow and unhappiness, all misunderstandings should take second place; in the face of death you have to be able to rise above any grudge. Of course, Anna Moiseyevna was a bad lot, a hard, heartless woman, but Lyova loved her and probably in her own way she loved him. After all, when they took him off his important job and transferred him to a place like Miass, she could have rejected him, she could have divorced him, but she didn't, she followed him to the Southern Urals. Anyway, it's too late to judge her and Lyova, they have gone. If it comes to that, we shouldn't judge mother, either, it was her nature.

Naturally, neither mother nor father, nor any of us, could get Lyova out of our minds, but even so life gradually got back to normal. That's one of the amazing things about life, no matter how many twists and turns and dislocations it goes through, it always ends up back on course.

Several unhappy months had passed, perhaps as much as half a year, or slightly less, when, what do you think, we received a letter from the village of Dikanka in the province of Poltava. You know Gogol's *Evenings on a Farm near Dikanka*? Well, it was the same place and the letter was from Anna Yegorovna, Lyova's old domestic help, who was asking if she could come. Olya was still with her, since she had brought her from Chernigov, and she didn't know what to do with her, she had no home of her own, people wouldn't take her in with the child, her family were all at work and there was nobody to leave the child with, and, as she wrote, without beating about the bush, 'there's no way out'. She was asking if she could come and discuss what to do next, as she put it, and she gave her address.

A tall order! Mother didn't want to know anything about it. 'What has this child got to do with us? Is she family? Is she Lyova's daughter? Didn't her mother have any family? Where are her grandmother and grandfather, uncles and aunts? Why us?'

'There probably are relatives,' I agreed. 'But perhaps Anna Yegorovna doesn't know where they are.'

'She found us all right, she can find them!'

'But suppose she doesn't?'

'She can put her in a children's home, she wouldn't be the first, or the last.'

'Lyova loved the child.'

'Loved! He loved that Moiseyevna woman, too, didn't he? Are you trying to saddle me with that child? I won't have it! Never!'

I certainly wasn't thinking that we should take the child in. Where would we put her? But I couldn't look the other way, either. Anna Yegorovna was a complete stranger and she hadn't abandoned the child, though she could have done, what was Olya to her – I dare say she had nannied plenty of little girls like her – yet she hadn't abandoned her. If she could have found Anna Moiseyevna's relations she would have done, which meant she couldn't find any. The phrase in her letter 'there is no way out' was particularly alarming.

I thought she couldn't put Olya into a children's home because she hadn't got the proper papers, and there was nothing you could do with the child if you hadn't got the proper papers. What was left? To take the child to the railway station and leave her there to be found and put into a children's home? Anna Yegorovna wasn't the sort of person to do a thing like that, of course, but circumstances can push even the best people to extremes. So I decided to talk to father. He hadn't seen either Olya or Anna Moiseyevna and he didn't get involved in my arguments with mother over it.

When I found myself alone with him I asked, 'What should be done about Olya?'

'Take her in?' he asked, looking at me.

From the way he said it and the way he looked at me, I knew he felt for the child.

'How can we take her in?' I said. 'Mother's got enough to do with us and Dina and Sasha and Igor. But we must do something for the child, and we have to help that woman. Perhaps we could look for Anna Moiseyevna's relatives.'

I told him what I thought about the question of papers and my fear that in the end the little girl would be left at the station, because Anna Yegorovna had no other way out. I saw the effect this thought had on him, like me he was picturing that little girl abandoned at the station and the picture became fixed in his mind, as it had in mine. Although he only said three words in reply, 'We must think', I knew he was on my side.

The same day, or maybe it was the day after, the subject came up during supper of a job I had to do on my next day off. I don't remember what the job was, you can't remember every minor detail of everyday life, but you know how small jobs pile up for your day off.

Mother said, 'Boris, don't forget to do so and so on your day off.'

To which father added, 'Boris has to go to work on his day off so that he can take two days off next week.'

'Why?' Mother was immediately suspicious and from her tone it was clear she had guessed father was up to something she didn't know about.

'He needs more than a day to get to Dikanka and back,' he replied.

'Did he lose something in Dikanka, I'd like to know?'

'Something must be decided about the little girl, something has to be arranged for her.'

'Decide and arrange all you want,' mother declared. 'But leave me out of it. I don't want to see her, I saw all I wanted of her in Chernigov.'

'Rachel,' father said, 'you needn't get excited, nobody's going to involve you. But we're not animals, Rachel, we're human beings, we can't abandon a child in such a situation. Boris will go there to see what's what and help find her relations.'

Mother said nothing, as she could see that father had taken a categorical decision. He rarely took such decisions against her will, but when he did they were final and couldn't be reversed. I went to work on my next day off, arranged to have two days in the following week, and got ready for the trip to Dikanka. But there was no need for me to go, after all.

A day or two before I was supposed to leave, I came home from work and who should I see, sitting on a bench, but Anna Yegorovna and Olya. Actually, Anna Yegorovna was sitting on the bench, with a large bundle next to her, and Olya was playing at her feet, digging at something with a rake. A little way off, playing on his own, was Igor, who was three by then. Olya, it seemed, was also playing on her own, but the two children kept glancing at each other, which made it clear to me just how things were. Mother hadn't introduced them to each other, she hadn't said, go and play together, children, perhaps on the contrary she had kept them apart, perhaps she had said to Igor, 'Play near the door so I can keep an eye on you, and don't go anywhere.' From the fact that Anna Yegorovna was sitting alone on the bench with Olya playing at her feet, and that they were in the full blaze of the sun, though it was getting towards evening, it was also obvious they had been there a long time, despite the heat, Anna Yegorovna in a warm coat, her headscarf pulled down on to her shoulders, and next to the bundle on the bench Olya's coat and beret. They were both dressed for winter, they'd come with all their belongings and looked like refugees. I realized that mother had received them exactly the way Anna Moiseyevna had once received us. Mother was a good person, even an exceptional person, but she was also quite vindictive and never forgot an injury. I wasn't even sure if she had given them anything to eat, but when I saw Anna Yegorovna take out a hard-boiled egg, peel it, put salt on it and give it to Olya, I knew.

Mother was in the kitchen and I could see from her face

that she would never let them into the house, she would stand firm on this.

'Have they been here long?' I asked.

'They've been sitting there since morning,' she replied, clattering saucepans and not looking at me.

'Have you given them anything to eat?'

'Am I running a restaurant?'

I went outside and said hello to Anna Yegorovna, stroked Olya's head, sat down and asked, 'Where is Olya's birth certificate?'

'I have it,' she replied, and got it out of her coat, wrapped in a piece of newspaper. I opened it up and read 'Mother, Anna Moiseyevna Gurevich; father, Alexander Petrovich Palevsky' – he must have been Anna Moiseyevna's first husband.

I had been wrong to suppose that Anna Yegorovna hadn't put Olya into a children's home because she hadn't got the proper papers, but I just couldn't bring myself to ask her why not. What was so terrible about a children's home? I've known plenty of decent people, many highly qualified, who had been raised in children's homes, but to ask this woman, sitting in the blazing hot sun in her winter coat, why she hadn't handed over a strange child to a children's home, but had kept her herself, took the trouble and worry on herself, I couldn't bring myself to ask it. It wouldn't have been a question but a suggestion that she should have put Olya into a home, but she hadn't come to us for such a suggestion, she could have done it for herself, without our advice, and she hadn't.

I asked her whether Olya had any grandparents or uncles and aunts.

'There must be some in Kiev,' she replied, 'but I don't know how to find them.'

'How did you find us?'

'Through people from your town.'

I didn't try to find out exactly who, there were plenty of them in Chernigov and Lyova had kept up relations with some of them. Anna Yegorovna might have known their addresses, or simply met them in the street, it wasn't as though it was such an enormous town, hardly a capital city. Anyway, that wasn't important. Nor was it important how she had found us. The main thing was that it was to us that she had brought the little girl. If she had wanted to, she could have found Anna Moiseyevna's relations, the woman was no fool. Instead she had come to us with Olya. Why to us? I often wondered about this later. How had her mind worked? Perhaps you can make more sense of it than I can, but what I think is that she had seen mother and myself when we were in trouble, and now it was Olya who was in trouble, and people in trouble are drawn to each other. True, we were strangers to Olya and she was sure to have relatives of her own, but the higher truth was in this woman's act, she had seen us when we were bereft, and she knew we could not be indifferent to Olya who was bereft now.

Father came home from work, Dina and Sasha came home from school, and we all sat down to eat, together with Anna Yegorovna and Olya. Mother was simply passed by, and she realized that not one of us would sit down at the table without the other two. But she wasn't the sort of person who would give in so soon and, without clearing away or washing the dishes, she went straight round to grandfather and grandmother, where of course the whole thing was debated. Grandfather soon came round to have a look at Olya and to take part in the family council.

Anna Yegorovna cleared the table and washed the dishes, Dina played games with Olya and Igor and the house became noisy – one child is only one, more than one is a whole crowd. Sasha didn't play, he just watched Olya silently and pensively. How old would he have been, eleven? Still a small boy, but already he was sensitive to other people's sorrows, and he could tell immediately if someone was unhappy. I think mother left the house not only as a sign of protest, but also because she couldn't take Sasha's look, which she felt as a reproach to her.

So, while Dina played with the children, grandfather, father and I examined and discussed the problem from all angles, and we reached the decision that Olya would stay with us in the meantime, and I would try to locate Anna Moiseyevna's relatives in Kiev. Mother, of course, would oppose this, but we would convince her, and if we didn't manage to convince her, then Olya would go and stay with grandfather and Uncle Grisha, who was still living there as before.

We called Anna Yegorovna in and explained our decision to her. She sat on a stool, smoothed out her apron carefully, listened to what we had to say, thanked us politely and with dignity, and then asked, 'And what will you do about me?'

In other words, she didn't want to leave. Maybe she didn't want to leave the little girl, perhaps she was attached to her and was afraid we would get shot of her, or maybe she hadn't got along with her family in Dikanka. But we didn't need her either, we had never had domestic help, we couldn't afford it and, anyway, we weren't that sort of people. Still, we saw that Anna Yegorovna was at a loss and we felt we must help.

Well, to cut a long story short, father found a job for Anna Yegorovna as a cleaner at the railway offices, and later on as a gate-keeper, which entitled her to a little room at the office building, and Olya meanwhile stayed with us. It was two or three months before I could get away to Kiev – when you're a master craftsman in a factory, it's not so easy to take a few days off. I didn't find any relatives of Anna Moiseyevna in Kiev in any case.

So, that was how our family grew by one more person, little Olya, which meant that, with Igor, the family was launched on the third generation.

12 ❖

While all this was going on, things were happening to me, too.

The girl in question was from our town, she had been to the Leningrad Drama School and worked in Kalinin in the theatre. In other words, she was an actress from Kalinin. She used to come to visit her parents when she was on holiday, and it was during one of these holidays that we got to know each other. What do I mean by 'got to know each other'? I already knew, of course, about Sonya Vishnevsky, I knew she was the great-niece of Khaim Yagudin, our scandalmongering ex-sergeant, and I had seen Sonya as a child, then as a young girl, I knew she was an actress, the only one from our town, in fact. We had musicians, even the famous conductor, People's Artist of the USSR, the pride of the town, I've told you about him already, but Sonya Vishnevsky was our only actress, so I could hardly not know who she was. But it was one thing to know who and what she was, and quite another to get to know her and to become good friends.

The fact that she was a professional actress already singled her out. The people of our town were ordinary working folk, with ordinary run-of-the-mill jobs, but here was an actress from the city of Kalinin, the ancient Russian city of Tver, as it used to be called. When she came she was the centre of attention, especially as she used to go around in a bright red sleeveless dress with shoulder-straps, her sun-tanned shoulders bare, and her hair was naturally the colour of copper, not hennaed. And what a figure! In our town they really appreciated women who had the right things in the right places. The town was famous for its pretty girls and even rivalled the town of Sumy in this respect.

Her parents moved to Dneprodzerzhinsk, but she went on coming to our town and stayed with Khaim Yagudin. Khaim Yagudin was very proud to have such a prominent relative, he called her his pupil and liked the fact that her appearance and behaviour shocked the citizens, those ignoramuses and block-heads. He condoned all Sonya's actions and the less they pleased others, the more they pleased him. It was precisely in her ability, so to speak, to offend public taste, that he regarded her as his pupil.

It wasn't really that way at all, however. Khaim Yagudin was a scandalmonger, a seventy-five-year-old hooligan, whereas Sonya simply liked to get things moving. She would spend the day lying in a hammock in the forest, sunbathing, and at night she would drag us off to bathe in the river. That wasn't our usual custom, normally we swam in the evenings, and during the day on our days off. Midnight bathing was Sonya's idea. It wasn't so easy for most of us, who had to get to work in the morning, while she had nothing to do but sleep all day in her hammock. We would build a campfire on the bank of the river and grill *shashlyki* – another of Sonya's innovations – and we would drink, though we knew how to do that already. Sonya was good fun and good company, she could listen well, nothing shocked her, and she could even tell the sort of joke that a man might not risk telling. If it was cold, she would take someone's jacket off him, and then to make sure he didn't freeze, she would put it round him, too, and sit with him in an embrace. She preferred male company, there weren't any girls in the town who would have been suitable friends for her. They were timid and shy, chickens, she called them, the only one she could get on with was the midwife, Liza Elkin, who was also bright and liked company and was easy-going. As it was hard for Liza, being a midwife, to take part in our nocturnal vigils, Sonya was surrounded by an entourage of bachelors. I didn't exactly take a back-seat, you understand, I wanted Sonya to like me, I showed off my strength, drank quantities of vodka, carried Sonya into the water in my arms, dived off the railway bridge from the highest girder, did the swallow dive and somersaults, and Sonya was in ecstasy, clapping her hands and kissing me in front of everyone. We would lie on the sand, me in my bathing trunks and she in her swimming costume, both of us twenty-seven, me no longer a boy and she no longer a little girl. And what is supposed to happen, happened.

It was all done without affectation. Sonya looked at these things simply, she liked me and wanted me, and I felt the same way about her. So what if I wasn't her first. We didn't talk about that, her past was no business of mine. Was she supposed to wait for me to appear on her horizon? Anyway, I hadn't waited, either.

As a matter of fact we were in bed for a solid month together, we just couldn't get up, and the less I talked, the more she talked. I was this and that, there was nobody else like me, what had she done to deserve such happiness and so on. I took all this at its face value, and at that moment it was all true, she liked me and I liked her.

Well, when two people in a small town like ours suit each other and rush into each others' arms, as you can imagine, it doesn't stay a secret for very long. Sonya didn't make any secret of it, in any case. She saw nothing shameful in our relationship, what shame could there be in love? So we were both in the public eye, though I wondered what conclusion I was meant to draw from that?

As for Khaim Yagudin, the affair was a pure gift to him, especially as it took place in his house. He seemed to think that it was he, not we, who were slapping public opinion in the face, he did whatever he could for Sonya, really spread himself for her. In the mornings, when Sonya and I were still asleep, he would keep everyone quiet in the house with his stick, in case, God forbid, they woke us up, though the banging of his stick did that job all too well. He made his domestic help clean and polish Sonya's room, change her bed-linen and supply fresh towels. Actually he liked to bring her a fresh towel himself, and there was something else he liked to bring her, while she was still in bed, and that believe it or not, was coffee! Yes, seriously, coffee! God knows where he got that one from, but he seemed to think it was the smart thing, to serve a lady with coffee while she was still in bed in the morning.

He would listen for us to wake up, knock on the door, 'May I?' He would enter ceremoniously, his stick in one hand and in the other a tray with a coffee-pot, milk jug, sugar bowl, and two cups. He would put it down on the bedside table and every time he would ask, 'Black or with milk?' even though he knew we only drank it with milk – you couldn't drink that swill without milk, you can guess that it was either chicory, at best, or just plain carrot coffee.

'With or without sugar?'

'With.'

'One or two lumps?'

'Two.'

He would pour out the two cups of coffee, add the milk and drop in the lumps of sugar which, mind you, he picked up with tongs, not his fingers. He liked to show what refined manners he had.

His own children, who were good, hard-working people, grown-up now, he slighted and humiliated, and he hung like a millstone round their necks all their lives, whereas for Sonya, his third cousin twice removed, a distant relation, who came to see him once a year, he really spread himself. Sonya flattered his vanity.

She was condescending towards the old man. If it gratifies his pride, she used to say, let him do it. Behind his back she made fun of him, but face to face, God forbid, she was sorry for him and was tender and attentive. For instance, when it rained or there was bad weather and we didn't go to the river, we would stay at home and she would put him at the head of the table, making him, so to speak, the central character, and say, 'Uncle Khaim, tell us a story.' And Uncle Khaim would start with his cock-and-bull stories and God knows what, about how he was such a hero and how cavalry generals and artillery generals celebrated in his honour, just as if they were his bosom pals and best friends.

Most of all he liked to reminisce about His Highness the Prince of Warsaw, Count of Erivan, General Field-Marshal Ivan Fedorovich Paskevich, the very one who fought the Turks and took Erzerum, then fought the Poles and took Warsaw, and later still fought the Hungarians and took Budapest. He talked about Paskevich, too, as if they had been the best of pals, drinking companions, partners at the card table, and comrades in amorous adventures.

I'm sure you appreciate the distance between a sergeant and a field-marshal, between Khaim Yagudin and His Highness the Prince of Warsaw, Count Erivan? That's not the point. The point is, His Highness died in 1856, before Khaim Yagudin was even born. Khaim talked about him as though he had spent the best years of his stormy youth in his company.

The fact was that Prince Paskevich had once owned the town of Gomel, his gorgeous palace is still there, and the whole of our district, our town being nearer to Gomel than to Chernigov, regarded itself as being connected with that great celebrity since time immemorial, and Khaim Yagudin, more than anyone, felt himself to be almost a relation. There were all kinds of legends, tales, anecdotes, and fairy-tales about Paskevich, and we all knew them, but Khaim Yagudin told them as though he had actually taken part in them himself. We knew he was an out-and-out liar, but Sonya found it interesting, she listened, laughed, showed amazement, and the more she listened and laughed and showed amazement the better the old boy liked it.

Once I told Sonya that Paskevich had died before Khaim Yagudin was born, but she replied without concern, 'So what? He's a great story-teller.'

So she let him lie and spin his yarns to his heart's content, and he adored her all the more, he worshipped her. The one thing she wouldn't allow him to do was to keep his children and grandchildren away from the table, considering them, as he did, not good enough for such élite society. He didn't dare to disobey, he submitted, and everyone sat down at the table, everyone had to listen to his nonsense. The whole town knew about our relationship, the whole town knew that Khaim Yagudin served us coffee in bed.

The only conclusion I could draw from all this was that we should get married. But what was I and what was she? I was a shoemaker. True, I was taking courses at the external department of the Leningrad Institute of Technology. Why an institute of technology? Because the Cooperative Industry Institute that I had entered was turned into one in 1939. Anyway, I was already in my fourth year and about to become an engineer and workshop chief, but I was still a common or garden cobbler, whereas she was an actress and not just anywhere, but in one of the most ancient theatres in the country, in Kalinin, on a level with Moscow and Leningrad. Who could say, she might even become a People's Artist of the USSR?

How could I possibly propose to her in those circumstances? If only she had given me a hint or an indirect question about what was in store for us, but she hadn't, no hints or questions, direct or indirect. Why was that? Was she used to casual affairs, was it that she was completely devoted to her art and all the rest was just a nuisance? Didn't she see any future for herself in me? Perhaps she had someone else in Kalinin? I didn't know, but a fact is a fact, she gave me no reason to discuss our future, and I couldn't raise the question because I was too proud, she might think I was trying to use her to become part of her glamorous life, use her to get myself out of the boredom and monotony of the town. That wasn't the case, I really did love her, but my vanity prevented me from proposing to her.

Her departure reinforced my position. It was hard to get rail tickets at that time, especially as she would be getting a through train. I ran to the station and managed to get her a ticket for a first-class seat, and I enjoyed doing this. I was hoping that our last evening, our last night, we would spend together, that I alone would accompany her to the station, especially as her train was at five in the morning. Not a bit of it! In the evening it was the campfire and *shashlyki* and night-time swimming.

At two o'clock I said to her, 'Sonya, you've got to get your things ready.'

She was unconcerned, 'I've got time.'

It was already four o'clock when we went to her place, and in fact she got everything ready in twenty minutes. The whole gang accompanied her to the station, she was laughing and gay, the train arrived, she kissed everyone good-bye, including me like anyone else, got into the train, which was an express and would wait for only two minutes, and called out from the steps, 'Don't get bored without me!' The train steamed out of the station, and I was left there, with a heavy heart.

It got still heavier as time went on. Surely it hadn't been just a summer fling? It was hard for me to accept that – I really did love her. That had never happened to me before, she was my first love. After everything that had happened between us, after all our nights together, and everything we had said to each other, she hadn't promised to come again, nor invited me to visit her, she hadn't asked me to write to her, in other words she had cut me off and that was that.

Of course, I didn't let anyone see how I was feeling, and nobody noticed, except mother. Naturally, mother knew about my romance with Sonya but she never once brought it up with me, as in our family we looked on such things simply and without humbug, especially as I was getting on for thirty, and although I knew perfectly well mother wasn't in favour of Sonya, she didn't say, 'Thank God Sonya's gone.'

A month or two went by and I received a letter from Sonya. There was nothing special in it, just 'Hi, Borik', which was what she called me. 'How's life, how's the gang, I think of you all, I love you all, I miss you all, give them my regards, drop me a line.'

Nothing special, but it was a letter, all the same, and she had written her address on the envelope. So it wasn't all over, it hadn't been an infatuation or a summer fling. It took me a week to write a reply. What could I write about? She wasn't interested in what was happening in the town, still less in my work, but I was hesitant to write about my feelings and anyway I didn't know how, so I just wrote, 'Everyone misses you, me most of all.'

Her reply didn't come right away, but it came all the same. Again there wasn't too much detail, just friendly, though it was a bit more substantial and businesslike, she was working on a big part, so she asked to be forgiven for writing so briefly, and also she was spending a lot of time over getting a room she had been promised. Anyway, it was the beginning of a correspondence.

There's something strange about corresponding with a woman that I can't explain. Being apart creates distance, yet at the same time it brings you closer, you miss her and all kinds of thoughts come into your mind, and then suddenly you get a letter, you read it and you find that she's thinking about you, too. It's always nice to get a letter from family or friends, but what does a relative tell you about? His troubles. When does he write to you? When things are bad.

Friends and acquaintances in this day and age don't write at all, or if they do it's only to let you know they're still alive, which explains the craze for greetings cards of all kinds. I'm sure I receive them four times a year from at least fifty people, and there's nothing you can do about it, you have to reply to them all. But that's just by the way. There's this strange thing about letters from women, that when you don't get one for a long time your heart pines for one, and when it does come your heart flutters. Sonya didn't write anything very special, still, when a woman is four hundred miles away, even the most insignificant things become significant.

In January 1940 I had to go to Leningrad for a session at the Institute. I wrote to Sonya about it, and she wrote back that I should visit Kalinin on my way. So, after the session, on my way home I stopped off in Kalinin. Sonya met me, she had received my cable, she was wearing a fur coat and fur hat, her cheeks were red and she was excited, she kissed me, but not properly, she laughed and said 'Later, later, there's plenty of time.'

I needed to have my ticket stamped for the next morning, but she was in a hurry to get to a rehearsal, and it was somehow awkward to show such foresight; to visit your beloved and the first thing you think of is your ticket. It's tactless.

We took a tram to her place. She settled me there and dashed off to the rehearsal. She had taken a room in a rickety old house, such as you wouldn't find in our town and, after all, Kalinin was the provincial centre. Moscow was to the right and Leningrad to the left, yet here was this peasant hovel. The room was minute, and to get to it you had to go through the owners' room, an old man and his wife, both absolute drunkards, living in neglect like beggars. Sonya's room was clean, that's true, but I was staggered by the disorder. She had a wooden trestle-bed with a hair-mattress, a bedside table, a little kitchen table, her things were in her cases, and instead of curtains the windows were covered with newspaper. I realized that she hadn't got a place of her own, everything was someone else's, temporary, borrowed. What is the life of an actress but wandering? Yet her life had seemed so different to us at home.

Three hours later she was back, gay and lively. 'We have the whole evening, what shall we do?'

'Whatever you say,' I replied. 'We should celebrate the occasion.'

'I'll take you to Seliger's for supper.'

'Sounds fine. I just want to see as much of you as possible.'

She laughed. 'I missed you, too.'

The restaurant was at the Hotel Seliger, a very pleasant restaurant to look at, and the hotel itself was a new building in the thirties style, the waiters were in black suits and black bow-ties and the waitresses wore white peasant-style hats, everything was done properly, there was vodka, all sorts of wine, a menu on which the chief item seemed to be beef in all its variations, beefsteak, beef stroganoff, braised beef. A waiter came up holding a pad with his pencil at the ready, he was very attentive to Sonya, and the people at other tables were looking at her, too, not just because she was a striking-looking woman, but because she was a local personality.

We drank, the band played, and I asked Sonya to dance, as others were dancing, but she said, 'Not in this hole.' I had made a blunder, it wasn't done for her to show herself off in a place like this.

'Sorry,' I said. 'I haven't got the hang of things here yet.'

'It's nothing,' she replied, brushing it aside.

She told me about her work. The theatre was dominated by ancient actresses who should have been got rid of ages ago to make room for younger ones. But they wouldn't go, they went on playing seventeen-year-olds at the age of fifty. Meanwhile, Sonya had finally got a really good part and she would show those old wrecks the meaning of real theatre. She was pre-occupied with the whole question, and I listened with pleasure as she talked about it, it was all so strange and sudden and unbelievable to think that here I was, sitting next to her.

We took our time getting back to her room. We walked and she showed me the town, the Volga and the old buildings.

In the morning she got some hot water next door for tea which she poured straight into glasses, she found a piece of stale bread in the table drawer and a hunk of ancient cheese, and that was our breakfast. Sonya didn't seem to think it meagre, to her it was the normal way to live. Maybe she hadn't any money, what with the wages actresses get.

I said tactfully, 'It's a lovely room, but to have to go through the owners' . . . '

'The room isn't lovely,' she said. 'It's a rat-hole, but the theatre pays the rent, and if I stay in a dump like this I have a better chance of getting a place of my own, in the end. I've been waiting three years already.'

You remember what things were like at that time. Nowadays you can think about what kind of flat you ought to take, whether you want a balcony or not, or if the district is suitable, what floor it should be on and whether you can count on getting a phone installed. In those days people waited years, even decades, just for a room in a communal apartment, any room, anywhere, as long as it was a room.

Suddenly Sonya smiled. 'Come and live with me, when I get my room.'

My heart missed a beat. 'Seriously?'

'Don't you want to?'

'Need you ask!'

'Darling, you ought to know I'm a lousy housekeeper.'

'We'll manage that, but why wait till you get a room?'

'Would you live here?'

'I can live anywhere, but I can get us a better room than this.'

She took hold of my chin and gave it a little pull, which

she liked to do. 'Borik, do you want me to have nowhere to live ?'

'What are you talking about ?'

'It's all right,' she said, 'I'll come in the summer and we'll discuss it. Don't sulk, Borik, it's the best thing to do.'

Why it would be the best thing to do, I didn't ask. I was in the seventh heaven, my dream had come true, and if I had to wait, I'd wait.

I left in that mood and remained in it right up to Sonya's arrival in the summer. We corresponded, not very regularly, it's true, she wrote about the theatre and her all-out war on the old women, though her letters were light-hearted, amusing and good-natured. It depended how she was getting on with her colleagues at any moment. The chairman of the local committee, who was a cunning fox, was a sweet thing when he was trying to get her a room, and the director, who was a psychopath, became a genius if he praised her at rehearsal. There was nothing malicious about her, her approach was, if you were nice to her you were an angel, if you weren't nice to her, you were an untalented son of a bitch. Incidentally, I noticed later that she could drink vodka with the same son of a bitch, put her arms round him and kiss him tenderly. She wasn't being a hypocrite, it was just that he was a colleague, a work-mate, he served art and it so happened that among those who serve art you also find the odd son of a bitch.

Sonya promised to come in June, then she put it off till July. I was upset by that, because I was hoping she would be there to adorn our family celebration. What celebration ? I'll tell you.

13 ▧

My parents were married in June 1910, which meant we ought to have celebrated their silver wedding in 1935, but you know where father was at that time.

Then in the summer of 1940, Genrikh announced that he would be home on leave in June, and Lyuba and Volodya were planning to come, too, so the whole family would be here. I got the idea that we should celebrate our parents' thirty years of married life, especially as father was also fifty in 1940, and thirty and fifty seemed memorable dates which we ought to celebrate.

I very much wanted Sonya to be here for the celebration so that I could introduce her to the family, she being a gay and sociable girl, everyone would like her. But she was tied up on tour and put off her trip home until July, so the celebration I had dreamed up had to take place without her.

As I said, the whole family was going to be here. The problem was Yefim and Natasha. Although it would also be a good opportunity to introduce Natasha to her husband's parents, at last, I've already given you an idea of the sort of man my brother Yefim was, always busy, always doing something that can't be put off, the factory wouldn't manage without him for an hour. As you know only too well, nobody's indispensable. With Yefim, it was the work that was indispensable, and the factory was just launching their gas-driven tractor.

I wrote to him. Surely, I wrote, our parents deserve a little attention from us, after all they've been through? Surely you can manage to take two days off for the sake of such an important occasion? Think of what they have done for us, and don't forget father will be fifty this year.

Yefim replied that he and Natasha would come on the appointed day.

I should explain that silver and golden weddings were not normally celebrated in our part of the world. I don't remember a single case. I do remember hearing as a child about such things being done in the Brodsky family, Brodsky being a millionaire sugar-baron in Kiev. They used to say the Brodsky family celebrated silver weddings, golden weddings and even diamond weddings, which came after sixty years of marriage. I'm not sure the Brodskys were all that long-lived, but there were always stories of that sort about millionaires. They used to say, for instance, that when Brodsky drank his tea, he didn't do it like a poor man, without sugar, or like a well-to-do man, with a lump of sugar on his tongue, or like a rich man, with the sugar in it, but instead they gave him a block of sugar with a hole in the top for the tea. I mention these fairy-tales only because silver, golden and other kinds of weddings were not the normal thing with us. We didn't even take any notice of birthdays, at least in grandfather's and our own family. Life was work and worry, holidays were for relaxation, in the old days religious holidays, and now our Soviet holidays.

I didn't tell mother and father anything as I wanted to surprise them. Let them all arrive, I thought, that in itself will be an event, as it had never happened before, though I must admit mother was always quite reserved about her children's visits; she thought, they've come, thank God, they should come to see their parents occasionally. This time there was a new situation, as Genrikh hadn't come alone, he brought two of his service friends with him, one of them his own commander.

Mother had a special attitude to Genrikh. He was the only

good-for-nothing of all her sons, he had had many scrapes, as I've already told you. She gave him more smacks round the face and clips round the ear than she gave all the rest of us put together. Never mind the school, the whole street heaved a sigh of relief when they took him into the depot training school and gave him something to do, and the street heaved a sigh of relief for the second time when he went into the army, to the flying school; they thought military service would straighten him out. But what military service! A pilot! Every day up in the air, every minute he was close to death. In fact, mother ought to have had time to get used to the idea, he'd had three years in the Air Force, and before that he had been in the local air-defence club, then he was a trainee pilot, then a parachutist, and on Air Force Day he took part in the group jumps at Chernigov. But that was sport, even though it was a dangerous one, and some of the other lads from the depot had taken part, too. Now he was something else, an Air Force pilot! He'd been at Khasan (in the Soviet-Japanese skirmishes of 1938), and at Khalkhin-Gol (same thing 1939), and only three months before, in March, the war with the White Finns had come to an end. When that war was going on, mother nearly went out of her mind; they'll send him to the Karelian Peninsular, she said, and he's such a hothead, everyone knows he's a typical Rakhlenko, a copy of Uncle Misha, the same Tatar face and slanted eyes, he'll get into the thick of the fighting and get himself killed. But they didn't send him to the front, the Finnish campaign ended without him, and mother saw him at last, alive and well. Now he had come, and not alone, but with friends, other pilots, and on top of that, one of them was his own commander! Such guests!

Genrikh's arrival with his comrades was an event not only for mother, but for the whole town. Nowadays being a pilot is a common enough job. But in those days! Chkalov was to the thirties what Gagarin was to the sixties. His flight over the

Pole to the USA was like the space flights of today. Well, what do you know, Genrikh's an Air Force pilot, our own little Ivanovsky kid, who used to run around in the streets, old Rakhlenko's grandson, the tough one! And there were three of them. Three pilots! A crew of three, like all the famous crews.

There they were, three pilots, wandering around the town in their polished boots and forage-caps, with pips on their collars, young and handsome and smart, just like in the movies. The whole town knew they were bachelors, that the commander, the one with three pips on his tabs, was called Vadim Pavlovich Sokolov, and that although he was still very young he had the Order of the Red Star. According to Khaim Yagudin, it was after this Sokolov that our pilots were known as *sokols*, or hawks. Khaim Yagudin mooched up and down the streets, especially the main street, Great Alexeyev, and also our own Sand Street, trying to be seen by the pilots, so he could give them a full salute, which they would return.

It was also well known to everyone that the second pilot's name was Georgy Koshelyov, and as Khaim Yagudin explained, Georgy was named for St George the Victorious, so it followed that Koshelyov came from an old military family.

Nobody was particularly interested in Khaim Yagudin's conjectures. What they saw were three fine young fellows, three Air Force pilots who looked as if they'd stepped straight out of the movie-screen. Everyone admired them, willingly let them go to the front of the queue in the shops, at the cinema, at the barber's, where Bernard Semyonovich provided for each one of them a fresh robe and an individual, hygienic packet with a shaving brush and napkin, and after the shave a hot compress, and after the compress a face massage, then another compress and last of all some French eau-de-Cologne that he had kept since before the First World War, so he said.

Grandfather Rakhlenko took one look at the airmen's

army-issue boots, told them to take them off, measured them all, and set about cobbling them new ones. He wasn't working in the factory any more, but he did a bit now and again at home – 'a heel, a *shmeel*, do grandmother and I need so much?' He still had two or three pieces of hide from his old days as an artisan, and he made the boys such chrome-leather dress boots, that even I, a specialist shoemaker, had to admire them.

Naturally the local air-defence club used the pilots' visit as an occasion to put a bit of life into their own activities. The fact was, apart from collecting membership fees, the air-defence club didn't do much at all. Now came this opportunity! They organized a meeting, and Vadim Pavlovich spoke about the achievements of Soviet aviation, about the amazing flights of our glorious pilots; he touched on the history of aviation and its prospects for the future. After that meeting, a lot of boys and girls signed up for flying school.

In other words, once again our town didn't disgrace itself, but showed that it was living in the twentieth century.

You can well imagine what was going on on the dance-floor. Our dance-floor was in the garden of the railway club. On weekdays they danced to records and on Saturdays and Sundays there was a brass band to dance to.

It happened to be a Saturday when the airmen came to the dance-floor for the first time, and the band struck up the Air Force march in their honour, 'Still higher and higher and higher'; they repeated it several times, and people danced the fox-trot to it. Naturally, all the girls wanted to dance with the airmen. The bolder ones went up to Genrikh, as he was an old acquaintance, and he then introduced them to his friends, and if the band happened to strike up at that moment, they simply had to invite the girls who were standing next to them to dance. There was a lot of activity, the girls refused their usual partners and danced with each other opposite where the airmen were standing, hoping they would cut in. They got up to all kinds of tricks, but no special friendships were started, none of the pilots walked any of the girls home, they kept themselves free but respectable. Genrikh danced with all the girls, not with one in particular, as he had a girl where he was stationed and he didn't want to start anything with any of the local girls. As for Georgy Koshelyov, the triumphant reception and all the pomp and ceremony rather overwhelmed him, as he wasn't used to being in the limelight, he was a shy lad.

It was my sister Dina who was really to blame for our local girls' lack of success. Even though she was only fifteen, I've already told you what she was like. Well, Vadim Pavlovich Sokolov announced, as a joke, that he would escort Dina to the dance and she would be his lady for the evening. It seemed very gallant, a commander with his medals. He was of medium height, thick-set, broad-shouldered, looked rather like Chkalov, he had the same large features, and though he was only twenty-five, as far as Dina was concerned, he was an old man, ten years older. His line was to let the young dance and flirt with each other while he, being an old man, would dance with this young girl, she would be his lady, he would court her. Everyone was supposed to know the courting was in fun, but in fact it gave him the excuse to keep the other girls at a distance. We had come in a group and we left in a group, Vadim Pavlovich, Georgy Koshelyov, Genrikh, Dina and myself.

Although the evening hadn't been a success for the local girls, I don't think they gave up hope, as there was still a whole month ahead.

Genrikh spoke very highly of his friends. Georgy Koshelyov was an orphan and had been raised in a children's home, and Genrikh had wanted to bring him to meet us. Vadim Pavlovich was also on his own, he had recently left his wife, he had walked out with just what he had on, he was living in the barracks, his wife was a bad lot, so it was a good thing

Vadim Pavlovich had divorced her. So, like anyone else, it seemed they had their humdrum problems, too. Nobody else knew about these worries. To the whole town they seemed like a holiday.

Then Lyuba and Volodya arrived. Lyuba was already a doctor and Volodya, who had finished the Army Medical Academy three years earlier, was also in uniform, though instead of pips he had the bars of an Army Medical Officer, Third Class. So we had four servicemen in the house – it was almost like a barracks. Finally, a week later, Yefim and Natasha arrived.

We put Genrikh and his friends in the living-room – as guests they got the best and we squeezed in as well as we could. I gave up my room to Yefim and Natasha; though they were family, they were very rare visitors. Lyuba, Volodya, Igor and Olya went to grandfather's, though he hadn't a lot of room, if it came to that, what with Uncle Grisha and his family, six in all, and Uncle Lazar and Daniel. Dina had to sleep at Ivan Karlovich's and I went to the Stashenoks, which meant that Ivan Karlovich and Stanislava Frantsevna and the Stashenoks all became involved in the turmoil. In fact, the whole town became involved in the turmoil.

Yefim and Natasha arrived on a Saturday, the very day we had decided to 'have the spread', which was the formula I used to camouflage the anniversary celebration we were about to have – once in a blue moon the whole family got together, so we ought to mark the occasion with a few drinks. I had of course let my brothers into the plan, but nobody else knew about it, except one man, who guessed what was going on, and that was father.

'You're proposing to celebrate my birthday?' he asked.

'Well, why not?'

'We never take any notice of anybody's birthday, there's no need to do anything about mine, either.'

'Nobody else has reached fifty.'

'Even so.'

'But it's your birthday, the head of the family. And it's also your thirtieth wedding anniversary, have you forgotten?'

'No, I haven't forgotten, but it's not a good moment.'

I knew he was thinking of Lyova, what kind of anniversary would it be without one of his sons there? But Lyova was gone, we had mourned him, we hadn't forgotten him and never would, still, you can't go on mourning forever.

'Look,' I said, 'for the first time in years the family is reunited and so many things have happened. Lyuba's finished her studies, Yefim has brought his wife to meet us, and Genrikh has brought his friends. Can't we drink a glass of vodka?'

'All right,' father nodded. 'But no anniversaries.'

I made allowances for his modesty, but I didn't abandon my plan, and took steps, as you shall see.

The table was laid for forty people, in the yard outside the house. There were grandfather and grandmother, Uncle Grisha and Uncle Yosif and their wives, and Uncle Lazar. Relations with Yosif weren't so great, as he kept himself at a distance from his poor relations, but still he was mother's brother, so he had to be invited. Then, of course, there were mother and father, Anna Yegorovna, Yefim and Natasha, Lyuba and Volodya, Genrikh, Vadim Pavlovich, Georgy Koshelyov, Ivan Karlovich and Stanislava Frantsevna, Afanasi Prokopyevich Stashenok and his sons Andrey and Petrus with their wives Ksana and Irina, then me, Dina, Uncle Lazar's son Daniel, then, if you remember, mother's friends the Kuznetsov sisters, with their husbands and Sidorov, the former manager of the shoe factory, who had happened to drop in on us on a visit from the Machine and Tractor Station, and of course we couldn't let him go away. Forty people in all, and that's not counting all the children who were buzzing round the table, Sasha, Olya, Igor, Uncle Grisha's children,

Stashenok's grandchildren, the children of the Kuznetsov sisters.

But you can imagine how it is in a small town like ours. If, say, Lyuba had told an old school friend to drop in during the evening, you could be sure she would come with more friends who would want to congratulate Lyuba on graduating, and also grab the chance of sitting next to the airmen at the table. And if Genrikh had said the same thing to one of his old pals from the training school or the depot, he would bring a few more pals with him to celebrate their friend's visit. And I had invited some of father's old workmates from the shoe factory. What is a little town, anyway, it's just like a village, the band strikes up at one end and the people start dancing at the other, especially as this was the south, and it was summer, and you could smell the cooking all the way down the street. The old widow Gorodetsky turned up, though nobody had invited her, and the miserable butcher Kusiel Plotkin shuffled in, after all father had started off working with him. Khaim Yagudin showed up as father's uncle, if you please, though he was about as much an uncle to father as the Mikado was an aunt to me. The barber Bernard Semyonovich looked in, no party could get along without him, and Doctor Volyntsev, who had saved mother's life and Sasha's, and the teacher Kuras, a most respected gentleman, and teacher of all subjects, and Oryol came, too, he was still a chemist, though of course not in his own business now, he was working in a state pharmacy.

We added more tables and squeezed up together. There was room for everyone and food for everyone, the baking and cooking had been going on since morning, with mother, grandmother, Uncle Grisha's wife Ida, Anna Yegorovna and Madame Yanzhvetska all working away. You remember Madame Yanzhvetska, the former owner of the hotel? Her hotel had been requisitioned in the Revolution and turned into the Peasants' Club, then the Collective Farmers' Club, and she had worked there as cook in the communal dining-room, as well as barmaid and cashier, but she wasn't working at all now, as she was seventy-five, single and very dignified. She wore an enormous hat with a bird's nest on top and she carried an old-fashioned handbag and parasol. People felt sorry for her and she was invited to all the parties, to join in, to lay the table and help in the kitchen, though the women in our household, I would have you know, needed no instruction in cooking! On this occasion we had only the best, chopped herring, grated radish, chopped liver, *gefilte* fish, stuffed goose-neck, chopped eggs in goose-fat, roast chicken, salami, mutton and veal brawn, noodles, compote, everything home-made, cucumbers and tomatoes straight from the garden.

The noise round the table was terrific. It was a very mixed company, young and old, locals and visitors, family and out-siders, friends and people we'd never met, and there were plenty of talkers among them. Khaim Yagudin, if you gave him the chance, wouldn't let anyone else open their mouth, the old woman Gorodetsky could shout down the whole mar-ket, and Bernard Semyonovich always had plenty to say, he was the town's oral chronicler, for years his barber shop had been the club and newspaper of the town.

The teacher Kuras liked a discussion, and Uncle Lazar was apt to become philosophical after he'd had a glass or two. The older people tried to get medical advice from Dr Volyntsev and Volodya, especially as it was known that he was doing so well, and of course they all wanted to have a chat with the airmen. Everyone had something to drink, some more than others, some drank vodka, others wine, some beer and others soda water, but whatever they drank, it went to their heads just the same. The women bustled about the table, someone would need a plate, someone else a fork or a chair, and then it turned out that some crank wouldn't eat *tref* and had to be reassured that everything had been made at home, that there was no pork in the house, there was nothing to worry about, if he ate the fish he wouldn't go to hell, but straight to heaven. Then they had to keep running to the kitchen to see nothing was burning, and they had to make the guests eat up before everything got cold, and shout at the children to get out from under their feet or someone might get scalded, God forbid!

Nobody was in charge of the proceedings, we hadn't appointed a master of ceremonies, there were no speeches, everyone just enjoyed themselves in their own way. But I wanted it to be a festival for my parents, I wanted to do them justice on such an important occasion, so I stood up and asked for silence, having earlier arranged with Yefim, Genrikh and Lyuba, who were, so to speak, part of my scenario, that they would each get their neighbours to stop talking. Everyone became hushed; they were all curious by nature so they were wondering why I wanted them to be quiet all of a sudden, at such a gathering, when the proper thing was to have a lot of noise.

I spoke. 'Dear friends! In the name of everyone gathered here tonight round this table, allow me to welcome our dear guests Vadim Pavlovich Sokolov and Georgy Koshelyov, both glorious airmen, and I ask you to raise your glasses to their good health!'

The airmen stood up and clinked glasses all round, people got up and went round to drink their health, and again there was a din and a racket and disorder. But Vadim Pavlovich went on standing, with a full glass in his hand, and it was clear he had something to say, so everyone went quiet again, as they wanted to hear with their own ears the words of the famous pilot.

'My comrades and I thank you with all our hearts for your hospitality. But Boris Yakovlevich made the wrong toast. The first toast should be to our host and hostess, to dear Rachel Abramovna and Yakov Leonovich, especially as today is their thirtieth wedding anniversary!'

Everyone clapped and cheered and congratulated mother and father, who both stood up and bowed.

'Thirty years,' Vadim Pavlovich went on, 'is a long time, and it is wonderful to see Rachel Abramovna and Yakov Leonovich looking so young and healthy and handsome, they could both join the Air Force right away!'

The teacher Kuras leant over to me and said, 'He's an intelligent man!'

'We will understand if they don't join the Air Force, they don't want to be up in the air when they've got so much to do down here on the ground. We wish them success. Let's drink to their good health and happiness!'

At that moment, Madame Yanzhvetska, who was standing by the kitchen door, called right across the yard, 'Kiss!'

It was a bit unexpected. None of us had a clue as to how these occasions were supposed to be celebrated and whether fully grown adults should shout 'Kiss!' all of a sudden. This was Madame Yanzhvetska, however, who was something of an aristocrat, a former one, that is, the former owner of the former hotel, the one who went around in a hat with a bird's nest on top, she knew about etiquette!

So amid all the noise and the shouts of congratulation and the clink of glasses, mother and father kissed. And, you know, mother was energetic and gay about it, she even threw off her shawl coquettishly, her eyes were shining, her teeth were as white as they had always been, and her hair was still black, though it was tinged with grey. She stood next to father, and I can tell you they made a regal couple, my parents, they were both tall, made taller perhaps by the way they carried themselves upright. Above them was the blissful southern sky, and in front of them the same yard where thirty years earlier they had celebrated their marriage, and they could see the street they had walked along after the ceremony, young and in love, while the band had played and everyone danced and sang around them, and now again people were admiring them, and were happy for them and wishing them joy.

Then, as we had also arranged, Georgy Koshelyov got up and said, 'I have something to add. Yakov Leonovich is fifty this year! I wish him a happy birthday and many, many happy returns!'

Again everyone lifted up their glasses to father, and without any prompting from Madame Yanzhvetska mother kissed father again, and father's friends all kissed him and little Igor yelled 'I want to kiss you, too, Grandpa!'

Father lifted him on to the table, and then he lifted up Olya as well, so that everyone could see his grandson and granddaughter and the continuity, so to speak, of the family.

Then up got Khaim Yagudin, leaning on his stick. I felt uneasy, as you never knew what to expect from him, a string of nonsense at best, a scandal at worst. Luckily, it was neither.

He straightened out his whiskers, raised his glass and cried out, 'Here's to the health of pretty women, hurrah!'

I think it must have been the shortest speech Khaim Yagudin had ever made in his life, and it gave the urge to others.

Bernard Semyonovich, the barber, said, 'Every person is beautiful in his own way, but not everybody knows how to make it obvious. My job is to make my clients' beauty as obvious as two times two is four. Very rarely do you meet people who are so beautiful you're afraid to approach them with the scissors or the clippers. I have only ever known two such people, they are Yakov Ivanovsky and his spouse. Let us drink to their outstanding beauty. Long life!'

Then it was the turn of the teacher Kuras. 'Yakov and Rachel have their lives in front of them, they are young, they will have many more festivals in their lives to celebrate. Now, our deeply respected Abraham Isaakovich Rakhlenko is eighty this year. Abraham Isaakovich Rakhlenko was born in eighteen hundred and sixty, and this is nineteen forty. So, allow me to invite you all to raise your glasses to Abraham Rakhlenko and his spouse Bertha Solomonovna. And let me also say to their children, look at your mother and father, and let me say to their grandchildren, look at your grandparents, and let me say to their great-grandchildren, look at your great-grandparents, look and you will see an example for your own lives!'

Everyone who had lived their lives alongside grandfather and grandmother went up to them, as the teacher's toast had really been for those who had lived long and honourable lives. If they cried it was for what would never return, their youth and strength, their health and their hopes. Only grandfather didn't cry. I doubt if he had ever cried in all his eighty years. He wasn't the man he used to be, that's a fact, he couldn't fell a horse with a blow of his fist now, his beard was grey, he had sclerotic veins in his cheeks and he was stouter, but you could still feel the strength in his shoulders, which he always kept pulled back, and the clear mind and common sense were still there behind that white forehead. Grandmother was the same hale and hearty, clear-headed sort of person she'd always been. Have you ever wondered why it is that a man who lives a long life often has a wife who lives a long life, too? It can't be accidental, you must agree? A brother and a sister may not both live to a great age, but a husband and wife so often do, yet they have different genes, different heredity. I wonder why? But that's just by the way, let's get back to the celebrations.

Ivan Sidorov, our old manager and now a mechanic on a Machine and Tractor Station, said, 'This is a good family, they are good people. Abraham Rakhlenko has worked hard, and so have his sons Grigory and Lazar, and his son-in-law Yakov, and his grandson Boris, they're all good hard workers. With all the boots and shoes they've made in their lives you could supply the whole province and the two neighbouring ones besides. Nobody has ever seen them do a bad thing, so let's drink to the whole family, from the oldest to the youngest, from the grandfather to the grandson. And not for the last time, as they say!'

There would have been no shortage of people wanting to speak – as long as someone was prepared to listen, someone was prepared to speak. But as everyone had had plenty to drink and they were all chatting among themselves, and the young people wanted to dance, and as a matter of fact we weren't used to after-dinner speeches, I whispered to Yefim, 'Say a couple of words to round things off.' As I had opened the debate, so to speak, I thought I'd let my brother close it.

'Dear comrades,' Yefim began. 'In the name of the family, I thank you all for your kind words. Sitting here are people of different generations and different professions. But we're all doing one thing, in our own places, at our own jobs, to the best of our ability, we are all labouring for the good of our country. Let's wish everyone success in their jobs, and long life to those who have already done their valiant labour. Once more, thank you all!'

With these words, Yefim closed what you might call the official part of the evening. The unofficial part rolled along under its own steam, people finished up the drink and the food, cleared the table, the old folks chatted, the guests gradually left, and all that could be heard at last was the clatter of pots and pans in the kitchen. Genrikh and his friends and Dina and her friends went off to the dancing. I didn't go, I took back the tables and chairs and crockery we had borrowed from the neighbours, restored some sort of order, and went off to the Stashenoks, where I collapsed into bed. The Stashenoks always went to bed early.

Next day, Sunday, I spent with Yefim and Natasha. We went to the market and bought tomatoes, cucumbers, and strawberries, which we put into boxes so they wouldn't get crushed on the journey. We thought they needed the vitamins, as they never saw this kind of thing in Kharkov. After dinner, the whole family saw them to the station, put them on the train and sent them home.

On Monday father and I went to work, but Dina and Sasha were on holiday, and of course they looked after the guests. The work guests do is well known – the river, the beach, boats, the forest, and cinema or dancing in the evenings. As ours was a little holiday town, a resort you could say, we were quite used to people relaxing on holiday while we were at work, it even gave a sense of festivity to our ordinary working lives. And now our house was full of guests and full of young people, a kind of double festivity. Mother cooked for everyone, Dina and Lyuba helped her, and Anna Yegorovna, who had become virtually a member of the family, helped her, too.

Then one day mother asked me, as if by the way, 'What do you think, is Vadim Pavlovich a respectable man?' When mother asked something as if by the way, it never was just by the way.

I shrugged my shoulders. 'Can't you see what sort of man he is yourself?'

'I can see everything,' she replied mysteriously.

It sounded ridiculous. She was worried about Dina's friendship with Vadim Pavlovich, quite mistakenly. Vadim Pavlovich perfectly well understood the distance between himself and Dina, a distance of ten years.

I said to mother, 'There's nothing wrong in it, and there won't be.'

'You know so much, you see so much!' she replied briefly.

I began to watch Dina and Vadim Pavlovich more closely, I found some time to lounge on the beach with them and, believe it or not, mother was right, Dina had fallen in love with Vadim Pavlovich. Can you beat it! A kid of fifteen and in love! It shouldn't have been surprising, he was a good-looking boy, an Air Force pilot, admired by the whole town. The point was, Dina hadn't fallen in love secretly, the way young girls usually fall in love with older men, but openly, like his equal, she seemed to grow up and become independent overnight. She didn't hang round his neck and chase after him, instead she became the inspiration of the group, the centre of attraction with her beauty and talent, and suddenly they all saw her as a grown-up girl, a young woman. She had none of the rudeness that had set mother apart as a young girl, but in the depth and seriousness of her feelings, she was mother's equal – if she fell in love, she fell in love.

Could Vadim Pavlovich resist the delights of young love? How could he not be carried away by this beautiful girl? I have never seen a girl as beautiful as Dina, and I never will. Only fifteen, but what stature already, what a figure, what carriage, what hair, what eyes! To give him his due, Vadim Pavlovich was a real man, he understood his duty, and talked it all over with Dina. I wasn't there at the time, but after that talk Dina told mother that in a year's time, when she was sixteen, she would marry Vadim Pavlovich, or rather Vadim, as she called him.

'Isn't that a bit early to be getting married?' mother asked.

'And how old were you when you and father got married?'

'Things were different in those days.'

Mother was reassured by the year's postponement, a lot could happen in a year, a lot could change, Vadim Pavlovich would soon be going away and Dina's infatuation would pass.

There was no awkwardness, it didn't go beyond mother and myself. The young people had decided to get married in a year's time, they would write to each other, and meanwhile they would carry on their friendship in company, in view, and there could be nothing wrong in that. Personally I was very pleased at their friendship. I didn't know how it would end, perhaps in nothing, but I was glad Dina had fallen for a boy like Vadim. Despite her appearance and talent, Dina was a trusting and simple-hearted soul. If mother, with the character she had, needed a man like father, then Dina needed a man like Vadim, strong, reliable, independent. Anyway, what is ten years between a husband and wife, it's nothing, actually, it's all to the good, and in any case, they weren't getting married straight away. Yes, I was very pleased Dina had fallen for a real man, not some young kid.

The time flew by. Soon Genrikh, Vadim Pavlovich and Georgy Koshelyov left, then a week later Lyuba and Volodya, and the household returned to its usual size. The holidays went on and Sonya arrived.

14

Sonya arrived and again it was the gang, the *shashlyki*, the night-time bathing and our nights together. Once again Khaim Yagudin strutted about, again he brought us his carrot coffee in bed, and it was no secret that things looked like heading for marriage.

I told Sonya I wanted to introduce her to my parents.

'What a good little boy!' she laughed. 'I'm to be inspected, am I? What if they don't allow it?'

'Don't talk nonsense. I just want to show some consideration to the old folks.'

'Okay, let's go,' she replied.

So I introduced Sonya to my parents; I presented her, though in those days it wasn't very usual, as I said earlier, people just got married and that was that. Lyova had done it and Yefim, too. I knew, however, that it would have been nicer for mother to have met their wives before the marriage, so that people could see that her sons wouldn't get married without their parents' blessing. She couldn't help it, she and father were both old-fashioned. So I decided to please them by bringing Sonya home.

Sonya brought sweets for Olya and Igor, and played with them and, as always, was bright and cheerful, but her charming manner clashed with mother's hostility. Mother didn't say a word but kept running out to the kitchen, making it look as if she was busy.

It was father who broke the tension. He laid his hand on mother's shoulder, so she had to stay at the table, and he kept it there while he talked about Leningrad, where Sonya had once studied at the Drama School. And mother gave in. It was amazing the way father knew how to calm her down, but that's something else. You know, father had only ever been to Leningrad twice, to visit Lyuba, but he talked about the place as if he'd spent his whole life there, the Nevsky Boulevard, St Isaac's Cathedral, the Kazan Cathedral, the Winter Palace, and he talked like a native, a born Petersburger – they all sound like walking tour-guides.

I'd stayed in Leningrad every year when I went for my exams, and father had only been there twice in his life. I had of course seen all the things he had seen, but I'd seen them in passing, I wasn't terribly interested in the sights, and I hadn't a lot of free time. Naturally, I'd been to the Hermitage and the Russian Museum, you couldn't not, and I'd seen the statues of the rearing horses on the Anichkov Bridge and the young muscle-men holding them in check – I must admit I didn't know they were called The Horse-Tamers, till father said so. It was curious that he had never once talked about Leningrad at home. When he came back he would tell us all about Lyuba and Volodya, which was what mother wanted to hear, but with Sonya he talked about the architecture of Rossi and Bazhenov and Kazakov, because that was something she was familiar with herself, the subject was appropriate. It was a sign of father's tact and good breeding.

I took Sonya home and when I got back mother said, 'Some pretty girl you've found yourself! Nothing but paint and powder! She's a Yagudin, don't you know what they're like? Only out for excitement, all layabouts and brawlers!'

'First of all,' I objected, 'she isn't all paint and powder, it's natural. And secondly, there are some things that I decide for myself.'

She made a wry face. 'Decide, decide. But just think for a minute, what would you be, living with her? The cook? Her buttons are falling off, it's obvious she's never held a needle in her hand. Why don't you say something?' she turned to father. 'Haven't you got a tongue?'

'A cow has a long tongue, but it still doesn't know how to talk.'

'You don't know how to talk? Some hopes! About palaces he talked to her, all of a sudden everyone's got an education!'

'Boris is a grown man, let him decide for himself,' father said. 'The only thing I would say to him is, don't rush.'

I knew from those words that father wasn't exactly crazy about Sonya either, perhaps he liked her for herself, but not the idea of our future union.

But, say what you like, I was already pushing thirty and had the right to decide my own fate. I had always lived with them, they had got used to having me around, it was hard for them to accept the idea that I might leave them, and it was hard for me to do it, but I had to build my own life.

◆

I arrived in Kalinin and straight away got myself a decent room in a nice house. I was getting good money, as I'd fixed myself up with a job in the regional industrial soviet as a footwear production engineer. I would come home from work and make the bed, that was no problem, and cleaning was no problem, I would take a broom and sweep up, wash the crockery, all two glasses of it. Sonya ate at the theatre, I ate at work in the canteen, and as for breakfast and supper, you could soon boil up the kettle on the hob and you could pop out to the grocer's easily enough to buy something for a sandwich. I was glad that Sonya wasn't distracted from the theatre by these trivialities. Without doubt she noticed the efforts I was making, knowing that I had to work, too, and as I had an important job I usually worked late, on top of which I was in my last year at the Institute, so it wasn't easy.

Sonya was aware of all that, she appreciated me and sympathized, and even said to me, 'My darling, you're too domesticated, drop it, we'll manage perfectly without all that, who needs it?'

She refused to get married, she was even surprised when I suggested it, 'My God, what for!?'

Anyway, living together was just the same as being officially married, what difference was there? Children? Not a chance! Give up your most crucial years and you give up everything. It was understandable, she hadn't made her name yet, she hadn't become a National Artist, or even an Honoured one. True, there was no knowing when she would become one, but fine, let her have it her way.

She was living with me, but officially she was still registered at her old place, because if the theatre had known she was living in such wonderful conditions, they wouldn't give her another room.

Taken individually, all these points made sense, but taken together, they put me in a very uncertain position.

I went to all the performances, of course. Sonya was competent and talented, everyone said so, but it seemed to me she strained somewhat, she liked to strike effective postures on stage. I didn't tell her that, as I didn't want to hurt her, and anyway what did I know about the theatre, I could easily have been wrong. In fact she never talked to me about theatre as such, only about life behind the scenes.

You mustn't think her life was nothing but intrigues. She lived for the theatre and her art, but as I was such a philistine where her art was concerned, she could only talk to me about things of secondary importance. If it comes to that, I didn't expand on my own work, either. As if she would want to hear about shoe production and repair! If I were to have any unpleasantness, she would have backed me up, but then what unpleasantness could befall me working in bootmaking?

Her friends would drop in, actors and actresses, they were very funny about their enemies, the old has-beens, they cursed them in words I wouldn't repeat here, and put them into situations and poses of which the less said the better. They were a jolly crowd, a bit noisy, and also shameless: they borrowed money which they never paid back, they tried to get you to buy their drinks, and made you feel a fool. Sonya wasn't shocked by this, she just laughed and said, 'Don't be a sponger!' She had a generous nature, so she liked the fact that I was feeding the whole crowd. She wasn't petty, she was carefree and looked on life airily.

The revellers used to get together at her place, not mine, because of the old problem about her room. It would be crowded, noisy, filled with smoke, and the owner and his wife would stand right there in the doorway till they'd been given a drink. All this would take place at night after the show. Usually I didn't wait till the mob had dispersed, but would go home to my own place.

I found it hard to get used to her way of life. I remember once a theatre critic came from Moscow. Sonya entertained him as if he were top-class, but behind his back she laughed at him and called him a moron, though she was still hoping he would praise her in his paper, and in fact he did give her a mention: 'Vishnevsky gave an interesting, if controversial, account of this role.'

Or, for instance, on her birthday. I got myself ready, bought flowers, laid the table. That day she had to attend a concert and should have been back by nine. She came in at one in the morning – there'd been a banquet.

She saw the flowers and the table laid, and said, 'Darling, I'm a pig, I know, but you must forgive me. They knew it was my birthday, so the banquet turned into a party for me, they celebrated in my honour! The regional bigwigs were there.'

I don't condemn her, we just saw these things differently.

As I said already, I had got myself a job in the regional industrial soviet as a footwear production engineer. In those days, a man who knew the business but didn't have a diploma was called a workshop-engineer. I knew the business, and I was in my last year at the Institute, so my diploma was only a matter of time, and I was getting maximum wages. But they had some problems with their staffing schedules, my post wasn't official, and they were paying me from a vacancy they had in the supplies and sales section, even though I was working in production.

I liked my work, my trade, my speciality. You know, the first manager of our factory had been Sidorov, who knew the business, then after him they'd put in a manager who wasn't perhaps as good as Sidorov, but was at least qualified. In a little town, they know what everyone can do, they know each person's value. But here, in the regional centre, there was a mass of people who only knew how to do one job, and that was management, today they manage a laundry, tomorrow a shoe-factory, the day after tomorrow a collective farm. Why, I ask myself, does he have to be a manager? And the answer is, because he's on the party's list of regional appointments. He can be on his last legs, but he has to be assured of a management job. He doesn't know the business? He'll learn. He might make a mess of it? When he does, we'll talk about it. On top of that, industrial cooperatives were regarded as something second-class, mere artisans! So if they wanted to get shot of a dud, they'd send him to the artisans. At any event, I ran into plenty of incompetents. I had to demonstrate the most elementary things to them, and they would regard every sensible suggestion with suspicion, they were afraid of taking any responsibility. Why? Maybe because the next day they could be shifted to managing a grocery shop.

Then there was the paper-work. I would come to a work-shop, have a look at the production, point things out, put things right, everything would be nice and clear, everyone would be happy, and I would push off and report to my boss on the work I'd done. A couple of months later, I'd go there again, and everything would be just as it had been before, as if I'd never been there, and it turns out it's my fault, I hadn't written anything down! I hadn't left them a piece of paper. They would flatly deny everything: yes, I'd been there, I'd wandered around, said something or other, and the management would go for me because I hadn't put it down in writing! You understand? On every sole and heel I was supposed to write out a bit of paper, make a document, compose a report and God knows what. Maybe it's like that in every establishment, but I'm used to production, I'm not a clerk. The people who understood the business would come to me for consultation and advice, but they were workers, and my position didn't depend on them. It's true, the head of the industrial soviet, Vasili Alexeyevich Boitsov, valued me and always listened to my opinion, but between him and me, an ordinary engineer, there were several managers in the hierarchy, and the fact that he dealt directly with me only added to my difficulties, which he couldn't do anything about. He was a good man, but he was getting on, he'd been through a lot, and he was tired.

Those were the conditions and the general atmosphere in which I worked. Now let me be more concrete.

When Hitler invaded Poland, many Polish Jews fled to us. I met one in Kalinin, called Bronevsky, he was working as a rate-fixer in one of our shoe-factories. He was a man of my age, or a little more, of medium build, with regular features, and something of the European in him. Despite this European quality, he was always fussing about something, he had a lot of cheek, always running from one office to another, to the town soviet or the regional party committee, asking for one thing or another, whether it was housing or goods and services, things that were hard for everyone to get, though he seemed to think he had a special claim.

Still, he was a refugee with a wife and two children, in a foreign country, he'd had to run away from Hitler, not a nice situation, you'll agree. As for what he told us about the Germans, what they were up to, the mind just couldn't grasp it, it was impossible to believe. We knew from our newspapers, of course, that the Nazis were conducting an unbridled anti-semitic campaign, but after we made the 1939 Pact with them I seem to recall something in the papers to the effect that, once he'd occupied Poland, Hitler announced that Germany would proceed to the 'final solution of the Jewish question'. We were to find out later just what the 'final solution' meant, when six million Jews had been burnt in the ovens. However, at that time it sounded like a promise to end the excesses and restore order. It even occurred to me that maybe this had been brought about by pressure from us, that in signing the Pact we had made it a condition that the anti-semitic antics must cease. I even had the idea that quite possibly our propaganda had exaggerated and that the position of the Jews in Germany or in the occupied countries wasn't as bad as all that.

What Bronevsky told us was far worse than anything we'd heard or could have guessed. The Jews in Germany were outside the law, they had been deprived of all human rights, the right to work, the right to study, to own property, to say nothing of the right of free speech. They were forced to live in ghettoes, they were forbidden to go out after a certain time of night, they were forbidden to walk on the pavement, but had to walk on the road, they weren't allowed to use public transport, to marry Germans, to go to court, to enter specified areas in the towns. They weren't served in the shops, and they had to wear a yellow six-pointed star on their chests and backs. And that was all in addition to the pogroms, violence and insults they had to suffer. When the Germans occupied Vienna, they got all the Jews out of their houses and made them scrub the pavements, and do you know what with? Toothbrushes! They organized that as a nice little entertainment for the inhabitants of Vienna to mark their victory.

Things were still all right for the German Jews, as they could at least emigrate. Out of Germany's half million Jews, about four hundred thousand left, mainly for other countries in Europe, where the Nazis caught up with them later on. Where could three million Polish Jews escape to? Hitler had occupied Europe and he wasn't going to let the Jews leave, he was preparing his 'final solution of the Jewish question'. And if the Germans treated the German Jews that way, and they were the most assimilated Jews anywhere, having lived in Germany for centuries, with German as their language, and German culture as their culture, then, what fate awaited the Polish Jews, when the Nazis didn't even consider the Poles themselves as human beings? Whatever Bronevsky was like as a person, it was very much in his favour that he had got away from the Germans with his wife and children, he hadn't let himself become their slave, so with all his faults I sympathized with him, and through him I sympathized with all the Jews who had fallen into Hitler's power.

He was quite well trained, spoke Russian, albeit with a Polish accent, but perfectly well, he had visited the Soviet Union on company business, in fact he was a qualified foot-wear specialist, perhaps more on the commercial side, and here he was, working in production as a simple rate-fixer. He didn't like the job, and you can't blame him. A rate-fixer's wage is rock bottom. Still, when you've just come to another country, nobody's going to make you a minister straight away. You have to be patient, get used to things, become familiar with the other people and let them become familiar with you. He didn't want to wait, however, he had a touch of Polish middle-class arrogance, he was sure he knew more than anyone else. On the other hand, there was something in him of the cemetery beggar, the kind that follow after you, moaning and wailing, and won't leave you alone till you've given them something.

That was Bronevsky, arrogant like a Polish lord, and tire-some like a beggar at a Jewish cemetery, but I was sorry for him, I put myself in his shoes and helped him. However, he saw that I was in a good situation and demanded that I help him to get a transfer to the regional industrial soviet, the department of sales and supply, where he would be able to practise his proper trade, in supply and marketing. I was stunned! What was I, just an ordinary engineer. I was new here, too, how could I recommend the transfer of another new employee? As if they'd listen to me! It was pointless.

I told him so. 'I'm not a manager, I can't give you a job and I can't recommend you for one, we're both new here. First earn some authority, work well with the collective, show them your worth, and things will work out nicely, they'll give you work you're qualified for.'

Wasn't that reasonable? He didn't think so, he began arguing, and he argued unpleasantly, at a high pitch, without consideration for the other person.

Then suddenly he said, 'There's a vacancy for an engineer in the section.'

He meant my job. Being naïve, I didn't get the true meaning of what he was saying at that moment, and I calmly explained to him that, because of the rigid staff schedules it was sometimes necessary, in the interest of the enterprise, to register a worker in a vacancy, even though he was working in a different department, and in the case in question that had happened with me.

As a joke I added, 'Of course, if they fire me, there'll be a vacancy.' He said nothing. I thought I had convinced him, but I was wrong.

Bronevsky occasionally dropped in on me for this and that, it was always for something. Sonya wasn't usually in, she rarely was, except overnight, but if she happened to be there when Bronevsky called, she never tried to hide her hostility and resentment. He only talked about himself, complained about everything, and only saw people in terms of what they could do for him. When he heard that Sonya was in the theatre, he straight away asked her for complimentary seats for his children.

'Tickets are sold at the box-office,' she shot back at him.

Obviously, he shouldn't have begun an acquaintance with a request, but she could have refused more politely. The point was, he was someone from my world, not hers, and unfortunately our two lives were growing apart more and more.

In January 1940 I went to Leningrad to do my state exams and the orals, and I went back to Kalinin feeling good. Say what you like, I was a technical engineer after four years. I picked up a couple of bottles of wine and some goodies in Leningrad to mark the occasion. Sonya and I drank to it, she congratulated me and was pleased for me.

Then she said, 'I've got some good news, too.'

She showed me an order giving her a room in a new municipal block. It really was good luck. The room wasn't in an old house, but a new one, and there were only a handful of them, it was in the centre of town, with all mod. cons., and right next to the theatre.

'That's marvellous!' I was very glad for her; after all she had waited years for it.

'Now I'm not dependent on anyone,' she said. 'To hell with the lot of them. If I feel like it, I can swap it for a room in Moscow or Leningrad, now I'm my own boss. And you, my darling, if you do well at work, you'll have your own place by the autumn.'

'Are we going to go on living in separate apartments?'

'No, why should we? When you get your room, we'll trade them in for something together.'

'The house is controlled by the department, they wouldn't allow an exchange.'

'Who can say what they'll do? Let's wait and see. What are you thinking?'

I really was thinking. I had hoped that when she got her

room things would change, and that we would live together at last, we would make a home, be like a family, and for the sake of that I had put up with my position, which wasn't all that convenient or dignified.

She went on, 'You'll be living with me, but officially you'll be without accommodation, and they'll give you some at work. After all, you've just completed your studies, they'll have to give you something. Why miss such an opportunity?'

As a joke, I said, 'Aren't you afraid I might try to get your room?'

'I've never thought that, and I don't want to think it,' she was serious, 'though all kinds of things do happen, people split up and become enemies and you can't avoid squabbles over the accommodation. We have the great advantage that we're both independent, our meetings are always like a holiday, it's best that way, it's more secure, believe me.'

Again, I can understand her, and you must understand her, too. Remember what it was like in those days, remember what the housing crisis did to people, remember the delights of communal living and how people would do anything to get a room of their own and how they would hang on to it, in case it was taken away? Sonya had struggled to get her room and now that she had, it really meant something to her, and, since I wasn't out on the street, but had a roof over my head, I could live with her and wait till they gave me my own place.

All that was true, but I wanted our love to be something higher than the housing crisis, I wanted Sonya to love me more than her accommodation, that for my sake she would be prepared to let it go to hell. After all, my father had given up a lot more for my mother than a room in a communal apartment. He loved mother!

I realized that Sonya didn't love me like that, and never would. She was a decent person, but she lived according to different principles.

'Listen,' I said. 'Maybe I shouldn't move in altogether?'

'Don't you like being with me?'

'I do like being with you, but I'm not always with you, I'm not really involved in your life.'

She was thoughtful for a while and then said, 'Perhaps you're right. It's not a life for you. But it'll be hard for me to part from you.'

'Me too,' I said. 'But it would be bound to happen sooner or later, the sooner the better for both of us.'

I spoke the words calmly and I was even smiling as I said them, but in my heart I felt 'My God, is it all over?'

'Do what you think best,' she said. 'I loved you and I still do.'

She burst into tears at the station. 'You're a wonderful man, Boris, really wonderful, but I'm no good to you, and I did warn you. Don't think badly of me. I'll never forget you.'

'And I won't forget you,' I said. 'Be happy.'

So we had parted. It happens. Things just hadn't worked out, we hadn't clicked.

Incidentally, I saw her a few years ago in the Russia Cinema at the film festival. I'm about as much of a film-goer as I used to be a theatre-goer in the old days, but my sons are great film-fans and during the festival they rush all over Moscow with their tongues hanging out, and dragging me along with them. So there I was sitting in the Russia, I don't remember what the film was, when I noticed that a woman, who was no longer young, was looking at me. At first I didn't recognize her and turned away, then I suddenly realized it was Sonya! I glanced at her again, her face was wrinkled – what do you expect after thirty years? She was somehow dried-up, thinner, maybe she was on a diet, but her hair was fashionable and she was wearing trousers. Even though it had all happened so long ago, my heart fluttered. After all, I had loved her once upon a time.

When I turned round again, she looked away. The lights went down and I watched the screen. I couldn't restrain myself from looking again, but when I did I found she had left. Why did she leave like that, why didn't she want to meet me, we were both old folks by then, anyway? Maybe she went out because she was ashamed of looking old and wanted to remain in my memory the way she had been thirty years earlier. I don't know. Anyway, I only told you this as a kind of finale.

Where had I got to? Oh, yes, I had left Kalinin. They released me from my job, which was bad enough, but there was more to it than that.

When I had returned from Leningrad, Boitsov, the manager, called me in straight away and told me there was trouble. It seems I had set damaging production norms and I must immediately present a detailed written explanation. After Boitsov, I was summoned to the personnel manager's office. Her name was Kamenev and she was also head of the specialist section. She closed the door, took out the file on my case and began 'to fill in a few details' on my relations in Switzerland and so on. She was an extremely unpleasant, fat female; once upon a time she had held responsible jobs, but because she was ignorant and always causing trouble she had come down in the world, though she had managed to retain the habits of responsibility – no joke, especially in the personnel department. She always looked as if she knew everything about everyone and that she held their fate in her hands, which to a certain extent she did, as she was in a position to make things really difficult. Because I had been summoned by her, I knew that the trouble over the norms was going to be serious, but I didn't panic. They didn't know anything about the business, while I did, they were involved in production only by accident, whereas I had grown up in it. I told Kamenev that all the facts about my origins were in my file,

I had nothing to add and I hadn't got time to sit there chatting with her, so good-bye! She actually dropped her jaw in amazement.

Briefly, the affair came to an end in the following way. Things progress, new equipment makes its appearance, new methods of production, new jobs, so the rate-scales get out of date and need correcting. I had written to Moscow to ask for the amendments, they had authorized them, but they'd sent only one copy of the letter. We have several shoe factories in the province, but only one typist in the soviet, she always has a pile of work, so the instruction could lie in her tray for a month or even two months. To make sure the work wasn't held up, especially as I was going to be away in Leningrad, I went to the factory, got the norm-scales from Bronevsky, wrote in, by hand, the amendments I had got from Moscow, and told him to recalculate the rates. But he was busy running from one office to another trying to get rations and coupons, and recalculated the rates only partly – some he did, some he didn't. The workers protested, Bronevsky blamed it all on me, showing them the scales which had my handwritten corrections, as well as older, smudged corrections, which had been written in before mine. The whole thing had a very unconvincing look. They were even more convinced by Bronevsky's accusations against me, as I was away in Leningrad and wasn't there to explain myself. Bronevsky was so certain of my defeat that he talked to me as if I were already finished.

'Look here at this scribbling of yours,' he said. 'Who can read that? Where did you get the figures from, the top of your head? And what do these words here mean? You call yourself a shoemaker!'

Again I don't want to burden you with detail, but every department has its own particular terminology, sometimes the same things are called by different names, and sometimes different things are known by the same name, but these were subtleties which a non-Russian like Bronevsky wouldn't know, especially someone as over-confident as he was. I didn't argue with him, I just looked through all the figures, saw the problem, then went back and said to Boitsov, 'Don't worry, it's not our fault. Let's call a meeting, invite a representative from Moscow and sort the whole thing out.'

Boitsov may have been a bit tired, as I said earlier, but at the same time he was experienced and he could be decisive at critical moments. He also knew that it would look bad for the factory if he let them ruin me, and no manager ever likes that to happen. Maybe he just didn't want to see me ruined, as he'd been through enough himself. In any case, he agreed with me.

A representative came from Moscow, we called a meeting, invited the craftsmen from the factories in all the districts, and let Bronevsky say his piece. He made a blustering speech, accusing me of ignorance, and mentioning terms he didn't even understand. He tried to worm his way into the workers' favour by pointing out that there was a carpet on the floor of Boitsov's office, where we were meeting, yet the showers in the factory usually didn't work, and he kept glancing at Kamenev. He had obviously set it all up with the old trouble-maker, it was she who had put him up to this particular 'unmasking'.

I made mincemeat of him, I can tell you. The representative from Moscow confirmed that I hadn't made anything up, instructions had been sent from Moscow. The craftsmen ridiculed Bronevsky because he hadn't understood the terminology. Kamenev instantly changed course and declared that she wouldn't allow businessmen from Warsaw to blacken the reputation of Soviet specialists. In fact, that little intrigue did him no good at all. I don't know what became of him later. After the meeting, I put in a request for a transfer to my home town; my own factory had written to ask whether I could be sent back.

Boitsov didn't want me to go. 'How did we offend you?'

'You didn't,' I replied. 'Family circumstances, I have to go home.'

'Oh well, love can't be forced,' he said. 'I've been very satisfied with your work. Remember us kindly.' He said it sincerely and I was touched.

I replied, 'Thank you for your consideration, Vasili Alexeyevich, I'll always remember you.' So we'd said good-bye properly and warmly. And that was good, because every job is a part of your life, and you should part with it decently.

In March 1941 I returned to my own town, my own home, and my own factory.

What can I say? Hearth and home. Everything's in flux, everything changes, the saying goes, people come, people go, but still when you come home to the town you were born and raised in, it's the same as it was, the same winds blow, the same rain falls, and the sun that shines is the same one as in your childhood.

You can imagine how pleased mother and father were to see me. On the other hand, my affair had ended in failure, my hopes hadn't been realized. Father said nothing about it, asked no questions; it was a man's own business, we'd been together, we'd parted. Mother tried to behave the same way, but she couldn't keep it up and blurted out something about 'that coquette'.

Gently but firmly I interrupted her. 'She never was that and never will be.' We didn't speak about Sonya again.

After Sonya and Bronevsky and the unpleasantness at my other job, I felt the security and calm of our home with par-ticular pleasure and satisfaction. Father was fifty-one, mother forty-eight, a wrinkle more, a wrinkle less, even wrinkles are an adornment on a beautiful person. Thirty years they had lived together, many days, cloudy days and clear days, mostly cloudy ones. You've seen the way a lonely tree on the seashore puts its roots down to the earth through the rock? It can resist gales and storms and the fierce, merciless waves of the sea. My parents' love was such a sturdy tree. It supported them, and it supported those near to them.

In the evenings everyone would be at home, mother would be ironing, warming up the heavy iron with wide swings of her arm – you remember, we used to have big, tall irons which had coal smouldering inside them, you could see the embers glowing red through small slits. Mother would wet her finger and put it near the iron to see if it was hot, then she would fill her mouth with water and spray it over the linen, which gave off a pleasant, homely smell of steam when it was pressed with the hot iron. As a matter of fact, when we were children we loved filling our mouths with water and spraying it over the ironing, and if mother wasn't too rushed and was in a good mood, she let us do it as a great favour.

Father would unfold a contour map on the table and call Olya and Igor, who would come running with their coloured pencils.

The year before, Lyuba had wanted to take Igor, but mother and father had said, 'Next autumn he starts school, take him then, let him stay here for the time being, the air's better here than in Leningrad.'

That's what was decided, so Igor spent the last summer of his life with us. What can I tell you about him? He was pale-skinned like his father. Lyuba was also blonde, but darker, whereas Volodya came from the north, and Igor took after him, a stocky, chubby little boy. The difference between them was that Volodya had a lot of self-restraint, whereas Igor, believe it or not, was just like his uncle Genrikh, my dear young brother, and I've told you what he was like as a child and how the whole street complained about him. Igor was growing up exactly like him. He even fought the way Genrikh used to, jumping on his enemy with fists and feet flying, stunning him by surprise, a typical hooligan's way of

239 •

fighting, and he was no more than seven years old. All the trees and roofs and barns were his stamping ground. He was always getting a bloody nose, or bruises, scraped knees and grazed elbows.

At the same time, he was a nice child; when I used to read to him he would lean towards me and listen attentively. And, you know, he had a certain noble quality – for instance, he would never hurt Olya. She was already in the third grade, a quiet, shy girl. She'd had to overcome aloofness, even hostility, in the house, and on top of that, you could never keep secrets from the children on the street, whatever their parents knew they knew – whose daughter she was, who her real father was, and so on. The whole story was mixed up in their minds and magnified by naïve childish cruelty, so Olya had been made to feel an outsider in every way, and you'd think little Igor, only seven years old, would want to join the pack in teasing her, but not a bit of it. Instead he got into fights defending her and wouldn't allow anyone to hurt her.

We treated Olya well, too. Mother came to accept her in time, perhaps she felt that this child had brought with her the ghost of Lyova, who had died so pointlessly. They spoke very little about Lyova, but they thought about him a lot. When mother gave a sudden sigh, or father became pensive, they were thinking of him.

So, father would open up the contour map, which was a wonderful device for introducing children to geography. They only had blue dotted lines and a few circles on them, and you had to draw in where the Volga was, and the Oka and the Kama, and you had to fill in the mountains with brown pencil and the lowlands in green. But that wasn't the main attraction. We used to start all journeys from our town, so first we would search along the Dnieper for where Kiev should be, measure the proper distance from there northwards to where Chernigov should be, then we would move northeast and mark a little cross for our town.

'And now,' father would say, 'we have a fair wind for our travels.'

We would cross the sands of the Karakum, climb the Pamirs, and turn back to the Caspian Sea; everyone would find his own route and try to outdo the others. They were happy evenings. Father had played with us older ones like that, then with Dina and Sasha, and now with Olya and Igor.

I used to like listening to Vadim Sinyavsky's football commentaries on the radio. You know, I never played football myself, but I'm a fan to this day. Sasha would be reading. His illnesses and ailments were a thing of the past, he was well-knit but still fragile and tender, not effeminate, but rather gentle, compassionate and trusting. To be honest, I felt a bit uneasy about him. Those were grim, austere times, you needed to be strong and occasionally flexible. I didn't think Sasha would be able to adapt to life, just as father had been unable to adapt in his time. Yet the fact is, my parents weren't concerned about Sasha. Well, what do I mean by 'not concerned'? Parents are forever concerned about their children, but mine were worried about Genrikh, an Air Force pilot! What about Sasha? Of course things would be hard for him, as for any gentle-natured boy, but for the time being he was at home with his parents, and when he grew up, we'd have to see. Bringing up seven children had taught my parents not to be anxious about them. Still, I was worried about Sasha.

Anyway, that's how we would pass practically every evening. Sometimes mother sewed. I remember just after I got back from Kalinin she turned her pale blue crêpe de Chine into a dress for Dina. Things weren't too good in dress manufacture at the time, and anyway, what with our budget, you can imagine. Dina had already finished school and was preparing to go to the Kiev Conservatory in the autumn. With her voice and her appearance, she had a great future to look forward to. But appearance and age make their own demands.

'I've got nothing to wear, nothing to go out in, I'm ashamed to be seen by people.'

It was the usual kind of thing girls say when they are trying to wangle something out of their parents.

'Listen to her!' mother was mocking. 'Nothing to go out in, naked she is, ashamed to be seen by people! You're not thinking about people, my girl, you're hoping your airman will turn up! You think the crêpe de Chine will make him love you more? Your father fell for me when I was wearing a plain cotton frock!'

That's what she said, but still she altered her dress for Dina, and bought her some new shoes and stockings, everything in fact a girl needs so as not to feel inferior to the others.

Grandmother used to come round with letters from her grandson Daniel, you remember, the one grandfather had brought up, Uncle Lazar's son. Daniel was on active service with the frontier troops.

Every time she got a letter from him, she would come and say, 'You read it!'

We understood, Uncle Lazar would be sleeping after having had a drop. Uncle Lazar worked with me at the factory, he still drank as before, not that you'd find him in a ditch, but he had to have a drop or he couldn't work, in other words he was an alcoholic, a sick man. He liked to philosophize and he used to look for other alcoholics to have his discussions with. He also liked to read, not library books, you understand. No, he would go to the bookshop on pay-day and buy anything they cared to wrap up for him. He had heaps of books at home, gathering dust, he was so disorganized, but he was a decent man. In time he became something of a crank, which grandfather found harder to take than his drunkenness.

Grandmother suffered, too. She would squint at the loudspeaker and listen to the commentator Sinyavsky, especially his pauses – you remember his famous pauses – after which he would shout, 'Goal!' She would sigh and say 'Does he drink?'

'Drink? Why drink?'

'He's got a husky voice.'

Father would wink at me. Grandmother was talking about Sinyavsky, but she was thinking about Lazar.

They'd had no luck with Lazar, and they'd had no luck with Yosif, who'd dug himself in at the dental surgery and stayed clear of grandfather's family.

Uncle Grisha was a different matter. If you remember, he was our celebrity, the best craftsman at the factory, always among the leading Stakhanovites, always suggesting improvements in production methods, an inventor, his name appeared on the Roll of Honour and in the regional press, he had a nice, friendly family, a wife, three sons and a daughter. Uncle Grisha was twenty-five when he married, and my mother had been sixteen, so my cousins were like nieces and nephews to me.

Father would read Daniel's letter out loud, and grandmother would sigh and wipe her tears away. He was her favourite grandson, he had grown up without a mother and his father was a drunkard. Then, to get her mind off her sad thoughts, she would look at the map father was colouring in with the children.

'What beautiful hands you've got, Yakov,' said grandmother.

I remember one evening, from the next room we suddenly heard Sasha scream. Mother put down her sewing and went in there. It turned out that Dina had tied one of Sasha's teeth to the door-knob and given it a pull, you know the way children do that.

Mother pulled out the tooth with her fingers and said, 'Ninny! Look at you, here you are, planning to get married – better get some brains in your head first! Is that how you're going to look after your own children?'

Dina looked at Sasha with scorn, 'Mummy's boy!'

And so it went. Was I bored? Well, how shall I put it? All my friends had married and moved away, I was the only one left. At thirty I didn't feel like going dancing, I was chief of production, came home late, and I knew nothing outside factory and home, all my hopes were pinned on the summer when the vacationers would come, and there would be some of our own local people coming home on holiday. In fact, in late May some of my old friends, from childhood and youth, began to arrive, and they were all amazed to find me here, in the sticks, and me with a diploma, but without any prospects. They all said I should move to an industrial centre somewhere, and I knew they were right, but circumstances didn't permit me.

Without any doubt, my parents' material position had improved, but it wasn't exactly brilliant. Only Lyuba and Yefim sent them something. Genrikh was willing to do anything and his salary was getting better, but he was a young man, he wanted to do all sorts of things, and he'd got himself a motorbike, which in those days was the same as owning a car today.

As a matter of fact, my coming back home was very welcome, I had good wages, I was living at home, what did I need besides? A packet of cigarettes a day, the baths, the barber – the barber incidentally was still the same, Bernard Semyonovich, a bit aged, but still going strong. So I decided, let Dina start at the Conservatory, Lyuba will take Igor, meanwhile I'll go on helping my parents, after all Sasha and Olya were still small, they had to get on their feet, and in a year or two I'll push off, maybe to Kharkov, or Kiev, or Dnepropetrovsk, anyway to an industrial centre where I'd have more prospects. Of course, I wouldn't forget the family, I'd go on helping.

It wasn't fated to happen. On the twenty-second of June 1941, war broke out.

15 ❖

The war began on the twenty-second of June, and on the twenty-third I was called up and sent to Bryansk for posting.

What should I say? You all lived through it. I won't try to describe mother's state of mind, it was the same as all the other mothers' in Russia. Genrikh was in the Air Force, Lyuba and Volodya were called up as army surgeons, Uncle Grisha was called up, and Uncle Lazar's son, Daniel, was serving already on the western frontier. I would never have thought it would be far worse for those who remained behind. Those who were sent to the front and died, at least died on the battlefield, as soldiers. We know now that those who were left behind perished, but how could we know then? Could I have imagined that the Germans would reach Moscow and Stalingrad?

I've already mentioned that I did my training in the artillery, so it was to the artillery that I was posted, as a gun-commander. Then, during the winter on the Bryansk front, near Mtsensk, we captured a German officer; he was taken to the divisional headquarters to be interrogated by the divisional commander, Colonel Shchokin, himself. The German was being insolent, the interpreter was only a young girl, fresh from language school, she had to keep on looking in the dictionary, the German was pretending not to understand anything. The colonel was losing his temper, which was understandable, as our counter-offensive was taking place on the neighbouring western front and it was embarrassing for the divisional commander to have to send a captured enemy officer to army headquarters to extract the necessary information, thereby wasting precious time.

My artillery commander, who happened to be at the command-post, told Colonel Shchokin that he had a certain Ivanovsky in the regiment, a gun-commander, who spoke German like a native. That was true, father's native language was German and I spoke it as well as I spoke Russian. They brought me to the command-post, I went in, stood to attention, as I was supposed to do, and reported to the colonel that I was there on his orders. He told me to interrogate the German, to find out who he was and where he was from, what was his unit, what was in front of us and behind us, what was to the left, what was to the right, what was the name of his commanding officer – in other words to get the whole picture. To judge from the embarrassment on the interpreter's face and the smirk on the German's, I could guess what had happened and I decided I was going to crack the German, come what may. I told him I had been ordered to question him, and I suggested he should give precise, detailed and truthful answers. My first question was, surname, first name, rank, unit, and job. He took me for another German and asked me if I was.

I told him, 'I ask the questions, you give the answers, and be quick about it, if you don't mind.'

He nodded towards the interpreter and said he'd already answered all the questions he was going to.

'I'm not interested in anything you said before I arrived,' I replied. 'You will please answer my questions.'

Arrogantly he declared he would have nothing to do with a traitor and wouldn't say another word.

In Russian I asked Colonel Shchokin if he would let the prisoner stand up.

'Carry on,' he replied.

I ordered the German to get up. He got up.

I said to him, 'I'm going to ask you for the last time, are you going to answer my questions?'

He looked at me with contempt and said nothing. I'm afraid war is war and they weren't going to be allowed to treat us like that, so I gave him a punch in the face that sent him flying into a corner.

Colonel Shchokin said, 'Steady on, stick to the rules.'

I replied, 'Everything'll be all right, comrade Colonel.'

The German was lying in the corner, eyeing me and my fists like a rabbit. They're brave people, all right, when they're doing the beating up, but not when they're on the receiving end. I told him to get up, and he did.

I said to him, very calmly, 'If you don't answer me right now, I'm going to take you outside and shoot you like a dog, and if you lie to me, even one word, I'll still shoot you like a dog. Your life depends on the first thing you say.'

He answered my questions, I translated, the interpreter scribbled away, the colonel and the staff commander, Lieutenant-Colonel Lebedev, put more questions, which I asked in German, then translated into Russian, and we really took him apart.

After this incident Colonel Shchokin transferred me to divisional intelligence, with the rank of second lieutenant, especially as I had a higher education. But as you know, we didn't take prisoners every day, and intelligence is a job like any other, you have to work, so in time I became a straight-forward intelligence officer, a platoon commander in an intelligence company. As I could speak and look like a German, my job was to go behind enemy lines. The security organs tried to recruit me, but Shchokin, who was by then a general and a rifle-corps commander, wouldn't give me up, and I spent the whole war in military intelligence, first at divisional level, then corps, reaching the rank of guards major. And this despite the fact that I hadn't been a regular officer, that my father was from Switzerland and my parents were in occupied territory, hardly the best of personal records. At the front, however, they weren't too bothered about your background, it wasn't personal records that were doing the fighting, it was human beings; you were judged by what you were and what you could do.

People only know about intelligence from what they've seen in the movies. Our daring agent is operating right under Hitler's nose, dressed immaculately, clean-shaven and perfumed, leading Himmler, Bormann and Kaltenbrunner up the garden path, as well as Müller, the head of the Gestapo, and of course, as we know all their plans, it's easy to fight them.

The intelligence I was involved in was nothing like that, the army couldn't sit and wait until Himmler and Bormann were led into a trap in Berlin. An army acts, intelligence has to supply up-to-date information on the enemy, regardless of everything; we would go through snowstorms, blizzards, marshes and fords, wade through rivers, then dry out somewhere and have a quick change of underwear. They say you have to be bold, decisive and quick for intelligence work. That's true, but the most important thing is to be able to find your way, at night, without a compass, to be able to remember every bush, every tree, to be able to hear every sound, the slightest rustle, you have to be able to merge with your surroundings, to melt into them. As for boldness, well, when you're out on a search, you can't exactly hide yourself, you have to act.

My cousin Daniel was killed in the first battles of the war on the western frontier. At the same time, or shortly after, Uncle Grisha was surrounded with his unit and disappeared without trace. In 1942, my brother Genrikh was shot down and killed as a fighter-pilot; Vadim Pavlovich Sokolov and Georgy Koshelyov were also killed. They were heroes, aces! They had shot down many enemy planes, but war is war, and even aces get killed.

My sister Lyuba worked in a field hospital, I corresponded with her and with Volodya. I also kept in contact with Yefim, who was by then the manager of a factory turning out tanks, and a very important man.

As for the rest of the family, they were all in German-occupied territory. I realized the fate that had overtaken them, that had overtaken everyone who remained in occupied territory. During the war we saw what the Hitlerites did to the Soviet people. It wasn't violence by individual soldiers it was a broadly conceived and remorselessly executed programme of the destruction of entire peoples.

'Human life in the countries concerned is worth absolutely nothing ... A terrorizing effect can only be achieved by means of exceptional cruelty.' These words are from an order issued by Field-Marshal Keitel.

'If tens of thousands of Russian women die from exhaustion, digging anti-tank ditches, it interests me only in so far as the ditches for Germany have been dug or not.' Thus said Himmler.

'This vast expanse . . . must be pacified as quickly as possible . . . The best way to do this is to shoot anyone who so much as gives you a sideways glance.' That was Hitler himself.

Perhaps they were just casual phrases, you say all sorts of things in the heat of the moment, especially in wartime?

Have you got a copy of the transcription of the Nuremberg trial? You have? Look at volume 3, pages 337 and 338, you'll find this quotation from Hitler:

'In the near future, we shall occupy territory with a very high proportion of Slavs, and we shall not be able to rid ourselves of them very quickly. We shall have to destroy the population as part of our mission to protect the German population. We will have to develop the technique of destroying population . . . I have in mind the destruction of entire racial entities . . . If I send the flower of the German nation into the thick of war, shedding precious German blood without the least pity, then without doubt I have the right to destroy millions of people of inferior race . . . One of our basic tasks at all times will be to halt the development of the Slav races. The natural instincts of all living creatures urge them not only to overcome their enemies, but to destroy them.'

There, so to speak, you have Hitler's general programme, to destroy nations, above all the Slavs. What about the Jews? The destruction of the Jews served as a kind of laboratory, where the Hitlerites could try their hand and acquire experience for the mass extermination of the other peoples.

I repeat, I realized the fate that had overtaken my family and relatives and the people of my country. Yet I kept a glimmer of hope. Hope for what? A miracle? In such situations you hope for miracles, too. But not only miracles. My hopes were pinned on our Chernigov forest-land. According to tradition, Chernigov gets its name from the deep forest in which it was founded. Names like Sosnitsy and Starodub also suggest mighty forests. They were still there in the north of the province, where our town was. It was in the forests of Yelin, Zlynka, Novozybkov, Bleshnyansk and others, that the partisan group, led by Fedorov, was active. Fedorov, by the way, had been secretary of the Chernigov regional party committee before the war. Not far from us was Putivl, in the province of Sumy, where the famous Kovpak started his partisan activities. I pinned my hopes on the partisans, and on the forests, and on the character of the people back home. I knew they wouldn't give up their lives so easily.

It goes without saying that unarmed people, especially old men, women and children, are defenceless before armed soldiers. When people say, how could six million people let themselves be slaughtered like sheep, then they are either scoundrels or fools to say so, or they've never been under enemy bullets, or looked down the barrel of the enemy's gun, or heard the rattle of machine-gun fire. How many of our own prisoners of war perished in concentration camps, healthy young lads? What would you have them do? Throw themselves on to the barbed-wire fence? Crawl away under machine-gun fire? It's all very well to talk of heroism, as long as you're not lying in the freezing snow in a blizzard, with an electrified barbed-wire fence all round you, and guards standing on watch-towers with machine-guns at the ready, and they haven't given you anything to eat or drink for three, maybe four days in a row, and when they do, it's only a mouldy potato or a piece of rotten fish. As a matter of fact, people did escape from the camps, they did throw themselves at their guards, and creep up on the machine-guns, it all happened. As for those who couldn't escape, or throw themselves on to the barbed wire, or run unarmed at the machine-gun fire, we should not judge them, either. The instinct of self-preservation is supreme as long as there is a flicker of hope, and if there isn't such acts are purely suicidal – and there were plenty of suicides, too.

Our town was liberated in September 1943, and Yefim was there in November. He had been called to Moscow by the State Defence Committee and given an important assignment on tank output, which they knew he would deliver, as he was always as good as his word. Then, by the way, they asked him if he had any personal needs, they usually asked him that, and he usually said he hadn't. On that occasion, however, he asked for permission to visit his home, he wanted to find out what had happened to his parents. That was some request to make just at the moment he'd been given an urgent job to do, and in wartime when days, hours and minutes were vital. He had thousands of people working under him, he could have sent a couple of sensible chaps to the town, and they could have got to the bottom of everything for him. But you don't send agents and special messengers to find the pit where your mother and father were shot, or the ground which has been stained with the blood of your family, for that you go yourself. Naturally, if they had refused, he would have complied, but they didn't, they gave him a plane and a day for the journey.

Yefim spent the day in the town, then returned to his factory and wrote to me that all the family had been shot, not one of them had been left alive. Though nobody could be more precise than that, still it seemed likely that they had all perished.

A few months later, in January or February 1944, I got a letter from Lyuba. She had visited our town, as her hospital wasn't far from it, she'd spent two days there and had been able to find out a bit more: a commission was already at work on the atrocities committed by the Nazi German invaders and, according to Lyuba, the Jewish population had been exterminated, perhaps as much as a year before our troops had arrived. It also turned out that Uncle Grisha had managed to escape from German encirclement and get back to the town, where he had joined the partisans. The information about father differed, some said they'd hanged him, others that they'd taken him away somewhere as he was half-German. She didn't write a word about Igor, she couldn't bring herself to write about him. Poor Lyuba! Up to this day she doesn't believe he perished and is still hoping for something. More of that later.

In October 1944 I got two weeks' leave and went home. We were on the Vistula, at the Magnushev beach-head and we needed a 'canary', a prisoner who would talk, but somehow we couldn't get hold of one, the Germans were so deeply entrenched. So I went with some of the boys well behind enemy lines and picked up three at once. We spent four days behind German lines; German troops were everywhere, as you can imagine. Anyway, we got three of them, they were fishing in a stream, but they got hooked instead. For that operation we got some leave given to us, and I went home.

In the course of the two weeks I found out quite a bit.

Then later, after the war and demobilization, I went there again.

Step by step I put together the circumstances of my parents' deaths. It wasn't easy. The dead had turned to dust. But troops and people who had been evacuated were coming home and were asking about their families and friends from anyone who might be able to tell them something, grains of information, fragments of the truth. People were discovered who had miraculously escaped shooting, crawled out of the grave, gone to the partisans. In time, I put together a picture, certainly not a full one, but at least a probable picture of what had happened to my family. I don't intend to tell you the story of this ghetto, I don't know it, nobody does. It was a little one, and it was shortlived. No written accounts of it have survived, it doesn't figure in official documents, it was simply wiped off the face of the earth. Anyway, what is there to add to the history of the ghettoes, they have been described in hundreds of books. It was the same everywhere, they tormented and tortured the people, then they killed them. What can you add to that? I wanted to know about my own family, however, and I want to tell you about that. Of course, the circumstances they were in were exceptional, indescribable, a normal person can't imagine them, no account can convey how they were tormented and suffered and died.

A black night had fallen on the town. Many years I have wandered in that gloom, along the same streets, there and back and there again. And the ghosts of the tormented wander with me from house to house. There are no screams or moans, not a whisper, only a deathly silence. But I knew them all so well – father, mother, my sister, my brother, my nephews, grandfather, grandmother, my uncles – that sometimes it seems to me that what happened to them happened to me, too, and that when I'm talking about them I'm talking about myself. Even so, my story will only be a pale shadow of what really took place.

16 🕸

Why weren't my family evacuated? Well, at the beginning nobody thought the Germans would get as far as us. Of course, there was the first shock of their sudden attack and their rapid advance, but actually it was only rapid in the first weeks of the war, after which they slowed down to twenty or thirty kilometres a day. Then, our resistance grew, and in fierce defensive battles we hammered their regular troops and destroyed their equipment, and the Germans themselves admitted that in the summer of 1941 they lost more than half a million men and 3,500 planes. We delivered strong counter-blows and undermined their offensive capability so much that their advance was slowed to as little as two or three kilometres a day, and in several areas their main forces were tied down and marking time. This also put paid to their idea of finishing the war before the winter set in, it wrecked their plan for a *Blitzkrieg*.

The Germans were aiming their main thrust towards Moscow, that is, to the north of our town, and therefore the people didn't see the advancing German troops. On the contrary, they saw Soviet troops moving westwards, reinforcements for the armies that were delaying the enemy's advance, and this strengthened the town's belief that the enemy would not reach this far.

However, in August the Germans, who hadn't been able to break through on our western front, moved their main forces to the flanks. Their Second Army and Second Tank Group, totalling some twenty-five divisions, were moved south in order to get deep into the rear of our south-western front. Then our Twenty-first Army, in whose zone our town was, had to retreat to the south, towards the Desna, in order to avoid being encircled, and this meant that our town, suddenly abandoned by our troops, found itself between two enemy wedges, the Second Army coming from the west, and the Second Tank Group coming from the east.

As a result, the question of evacuation arose unexpectedly, not everyone was prepared for it, and much had to be left behind that couldn't be taken out.

The chance to leave, however, did exist. Escort troops were provided at the last minute, and people did get out. They had to hurry, they had to decide immediately.

My parents didn't make up their minds. Why? Mother didn't want to leave.

'Haven't I seen Germans?' she said. 'You think I didn't live in Basel, you think it was someone else? They're a civilized nation, cultured, decent people. You should see the way they all go to church and how they respect their dead – every Sunday they go to the cemetery in black suits, with their boots polished and carrying umbrellas. Perhaps you think I dreamt it? Anyway, never mind about Switzerland, here right next door you've got Ivan Karlovich and Stanislava Frantsevna, they're also Germans. Can you say one bad word about them? What about the German colonists? Has one of them ever swindled you by so much as a kopek? Everything they say about them is nonsense. Do they kill their wives, their old folks and their children? Show me one person they touched in 1918.'

That was the way mother thought. She is no longer with us, so we shouldn't judge her too harshly. Unfortunately, she wasn't the only one who thought like that.

Grandfather didn't want to go, either. He was eighty-one and grandmother was seventy-six. Evacuation? What, and be a burden to everyone? Grandfather was a proud and fearless old man, he had never run away from anyone, he had been born and raised here, he had already faced all kinds of misfortune, he was prepared to face new ones now. He didn't leave. Uncle Lazar said they must go, he discussed the whole thing thoroughly and philosophized about it, and didn't go anywhere. He was a weak man.

As for Uncle Yosif and his wife, they couldn't bring themselves to part with all their possessions; they counted on being able to buy themselves off, and were destroyed by their greed.

Finally, there was Uncle Grisha's wife. Where could she go with four children?

In all there were sixteen members of the family left, grandfather was eighty-one. Igor was seven.

The only one who was categorically in favour of leaving was my father. Though he was half-German himself, he wanted to get his family away from the Germans. But where to? Deep into the rear? As a half-German, and being Swissborn on top of it, things could be very hard for him there, too. Mother wouldn't listen to him.

'You want to go, go!' she said. 'I'm not moving one step from this place.'

Perhaps in due course he might have convinced her, but there was to be no 'in due course', everything had to be done in minutes, and these minutes were lost. The ones who got out were those who had waited for the escort troops at the railway station. Those who paused to think were left behind.

Then the Germans came. Their planes flew over in the morning, dropping a few bombs but doing very little damage, a couple of sheds were burned down at the New Market. Later that day their motor-cyclists raced down the deserted streets, while everyone hid behind locked doors and closed shutters. Only paralysed Yankel was outside, sitting on the porch as always, with his legs crossed, warming himself in the melancholy autumn sun, and smiling blissfully. He was an old man by then, and grey, but he still had the face of a child and a child's smile. A machine-gunner fired off a burst at him.

Paralysed Yankel was the town's first victim of the Nazi German invaders.

After that everything went according to a certain system: registration, sewing on the yellow six-pointed star, the order to move into the ghetto within twenty-four hours. The streets designated for the ghetto were Sand Street, Hospital Street, Trench Street, and the side-streets connecting them.

I won't describe the scene of the people moving into the ghetto, everybody knows what it was like. Bundles and bags, prams, frail old men, babes-in-arms, sick people on stretchers and in wheelbarrows. Nobody dared disobey. The minute the Germans entered the town, everyone knew they had been naïve, they knew what was coming to them.

One man only refused to submit, one man wouldn't leave his house and move into the ghetto. That was Khaim Yagudin, the ex-sergeant. He was already eighty, completely shrivelled, lame, yet he was still touchy and ready to make trouble. His children begged him to go with them, but he flatly refused. He rushed around the house, stomped about on the creaking floor-boards and out on to the rickety veranda, banged with his stick on the broken rail, and shouted and yelled, he didn't understand and didn't want to understand why he had to leave his own house. By what law? For what reason, he wanted to know? By order of the German commandant? Let him order his Krauts about if he liked, he was their commandant, not Khaim Yagudin's! If this commandant, this German-*shmerman*, wanted to know, nobody had the right even to enter his, Khaim's, house, even under the Tsar his house had been exempt from requisitioning as a billet, damn them, the swines, the sons of bitches! He wasn't going to budge, he'd show those sausage-makers!

What were his daughters and daughters-in-law to do? Stay with him? They had tiny children, should they deny them life because of an old man's obstinacy?

Khaim Yagudin remained in his house and met the Germans alone, standing in the middle of his 'drawing room', against the background of the enormous tumbledown cupboard with most of its glazing gone. He stood there, leaning on his stick, shrivelled and lame, his grey cropped hair thin on his head, his whiskers still red, and he looked at the Germans with his eyes bulging. Then he noticed the ghetto police and among them Golubinsky, the railway mechanic.

'Golubinsky, you rat, you've gone over to them!' Yagudin raised his stick and went for him.

He never got that far. A German officer took out his pistol and shot him. Khaim Yagudin was the second victim of the German Fascist invaders.

So there was a ghetto. I ought to mention that the Soviet Jews weren't even sent to Auschwitz or Maidanek, they were shot right where they were, on the spot. By the spring of 1942, those responsible for the extermination could proudly report that the area in question had been freed of Jews, it was *Judenfrei*. As a rule ghettoes weren't formed in the small towns, at most there were assembly points from which the people were dispatched for shooting. Ours was a proper ghetto, the only one, I think, so far to the east. Why did they create it? Because of the forest!

Of course there were enterprises in the town that the Germans needed, like the shoe factory, the garment factory, the tannery, the sugar refinery, in fact all the things I've told you about. However, all that was unimportant, they were going to exterminate the Jews without regard to anything. But the forest! Beautiful timber, enormous old pines and oaks – industrial felling here had long been prohibited as there was plenty of timber in the north. The Germans, though, didn't get to the north, and they needed the timber, so they started felling and transporting ours. What labour could they use for this? What did they find here? There were no timber-yards, no equipment, no forest roads, no timber-workers. There was nothing. What about mobilizing the local population? The men were all in the army. The collective farm workers? Who would work the land for them? There was only one other possibility, the Jews! There were several thousand Jews! Let them be tree-fellers, sawyers and cutters, they can be tractors and carry the timber on their backs, they can be cranes and lift the timber up on to the trucks with their bare hands.

Working for twelve hours a day and living virtually without food, people were dying after two or three months. That was just perfect! The timber was being got out and the Jews were being killed off. Naturally, it goes without saying there was shooting as well, the sick and crippled, children and old folks, but it was done as a matter of course, for disobedience, breaking the rules, a sideways glance, disrespect. As for the rest, let them go on working the timber, even if they're about to drop dead, they'll be shot in due course anyway. In this way the economic and the political aims were being achieved at the same time. And those in the factories could go on working, too, under guard of course, also for twelve hours a day and without pay.

There were at most one hundred and twenty or one hundred and thirty houses inside the ghetto, and into them they packed three thousand people, and then a week later another four thousand from near-by towns and villages. These are only rough figures, of course, nobody knows precisely. They slept on floors and tables, in attics, in barns and granaries, under awnings, or simply out in the open in yards or on the streets. It was already autumn, winter was coming on, the congestion was appalling, but there was nowhere else to go, they were surrounded by barbed wire, there was only one entrance to the ghetto, at the end of Sand Street, and that was guarded by soldiers in green uniforms, carrying machine-guns, with *Gott mit uns!* engraved on their belt-buckles.

More than fifty people found shelter in grandfather's house. Grandfather, grandmother, Uncle Lazar, Uncle Grisha's wife and children, my parents, Dina, Sasha, Olya and Igor, all the Kuznetsovs – their house was in Sand Street, but at the far end and outside the ghetto, so they had come to us, all twenty-one of them. There was old man Kuznetsov and his wife, their daughters with their husbands, their daughters and sons-in-law, daughters-in-law whose husbands were at the front, and finally half a dozen grandchildren. One of the daughters-in-law, Masha, was in her last month of pregnancy and gave birth soon after moving to us. Liza Elkin, the only midwife in the ghetto, delivered her in a back-room in case the Germans heard the baby's first cries, which could easily turn out to be its last. Next day, Masha took pity on her baby, she didn't stuff its mouth with a rag, some Germans who were making their rounds heard the baby cry, and the commandant, Stalbe, arrived. He looked at the infant, smiled, stroked its head and held something black under its nose.

Then he asked, 'Who delivered this baby?'

My grandmother Rakhlenko replied, 'I did.'

'Have you been doing this sort of thing long?'

'All my life,' she replied.

'Well, now, you can come with us, we'll be needing you,' Stalbe said.

He took grandmother away. She went in her black dress and black lace shawl, just as she used to go to the synagogue, and she even took her prayer-book with her, can you imagine!

An hour later the baby died. I've read somewhere that the Nazis usually killed off new-born babies with that poison.

After another hour grandfather was summoned to the commandant's office and told to take his wife's corpse away, my grandmother Rakhlenko had been shot for disobeying the order which prohibited Jews from taking any part in midwifery and forbade Jewish women to give birth. Grandmother's dress and shawl had been removed, her prayer-book had fallen a little way away. Grandfather was allowed to pick it up.

Grandmother Rakhlenko was seventy-six years old when she was shot outside the commandant's office, the fourth victim of the Nazi German invaders. She had saved Liza Elkin's life, more babies would be born in the ghetto, the midwife would be needed. Quiet and unnoticed in the house, grandmother was quiet in the face of death as she gave her children their last lesson, unnoticed. We had loved her, but I don't think we had said more than a dozen kind words to her in all her life, we hadn't given her all she deserved.

Apart from the Kuznetsovs, we also had the teacher Kuras living with us, and his wife, his daughter and granddaughter Bronya. Then there was the family of the old widow Gorodetsky – you remember, the poor widow from the Old Market. Her daughters had married friends of their brothers, also workers at the depot, two of them incidentally had married Russians and had children, but more about that later. The Gorodetsky family numbered twelve people.

There were also men and women from the town of Sosnitsy, able-bodied all of them. I want to emphasize that. The four thousand people who had been driven out of the other towns and villages were all able-bodied men and women, their children and old folks had been left where they were. There were eighteen children in the house, the oldest was Venya Rakhlenko, Uncle Grisha's son, who was seventeen, the youngest was Tanya Kuznetsov, who was four. Tanya had a different name, which I don't know, so I call all the Kuznetsov grandchildren Kuznetsov, just as I call all the Gorodetsky grandchildren Gorodetsky, though they had other names, too. Five of the children were made to march off to work, just like the adults, they were Dina, Venya, Sasha, Vitya, and Bronya.

The Germans didn't simply destroy the Jews, they wanted to exterminate them like animals, not like human beings; it was easier and simpler to treat them like cattle. To turn people into cattle, you first have to destroy what is human in them, you have to kill off everything that makes them human beings, above all you have to destroy their dignity.

They made them sew on the yellow six-pointed star, locked them up in the ghetto, forbade them to go out, except to work, and then in columns watched by soldiers and Alsatian dogs, they forbade them to contract contagious diseases, the sick were shot at once, they forbade them to give birth, the newly born were destroyed, as I've already described, they forbade them to bring food or firewood into the ghetto, they forbade them to eat or drink anything other than bread, potatoes and water, they turned off the electricity, forbade them to bring in flowers from the fields, or to teach their children to read and write, or to wash in the baths, and women were not allowed to use make-up. Dozens of prohibitions, and for breaking any one of them, you were shot.

All the furniture had to be listed, and if so much as a bedside table was left out, you were shot. They ordered all objects of gold and silver to be handed in, ornaments, rings, brooches, money. This was done, but not by everyone and not everything, after all when you're being robbed, you try to save something. So there were continual searches, everyone had to kneel facing the wall and anyone found in possession of money or valuables was shot on the spot. One such was Sima, a daughter of the old widow Gorodetsky, they found a worthless ring on her. Sima had two sons, Vitya and Motya, and right in front of them the Germans shot their mother.

A group of sixteen people were the fifth victims of the German Fascist invaders. I'll stop counting with them, I can't count all those who were exterminated.

17 ▨

Sixteen people were shot for 'deceiving the authorities', a fine of five hundred thousand roubles was imposed on the rest, and fifty male hostages, all fathers of families, were taken until the ransom was paid. Kuznetsov's son-in-law Meyer, a baker, was taken from our house. It was impossible to find five hundred thousand, half a million, after everything had already been taken from the locals, and those who had been driven here from their own towns had brought nothing at all. Where could such money be found, anyway? There were rich people, certainly, Uncle Yosif, for instance, but they were a handful, and as it happened they didn't give anything, for reasons you will learn later. The ransom wasn't collected and the hostages were shot. They were shot in the same pine forest where the summer vacationers used to come with their hammocks, by the veranda where Oryol used to sell his *kefir*, and where now ditches had been dug. The forest was alongside the ghetto, everyone heard the bursts of machine-gun fire and knew that their sons, and fathers, and brothers and husbands were being shot. It hadn't been possible to collect the ransom, the ghetto had already been stripped. To make up for it, when they were ordered to hand over anything made of fur, like coats, hats, collars, cuffs, they gave up everything to the last tuft, even though they were working in the forest at freezing temperatures.

The commandant of the ghetto was SS man Stalbe, the supreme master who decided who should live and who should die. The immediate control of the ghetto's affairs, however, was in the hands of the *Judenrat*, or Jewish Council, which the Germans appointed, and its chairman was my Uncle Yosif, the only one in our family who agreed to collaborate with the Germans, ignoring even the fact that they had shot his own mother. He had made an error in not being evacuated, and to make up for it he decided that, with all his wealth, he ought not to take a back seat, he ought to occupy a prominent position, so he became chairman of the *Judenrat*. It must be said that not all chairmen of Jewish Councils were like Uncle Yosif. A lot of them sabotaged the inhuman orders issued by the occupiers and did all they could to preserve and improve the lives of the people, for which they were duly shot. In the end all those who collaborated in the Jewish Councils were exterminated, good and bad, but we judge people by the way they lived, not by the way they died. Death can atone for much when it is a purposeful act. In Uncle Yosif's case it wasn't that. He died in a special way, as I'll describe later.

My father put on the yellow star and moved with mother and the children to grandfather's house, as ours wasn't inside the ghetto. As his mother was pure German he was what the Germans officially called a 'half-caste'.

Their treatment of such people wasn't very clear, it seems. Some they killed right away, others they killed in due course, and others still weren't touched at all but were allowed to live outside the ghetto and not wear the yellow star.

The *Gross Wannsee Protocol*, you know what that is? You've heard of it, but you don't remember. Well, I've collected a file of extracts from various documents, all of them published. These are the most interesting ones.

Why are they interesting? Because they show the vileness to which people can sink. The *Gross Wannsee Protocol* is among them.

According to this *Protocol*, 'persons of mixed origin' were divided into two categories: half-Jews were first category, and quarter-Jews were second category. The first category counted as Jews and were subject to extermination, the second counted as Germans and were not subject to extermination, except in the following instances. I quote: '(a) unfavourable racial features, making the individual look like a Jew; (b) bad police record, showing that the person regards himself as a Jew and behaves accordingly.'

There were many other points in the *Protocol* to make quite sure that nobody, God forbid, should escape shooting, but it was issued at the end of January 1942, and whether or not it reached all executives, especially in areas of military operations, is uncertain. I doubt it. In our town, for instance, two half-Jewish women survived, I met them and talked to them. There had been six of them originally, they had been arrested, interrogated, released, re-arrested, sent to Chernigov, brought back, taken back again. Four of them were eventually shot, but these two remained alive as evidence that the *Gross Wannsee Protocol* was not observed everywhere.

If I could find these women alive even after the war, then in 1941, when everyone was being herded into the ghetto and those six were left outside, the whole community would have known about it, especially as two of the widow Gorodetsky's daughters were married to depot workers, and their children, who were half-Russian, were not put inside the ghetto; the mothers were put inside, but not the children, they were left with their Russian fathers outside, though eventually they were shot, too.

My father could have declared himself to be half-German, but he didn't, he registered himself as a Jew and went into the ghetto with the rest of the family. The Nazis didn't go out of their way to find people they could be kind to; if you wanted them to show mercy you had to make an effort; if you didn't make an effort and considered yourself a Jew, then you could be a Jew and share the fate of the Jews.

What did mother feel about this? Apparently she didn't insist that father get out of the ghetto. I think I understand her. They still didn't know what 'the final solution of the Jewish question' meant. They had seen the ditches dug in the forest, every day they went past them, but they still had no idea that those ditches were their future, their fate. True, death dogged them at every step, they were starving, the work was beyond their endurance, and there was the shooting for no reason. Nevertheless, they were still together! Certainly mother must have known that six half-Jewish women had been allowed to stay outside the ghetto, but like everyone else she also knew they were always being dragged to the police for questioning, taken off to Chernigov, brought back and taken away again, and that their fate was uncertain. Mother was afraid for father. Even if he managed to get out of the ghetto, there was no knowing what lay in store for him, they could cart him off somewhere and she wouldn't know how he was. She must have felt it was better for him to stay with her, the children were also with her and she would be able to protect them, she thought. In those dark days, everything had been destroyed, only the family remained, they clung together as they had clung together for thirty years. They had been through so much, they would go through this, too.

Like father and Dina, mother worked in the forest, and it was the most exhausting work. The distribution of jobs was in the hands of the *Judenrat*, whose chairman was Uncle Yosif, mother's brother, and with his help she could have got a job doing something in a factory. Mother didn't like Yosif, but when it's a matter of life and death you don't let that stand in the way. However, father and Dina worked in the forest, she wanted to be with them, and so she was.

Every day, at four in the morning when it was still dark, columns of workers formed up on the street, shouted and cursed at by the police, lashed, whipped and beaten with rifle-butts, and menaced by snarling dogs. Move, move, move! Don't stop to think! Form ranks of ten, join hands! You're too slow – a bullet! Forward, march! At the double, at the double! Faster, faster! Someone falls behind – a bullet! And so on until they reached the forest. Then twelve hours of hard labour, and anyone who dropped from exhaustion at work got a bullet. Anyone who lagged behind on the way home also got a bullet. They staggered back in the dark of the late evening, carrying those who couldn't walk, stumbling along through the mud and snow, then along the middle of the street, which was deserted, either because of the curfew which applied to the entire population, or perhaps because the inhabitants were scared to go out after dark.

Once, when the exhausted column was dragging itself along the dark empty street, harried by the police, my mother noticed Golubinsky's wife on the pavement. You remember her? She was married to a depot mechanic and had been in love with my father once upon a time, she used to go to see him when he worked in the butcher's shop. There she was, dressed in a good winter coat and warm headscarf, walking along the wooden sidewalk alongside the column, looking at father. He wasn't the handsome Yakov Ivanovsky they used to call 'the Frenchman' any more, now he was a skeleton in filthy rags. But she still recognized him, and she walked alongside the column, looking at him. How she looked at him I can't say. With love? What love could she have felt after thirty years? Maybe she was remembering how she had been in love? Maybe. Sometimes the memory is stronger than the thing itself. Maybe she looked at him with pain, pity, sympathy. I don't know. But I do know how mother felt about it.

In a loud voice, so that a lot of people, including no doubt the Golubinsky woman, could hear, she said, 'Policeman's whore!' – her husband was the chief of the ghetto police.

The fact was, Mrs Golubinsky wasn't just looking for father. Certainly, people's lives connect in the most unusual ways. In this case, however, there was nothing unusual. It was a small town, the people had lived together all their lives, everyone knew everyone else, and though the ghetto was cut off from the rest of the population, they all knew what was going on inside it. There was nothing odd in the fact that the Golubinsky woman was standing on the street just at the moment when the column of labourers was being herded back from the forest, and that she was looking out for my mother and father. The unusual and surprising thing was something else: she was searching for my mother and signalling to her by her glance that she wanted to talk to her. Mother understood, and although she had once regarded Mrs Golubinsky as public enemy number one, she nevertheless went to meet her, despite the fact that any contact between the inhabitants of the town and the inmates of the ghetto was forbidden on pain of shooting.

After the war, no, actually it was during the war, in 1944, when I went there on leave, I met Mrs Golubinsky. Her fate had been a sad one. Her husband had taken part in Nazi exterminations, and been hanged for it by our people. That was what he deserved, he had been a beast. The best thing for her to do would have been to go away somewhere else – the people who had witnessed her good deeds were dead, and only people who had seen her husband's crimes were still alive, and you can guess their attitude to her. As I said, she ought to have gone away, but she didn't, perhaps she hadn't the strength left. She was a broken woman, quiet, withdrawn, probably a bit touched in the head, I couldn't make sense of how she and mother had managed to meet, her husband might have killed her for it. Anyway they met, and this is what she said to my mother. 'Rachel, they've let out the half-Jews in Chernigov, there's an order that they mustn't be touched, they must let your Yakov out, too. They need a store manager at the depot, tell Yakov to speak to Ivan Karlovich, he'll be out of danger working with him.'

Mother never changed her attitude to people, yet, can you

imagine, she trusted Mrs Golubinsky, the wife of the police chief, the wife of a hangman and traitor. She trusted her and she made up her mind, if they took Yakov to work at the depot, in the railway stores, that meant they wouldn't send him away anywhere, he would still be here in the town. He could be saved, he must be saved. Whatever lay in store for herself and Dina and Sasha, father had to be saved.

She said to father, 'Go and tell them you're half-German.'

'I won't,' he said. 'Your fate is my fate.'

She insisted, she even wept. 'I beg you, Yakov, don't torment me! Go to Ivan Karlovich, leave this place, you must live. If you can save yourself, maybe you'll be able to save us, too.'

She didn't believe what she was saying, she knew it was impossible to save them. She also knew that father would never leave them for his own sake, though he might for her sake and for the sake of the children and grandchildren.

Father also knew it was impossible to save them, and without them he didn't want to save himself.

He said, 'Rachel, I've told you. Let's say no more about it.'

Mother, however, acted on her own. There were three German commandants in the town. The military commandant was Lieutenant Reinhardt, then there was Stalbe, the commandant of the ghetto, then Captain Le Court, commandant of the railway station. You would think that as military commandant Reinhardt would be the senior officer. That wasn't the case. Stalbe, as commandant of the ghetto, was subordinate to his S S chiefs, the fate of the Jews was in his hands, he had his job to do, and Reinhardt didn't interfere. As for Le Court, he controlled a limited area, the railway, and so he would seem to have been the third in line. But that wasn't the case either. Our station was on the edge of a front-line zone, at the junction of two army groupings. The Germans guarded it most carefully and were prepared to sacrifice all the other enterprises, including the timber, for the sake of the railway. Everything was subordinated to the interests of the railway. That's what determined Le Court's position. He was the most powerful officer in the town, as well as being the most senior in rank. He was an independent man, energetic and, possibly, not a pervert and sadist like the others, but he had a difficult job to do. The station staff and nearly all the technical personnel had left with our troops, the Jews had all been cleared out of this vital strategic establishment, and were brought in from the ghetto only to load and unload wagons, or to clear the tracks after bombings. But the station had to work day and night, convoys were passing through one after the other, labour was needed, it was a big depot, locomotives were changed, repaired, and so on. A number of railway troops had been sent, but there weren't enough specialists. Among those who remained was our neighbour, Ivan Karlovich. He was a good technician, he'd spent his entire working life on the railway, he knew the job, knew the people, as well as being a German, he spoke Russian and German. Le Court couldn't have asked for a better assistant, and he valued and trusted him in everything.

What can I say about Ivan Karlovich? Was it fear or conscience that made him work for the Germans? I don't know – the fact is, he did. As a German, his position was complicated, as you can imagine, he was caught between two fires, between the anvil and the hammer. There's nothing I can say about him, I can only state that he went on working on the railway and enjoyed the confidence of the commandant, Le Court. It was to Ivan Karlovich that mother turned.

As you know, grandfather's yard was next door to Ivan Karlovich's garden, they were divided by a solid fence, which now had barbed wire on it. There was an order forbidding Jews even to talk to non-Jews on pain of shooting, but mother managed to meet Ivan Karlovich. Igor had a place where he could crawl through into the garden, he went to Ivan Karlovich and told him grandmother Rachel was waiting for him at the fence.

Ivan Karlovich came out to her, which you must admit was quite an act on his part, he needn't have come, he could have handed Igor over to the police and compelled the commandant's office to repair the fence so that nobody, big or small, was able to get through into his garden. He did nothing of the kind, he came to the fence and listened to what mother had to say.

'Ivan Karlovich,' she said. 'You know Yakov well. He has refused to declare that he's half-German, he doesn't want to leave us. But he's done for, Ivan Karlovich, he'll be dead in two weeks, if you only saw him. They're leaving the half-Jews alone, as you know, they haven't touched Borisov's wife, or the Nedzhvetskys or the grandchildren of the widow Gorodetsky. They declared what they were themselves. But Yakov won't, he's afraid we'll be done for without him. He's killing himself because of us, he can't take this kind of life. Let me also tell you that he not only has a German mother, but his father is half-Russian. Help us, Ivan Karlovich!'

On this occasion mother repeated the legend about old man Ivanovsky's mysterious origins.

'I'll have to think what can be done,' Ivan Karlovich said, and he added, 'And you must try not to meet me here again, Rachel Abramovna, it could end badly.' That's all he said.

A little while later, as Mrs Golubinsky told me, Ivan Karlovich found an opportunity to tell Le Court that a local inhabitant, Yakov Ivanovsky, who was living in the ghetto, was in fact half-German, he had come here from Switzerland for romantic reasons, he had fallen in love with a beautiful Jewish girl, and he called himself a half-Jew, which was doubtful when you considered that his name, Ivanovsky, was the most common name in Russia. He had influential German relations in Switzerland, he was an extremely respectable and honest man, he'd worked for many years in the depot stores and knew the job perfectly. The old store manager had left and it was no good replacing him with a German who couldn't speak Russian and wasn't able to handle the spare parts. Among the Russian employees he couldn't see a suitable candidate, in fact he couldn't entrust the stores to anyone but Ivanovsky.

Le Court got in touch with Stalbe and asked for Ivanovsky. Stalbe objected – every inhabitant of the ghetto was his catch. Le Court insisted and two SS men came for father. Everyone was sure they had come to take him away for shooting, only mother remained calm, she realized this was Le Court's doing. And, indeed, father returned soon after – with his face beaten and bloody and a gash in his shoulder. He said they wouldn't let him leave the ghetto, they didn't believe he was half-German and they gave him a few knocks for trying to trick them. So there should be no more of this, once and for all. Mother believed him, she knew they beat people up for any reason and for no reason.

What had in fact happened was told to me by Mrs Golubinsky. They brought father to the commandant's office and questioned him. There was no need for an interpreter. In the course of the questioning it was established that father's mother was in fact a German from Basel, with the maiden name of Haller, and that he did have relations in Switzerland who were pure-blooded Germans.

All this took place in November 1941, before the *Gross Wannsee Protocol* had come into existence. The position of half-Jews was not yet clear, and anyway this was no ordinary half-Jew, a half-Russian, say, or a half-Ukrainian. German blood was flowing in this man's veins, and to look at he was a pure German, born a Lutheran Christian, and the doctor established that he wasn't circumcised. On top of all that he was in demand by none other than Captain Le Court himself, a man invested with extreme authority. They told father he would be working on the railway, he could live outside the ghetto, but he must report every day to the police.

Father asked, what about his wife and family? Wife?! Family?! They would stay in the ghetto, and he would not be allowed to associate with them. In other words, it was life for him and death for them. Father declared that either they must let his family out with him or he would go back into the ghetto.

Stalbe replied, 'Your wife's a Jew, her place is in the ghetto. Your children are mongrels, their place is in the ghetto, and you're a mongrel, too, and your proper place is in the ghetto. Or maybe you consider yourself a German?'

Father, who was a quiet man, and who was worn out by the heavy work, by hunger and illnesses, in tatters, filthy, at the end of his strength, replied, 'Mr Stalbe, if you are a German, I am a Jew.'

What an answer! Can you imagine! Stalbe could have shot him on the spot, but he didn't. He lashed out with his whip twice, once on the shoulder and once on the face. You know what their whips were like, don't you? They were a steel switch bound with leather, you could kill a man with one. But father stayed alive. Stalbe ordered him back to the ghetto and reported to Le Court that Ivanovsky had refused work on the railway, he considered himself a Jew and as such was liable to the normal measures being applied to the Jews. Father told mother nothing of this, he told nobody, he only said that they weren't letting him out of the ghetto and that for trying to trick them he had got a couple of knocks. Mother drew her own conclusion from father's story, which was that they must prove at all costs that father was telling the truth, that he really was half-German.

I can't remember if I've mentioned that father had kept his Swiss passport. Why he had kept it, I don't know. Maybe because it was the one document he had which gave him a link with his motherland, or perhaps he'd kept it the way orderly people always keep their papers. Mother got hold of the passport and asked grandfather how things stood. Grandfather immediately came to the conclusion that Yakov was still a foreign subject. Whether that was enough to save him or not, grandfather wasn't sure, I doubt whether he even realized that Switzerland was a neutral country, but he did realize that there was just a chance, especially as someone as powerful as the railway commandant was going to a lot of trouble to get hold of him.

Grandfather decided to show the passport to Yosif. Mother objected, 'Yosif will hand over the passport to Stalbe and everything will be lost.'

'He won't give it to Stalbe,' grandfather said. Mother didn't trust Yosif, she knew him for what he was, but she did trust grandfather, and there was no other way out.

Yosif thought about it for a long time. He understood politics better than grandfather, he knew that with this passport Yakov wasn't just a person of mixed origins, he was a foreign subject, and of a neutral state, what's more. Yosif faced a dilemma, should he tell Stalbe about this passport or not?

Suppose he were to tell him, Stalbe would undoubtedly destroy the passport so that he could destroy Yakov later, and undoubtedly he would approve of Yosif's action. But what good would it do Yosif in the long run? He already had Stalbe's goodwill, as well as his trust, he had even been issued with a Walther automatic in case someone attacked him in the ghetto. Yes, Stalbe trusted him today, but tomorrow, without batting an eyelid, he could send him into the forest to be shot. The most obedient Jewish Councils had been destroyed together with their ghettoes elsewhere. Stalbe's goodwill was only a temporary gain, it offered nothing for the future. On the other hand, a half-German brother-in-law with rich and powerful relations in Switzerland – there was a future there. True it was vague and uncertain, but still it was a future, it was a straw for a drowning man to clutch at.

Yosif said to grandfather, 'I haven't seen this passport, you haven't shown it to me, you haven't seen it, either, Rachel didn't give it to you. Tell her that. She should give it to Ivan Karlovich as her own affair.'

Mother was afraid to give the passport to Ivan Karlovich, for the first time in her life she couldn't make an independent decision. How would it end if she interfered, if she turned to Ivan Karlovich? Suppose it was like the last time? Should she hand over the Swiss passport? Suppose it got lost?

It's easy to understand mother's hesitation, one false step and it would be the end! Every day there were shootings, killings, torture, and she so wanted to go to Ivan Karlovich and beg him to get Yakov out of it all. On the other hand, the last time she had given Stalbe an excuse for beating Yakov, wouldn't she now be giving him an excuse for doing something much worse, if she handed over the passport to Ivan Karlovich?

Then suddenly news filtered through to the ghetto that they were killing the Jews wholesale in the neighbouring towns and villages, including the families of those who had been transported here to work.

Can you imagine it happening? Every one of the four thousand people who had been brought here had left behind their children, their fathers and mothers, brothers and sisters. They can't all have been shot and thrown into a ditch, surely?

At first nobody believed these rumours, they didn't want to believe them, they were afraid to believe them, especially the old men. Why should the Germans do this? After all they need the labour, they are forcing people to work like oxen, why should they kill them? Who's going to fell the trees, unload the trains, clear the railway tracks after the bombings? Who's going to work in the factories and mills? True, there's lawlessness here, but that's because of that bloodthirsty beast Stalbe and his henchmen. True, there are the appalling regulations, but there is a war on. True, God is punishing his people for their wicked sins, but when and where has anybody ever seen women and children killed just like that, and for no reason?

That's what the old men said, though not all of them. Not my grandfather Rakhlenko, and these rumours filtered into our house before the others heard them.

The first signal came from Anna Yegorovna, Olya's nanny. Anna Yegorovna worked in the kitchen at the German officers' mess, in what used to be the Collective Farmers' Club. The dining-room was downstairs, and upstairs they had a casino, a sort of place of entertainment for the officers and gentlemen. The staff came from the local population, and police chief Golubinsky had put Madame Yanzhvetska in charge – you remember, the former owner of the hotel. She was an aristocratic lady, as I mentioned earlier, very imposing, she knew etiquette, and how to lay the table and serve, in a word, she took good care of the officers and gentlemen. Golubinsky didn't doubt her reliability, and he even promised her that in time she would be given back the hotel which the Bolsheviks had requisitioned illegally. Old Madame Yanzhvetska picked her own staff, including Anna Yegorovna for the kitchen.

However, things didn't work out with Madame Yanzhvetska quite the way Golubinsky had hoped.

She knew her job all right, she knew how to wait and to cook, she was thorough and demanding, and her imposing appearance did indeed lend a certain respectability to the establishment. Mind you, nobody there had any use for respectability. Who needed respectability and etiquette when the gentlemen-officers got themselves stinking drunk on any excuse, or none at all, and when they thought it the thing to do to behave like pigs? One day, they told Madame Yanzhvetska to get hold of some women for them. She replied that there weren't any women like that in the town, and there never had been. With loud guffaws and coarse and obscene expressions, they said all women were like that.

At this, Madame Yanzhvetska drew herself up and declared that in the course of her long life she had seen many officers, both Russian and Polish, and they would never have allowed themselves to speak about women in that way, because an officer is first of all a gentleman. Only louts would speak like that about women, especially in the presence of an old woman; only animals, even if they were wearing officers' uniform.

That's what Madame Yanzhvetska told them! She probably had a few more things she'd been saving up to say, she'd seen a good deal of that scum. But the officers and gentlemen didn't give her a chance to finish. They threw her out of the window, from the first floor, which, as you can guess, was quite enough for an old lady of seventy-five. That's how Madame Yanzhvetska ended her days. She had been a proud and worthy woman, may she rest in peace!

Well, the first signal about the exterminations came from Anna Yegorovna, indirectly. She met Olya, to give her some food to bring home, and she said to her, 'Tell Granny I'm going to take you to Dikanka.'

'What for?' Olya asked.

'Because you'll die of starvation here, that's what for.'

Olya didn't tell mother this. Anna Yegorovna wanted to save just her, but what about the others? What about Igor?

Next time they met, Anna Yegorovna repeated what she'd said, and this time she threatened Olya that if she didn't tell her granny, she wouldn't bring any more food. So Olya had to tell mother, and mother told father and grandfather.

Father decided right away, 'Let her take her, she'll die of starvation here.'

Then grandfather said, 'They'll kill her before she dies of starvation. They've already killed off all the children in Sosnitsy and Gorodnya.'

This was the first time grandfather had ever mentioned the

children being killed in Sosnitsy and Gorodnya, though he had known about it. He was in charge of burying the dead – the Germans were still allowing burials at the cemetery, without the burial ritual, of course, just for reasons of sanitation, and under police supervision. The cemetery was two miles away from the ghetto, so every burial meant an excursion into the outside world for the burial team, and burials were taking place at the rate of several a day. There was no shortage of the deceased, as you can imagine. The police got fed up having to drag along in the wake of every coffin, then to stand there waiting while the old men dug the grave, and anyway where could these old wrecks escape to? So they would leave them to it and go off and get drunk. It was in the cemetery that grandfather met some people from the outlying villages and heard what was going on around them, he found out that the Jews were being exterminated, but he didn't say anything at home, he didn't want to poison their lives more than they had been. He only told them when he knew that the extermination was approaching their ghetto. It was clear now that Anna Yegorovna was saving Olya from shooting, not from starvation, so they gave her the child and she went away with her to Dikanka. The rumours had become a reality, the future was staring the inhabitants of the town in the face. Once again mother decided to do something.

18 ▨

Just at that moment Uncle Grisha turned up in the ghetto. He managed to infiltrate himself into the column returning from work as it was leaving the forest. Like the rest of them, he was in rags and wearing the yellow star, but he didn't attach himself to the family as they would have recognized him and as an escaped Red Army soldier he couldn't afford to get caught. He joined up with some people from the other towns who didn't know him, especially as he was just as filthy and gaunt and exhausted as all the rest. It was a cold December night, the guards were freezing and hurrying to get home, and Grisha wasn't noticed. He spotted Dina in the column, caught up with her, indicated that she mustn't recognize him, and went into grandfather's house with the others.

Grisha told them his story briefly: he had managed to get out of German encirclement, he was wandering in the forests and next morning he would return there. It seemed plausible. The truth was that Grisha had come from the partisan unit led by Ivan Antonovich Sidorov, the old manager of our shoe factory. Sidorov was living openly, the Germans left him alone, thinking that, as he had once been imprisoned by the Soviet authorities, he had a grudge against them. They even offered him various jobs, which he declined on grounds of ill health. In fact, Sidorov had remained in occupied territory on the orders of the party district committee. The Germans were eventually tipped off as to his real identity, but they didn't manage to arrest him before he slipped away into the forest.

I won't say anything about the partisan movement in general, or in particular about the movement in our locality, which was at the junction of the Ukraine, Byelorussia and the Russian republic, as everyone knows about it. The partisans inflicted heavy casualties on the enemy, the very fact of their existence was an inspiration to the people, they compelled the enemy to divert his combat forces, they helped the army with intelligence, they were extremely successful in their operations against the enemy's lines of communications – you must have heard about the partisan 'rail-war'.

Partisan diversionary and intelligence groups began operating in our district as early as the second half of July. Not far from us was the famous Koryukov partisan district, which the Germans were afraid to enter and where they put up signs saying 'Partisan Zone' and made wide cuttings in the forest to protect their transports from surprise attack.

Even before the Germans arrived, Sidorov had dumped food supplies and some weapons in the forest. Being a canny, intelligent peasant, he was careful in the people he picked, locals he knew well at first, and later on escapees from German encirclement, once he was sure of them. One of these was Uncle Grisha, though Sidorov had no doubts about him, as he knew him well from their factory days. Grisha could turn his hand to anything, and became a great demolitionist, highly valued by Sidorov. The unit had its job to do, in very difficult conditions in the enemy's operational rear where there were strong enemy forces, and so Sidorov could permit Grisha to visit the ghetto only in January or February of 1942. He may even have sent him there, as he had his eye on our town, on the railway station, to be precise.

Grisha confirmed that the Jewish population in the surrounding districts was being exterminated and that the same fate awaited our town. So the people must prepare themselves either to die or to fight.

I think many of them must have been surprised. How

could anyone talk of fighting? Who against? What with? Sticks? First you have to get hold of some weapons, learn how to use them and then wait for the right moment, wait for the turning-point in the war.

On the other hand, it was no good waiting, the hour had already struck. Brilliant engineers, chemists and doctors of Hitler's Reich had devised an entire industry, with gas-chambers, crematoria, gassing-vans, grinding-mills for human bones. Socks and shirts that had been taken off the bodies of murdered children were already being dispatched back to Germany, along with the gold crowns and bridges that had been torn out of victims' mouths, and women's hair to be used for stuffing mattresses, and the ash of the cremated for fertilizer; lampshades were already being fashioned and books being bound with human skin – after all, Germany was the birthplace of printing! The death industry was gathering force and the people had to prepare to defend themselves, to defend themselves with their bare hands, to die in the act, but to die with honour.

Grisha spent the night with his sons, Venya, Tolya and Edik, and with my sister Dina and my brother Sasha. None of them have survived, so I don't know the details of their conversation. That night, Grisha met some other people he knew well and I think they talked about the same thing. Grisha chose four people to form a unit, they were young, fit and bold, among them Yevsey Kuznetsov, Masha Kuznetsov's husband, a strong man, a driver by trade. Of course Grisha would have liked to take his son Venya with him, he was already a tall, healthy seventeen-year-old, and fearless like all the Rakhlenkos, but Venya was needed here. Grisha would have stayed in the town himself, but as a Red Army escapee he would have to live illegally, which would have been prac-tically impossible within the compass of only three streets.

Next day Grisha went back into the forest, and two days later the people he had chosen slipped away from their work to an appointed place where he met them and took them to Sidorov.

Little Igor went with them. Grisha showed him the way through the forest, after which he came back to the ghetto, and from that day he was its link to the partisans. He was desperately brave, a completely Russian child in appearance, he had spent his life in the town and spoke like everyone else there, a mixture of Russian and Ukrainian. He knew the villages that lay along his runs from the ghetto into the forest and back, and he could always make up an excuse if need be, though there were enough homeless boys wandering around!

As for my father, Grisha insisted that he must go and manage the railway stores, as Ivan Karlovich had proposed. 'We need one of our own men at the station,' Grisha said. 'You'll be that man.'

This put the question in an unexpected light. Father had firmly decided not to leave the family. When their time came he would die with them. He wasn't afraid of dying outside the ghetto, either, but do you know what was bothering him, what was holding him back?

'If I'm caught,' he said, 'Ivan Karlovich will suffer, as he went out of his way for me.' That was father all over, he couldn't cause trouble for someone else, especially someone who had saved his life.

Grisha replied, 'Don't worry about him, he'll be all right, he can't be responsible for everyone who works at the depot.'

Mother said nothing. She realized that Grisha wasn't advising Yakov to go and work on the railway by chance, it was what Grisha's chief wanted. Yakov would have to help the partisans, and she knew how many people in the outlying villages had already been hanged and shot on suspicion of being in contact with them. She sympathized with the partisans and hated the Germans, but she thought father was no good at such things, he would get caught straight away and they would torture him. But to stay here was certain death, too. He must get out of the ghetto, come what may, and then see what happened. Perhaps they'd send him off to Switzerland as a foreigner. Let him first get out and then she would persuade Grisha not to involve him in anything, to leave him in peace and give him the chance to save his own life.

So she said, 'Yakov, you must do this.'

Father, however, saw it as his duty to die together with his wife, his daughter, his son and his grandson. He didn't know if he could be useful in the struggle by working out there, in the railway stores. What he did know was that, if he went to the stores he would be leaving hell, and Rachel, Dina, Sasha, and Igor would remain in hell, and father couldn't leave them there.

I'll tell you this, nobody knew mother as well as father did, and in a way that nobody else could.

I remember one wonderful mushroom season. The Stashenoks were bringing white mushrooms home by the bucketful, drying and salting and frying them, and you could smell them all the way down the street. One morning at dawn we went into the forest, too, we took Dina with us, she was probably no more than five or six at the time. The best kind of mushrooms grew beyond the ravine, but it was too far to go with the children, they'd get tired, so we decided to turn off into a young pine wood, where there might be another sort.

Mother and Dina went on in front, the sand was still damp from the dew and mother's footprints were deep, Dina's were hardly visible, she weighed practically nothing. They stopped to pick a white mushroom that was growing right in their path. Mother stood up and went to one side in case there were more growing there, then all of a sudden she gave a shriek, clutched hold of Dina and, pressing her awkwardly, sideways to her, she froze in terror.

'Silly fool,' father laughed. 'It's only a grass snake.'

Mother had gone white, she stood there unable to take her

eyes off the bush and in a quiet, pitiful voice, she asked, 'Is it really a grass snake, Yakov ?'

That voice came as a surprise to me, I had never heard her speak in such a pitiful, helpless voice, it was the voice of a weak woman, not masterful and decisive, like my mother. We didn't know that she could be frightened and beg for protection and complain. Only one person knew her like that, and that was father. So he forbade her to give his passport to Ivan Karlovich. This time mother didn't disobey him.

Father remained in the ghetto. Like all the others, he was starving, barefoot and in tatters, he had boils and sores, he felled timber in the freezing cold, loaded it on to trucks, unloaded wagons, cleared the tracks, collected unexploded shells. He did what all the rest were doing, he was dying in the forest, dying in his own house, he ate the same as everyone else, nothing, he came back to the ghetto late in the evening, carrying his exhausted comrades on his back in case they fell by the wayside and got shot by the guards. Mother and Dina were still going to work, only Igor stayed at home, and soon Olya would return to the ghetto.

Someone in Dikanka gave Anna Yegorovna away, she was arrested and brought back to us. Olya was taken to the *Judenrat* and Uncle Yosif acknowledged that the child was in fact from the ghetto, and it would be hard to condemn him for this as it was a fact that couldn't be denied. Olya was sent back to the ghetto, and Anna Yegorovna was hanged on the gallows in the town square, with a board round her neck saying 'She harboured a Yid'. That's how Anna Yegorovna died, a great woman, long live her memory!

The facts I'm relating are all firmly established. As you can imagine, they represent only a hundredth or a thousandth part of what went on in the ghetto. The rest went to the grave with the people. However, there was something that was a secret even inside the ghetto, and it is for the sake of this that I'm telling the story, otherwise the story wouldn't be worth telling. It was the same everywhere, people were exterminated, the exact way they were exterminated is neither here nor there, whether they were first made to lie in the ditch and then shot, or shot first and then thrown into the ditch.

I have very few facts about the story I want to tell now, the facts I have allow a certain amount of guesswork and supposition. These guesses and suppositions may be right or wrong, precise or approximate, but without them we won't understand the later events, which are the main point of everything I'm telling you.

Our neighbour, the saddler Stashenok, was friends with my grandfather and, as you will remember, he used grandfather's sheds for storing his hides. These sheds had cellars, which had been dug during the Civil War to hide the leather goods from marauding gangs. The cellars were well camouflaged under double floors and the Germans had no idea they were there. Even as children we didn't know of their existence. Then one day, there in those cellars, Motya Gorodetsky and the teacher Kuras's granddaughter Bronya blew themselves up, both of them aged fourteen. The Germans didn't hear the explosion, grandfather buried the children at the cemetery, the S S weren't concerned about what people were dying of, they didn't ask to see a doctor's certificate.

How had Motya and Bronya blown themselves up? Maybe they were playing with a mine they'd found, or a grenade? They had no time for games, and grenades weren't just lying around the town, you might find them in the forest, but then strolls in the forest weren't encouraged – for strolling in the forest a child would be shot immediately. If the children had gone in search of bombs in the woods on pain of shooting, and had brought them back into the ghetto, also on pain of shooting, you can be sure it wasn't because they were playing games.

Even so, I don't think they found these bombs and grenades in the forest, I think they made them. No, I'm serious. A bomb can be a bottle of kerosene wrapped in a rag, a grenade can be a can of nuts and bolts, or just a piece of sawn-off tubing, packed with dynamite, and they could have made bombs and grenades of that sort, even without the aid of a chemistry text-book or the Brockhaus and Efron Encyclopedia. Although they were only children, they realized that these weren't proper weapons. Now another fact: Kuznetsov's grandsons, Vitya and Alik, were caught taking machine-guns off vehicles that had been left by their drivers. If Stalbe had known why they were taking the machine-guns, he would have had half the ghetto shot, for sure; instead he took it for a childish prank and ordered only the naughty boys to be shot.

Mother's friend, Emma Kuznetsov, together with her daughter Fanya and Grisha's wife, Ida, a mother of four, were all shot for trying to smuggle a uniform out of the factory. Maybe they were hoping to barter it for food? They hadn't had anything of their own for a long time, it had all been taken off them or they had already bartered it. A head of cabbage would cost you a new dress, for a dozen potatoes a pair of shoes, and a good watch would get you a loaf of bread. But you didn't take a uniform or boots or hides to the market-place to barter, you could trade with the police or the soldiers with such things, and not only for food.

I repeat, the facts are few and vague, you can interpret them in different ways, but there's only one conclusion to be drawn from them – deep in the heart of the ghetto, in the depths of that hell, resistance was rising. At first it was inept, primitive, naïve, but the people were nevertheless getting ready to fight, and that was the main thing. The seeds sown by Uncle Grisha had not been lost, in time you'll see their shoots.

One fact that is absolutely reliable is the conversation that took place between grandfather Rakhlenko and his son Yosif, the chairman of the *Judenrat*; it was reported to me almost verbatim.

Grandfather went to Yosif and said, 'Yosif, do you

know what they've done in Gorodnya and Sosnitsy?'

'Yes, I do,' Yosif replied.

'They'll do the same to us.'

'What do you suggest?'

'We must go into the forest,' grandfather said. Yosif knew that nobody could reach the forest, and that if they did they would perish there, and he knew that grandfather knew it perfectly well, too, and that he hadn't come to Yosif to find that out.

'What else do you suggest?' Yosif asked. In other words, lay your cards on the table, what do you really want?

'There are some peasants,' grandfather began.

'What peasants?'

'From one of the farms.'

'Well?'

'They'll hide us for gold.'

'They'd take the gold and hand you over.'

'They're reliable.'

'And where are you going to get the gold?'

'Haven't you got any?'

'Not for Grisha, I haven't!' Yosif said. 'Do you think I don't know he sent you here? Just remember this, Grisha is a partisan. If Stalbe finds out he'll shoot the lot of you, the whole family, and that's at the best. At the worst, he'll shoot every tenth person in the town.'

'I haven't seen Grisha since the day he was called up, where he is and what he's doing I have no idea,' said grandfather.

'Neither have I and I don't want to!' Yosif snapped. 'But I do know why you're trying to get hold of some gold. Listen, don't get mixed up in it. Who're you going to fight? Them? They've conquered the whole of Europe, they're going to conquer the world! What will you fight them with? Muskets? Rusty old sawn-off shotguns from the Civil War? Against tanks and machine-guns? If they find a single pistol among you they'll shoot everyone in the ghetto. It's easy for Grisha to stake your life on a card, he's in the forest. Innocent people will go to their certain death just because his snot-nosed sons want to die as heroes.'

'They're going to die anyway,' said grandfather.

'How do you know that?' Yosif retorted. 'All right, in Gorodnya and Sosnitsy something took place, but what it was, we don't know. I asked someone and he said "Yes, there was shooting." What for? "They tried to kill some Germans." Probably a few kids had got hold of some pistols, so everyone else was shot for it. And the same thing will happen here. If these kids don't come to their senses, I'll make them. Nothing's happened here, so far, and it won't! They need us now and they're going to for a long time. There's all the timber, in the spring they're going to start building a road, we can hang on till the autumn, they'll take Moscow, the war will be over and in peacetime they won't be able to do the things they can in wartime. We've got to bide our time, we've got to hold out.'

'The people from Gorodnya and Sosnitsy have had their children murdered, what have they got to bide their time for?' grandfather asked.

'We still don't know who was killed and who wasn't,' Yosif objected. 'They might have transported them to Poland, it's near the front here and they're afraid the Jews might help the Reds. So, tell everyone there's no need to panic or spread wild rumours. If Grisha turns up here again I'll turn him over to Stalbe, it's my duty, and if I don't carry it out they'll shoot me, too. And if his sons lift a finger, I'll turn them over to Stalbe. I'm responsible for seven thousand people here, I have no other choice.'

'It's already down to five thousand,' said grandfather.

'They're still five thousand human beings,' Yosif said. 'Don't get mixed up in this, father! If they find out about you they'll shoot not just you, but all the old men.'

Grandfather detected in this the fact that they were

murdering the old people as well as the children, though he
didn't need Yosif to tell him that. He saw right through Yosif.
Yosif was lying when he said they might have transported the
children to Poland, they had shot them. He'd lied when he
said some ghettoes still survived, they'd been liquidated
together with their inhabitants. He'd lied when he said the
Germans would take Moscow and the war would soon be
over, they'd said they would take Moscow already last
October. And Yosif wasn't going to save anyone's life, it was
all lies, he was a rat, he was only thinking of saving his own
skin. In the old days, grandfather would have said all this to
Yosif and got the truth out of him with his stick. But he
wouldn't get out of him with a stick what he needed to know
now, which was how Yosif had heard that Grisha had been
here and that the boys were up to something.

'Who told you Grisha is supposed to have come?'

'But you're saying he didn't come.'

'I didn't see him, but maybe someone else did. I'd like to
know who. After all, Grisha is my son.'

'Aren't I also your son?'

'You're all my sons, you and Lazar and Grisha. But I know
about you and Lazar, I don't know about Grisha and I want
to know.'

'You know a lot more than I do, but we won't talk about it.
You must go, father, but don't forget, I'm responsible for the
people here and I won't hand them over to be destroyed by
Grisha, though he's my brother, or to Venya and Dina, though
they're my nephew and niece, or to you, though you're my
father. You're not the only people who live on the street,
other people can see you, others are living right next to you,
Aleshinsky, Plotkin, the Yagudins.'

Whether Yosif had said all this on purpose or had said more
than he meant to, it was enough for grandfather.

'Fine!' he said, and left.

As you know, grandfather's neighbour was the saddlemaker Afanasi Prokopyevich Stashenok. His eldest son, Andrey, worked at the depot and lived at the railway settlement with his wife Ksana – you remember, Yosif tried to get off with her. The eldest son, Maxim, was at the front, the daughter Marya and the son Kostya worked at the depot. Irina, the wife of Petrus, the second son, and her three daughters, Vera, Nina, and Tanya, aged sixteen, thirteen and ten, were living with the old Stashenoks, and Petrus himself was at the front.

The Germans had ordered the Stashenoks to get out of Sand Street, as it led into the ghetto. They'd had to move into our old house on the next street, and their house was used to settle Jews driven out of other streets or other towns, probably seventy people or more were packed into it. There was Oryol the chemist with his daughter and four grandchildren, the wretched Kusiel Plotkin, you remember, the butcher father once worked for? His wife had gone to be evacuated together with his former assistant. And, another coincidence, the old man Aleshinsky lived there, too, the former hardware merchant father had also worked for in the shop. After NEP, Aleshinsky had worked at making roofs and, incidentally, had some goods tucked away that grandfather knew about. There was also the family of Khaim Yagudin, who'd been shot by the Germans, his children, grandchildren, and great-grandchildren, apart from those who were serving in the army or had got away in the evacuation, of course.

Among Khaim Yagudin's daughters I'd like to draw your attention to Sarah, the one who used to deal in diamonds and looked like Vera Kholodny as a girl. She was now over fifty, and there wasn't much left of Vera Kholodny. She'd spent most of her life in prisons and camps, she'd been on Solovki and the White Sea Canal, and how she survived I can't imagine. She turned up again just before the war, smoking, swigging vodka and using foul language, a thoroughly hardened criminal. She wasn't known as Vera Kholodny any more, but

Sonka Gold Fingers. She had stayed behind because she thought that, as someone who had suffered under Soviet rule, she could do well for herself with the Germans, and as she had already survived fire and water and everything else, she thought she would survive this, too.

The first thing she got from the Germans was a public flogging in the square, fifteen strokes of the cane on her backside for going out with lipstick on. She thought that, in the old way, she might manage to pick up a policeman, or even a German, and she wasn't bothered about regulations prohibiting people from using lipstick and make-up, so she got fifteen strokes and couldn't sit down for a month. Sarah learned nothing from this punishment, if anything it hardened her low, criminal character. She managed to worm her way into the confidence of the Germans, they made her a team-leader and, being the utter scum and swine she was, she taunted the people she was put in charge of and demanded bribes for not putting them on the heavier work. What bribe can you take from a dying man? His last crust of bread or scrap of potato. Scum that she was, she took it and left people to die. All in all, she was a true and faithful servant to herself and to the Germans, she was ready to sell anyone down the river.

Grandfather realized that she had told Yosif about Grisha. She could have reported it to the commandant, but what would have been in it for her? Maybe an extra bread ration. No, she reported it to Yosif, the chairman of the *Judenrat*, she told him his brother, an unregistered Red Army man, had turned up in the ghetto and then left the ghetto, and she was blackmailing Yosif with this fact, and that was why Yosif had made her a team-leader and why he had done nothing about the many complaints people had made about her. He was afraid she would tell Stalbe that he had concealed the fact that his brother, a Red Army man and partisan, had come to the ghetto.

I reckon that Yosif's hint to grandfather about Sarah had been on purpose. He knew grandfather wouldn't leave it at that, but he had been afraid of making a straight deal with grandfather. He wanted to get Sarah off his back, but he didn't want to be in debt to grandfather, so he gave him a remote hint, knowing that he would pick it up, which he did. More than that, grandfather did some checking up and was certain that Sarah knew about Grisha's visit. He had some suspicions about one or two other things, too, and took steps.

19 ❖

Grandfather wasn't able to act right away, he didn't have time. Soon after his conversation with Yosif, the first extermination was carried out in the ghetto. It must have taken place in February or March of 1942, some say it was winter, others spring, so I put it at the end of February, beginning of March.

It was announced that all crowbars, shovels and spades would be requisitioned for the building of the road. Rumours about this road had been going around for a long time, it was supposed to be a trunk-road going from north to south, and it was the one Uncle Yosif had mentioned to grandfather. The requisition made nobody suspicious, they'd long got used to requisitions. The tools were loaded on to a truck and driven off by the police – as it turned out later, to the forest, to the place where Oryol used to have his pitch, and where, after NEP, a snack-bar had been built, with a kitchen, a store-room and wood-shed.

The first 'action' was carried out on the inhabitants of Trench Street. At four in the morning the labour columns went off to the forest, and at four thirty, while it was still completely dark, SS men, with ghetto police and dogs, got the people out on to the street, supposedly to disinfect the houses against typhus. Using whips and lashes and rifle-butts, they drove the people out, threw them out of their beds, giving them no time to get dressed, old folks, men, women and children. The people carried the sick out on stretchers or on their backs, cripples hopped along on their crutches, while the Germans shouted and cursed and swore at them, and anyone who fell down and couldn't get up was shot where he lay.

Yet, despite all the rush, the cursing, the dogs, the whips and the shooting, not one person suspected that this was the end, that they had only a few hours to live. Every action was carried out to the accompaniment of cursing, beatings, whips and lashes, on-the-spot shootings, S S yelling at them to move faster all the time, faster, faster, they mustn't stop to think, run, run, run! Anyone who stopped for a second got a bullet! Faster! Form ranks of ten, faster, faster, join hands! Some of the women couldn't join hands, as they were holding their babies, so soldiers tore the infants from them and dashed out their brains on the road or against the side of a house. Move, you animals! The only infants left were those whose mothers managed to tie them to themselves with a shawl or towel. The main thing was speed. In less than half an hour eight hundred people had been driven out of the houses and formed up in ranks of ten, and all the time to shouts and curses, and barking dogs, shooting, and whips and lashes. The ghetto was not asleep, the people in the next streets heard everything, they were too scared to go out, and locked themselves in, as if locks and bolts were any protection.

The soldiers surrounded the column and marched it to the forest. Faster, at the double! The people ran, the children ran, the cripples hopped along on their crutches, the old, the sick and the helpless fell and were shot where they lay. The road to the forest, no more than two miles, was littered with corpses, which froze solid and rang like glass when they were being buried later.

The column was halted in the clearing where Oryol's veranda used to be, and split up into four groups of twenty ranks each. These were marched to the four sides of the clearing and ordered to sit down on the snow, leaving space between each group. The people sat down, as the dogs bared their fangs at them, and they still didn't realize why they had been brought to this place. If the Germans wanted to disinfect their houses, they should have moved them to other streets. What was the point of bringing them here?

They began to suspect what the point was when, after getting their breath back and calming down the children, they took a look around and saw, through the darkness and frosty, early-morning haze, watch-towers among the trees, with ladders fixed to them, and soldiers armed with machine-guns standing on top of them, S S men and police, also armed with machine-guns, posted all round the clearing, and armed soldiers and police with dogs in the spaces between the groups. Eight hundred people were encircled in a trap. Stalbe, a rigid schoolmaster, had thought out and carefully organized his first extermination. Similar actions had already been carried out in neighbouring towns and villages and Stalbe had studied the experience of his comrades-in-arms thoroughly, experience which his colleagues had shared with him gladly, generously, unstintingly like the comrades and gentlemen they were, hiding nothing from him, neither their achievements nor their errors. Stalbe supervised the action personally, standing on the veranda, surrounded by his staff, and observing with satisfaction that his plan was being carried out to the letter. The main thing was to have an exact schedule for the executors of the plan to work to, and to act with speed, not giving the victims a moment to get their bearings.

The S S picked out fifty men and ordered them to take crowbars, shovels and spades from the veranda and to clear and deepen an anti-tank ditch that had been dug to defend the railway station against light and medium tanks, so it was triangular in shape, or, in army terms, it was a 'partially excavated trapezoidal ditch'. Fully dug trapezoidal ditches are meant to hold up heavy tanks, whereas only light and medium tanks were expected here. The length of the ditch, seventy-five yards, was just right for the action that was about to take place, and its width of eighteen feet was more than enough, but a depth of only six feet was too shallow, ten would be perfect. So the ditch had to be deepened and cleared of snow, earth, brushwood and leaves.

When the fifty men went down into the ditch and began putting it in order, the people understood exactly why they were there.

The moon lit up the clearing and the people sitting on the dark snow, it lit up the machine-gunners on the towers and the police, carrying rifles, the dogs straining at their leashes, and the SS men pointing their machine-guns at the men working noiselessly in the ditch.

It also lit up Stalbe himself, as he stood on the veranda and silently observed the scene. Everything was going *sehr gut*, a model of order. The main thing was not to let the action turn into butchery, a German soldier doesn't take part in butchery, he engages in a properly organized operation. I can tell you, as an ex-intelligence man who's seen plenty of Germans, that they love words like 'action', 'operation', 'execution'. Order for them was like a symbol of the law, and in the name of the law they could murder women, old folks and children without a qualm. If order were disrupted, if children, women and old folks were to resist, that would cast doubt on the legitimacy of the measures being taken. Stalbe understood the importance of achieving unquestioning obedience, of making sure that the people would lie down in the ditch without complaint, that they would lie down, fully aware that what was happening was inevitable, for in doing so, they would confirm the legitimacy of it.

The men finished digging and got out of the ditch, put the crowbars and spades back on the veranda, and sat down where they were told to, on the snow under armed guard. After the action, their job would be to fill in the ditch.

Then, the first group was ordered to strip naked and lay their clothes at the edge of the clearing, their footwear together, their outer clothes together, and their underclothes together. But the people didn't obey the order, as they knew that every movement they made, every boot removed, every sleeve pulled off, was a step towards the ditch, a step towards death, so they sat, rooted to the spot. Again came the cursing, the whips and truncheons, the rifle-butts and the dogs, and the clearing came to life, the people howled and screamed 'Hangmen!' 'Murderers!' The children clung to their mothers and wailed 'Mama, don't leave me!' There was crying and moaning, and in reply came the whips and lashes and rifle-butts and barking dogs. Someone ran away into the forest and was shot down, there was no escape that way. Men and women threw themselves at the SS men and tried to seize their guns, they struggled and bit. Then, on Stalbe's order, the SS men joined the circle of machine-gunners surrounding the clearing, a burst was fired at the crowd and it scattered, then the machine-guns on the towers opened up and the clearing ran with blood, the people fell to the ground and pressed themselves flat.

Stalbe gave the order to cease fire and again soldiers went in with their clubs and whips and rifle-butts and forced the people up, again they divided them into four groups and ordered them to strip naked, and again they must hurry, faster, faster! If you couldn't undo your bootlace – a bullet! A child wouldn't let go of its doll – a bullet! So the people hurried, next to them were the dead and the half-dead, wheezing and convulsing, in front of them the muzzle of an automatic, and above them the whip and the lash.

Now Stalbe ordered everyone to undress. God was his witness, he had wanted to carry out the action in an organized fashion, he had wanted those waiting their turn for the ditch to be dressed and not have to freeze. God was his witness, he had tried to be humane, as far as circumstances would allow, but these people didn't deserve humaneness, let them sit naked in the freezing cold, let them sit there among the corpses, right there on the blood-soaked snow.

Order was restored and the schedule, slightly delayed, came into force again, though with some amendments. According to the plan, those being executed were supposed to lie down in neat tight rows in the ditch, they would then be shot from above by machine-guns, then the next lot would lie on top of them and so on, to the end. Because of their sabotage, however, it was necessary to drop that plan, and instead the naked people were made to run to the ditch, where they were shot in the back and fell into it, those who fell beside it being kicked in. Others were then made to take their place at the edge of the ditch and be shot in the back. The bullets didn't always hit the children, as they were small, so many children were thrown into the ditch alive, and the dead and injured fell on top of them, in one huge, bloody heap of writhing humanity, and above all it had to be done with speed, faster, faster!

There was now silence, broken only by bursts of machine-gun fire and pistol shots. The people were quiet, they knew their last hour had come and that nothing would save them. They went to the ditch in family groups and said their farewells, mothers embraced their children, fathers reassured their sons, old men and women mumbled prayers to a God who, yet again, hadn't come to their help. This wasn't the silence of numbness, it was the silence of a brave farewell to life, of contempt for death and for their murderers. There was only the crack of pistols, the rattle of machine-guns, the barking of dogs, and from the veranda the sound of Stalbe giving orders through a megaphone.

Often I've heard people say, how was it they could go to the ditch, climb down into it, lie down and wait for their bullet? Tell me what else they could do? Should they have run around the clearing like rabbits, or squealed like stuck pigs? Should they have shown their enemy their fear, their animal fear? No! Their death was fated, it was unavoidable, irrevocable, but they had to die with dignity. Their dignity was in their silence.

When they had all been shot, the fifty men who acted as gravediggers were ordered to throw all the corpses into the ditch and fill it in.

They picked up their spades. They were all strong men, they knew what was in store for them, they had nothing to lose and they had agreed everything among themselves while they were sitting on the snow, watching as their wives and children and mothers were being shot. So, crowbars and spades in hand, they rushed at the soldiers in a sudden movement and broke through the circle. The veranda shielded them from the watch-towers, so they were out of range of the machine-guns, and having broken through the circle they scattered in all directions in the forest. SS men with dogs chased after them, firing their pistols and automatics. Even so, some managed to get away. I met two of them after the war, I spoke to them myself and much of what I am telling you is based on their stories. Many of those who ran were shot and their corpses were left in the forest. The SS couldn't be bothered with them, they went back to the clearing and made the police fill in the ditch. Although the Germans sustained no losses, there were some slight injuries, cuts and scratches from the spades, and there was one serious injury, a cracked skull from a crowbar. Nevertheless, Stalbe, as an honest and well-organized officer, felt it necessary to report that the plan of execution had been disrupted by the resistance of those being executed, and a number of people had been shot while attempting to escape. The communiqué didn't sound very victorious and I doubt if Stalbe and his assistants won any medals for it.

The shots and machine-gun fire had been heard in the ghetto, as it was only two miles away, but the people working in the forest beyond the railway station, five miles away, had heard nothing, and when they returned late in the evening, they didn't find their families, nor could they go to their houses, as Trench Street was now fenced off by barbed wire. The ghetto now consisted of Sand Street and Hospital Street and the streets connecting them, and the number of people left was down to three thousand. In less than half a year, around four thousand people had been exterminated, either by shooting or by starvation and disease.

The houses on Trench Street were sold, together with their miserable contents, to the inhabitants of the outlying villages. It is a matter of shame and regret that there were people who were eager to buy the houses and belongings of those whose lives had been devastated through no fault of their own.

They took the clothing and underwear of those who'd been shot to the garment factory and their shoes to the shoe factory, where everything was sorted and repaired and then put on sale in the German shop. The girls doing the sorting recognized the clothes and shoes of their relatives and friends.

Stalbe sent the *Judenrat* a bill for eight thousand roubles in respect of bullets and other expenses incurred by the authorities in the course of the action.

So, the first extermination had been accomplished in our town. Many people hanged themselves as a result of it – ropes hadn't yet been requisitioned. Fathers and mothers whose children had been exterminated hanged themselves. Several families decided not to wait for the same thing to be done to them and hanged themselves. A father would kill his wife and children, and then himself, or a mother would kill her children and then hang herself. Uncle Lazar hanged himself, he couldn't take any more of it, he didn't want to lug timber for the Germans any more, he didn't want to have to bury children alive, or go down into the ditch himself, so he found the courage to die. He hanged himself at night in a shed. Grandfather removed the noose and buried him at the cemetery next to grandmother. Some people escaped into the forest, and the SS shot their families for it, and if there was no family left to shoot they shot every fifth person in their work-team. And they introduced morning roll-call.

At the first roll-call, Stalbe announced that if anyone ran away, everyone in that house, as well as the whole family, would be shot, and every third member of their work-team.

'Don't go to the partisans,' Stalbe told them. 'You'll die of cold and hunger in the forest, the partisans don't accept Jews, they'll leave you in the forest to the mercy of fate. Work hard and there'll be no more actions. The action was made necessary by difficulties in food supply in the winter, it became necessary to reduce the numbers in the ghetto, it was a hard measure, but there's a war on, young Germans are dying at the front, the population of Germany is also suffering hardships, you must try to understand that. The problem of food supplies has now been solved, there will be no more actions. Work! And report anything you hear about the partisans. There will be a reward for every piece of information.'

Soon after this, Uncle Grisha turned up in the ghetto again and gave a detailed account of the action, having heard it from those who had escaped and joined Sidorov's unit, and he added that the fate of the ghetto had been decided, the next action was to be expected any day, they must get out into the forest, though it was impossible without weapons, as the cordons had been strengthened. Those who didn't manage to get out would need weapons, too, so as to resist when the action came.

As I now understand it, and as Sidorov told me later, the intention was to form a partisan unit out of the inhabitants of the ghetto. At first it would be a combat unit, then, under the protection of combatants, it would serve to safeguard the families, the women and children. The idea was unrealistic, utopian. Can you imagine, in the spring of 1942, when the balance was still in the Germans' favour, trying to move hundreds of women and children, pure fantasy! Still, many great deeds were born in fantasy, weren't they?

To carry out this fantastic plan, weapons would be needed. A few stolen grenades and pistols and home-made things didn't amount to anything. They needed real weapons, and plenty of them. They could only be got at the station, where the supply convoys were unloaded, and for that there had to be one of our own men on the spot.

It was obvious that Grisha had father in mind, though he didn't say it in so many words, he didn't want to force him to do it. The path that Grisha had taken, and that his children and his children's comrades had taken, was a dangerous one, and could only be taken voluntarily. On the last occasion, my father had refused to take that road and Grisha didn't want to insist on it any more, he didn't even want to mention it. It was mother who mentioned it.

'Yakov!' she said, 'you must help our children. If you don't, nobody will.'

She said it with a heavy heart, knowing that Grisha wouldn't say it. Father knew from the way her voice trembled that she meant it.

My father and mother weren't fighters. They were brave people who had shown their bravery in the assertion and defence of their love and their family. Their love had been their whole life, they ought to die together, too, and their one desire was to go to the ditch together. Now they were faced with dying apart from each other and in different ways. But when mother spoke those words, she was already a different person, she knew what she was sending her husband to, and she was ready herself for whatever happened.

Again through Igor, father sent Ivan Karlovich his Swiss passport, together with a note saying he would try to get a permit to go to Switzerland, and meanwhile he asked Ivan Karlovich to fix him up with a job at the depot.

I don't know what happened between Stalbe and Le Court on this occasion, but the fact is they let father out of the ghetto and put him in charge of the depot stores.

How father said good-bye and left I don't know. How he went out of the house and went along our street, dragging his feet through the heavy sand, I don't know. It really was the end. He was forbidden to appear in the ghetto or to be seen with anyone from the ghetto. He had to report to the police every week, and his documents, as a Swiss citizen, were sent to the Fourth Section of the Gestapo in Berlin, under Adolf Eichmann. Father lived in a cubicle at the stores. Both the stores and the cubicle have survived, I went to see it with my wife on our first visit.

Yes, I got married, but I'm afraid it might divert me from the main story if I tell you about it. No, there's no secret, what do you mean? If you want to know, fine!

20 ▨

My wife, Galina Nikolaevna, or just Galya, as she was during
the war, was a telephone operator in battalion signals. She
joined the army after one year of teachers' training college.
That was pretty uncommon, usually they joined from school,
after eighth grade, or even sixth, and despite the education
she had, she didn't become a wireless operator, but joined the
ordinary telephone operators. The course for wireless operators was six months, for telegraphers it was four months and
for telephone operators only one month. Galya wanted to get
to the front as quickly as possible, she did her month's training and they sent her to a unit right there where she had been
trained, in Stalingrad.

Books and movies have created the image for us of the
girl soldier at the front as a fine, strong young girl in a tunic
and skirt, boots and forage-cap, ear-flaps and sheepskin coat
in winter, a dashing pointswoman with a flag. There were, of
course, some like that, but not many. Galya was tall and thin.
In 1941 and 1942, they often issued the girls with men's
uniforms, even men's underwear, shirt, underpants, trousers
with flies, buttoned undershirt, felt boots. They might save
a girl's life, but she could hardly look like Venus de Milo in
them. Though whatever you put on Venus de Milo she would
still be Venus.

Real love did occur at the front, but many felt 'the war
would excuse anything'. What was it like for a girl among the
troops? Hospitals were one thing, most of the personnel were
women, there was hot water, sheets on the beds and so on, and

anyway the men were wounded and sick and needed looking after, a girl didn't depend on them. Battalion signals were another matter, men all round; the girls didn't even live together, but would be sent out to command-posts and observation-posts, to corps or division, regiment or battalion. A girl could be alone there, and sometimes her need for protection, for a strong male arm and a little basic comfort, would get the better of her. And the fact was, even a company commander had a separate hut of his own, or a dugout.

However, Galya came through with flying colours, as they say. There were two of them like that, Galya and her friend Nina Polishchuk, both from the same town, the same institute, they'd gone to school together, they both became telephonists and ended up in the same unit. They were the sort of girls nobody would take liberties with. In Nina's case that was easy, as she was ugly, short and sharp-nosed, whereas Galya was tall and good-looking, with big eyes, and a lot of men liked her, but she was independent, that's the point. Maybe she didn't have what some of the girls in the battalion had, but the soldiers helped her, they took care of her, she was a brave girl, she stayed at her switchboard to the very last, and she got two Red Star medals, not bad for a telephonist!

Books and movies have also created the idea that the most important person in army signals is the wireless operator, and if it's a girl wireless operator, then she's the heroine of the piece. I should tell you that this is also not quite the way things were.

Radio requires no wires so the distance is covered without any danger to the wireless operator, who is vulnerable only at the spot where he's working. A telephonist has to carry the wire across the battlefield, often in the enemy's view, he can come under fire from the air, or from artillery, and he can be sniped at. If contact is broken he has to restore it immediately, as the troops cannot be left without control, and the repair has to be carried out also under enemy observation. A telephonist can camouflage himself and take advantage of the terrain, but sometimes that isn't possible, especially at the approach to a command post, where the wire has to be raised up.

You probably think the girl telephonist operates the switchboard and that the wire is fed out and repaired by men. That's true, but if there's a fault, the operator also has to help repair the line. Women fed out the line and carried the reel under battle conditions. As a rule, the signals centre would be established at the command post in, say, a dugout. But what sort of dugouts were there at Stalingrad, you might well ask! The girl telephonists dug their own fox-holes there, and sheltered in them with their equipment, they ran out the wire themselves and did their own repairs under bombardment. After 15 October 1942 the order came to evacuate all the girls to the left bank, as conditions had become unbearable, but a delegation of girls, including Galya, went to Chuikov and asked to be allowed to remain on the right bank, just like everyone else. So they stayed and fought and died. No other town saw as many heroes as Stalingrad, but how many Stalingraders were awarded that title? The title of hero was handed out lavishly only later, when we were going forward on the offensive and winning, but not at the beginning when we were defending ourselves and when the Unknown Soldiers were dying. A lot of the girls in the signals were left behind in the soil of Stalingrad. May they never be forgotten.

Again you might say, if telephone communication is so dangerous, why not use radio, which is anyway more reliable? More reliable, yes, but don't forget that during the war, especially at the beginning, radio communication wasn't perfect, on top of which the enemy can listen in, so you have to put everything into code and then decode it, all of which takes time, which is the one thing you haven't got in battle conditions. I can tell you this, any commander preferred the telephone. Just psychologically, by the tone of a conversation or the force of his personality, a commander could have a much more direct immediate influence on a subordinate over the telephone. For a battle commander, the telephone was second only to a face-to-face exchange. As for the artillery battery, telephone is the only possible means of communication, there just isn't time to start decoding cables when you're directing fire.

Galya actually started off in an artillery battery, even though it wasn't usually done to post girls to firing positions. But that's what happened with Galya, she ended up in the artillery and that's where we met. Later on they transferred me, as I said, to intelligence, and she was sent to battalion signals, but we were both in the same division, and we met; not often, but still, we did meet.

Anyway, one night, it was either November or December 1942 and still in Stalingrad, we both landed up in the cellar of this bombed-out building, some sort of store or warehouse next to a blown-up railway siding. The rest of the building had been blown to bits and only this part remained intact, together with the cellar underneath it. Troops from different units were packed in there like sardines, grabbing a few hours' shut-eye, not an inch of space left. My men managed to find me a dry place next to the wall, not too near the door. And then Galya and Nina turned up, chilled to the bone, poor girls, straight out of a blizzard, straight out of battle, and there was no room for them, everyone was lying down, you couldn't move. But you know what General Guderian said: there are no desperate situations, only desperate people. He was right. Everyone squeezed closer up together to let the girls lie down. Naturally, they slept in the clothes they were wearing, buttoned-up breeches and boots. It was a concrete floor, so I laid out my ground-sheet, covered Galya with my greatcoat and wrapped my arms round the poor thing. She warmed up, looked at me, smiled and fell fast asleep, and despite the rumbling overhead and the trembling walls, she slept peacefully. I had this feeling of tenderness towards her, and I seemed to be both asleep and awake – I would drop off, then I would hear her breathing and see the child-like quality of her face.

Before morning, there was a shout at the door: 'Tokareva, Polishchuk, outside!' Galya woke up, shook herself, then she and Nina Polishchuk got up, picked up their rifles and telephone sets, said good-bye and left.

After that we saw each other occasionally, as before. I liked her and I thought she wasn't entirely neutral towards me, though she gave no sign either way. In 1943 she was twenty and I was thirty-one, an ordinary lieutenant in intelligence with no distinctions, apart from some chevrons I'd earned for getting wounded. Not that she minded, she was indifferent to status, but evidently she'd taken an oath to behave herself, and I felt I couldn't make a pass at her, I didn't want her to see me as someone just out to get a bit of skirt. I behaved towards her like a friend, and she was friendly to me. She was friendly to everyone, but it was a friendliness that kept men at a distance, you know how clever women can do that.

With Galya, however, it was part of her job. During battle, everybody, especially corps headquarters, needed the telephone. There were only two telephone lines, a direct line and a by-pass, but there were forty connections on the switchboard with an important commander at the other end of each one, demanding to be connected with this division or that unit. And all demanding at once! What do you do in such a situation? It requires skill. Suppose the artillery commander is on the line and the HQ commander rings, you can't interrupt the artillery commander, but then you can hardly refuse to connect the HQ commander, either. Somehow, you have to appease him. You say, one minute, please, Colonel, I'll connect you right away, just hang up for a moment and I'll get the division on the line and call you back. Then, just as nicely, you say to the artillery commander, 'Vasili Fedoro-vich, I have a long line of people waiting, they're getting angry.'

Such situations arose all the time, she had to appease everyone, never offend anybody, she had to know exactly how to speak to them all, a girl of only twenty and she had to be a diplomat! You don't think it was an accident that all the switchboard operators were women, do you? A corps com-mander would only have to hear a man's voice at the switch-board and he would start feeling agitated and get on his high horse. A girl on the switchboard in battle conditions is like a nurse in hospital. A girl who's been through that kind of schooling learns how to deal with people and how to present herself.

You remember May 1943? It was the first May after Stalin-grad, the great turning-point of the war. There was that sud-den lull at the fronts, we were pulling ourselves together after our victory, and the Germans couldn't pull themselves together after their defeat. May 1943 was special in every way, it wasn't like any other. You'll say that May 1945 was another Great May. True, that was a national, universal victory. But for us front-line soldiers, May 1943 was some-thing unrepeatable, we felt like different people, we felt our own strength and confidence, for the first time we could take a breather, get ourselves shipshape, take a bath and get clean after two years of exhausting and bloody war. It was our first real breathing-space and we had earned it with our blood and our lives. For the first time in the war we could celebrate May Day, we had the right to a holiday. And orders came, promoting me to first lieutenant and awarding me the Red Banner, and there were decorations and medals for my men, as well.

We were to the west of Voronezh, towards Kursk, in a

village that had barely been touched, if you can imagine it. Voronezh had been blasted to smithereens, the surrounding villages had all been burnt, but this one had survived by some miracle. It was large and the huts were intact, the bath-houses were heated up, the quartermaster doled out something special for the holiday, we had victory rum and victory chocolate. The main thing was the signals people were also in this village, and Galya was with them. She had some time off, and it wasn't 1941 any more, it was 1943; she wasn't wearing a quilted jacket and trousers now, but a blouse and skirt, and boots, her hair was done, and she looked fine. She visited us in the intelligence unit to grace our modest celebration.

And this was my show, it was my company, they were my soldiers round the table, I was the officer in command. I wasn't a regular army-man, I was really a civilian, I never liked hierarchy, but the army is the army and, say what you like, I was their commanding officer, I was good at the job, and my men wanted to work with me. Naturally, I was demanding, you had to be, but I wasn't a stickler about a button being undone, or a collar not being just right, or how a man saluted or stood to attention. You often got a slovenly little peasant who was a real soldier, which wasn't always true of men who knew how to stand and look you straight in the mouth.

But that's all by the way. So, I've already given you the background to May Day, 1943. We had a festive table, with rum, stew, sausage and chocolate, and there was Galya, like a queen, and there was I, a first lieutenant, it really looked as though we were a couple. Anyway, that's how my men saw it, especially as she had come as my guest, they put two and two together and gradually they all began to disperse, dis-appearing as if they had things of their own to do elsewhere, leaving the two of us alone together, though, believe me, I didn't make them go, not the slightest hint. Maybe I did want to be alone with Galya, but I would never have spoiled the holiday for the others, this was a holiday for everyone, and as their officer I could order them to stay at the table and enjoy themselves. On the other hand, if Galya had wanted it that way, she could have changed the situation herself, she could have got up and said that, as long as everyone else was leaving, she would leave, too, and then I would have made sure they all stayed. But she didn't get up, she didn't make me stop the others from leaving. We were left alone.

I noticed that, in spite of her holiday mood, Galya was preoccupied, it would show fleetingly in her face, disappear and then return again.

'Where is Nina?' I asked her.

If she had come alone on such an occasion, without the friend she wouldn't part from throughout the war, and she was worried about something, it seemed likely that the friend was the problem.

'I don't know,' she replied.

How could she not know where her best friend was, after all, they lived together? Obviously, something had happened between them, they'd had a fight or quarrelled, these things happen, but what business was it of mine? Friends quarrel and make up, that's the way things go. But my mind was occupied with other thoughts, I put her uneasiness down to the situation: she was here alone with me, she knew something was going to happen, maybe she was making up her mind.

I took hold of her hand and asked sympathetically, 'Have you had a fight?'

'Yes, we have,' she replied, without taking her hand away. It trembled slightly and I held it tight.

'Never mind, you'll make up,' I said.

I could feel the warmth of her hand, the softness of her palm, her nearness. It had been so long since I had held a woman's hand. I pulled her close and kissed her.

'Comrade First Lieutenant! Please!' she said.

It's normal for a girl to resist, even if only symbolically. I wanted to kiss her again, but she freed herself from my arms.

'I asked you not to, Lieutenant!'

It wasn't the official way she spoke to me that stung, nor her irritable tone or the fact that she pushed me away, it was the way she did it, in such a familiar, skilful movement, as I saw it. I had an unpleasant sensation, a feeling of injustice. If she knew how to free herself from a man so confidently and firmly, it must mean she also knew how not to free herself, when she didn't want to.

Nevertheless, in a friendly way, I said, 'Come on, Galya, why the struggle?'

She got up.

'I thought you were different, but I see you're just like the rest. You, *First Lieutenant*!'

I sensed in the way she said 'You, *First Lieutenant*!' that she wanted to hurt me, as if to say, at the command post she had to do with generals, and here was this raw first lieutenant, who'd only just got his new rank that very day, and already he thought he could do as he liked.

Had it gone to my head? I swear, nothing like that had ever happened to me before. I couldn't understand it myself.

'Isn't a lieutenant good enough for you?' I said crudely.

'You're not like the rest, you're worse. At least they don't pretend, they're not hypocrites,' she said, and with that she left.

I drank another glass of rum and went to bed.

Next day I analysed the whole episode and I realized I'd behaved like a louse. I had to apologize for insulting her. Of course, there could never be anything between us, that much was clear, but after all we had been friends for a year and a half, we had shown respect for each other, we shouldn't part in such an uncouth way, we must remain human beings. I would tell her I'd had too much to drink, I'd behaved like a lout, she must excuse me, forgive me, forget it and let's be friends like before. She'd behaved well, and she would have behaved even better if she'd slapped my face. She was a clever girl, she'd understand, she'd forgive me. I felt better after I'd decided to apologize to her, and with a light heart I set off for the other end of the village, where the signals girls lived.

I got there and there was no sign of Galya. Nina Polishchuk, the friend I've told you about, was there, and another girl. I called Nina out and asked her where Galya was. She shrugged her shoulders.

'Don't know.'

I got the impression that she didn't want to know. Just like Galya the night before. Except that Galya had shown disquiet and anxiety, whereas Nina looked annoyed, angry and stubborn.

Nina Polishchuk also had a good reputation, both as a girl and as a signalwoman, but she was quite different from Galya. She was small and dark, with a long nose, nothing to look at, a good telephonist, but again not like Galya. Not a scrap of diplomacy, or courtesy, or mildness. On the other hand she was precise, quick on the uptake and efficient. She spoke in a dry, official, rather abrupt way, but she never forgot a thing and she knew her way round the HQ set-up perfectly, she was decisive and as her decisions were generally the right ones, most people were prepared to let her dictate, and though there were conflicts in the early days, and they even had to take her off the main switchboard, gradually people got used to her, especially the corps commander, who preferred working with Nina to any of the other telephonists, because Nina would do anything for him. Galya would also do anything for the corps commander, but she was also nice to other people, saying, excuse me, would you please finish, the general needs the line, then telling the general she would call him right away, so he would have only a minute to wait and the other caller would have a chance to finish his conversation. Nina would cut off anyone else instantly, if the commander needed a line, though when he'd finished she never forgot who she'd cut off and she would ring back and ask if he wanted to be re-connected.

Altogether she had such an independent and brusque character, and was so quarrelsome, that you really had to adapt yourself to her, but once you did, you could get along with her just fine. At any rate, Galya had made friends with her, and now they'd fallen out, just like that.

I asked her point-blank, 'What did you quarrel over?'

Nina asked me how I knew they had quarrelled and what Galya had said to me about it and so on, but I won't burden you with the details, especially as we've spent far too long on this episode already, so I'll just give you the main point.

It all started over the Norwegian writer Knut Hamsun. Can you beat that! Actually, it was a lot more serious than you might think at first glance. It wasn't that they had quar-relled over Knut Hamsun as such. They were both educated girls, well-read, student teachers, preparing to teach litera-ture, they knew all the writers, including Knut Hamsun. To tell the truth, I'd never even heard of him until then, he never figured in any syllabus – I'd read pretty well only what the syllabus required, and it hadn't required Knut Hamsun.

Like every other writer, Hamsun had his admirers and his critics. Galya recognized him as a major artist, but claimed that his heroes were isolated, unattached, egocentric, spiritu-ally sick and mentally ruined. She quoted Plekhanov and other Marxist critics to show that they had long ago exposed the reactionary tendencies in Hamsun's work, she said that Hamsun was concerned with the evil in man, unlike Leo Tolstoy, who glorified the good, the kind, and the noble. But Nina argued that only Knut Hamsun knew how to reveal the real human mind. Now, Nina's father was a scholar, a philologist and specialist on Hamsun, something he'd been given a really hard time for, being accused of defending Knut Hamsun's reactionary views. So Hamsun for Nina wasn't just Hamsun, he was a great writer her father had suffered for, and she took any criticism against him very badly. As her closest friend, Galya tried to keep off the subject.

But then it so happened the Germans dropped some leaflets. They were always dropping them and usually we took no notice, they were always full of junk, but on this occasion they dropped one which said that many leading European figures, including the famous Norwegian writer Knut Hamsun, were giving full support to Hitler, and they quoted some of his remarks to prove it, though I don't remember what, as if anyone could remember the rubbish that went into Fascist propaganda.

I read a few of Hamsun's things after the war, *Hunger*, *Pan*, *The Wanderer Plays with Muted Strings*. Of course, I'm no literature specialist or critic, and I can't judge whether Nina or Galya was right. There's no question, these books are powerful and impressive. On the other hand, Hamsun did collaborate with the Germans after they had captured Norway, he did give them active support, and the Nazis did use his name widely for propaganda purposes. After the defeat of Nazi Germany, he was put on trial as a traitor and boycotted by the cultural world. That's a fact you cannot escape. You have to agree that if a world-famous writer collaborates with the Fascists while they are enslaving his own country, it can't happen by accident, and Galya was right to accuse him of being reactionary.

But, to return to events.

So, the Germans had dropped these leaflets, which mentioned Hamsun, Galya got hold of one of them and showed it to Nina, as if to say, look at this Hamsun of yours!

Nina, of course, bristled, it couldn't be true, Hamsun wasn't that sort of person, the Germans had invented it, it was a forgery.

Anyway they argued, and the argument took place in the hut, with the other girls present, the leaflet went from hand to hand, and this fact got to the head of the political section, Lieutenant Danilov, who knew as much about Hamsun as I did. What he certainly did know was that these leaflets ought to have been handed in, and also that they were not to be handed around to others as an object of discussion. He summoned the girls and questioned them, Galya and Nina included, and they all confirmed that Galya had brought in the leaflet, which she didn't deny, even though she knew what was threatening her and how it might end. This explained her anxiety the night before.

Of course, I saw it all, I sized up the situation and knew what was behind it.

I went to Danilov. 'Look, Lieutenant,' I said. 'That leaflet is mine, I picked it up. Why did I hang on to it? Because it mentions the well-known writer Hamsun. I showed it to Galya Tokareva, after all, she did languages. And she showed it to Polishchuk, as her father is a professor, actually a specialist on Hamsun. It's all due to my curiosity. I just wanted to understand, to have it explained. You don't think I was going to distribute a German leaflet?'

'Then why didn't Tokareva' – that's Galya – 'tell me you had given her the leaflet?' he asked.

'Danilov,' I said. 'Would your girl split on you? You know Galya! Look, I'll give you any explanation you like, in writing, if you want, but, please . . . Or better still, tear that disgusting rubbish into little pieces, you can pick up as many as you like in the fields, but just don't ruin my life, or the girl's life.'

'No,' he said. 'I can't just tear it up like that.'

He picked up the phone and called Galya. 'Tokareva! Get your replacement and come and see me immediately.'

Galya arrived and sat down. Danilov asked her, 'Where did you get this leaflet?'

'I've already told you, I picked it up on the street.'

Danilov pointed at me. 'But the first lieutenant maintains he gave it to you.'

'I don't know what the first lieutenant maintains, and I don't want to know,' she said.

Danilov then picked up the leaflet, tore it into small pieces and threw them into the waste-paper basket.

'I can quite understand that you want to protect your first lieutenant, but let me advise you next time not to accept gifts like that from a first lieutenant or anyone else. As for you, comrade First Lieutenant, don't give any more gifts of that nature.'

'It wasn't a gift,' I said. 'I showed it to her in the course of a discussion on Hamsun.'

'And you acted improperly,' he corrected me. 'You placed Sergeant Tokareva in a false position, but in view of the fact that you're a combat officer, I'm closing the case. I regard it as an unpremeditated act, and I warn you not to let it happen again. Right, you can leave now, and I don't want to have to see you again!'

As a matter of fact, Danilov told me later that he knew straight away that I was lying to get Galya off the hook, and he was pleased, as he didn't want to ruin such a nice girl, but he hadn't known how to deal with it, and my statement came just at the right time. I don't know if he was telling me the truth, but at any rate he behaved decently in this affair. If someone else had been in his job, Galya could have been in for a really rough time.

Anyway, it was all over, Galya and I came out, and she grinned. 'Thanks! What do I owe you for that, now?'

'Galya,' I said, 'don't say that. You shouldn't. Last night I behaved like an animal.'

'I'm not talking about last night, I'm talking about today,' she interrupted. 'Yesterday's been and gone. But today you turned up here as *my* first lieutenant, after all, that's what Danilov said, "You're protecting *your* first lieutenant." Maybe you told him I'm your "battlefield wife"?'

'I had no reason to tell him that,' I replied. 'You don't

317 ♦

seem to realize just how serious this was and how it might have ended.'

'Don't put yourself out,' she said. 'I've got someone who'll worry about me.'

'Just as well,' I replied. 'He'll come in handy next time. Give him my regards, and take care of yourself!'

With that we parted. I took no notice of her hint about a protector. I knew it was our general, the corps commander, he thought highly of her and would have defended her. That wasn't the point. After two years at the front, your nerves get frayed, even at twenty, but she was a sensible, intelligent girl, probably I could have persuaded her that I really was sorry for what had happened the night before. But I didn't get a chance. Soon after, the battles on the Kursk arc took place, we moved forward, there was the summer campaign, Belgorod, Oryol, Kharkov, then the winter campaign, Kiev, Korsun-Shevchenkovsky, Rovno, Lutsk, Proskurov, Kamenets-Podolsk. Then another summer campaign, through Byelorussia, into Poland, at the end of July and early August 1944, when we forced the Vistula and seized the air-heads in the Magnushev district. In that period of just over a year, I caught a glimpse of Galya in corps HQ twice, then they transferred the signals battalion commander to army HQ, and he took Galya with him. As long as she was in army HQ, obviously I couldn't see her. Later I heard that as soon as the war ended she was demobilized, as they were releasing ex-students to continue their studies. I still had a year to serve in Germany with the occupation.

We were stationed at Reichenbach, not far from Chemnitz – it's now called Karl Marxstadt – and life went on. But I couldn't get Galya out of my mind, she had made a place in my heart, I couldn't forget the night we'd slept together in the ruins of Stalingrad, that memory would stay with me forever. True, in Reichenbach I had an affair with a woman doctor.

She was a captain in the medical corps, a good-looking girl of twenty-eight, a solitary like me, bright, intelligent, educated, decent and very dignified. She used to come to me from Erfurt, where their hospital was, and I used to go to her in the Opel Olympia car that I had. Did she love me? I think she did. But she was altogether restrained, especially in the expression of her feelings, though perhaps that was in response to my own restraint. She was very sensitive, and I was conscious that Galya stood invisibly between us. The affair with the doctor didn't come to anything. In July 1946 I was demobilized, I returned to the USSR and went to Moscow, where a friend of mine from the front, Vasya Glazunov, who was working in the commissariat for light industry, had promised me work, perhaps even in Moscow. Of course permits for Moscow weren't easy to get, but anyway, he'd said, come and we'll think about it, we'll come up with something.

There were other people at Vasya's who'd been scattered by the war, they had wanted to get home, but like so many, found they no longer had a home to go to. Everyone was trying to rebuild their lives anew and make new contacts, but still they couldn't forget the old ones that had been forged in blood and heavy army service.

Anyway, there we were at my friend's place, reminiscing and checking up on who was where, when suddenly one of them said, 'Hey, do you remember Galya Tokareva, the telephonist, she was with us at Stalingrad, and then went to army HQ?'

My heart stood still.

'Well, anyway,' he went on, 'I saw her, ran into her at Yaroslav Station, she's living somewhere near Moscow and works in Moscow.'

'Where does she live, where does she work?' I asked.

'No idea,' he replied. 'I hardly knew her, she didn't even

recognize me. I had to remind her of our corps, the signals battalion. I asked her how she was. "OK," she said, "fine." She had on a fur coat and hat, quite a lady!'

What can I tell you? I spent the whole of January 1947 at Yaroslav Station, every day without missing one. From seven in the morning I met the suburban trains and from five o'clock to midnight I watched them leave. Sometimes I even stood there throughout the whole day. There were the January frosts and the thousands of people and more than one platform, and it got light late and dark early. It was hopeless. No Galya. I made inquiries and found out that Galina Nikolaevna Tokareva had been born in Stalingrad in 1923. No such person was registered in Moscow, so she was obviously living near Moscow, but where?

February came and I waited all through February, though I knew it was pointless.

And then I met her! It was a Sunday morning and she was coming back from Taininka, where her parents lived and where she was registered, though in fact she was living in Moscow. She had a room which she shared with a friend and she was in her third year at Moscow University, in language and literature. On Sundays she went home to her parents, and now she had come in to shop.

I said, 'May I come with you? I was going to shop anyway, and I'm a visitor here.'

'Have you been in Moscow long?' she asked.

From the way she asked, I had the feeling she already knew.

'Oh, about a month or so,' I replied. 'Why do you ask, have you seen me, or something?'

'Yes, I've seen you.'

'Where?'

'Here, at the station, twice.'

'Why didn't you come up to me?'

'You were waiting for someone and I didn't want to be in the way.'

'I was looking for you.'

She was quiet for a moment, then she said, 'I knew you were looking for me, but why?'

'Galya,' I said, 'all I can offer you is myself, as I am, here. I love you, I've always loved only you, I searched for you and now I've found you.'

'And I love you, too,' she answered. 'I knew we would meet, and you're still like the little boy you always were.'

We've been together now for thirty years, and they seem like a day. We have three sons, Yakov, Alexander and Genrikh, and we've already got grandchildren, Igor and Dina, named in honour of those who are lying in the cold ground.

Why did my sons register themselves as Jews? Out of respect for me? No, I don't think so. They respect their mother just as much. No, the point is, the son of a Georgian father, for instance, and a Russian mother will, as a rule, register himself as a Georgian, or the son of an Uzbek man and a Russian woman will sign himself an Uzbek. After all, the wife and children take the father's name, not the other way round. I think my boys did the right thing.

Well, that's the story of my marriage and now I can get back to the main story.

21

They say that in the spring of 1942, people were dying in the ghetto at the rate of fifteen or twenty a day because of raging dysentery. Stalbe received instructions 'On the burial of dead horses, cattle, dogs and Jews found littering the roads', and he ordered that all the dead be buried immediately. It was spring, corpses were decomposing and they were supposed to be buried at least six feet deep. The problem of coffins was made easier by Jewish custom, which prescribed the burial of the dead without a coffin, but wrapped in a shroud, so the coffins were brought back to the ghetto for new corpses, and there were enough coffins. But then there weren't enough shrouds, so Stalbe ordered burial without them, and the shrouds were brought back to the ghetto for the new corpses to be wrapped in. His orders were carried out, coffins and shrouds came back to the ghetto.

As I understand it, the Nazis had gone through their first phase of ardour and enthusiasm for mass killing, beatings, mockery and taunts, and the whole thing had become a habit with them. In the early days, they had found a few thousand people, mostly women, children and old folks, it is true, but nevertheless strong and healthy and full of life and vigour, and they'd had to be especially alert and use extreme savagery in order to turn these people into labouring cattle. What they had to deal with now was not seven thousand, but a little over three thousand wrecks, emaciated, debilitated, filthy, stupefied, tattered, frozen, crippled creatures that could hardly drag themselves along the ground – you wouldn't call them human. They were dying in the ghetto and in the forest, and the main thing, now after the actions, was that they knew they had no escape from death, they firmly believed this and they had come to accept it. They had become used to the idea that they could die at any moment, they would die without complaint, and there was no need to waste a bullet on them, one crack of the whip would do the job. The aim had been reached, the regime was being obeyed automatically, fear had been beaten into them firmly and forever.

So if those returning from work used to be searched thoroughly, now it was done just anyhow, carelessly, and with revulsion, as it was disgusting to have to touch these lice-ridden creatures, covered with sores, even to look at them made you sick, especially then, in April, when the tiring spring sun warmed up the blood, and made you want to lie on the grass or go for a drink, and soldiers on leave were going by with their trophies – the Russian goods they'd picked up – and with their iron crosses, and here you were, having to poke around in this shit and stink. True, you could always arrange a little entertainment by making them strip naked and roll in the dirt, or make them do gymnastics, the knees-bend, perhaps, all of them together: 'Knees bend! Stand up! Knees bend! Stand up! Ten times! Twenty times! Thirty! Fifty! A hundred times!' Till they drop dead. Or you could make them dance, naked, of course. After work, of course. The waltz, for instance. One S S man played 'The Vienna Woods' brilliantly on a mouth-organ, and if any blockhead or swine or saboteur got out of step, he'd get his last lash of the whip. One of their own dances was even better, even merrier. It was real entertainment, terribly funny. Like the circus, the movies, and the cabaret, all in one! You should have seen those skeletons jump up and down, and throw their arms and legs about, or put their thumbs under their armpits and stick out their skinny little chests, and of course some of them would fall, and it would be necessary to dispatch them to the cemetery with a lash or two.

But even shows like these could pall after a while. Who could then be bothered with inspections and searches? If in the early days coffins had to be carried out one at a time and each lid lifted one at a time, now they only ordered a lid to be lifted in an extreme case, and as for unwrapping a shroud, that was out of the question, especially as the corpses wrapped in them had died from infectious diseases.

However, according to the two men who, you remember, had managed to escape during the action, it was actually in shrouds that weapons were brought into the ghetto.

Grandfather lived at the cemetery. When you're burying fifteen people a day, you're not going to run two miles each way fifteen times, and Uncle Yosif convinced Stalbe of the need to divide the labour: one group to collect the corpses in the ghetto, another to carry them to the cemetery and go back with empty coffins and shrouds, and a third lot to dig the graves, bury the dead, and live at the cemetery as watchmen. Two policemen were attached to the burial team, both locals I used to know. One was Morkovsky, who used to be the head of the state insurance office, the other was Khlyupa, a vet's assistant, who was still a young man, as a matter of fact. They were both absolute scoundrels, you realize, but they'd completely sold themselves to grandfather for illicit vodka and lard.

Vodka? Lard? Where did grandfather get hold of vodka and lard? He himself was dying of starvation, and so were his children and grandchildren. How could there be any question of lard and vodka? Nevertheless, grandfather had vodka, and he had lard, and he had something more substantial than vodka or lard. I mean gold. Where did he get the gold from? From those who had it. What the Germans had failed to get by shooting hostages, with their automatics and machine-guns, grandfather did manage to get. Hungry and cold, stripped of all rights, every day he was burying ten or fifteen dead, he buried his own wife and son, and he had one foot in the grave himself. I tell you, if an old man of eighty-two could find in himself the strength to obtain weapons in those conditions, and if in those conditions he could do everything possible to defend the dignity of his fellow citizens, then God and nature must have given him a mighty spirit and a powerful will.

As I told you earlier, grandfather had intended to get gold from his son Yosif, but without success that time, though he did confirm that Sarah Yagudin knew about Uncle Grisha's visit to the ghetto, that she knew the boys were cooking up something, that she was blackmailing Yosif with this, and that Yosif, being the head of the *Judenrat*, was afraid of her. Grandfather told my mother about it and they decided to take steps. But then the action took place, eight hundred people were shot, and they took their steps only after the action, and after one other event I want to tell you about now.

There's no denying that in the war against the civilian population the Germans achieved a lot, on that front it was victory all the way. Naturally, their opponents were unarmed. Millions were killed. They weren't all brave, but there were heroes among them whose names we don't know, for the most part. But if you're talking about the ghetto, the first monument ought to be to the children, for they were the most fearless. Showing incredible bravery and daring, they brought food into the ghetto. Many of them paid with their lives for a crust of bread, a handful of flour, a potato, a beetroot, but that didn't stop them. On half a pound of bread a day, and less than a quarter of a pound of peas a week, the inhabitants of the ghetto would have been dead within three months. They didn't die, they had to be exterminated. The first battle was with hunger, the children were the first to fight it, and they won. They knew where the gaps were into the neighbouring streets, they could crawl through any crack, they rummaged in scrap-heaps, stole from stores and bunkers, from German motor vehicles, they traded things for bread, or bought it if they had money, and they brought everything back to the ghetto, down to the last crumb. Imagine. When a hungry man finds a piece of bread his first impulse is to eat it up. What would you expect a hungry child to do? But, as I said, they brought every last crumb back to the ghetto. These children became grown-ups at seven, and at eight they died, as grown-ups.

Our family was in a slightly better situation. At one time, Anna Yegorovna had helped by feeding Olya. But Anna Yegorovna wasn't around any more, God rest her soul. Anyway, the little she had brought would hardly have done for all of them. She was starving herself. The Stashenoks did most to help. It was only thanks to them that our family survived that terrible winter. They lived in our old house; in the old days we used to be able to get to grandfather's from there by going through Ivan Karlovich's garden, but now it was impossible, you got a bullet if a sentry saw you. But Igor had a way through into Ivan Karlovich's garden, and from there another one under the fence into our yard. He used to steal along to the Stashenoks at night, they would give him whatever they could and he would come back by the same route. By the way, it was in their house that Anna Yegorovna and Olya used to meet. If the police had got wind of that, they would have shot every Stashenok they could lay their hands on. But the Stashenoks were true human beings, they didn't stoop before the Germans, they put human obligation above fear.

Still, they didn't have a food store or a grocery shop, they were giving of themselves, they were sharing what little they had of their own, they gave their last to help their friends who were perishing in the ghetto. And they had three grand-children of their own who also had to be fed.

Another source of support, temporary, but real none the less, came from another quarter.

Grandfather's house was the first house on Sand Street. Stalbe put gates at the end of Sand Street, at the exit to the forest, and closed off the end of grandfather's property, so grandfather's house became the last in the street. Beyond it stood a solid fence with barbed wire, and beyond that there was a fruit and vegetable depot, abandoned, of course – as if there would be any fruit or vegetables around! The inhabit-ants had picked out whatever could be eaten and our own authorities had distributed it, so the enemy shouldn't get at it. The rest had rotted and just lay littered about among the empty barrels and boxes.

Again because it was spring, the authorities imposed strict sanitary conditions, and the *Judenrat* was ordered to put twenty men on to cleaning up the depot, and their team-leader would be responsible for looking after the produce. What produce? Mouldy cabbages, frozen potatoes, rotten apples? That's right! They had to sort the stink and decay into heaps, when it would be handed over to the *Judenrat* as part of the food allocation.

Uncle Yosif put Gorodetsky's brother-in-law, Isaac, in charge of the team, as he had handled state purchasing at the depot before the war and he knew a bit about fruit and veget-ables, so though everything had gone bad and stank, he might still be able to save something of use to the ghetto.

At the depot, before the war, they used to make strawberry filling for sweets. They would put the strawberries in barrels, pour in some substance that turned the contents into a white mass, which didn't spoil, then send off the barrel-loads of filling to a sweet factory in Chernigov. And in one of the cellars, hidden under a heap of empty boxes, Isaac found several of these sealed barrels of strawberry filling. He may have known they were there, perhaps he had hidden them himself, I couldn't say. Nor do I know how our boys found out about them, but the fact is they did, and they decided to get them out. Each barrel with fifty pounds of filling in it was enough to save several dozen people from death by starvation.

The boys dug a tunnel from grandfather's cellar to the depot, they reached the barrels and, using cans and buckets by night, they brought out the filling to the ghetto.

I had a look at this tunnel later, or rather at what was left of it. It was about fifteen feet long, they had dug it at night, and they had made it wide enough to carry a bucket along, and reinforced it so the roof wouldn't fall in. It may sound like a miracle, but those children dug that passage, they brought out the filling, the people in the house cooked it to make *kissel* and they all lived on it for nearly a month. But all good things come to an end, and an end came to the life-saving *kissel*. The SS got wind that something was going on and during the night, while the boys were taking the filling, they burst into the depot.

The children made their raids in twos; one would climb down into the cellar where the barrels were, fill the cans and pass them up to his companion, then he would climb out and the two of them would crawl back with the laden cans. On this occasion, it was my brother Sasha and Ilya, one of the Kuznetsov grandchildren, who had gone. And the SS swooped. The children had already agreed that if they were captured, they wouldn't let on about the underground passage, whatever the cost, they would die first. If the SS found the cellar and the passage from it, they would shoot everyone living in the house. So when the boys saw the Germans, they didn't make for the underground passage, though they could have saved themselves just by diving for it, instead they went in the opposite direction, hiding themselves behind the empty boxes and barrels. The SS men followed them, firing as they went, and they caught them just as Sasha was climbing over the fence and helping Ilya to scramble up after him. They shot Ilya while he was still on the ground, and Sasha died where he was, hanging on the fence. Sasha was fourteen, Ilya twelve. The Germans found the barrels with the strawberry filling, but they never did find the underground passage.

That's how my little brother Sasha died, a gentle, fragile boy with blue eyes. There had been no need for me to worry about him, he had turned out to be a real man. Long live his memory, and long live the memory of all those who suffered and perished!

Meanwhile, at the time all this was going on, Sarah Yagudin had come to our house and demanded some strawberry *kissel*. When a household of fifty people can keep themselves going for a month on *kissel*, the neighbours are bound to hear about it, especially if they've got nothing to eat themselves. But even in those conditions, people didn't take the food out of each other's mouths. Each person ate whatever he could get hold of, whether he traded for it, or stole it, or bought it outside the ghetto. The *Judenrat* had a common soup kitchen, but the crust of bread that a man found for himself at the risk of his life was his own, he could share it with someone else or not, as he chose, that was his affair, it was his right. But in this case, the sweet filling was stolen, if you started dishing it out to everyone the Germans would uncover everything immediately. So the inhabitants of our house kept it secret, except that, as I said, it was impossible to keep it a secret in those circumstances. The neighbours knew, but they kept quiet, they didn't ask any questions, they also knew that they would all be done for, unless they were loyal to each other. Only Sarah didn't want to know anything about loyalty, she broke the secret, she had the cheek to come to my mother and demand to be given some *kissel*, or some of what it was made from. It wasn't that mother grudged her a dish of *kissel* – as it was she was sending filling for the sick people in other houses – but here was this insolent slut, this blackmailer, this criminal, if you gave her your finger, she'd take your hand. Mother sent her away. That night the guards caught the boys red-handed and Sasha was killed, and mother was quite sure that it was Sarah's doing.

I told you about Uncle Grisha's first visit to the ghetto. Even then, mother and grandfather realized that Sarah had reported it to the *Judenrat*. Then, when Bronya Kuras and Motya Gorodetsky blew themselves up in the cellar, trying to make a bomb, Sarah asked mother, 'Rachel, how did Bronya and Motya die? I saw them that morning and they looked fine.'

'Open your eyes,' mother replied. 'Can't you see people are dying all around you? One minute they're alive, an hour later they're dead.'

'Yes,' Sarah agreed. 'But not with bangs and explosions.'

'You heard?'

'People talk.'

'People talk nonsense.'

'If this nonsense reaches Stalbe, it'll be hell to pay for somebody!' Sarah threatened.

'And it won't do much good for whoever tells him, either,' mother warned.

Sarah took no notice of the warning.

When Uncle Grisha came back to the ghetto, after the action, Sarah turned up at our house the same evening and scoured the room with her eyes. Uncle Grisha was down in the cellar with his sons and she didn't see him, but she still asked mother, 'Well, where's your partisan?'

'You want him?'

'I don't want him, but Stalbe does.'

'You're very nervous, Sarah,' mother said. 'It's not good for your health. Here, have some sedative drops.'

And she took a bottle out of her pocket, an ordinary medicine bottle, and offered it to Sarah.

'Try it, it'll do you good.'

Sarah gave her a suspicious look.

'You try it first.'

'You're doing yourself out of it,' mother said, as she took a mouthful.

Then Sarah took a mouthful and discovered it was vodka, real vodka! And she sucked on the bottle till it was dry, she didn't want to let go of it, and went on sniffing at it. They shot you for possession of spirits in the ghetto, and here they had vodka, home-made! To hell with them and their shooting, let them shoot, there was vodka! Vodka! That this miracle should have befallen her! Would she ever have got it from Stalbe, or Yosif, or the shitty *Judenrat*?!

'Just remember, Sarah,' mother told her, 'there are no partisans here, there never have been and it couldn't happen. Get the whole idea out of your head and don't repeat such nonsense.'

Sarah was merry from the vodka. 'Fine, Rachel, you and I'll get along together just fine, don't worry about a thing.'

But the next day, or maybe the day after, Sarah turned up again and asked for more vodka and, as if that wasn't enough, for tobacco, too.

'I haven't got any tobacco, and never had any, I don't smoke,' mother told her. 'And there's no more vodka, either. I gave all there was to you.'

'You're lying!' said Sarah. 'I can see right through you. Where do you get the vodka?'

'It was from before the war.'

'Another lie! That vodka was fresh made, you can't fool me. Where do you get it?'

'I'm not telling you,' mother replied. 'I don't intend to get anybody else involved.'

'Well, if you won't tell me, you'll tell Stalbe, all right!

You'll tell him about the vodka, and about your partisan of a brother, and you'll tell him what your children and your nephews are up to in the cellar.'

'What is it you want, Sarah?'

'I want vodka, and I want a smoke!' Sarah answered. 'You'd better get me some vodka and tobacco, or the same thing'll happen to you as happened to your son!'

You see? The reptile herself admitted she'd had a hand in the murder of Sasha and Ilya, she had led the Germans to the depot, that's why they were so kind to her, that's why Yosif was scared of her.

'Listen to me carefully, Sarah,' mother said. 'I'm not afraid of death, I should have gone long ago. If you talk to me that way then we have nothing to say to each other. You go to Stalbe, maybe he'll give you a drink. You'll get nothing from me that way. Now clear out!'

'All right,' Sarah said in a conciliatory way. 'All right, Rachel, keep your hair on. Let's talk woman to woman. Get me vodka and something to smoke.'

'A smoke I can't get.'

'Bugger the tobacco, get me the vodka.'

'They don't give it away, you know.'

'What do you need?'

'Don't you know what they want in the villages? Stockings, shoes, blouses.'

'A blouse, I can get a blouse,' Sarah announced, obviously she'd already thought of someone she could get it from.

'I'm not prepared to bring it through here, the guards will catch us, we'll get shot,' said mother. 'Come tomorrow night to the cemetery, to my father, bring the blouse and you'll get your vodka.'

Next night, Sarah went to the cemetery, where grandfather and six old men from the burial squad were waiting. The police had gone home to the town, where they always slept.

The seven old men judged Sarah Yagudin for extortion

from starving people, for the denunciations she had made, for the deaths of Sasha and Ilya, and they sentenced her to death. Grandfather carried out the sentence, by strangling her with reins. The old men buried her outside the fence.

The S S brought in the whole of Sarah's work-team and all the people who lived in the same house with her, to try and find out where she had got to, but nobody in the team or the house had any idea. Uncle Yosif managed to convince the S S that she had run away. Why should anyone be surprised, she was a hardened criminal, she had escaped from proper places of detention, why not from here? It would be easy for her. And Stalbe believed it, though he gave warning that next time anyone escaped, their entire family would be shot, and their work-team, too.

But in the ghetto, those who could still think and use their imaginations knew what had happened to Sarah, and they realized that there was another force at work in the ghetto, apart from Stalbe. It was a force that punished traitors.

Just how grandfather managed to get hold of money and valuables, or how much there was of it and who he got it from, I don't know, as none of the witnesses survived. There was a witness to what was going on in our house who did survive, and you'll find out who that was later. I don't know what was going on in the other houses, or how grandfather got gold from his son, Yosif.

According to one version, grandfather went to Yosif and said, 'Your assistant, Sarah, has gone into the forest. I showed her the way. I can show it to you, too.'

Yosif became alarmed and gave grandfather his gold. According to another version, which I think is more likely, Yosif wasn't scared at all, he refused point-blank, but his daughter, Raya, stole the gold from him on the orders of my mother, who then gave it to grandfather. What else he managed to collect in the ghetto I have no idea, certainly nothing very valuable, not the English Crown Jewels or a diamond from the Kremlin collection. Wedding-rings, earrings, brooches, cuff-links, table silver, gold crowns from teeth, Tsarist gold ten-rouble pieces. And it didn't come by the caseful or the trunkload, it was scraped together after the Germans had taken everything else, and what they didn't take had been bartered for food. Even so, grandfather managed to collect something, which he was able to exchange for weapons. Who had weapons, or who got them for grandfather, I also don't know – grandfather took that secret to the grave with him. In any case, the exchange was made by a complicated route, through a man grandfather trusted, who lived in the village of Petrovka, four miles from the cemetery.

Of course, I can't confirm it, but I think, I'm even sure, that grandfather's illegitimate son may have had something to do with it, perhaps he was the man grandfather trusted. It was surely no accident that he lived in Petrovka. But as it can't be proved that it was him, we'll refer to him simply as grandfather's agent. This man bought the weapons in the town, as there was hardly a German soldier who could resist gold. There wasn't a lot of gold, and there weren't many weapons. The most valuable were four Schmeisser sub-machine-guns, first-class, lightweight, with a magazine for thirty-two rounds instead of a pan like ours had, also some rifles, pistols, and hand-grenades. Not a lot for making war on Hitler, but they played a decisive role, because the boys learned how to handle weapons. Until then, they had no idea. Is the bullet in the clip? What then? What are these numbers for, one hundred metres, two hundred, three hundred? What's this? The breech frame? And this? Oh, the feed-box cover. What do you do if the weapon misfires? How do you throw a grenade without getting hit by the shrapnel yourself?

Uncle Grisha came a third and a fourth time and taught his sons Venya and Edik, and my sister Dina, and they taught others. Resistance starts the minute a man has a gun in his hand. The first weapons were got by grandfather, there weren't many, but without them the people would have been power-less later on, when a lot more came into their hands.

The police guessed, of course, that grandfather was doing business at the cemetery. He wasn't bringing the vodka and lard and bread out of the ghetto, you couldn't find a cat or a dog left to eat there. Someone must be bringing the food and drink to him at night, he was buying it or trading it, so there must be some money around, or some goods! It didn't occur to them that the old man might be acquiring weapons. He must be piling up grub, the old swine, and a lot of it, seeing how much he forked out. They guarded these Jewish devils all day long, maybe they brought goods in the coffins instead of corpses? No, they took out the corpses, unwrapped the shrouds and put the corpses in the grave, muttered some words or other, and covered them over with earth. The corpses were naked, on the commandant's orders. But still, all this stuff didn't fall from the sky, it wasn't manna from heaven. They may have been alcoholics and rogues, but they weren't stupid. Morkovsky was an insurance agent and Khlyupa was a vet's assistant, they were educated, they put their heads together and they reckoned that if the old man could dish out so much to them, in the way of bribes, how much stuff must he be sending back to those Yids of his, how much must he be paying for it, and what with?

It was only to be expected, regardless of how devious grandfather was. And grandfather wasn't to blame, he didn't make any slips, but the circumstances were too much. Maybe he even sensed something in the police, he had an instinct about people, but on the other hand the police weren't idiots and they managed to fool grandfather, the swines.

One evening, as usual, they set off as though to the town, but they didn't go far. They hid and waited for grandfather to come out of the watchmen's hut later and saw him go into the forest. They followed. Grandfather sensed something, maybe he heard footsteps or the crunch of twigs, he stopped and listened, the police stopped and hid. Grandfather waited a while, started off again, then apparently realized he was being followed, turned round and started to go back. The police blocked his path.

What really happened I can't say. Descriptions of the scene have been given to me, but whether they correspond to the truth I don't know.

The police searched grandfather and found nothing. Take note of that: grandfather was going to get weapons, yet he had nothing to pay with. Everything had been paid for in advance – the gold, the valuables, the money that he'd collected, he'd given it all straight away to his agent. That was the right thing to do – where could he have hidden it all, to be able to take it out of the ghetto bit by bit? The longer it was hidden, and the more often he'd have had to take it out of the ghetto, the sooner he'd have been caught. Grandfather had given everything to his agent in Petrovka, where it was in no danger, or at any rate in far less danger than in the ghetto. How could grandfather have trusted this man so much, that he would put the fate of the ghetto in his hands? This is another reason for thinking that his agent was his son.

When the police found nothing on grandfather, they ordered him to keep moving in the direction he'd been going in, so as to bring them to the man he was expecting to meet. They started pushing him with their rifle-butts and he went further along the forest path, with the middle-aged ex-insurance agent Morkovsky behind him, and behind Morkovsky, Klyupa, the vet's assistant.

Grandfather walked as far as he intended to walk, then he suddenly turned round, grabbed Morkovsky's rifle, and yelled at the top of his voice, 'Run, Mikola!'

He brought the rifle down on Morkovsky's head, Morkovsky fell, but Khlyupa managed to raise his rifle and fire.

Grandfather fell.

But before he fell, he yelled out again, 'Run, Mikola!'

Khlyupa shot at him, lying dead as he was, then lifted up Morkovsky, who was still alive, though his skull was fractured, and dragged him to the watchmen's hut. He had two rifles over his shoulders and his fellow-policeman in his arms.

Now, in fact, Mikola hadn't run away. This is a third reason for thinking he was grandfather's son – he had grandfather's character. He caught up with them near the watchmen's hut, shot them both, took their rifles and bullets, their knives, uniforms and documents, and left.

The S S came in force the next day, plus Gestapo men with dogs, and Stalbe himself. Two policemen had been killed, and the old Jew, Abraham Rakhlenko, had obviously gone off with the partisans. Then the dogs discovered grandfather's body. He was lying on his back with his eyes closed, and his hands folded on his chest. Take note of that! It meant that Mikola had returned, he'd had nothing to dig a grave with, nor time, and anyway there was good reason not to, as grandfather's disappearance would have provoked the killing of his family. And the way he was when they found him is a fourth reason to believe that Mikola was his son.

After the war, I went to Petrovka to try and find this man, who was actually my uncle, or his children, who were my cousins, and I wanted to find the woman grandfather had loved long ago in his youth, and who had given him a son. But instead of a village, I found only charred chimneys, the village had been burnt to the ground by the Germans in 1943, and every single inhabitant had been shot for having contact with the partisans. So if that man was grandfather's son, he only outlived his father by a year. Their fate made them equals.

They buried grandfather and, although there was no evidence that he'd had anything to do with the deaths of the policemen – if anything, the evidence was that he'd been killed with them – they shot the whole burial team, all fourteen of them. They included Kusiel Plotkin, the butcher, and the roof-maker Aleshinsky. As you see, he picked his team from people he knew. I'm sorry, I know this is no place for humour, but it amuses me that grandfather picked his own people for the burial team: he'd get the weapons, but others would wrap them in shrouds, put them in coffins, and carry them back to the ghetto, and these others had to be people he could rely on.

22 ▩

Meanwhile, Uncle Grisha went on forming his detachment. It had been decided that Sidorov would supply six men, and that Grisha would take ten from the ghetto. He chose the ten, and once again he didn't take his own sons, nor anyone else who could handle a gun, as they would be needed there. He only took those who still hadn't learned, he would teach them in the forest. The boys, who were all young and relatively healthy, were from the shoe factory, the leather works, and other towns.

The question was how to get them out of the ghetto? It was easy enough just to go out, but what then? Many of the restrictions in the ghetto weren't being so strictly observed, and they were turning a blind eye to quite a bit, but an escape, any escape, would be seen as contact with the partisans. If anyone escaped from the ghetto, the rest would be severely punished.

There was one way – the *Judenrat* could list the names among the dead. Mother sent Dina to the *Judenrat*. Why didn't she go there herself? It's hard to judge. I think, after grandfather's death, she held all the strings in her own hands and she probably felt she shouldn't be, so to speak, on the surface of events. One false step and she'd be lost, the loss of one meant the loss of them all, the two streets, several cross-streets, three thousand people – they all saw and heard everything. Maybe mother couldn't have dealings with Yosif – after all, it was she, apparently, who had put his daughter Raya up to stealing his gold and giving it to grandfather. In any case, the fact is, it was Dina who went to the *Judenrat* to see Yosif.

Emaciated by hunger and cold and the unbearably heavy work, tattered and filthy, Dina was still a beauty. You can imagine what awaited her among those beasts and thugs. But Stalbe at least deserves credit for sticking to the 'twelve commandments on the behaviour of Germans in the east'. You don't know them? I see you're not very well informed, but then, who is? Only specialists in the history of the Fascist Reich. The whole thing has become an academic subject. And that's all wrong! This is a lesson of history that should be taught to schoolchildren.

Anyway, the eighth commandment said: 'Keep yourself at a distance from the Russians, they are not Germans, but Slavs. Don't engage in drinking sessions with Russians. Don't enter into any relations with women or girls. If you should sink to their level, you will lose all authority in their eyes. Through his age-old experience, the Russian sees the German as a higher being.'

These commandments were compiled by state-secretary Backe, who was responsible for food-supply, but even so, Stalbe, an S S man, fully recognized them. If that's how the Germans saw Russian women, what was there to say about Jewish women? Shooting them, that was good order. Raping them, that was disorder. This protected Dina to some extent, but she was defenceless against everything else. Even worse, Stalbe had his eye on her: she was the daughter of that mongrel, Ivanovsky, the one Le Court had managed to extract from the ghetto, and also she could sing.

Singing was forbidden in the ghetto, the penalty for singing was to be shot. For carrying on a loud conversation you got fifteen strokes of the birch, but if you sang, they shot you, because if one person started singing, others would join in, and soon everyone would be singing, and singing would make them human again, but they were insects, and insects don't sing, as everyone knows.

As a matter of fact, in some ghettoes the Germans formed orchestras which played everything from popular folk tunes to 'Kol Nidrei', and in either the Vilna or Minsk ghetto, I don't recall which, they made the famous singer, Gorelik, sing Jewish songs. The prisoners were lined up in the square in their thousands, in tens of thousands, and Gorelik sang and the orchestra played tunes they knew from their childhood, and the people stood and wept. Then they were taken away and shot. And you probably know there was also a prisoners' orchestra at Auschwitz, which played the 'Tango of Death' as the people were being sent to the gas chambers.

But apparently Stalbe was not a sentimentalist, and anyway the scale here was different and the aims were different. Only three thousand were left of the original seven, soon the electric saws for felling the trees would arrive and that would be the end for them, too. And when that happened, Stalbe was going to have no disorder or sabotage! They would all lie down neatly, side by side!

In other words, singing was out of the question. But then that weakling, Reinhardt, the military commandant of the town, asked Stalbe to allow Dina Ivanovsky, the daughter of Yakov Ivanovsky, a person of mixed origins, to sing at a concert in the club.

I've told you about the club that used to be the industrial cooperative club, where once upon a time Dina performed in amateur concerts. With the permission of the military commandant, the town council formed an amateur theatre there for the local population. It was managed by a husband and wife, the Kuliks, old local schoolteachers, as a matter of fact I had been taught by them myself, and now here they were doing cultural work under the Germans. They mostly put on plays by Staritsky, like *Aza the Gypsy*, and various adaptations from Gogol and Panas Mirny. As it happened, the theatrical enterprise came to an end with a nice little show. During a performance, the police surrounded the theatre and detained all the young people, which meant most of the audience, and then sent them off to work in Germany, as so few had wanted to go voluntarily. After that, nobody went to the theatre – anyway, there was nobody left to go. That happened later on, but in the spring of 1942, the Germans ordered a big festival concert to be organized for their servicemen. Of course, it was no good putting on Staritsky for German servicemen, as they couldn't understand Ukrainian, so it was a case of playing musical instruments and dancing and singing. That's when the idea of asking for Dina Ivanovsky came up, she had the only voice that would surprise the Germans. Of course, she was imprisoned in the ghetto, but her father lived outside, free. Anyway, the Kuliks persuaded the mayor, the mayor persuaded Reinhardt, and Reinhardt asked Stalbe. You can imagine Stalbe's fury! First they managed to scrape the father out of the ghetto, and now they're after the daughter!

Stalbe immediately ordered Dina to be brought to him. She was brought.

Through an interpreter he asked her, 'Can you sing?'

I should tell you that Dina spoke German as well as I do, fluently. German was the third language spoken at home, on top of which Dina had spent a lot of time in Ivan Karlovich's house, where she studied music with his wife, Stanislava Frantsevna, and there they spoke German, and she did German in school, too. But in front of Stalbe, she gave no sign that she understood the language. It was dangerous to know German in the ghetto, as the Nazis could give you unpleasant jobs to do, for example, translating their inhuman instructions, which would make you in effect one of their assistants.

When the interpreter translated Stalbe's question for her, she sensed a trap and answered, 'I can't do anything.'

'But they told me you can sing well,' Stalbe said.

'I sang in school, but I forgot everything a long time ago.'

'But your former teachers want you to sing in the club.'

'I can't sing, I've forgotten how, my voice broke, I wheeze.'

She really did wheeze, everyone wheezed and coughed. Half-naked, they had to fell timber in the winter frosts, and in the rain in spring.

'Where's your father?' Stalbe asked.

'He works on the railway.'

'Surely he's a Jew?'

'No.'

'Probably he's trying to do something for you, too,' Stalbe said, as if he was thinking aloud.

I think that remark threw Dina off balance for a moment. Surely father didn't want her to sing in the club? To sing? In front of them? Surely father didn't want to please them?

Of course, it's easy for us to reason on Dina's behalf, to put the arguments and counter-arguments, and to take this decision or that. It was harder for her. She didn't know the true situation. Father was working at the station, but just why he was there was known only to mother, Sidorov, Uncle Grisha and grandfather. And now that grandfather was dead, only mother, Sidorov, and Uncle Grisha knew. Mother trusted Dina, but you must understand the conditions. If the Germans had suspected anything, they could have subjected her to the kind of torture that would loosen anybody's tongue. Dina only knew that they'd let father out of the ghetto, his case was being looked at in Berlin, mother was hoping they'd let him go to Switzerland, and I think that, however much Dina loved father, for her he was now outside her life, everybody who was not in that hell with her was outside her life. Father was saved, and thank God! He hadn't wanted to be saved, mother had compelled him, there was nothing to reproach him for, but he was already outside her life. She didn't think father wanted her to sing in the club, but even if he did, she still wouldn't sing in front of them! Never!

She knew that her life depended on one wrong word, but still she said, 'I don't know who is trying to do anything for me, but I've forgotten all the songs, and I've lost the ability to sing.'

'So, that means you don't want to sing in the club?'

'No.'

With that, Stalbe let her go and informed Reinhardt that Jews were not allowed to make public appearances, and even if it had been allowed, Dina Ivanovsky had refused to sing in the club. Reinhardt didn't insist, he didn't much like that sort of amateur activity and, in any case, who could tell what sort of performance this girl Dina would give, though her father, Ivanovsky, a person of mixed origins, seemed loyal enough at his job on the railway.

And that was that. There was no more talk about any singing, Dina continued working wherever they told her to, in the forest, clearing roads, unloading wagons, cleaning the barracks, and at night, together with Venya Rakhlenko, she taught the other kids to dismantle and assemble weapons. They say that she mastered the art herself very quickly. Of course, there was no firing range, nowhere to train, but one thing was sure, and that was, when the time came to use the weapons, the children would know how. Even before the war, Venya had got his Voroshilov Marksman's badge.

So now mother was sending Dina to Uncle Yosif to try and get him to register as dead ten men who would be going with Uncle Grisha to join the partisans.

'Whose names am I to put in the report?' Yosif asked.

Dina told him the ten names.

He wrote them down on a piece of paper.

'All right, I'll think about it.'

'No,' she objected. 'The first five have to be registered today, they're going tonight, and the rest must be registered to-morrow, they're going tomorrow night.'

'I'm not registering them today or tomorrow, but when I think it's necessary,' Uncle Yosif replied. 'And if I don't think it's necessary, then I won't register them at all. If they're caught, what happens to me?'

'You should have said that straight away. Why did you write down their names, then?'

'That was necessary, so I wrote them down. I want to know exactly who they're going to shoot every fifth one of us for.'

'Give me the list and forget about it,' said Dina.

'No!' Yosif shouted. 'It stays with me. And if you want to stay alive a little longer, don't meddle in this business. Now leave!'

'Give me the list!'

'Clear out!' Yosif yelled. 'You want to go to the ditch? I can soon fix it for you!'

'Give me the list!' Dina repeated.

'You want the list? What about this, then?' Yosif took a pistol out of his desk drawer. Yosif was violent by nature and was capable of anything, especially here, where he could act with impunity and where human life wasn't worth a damn.

'Put your gun down,' Dina said. 'I can suggest something different. You register the names as dead, and I'll get your gold back for you.'

This was something unexpected for Yosif, I think, as he regarded his gold as lost. And now, all of a sudden, it turned out it wasn't lost, it might be returned to him, and with it hope for salvation. He was no longer relying on his brother-in-law, Yakov, as his Swiss relations hadn't responded for quite a while now. And Yosif didn't believe in the partisans, they'd be slaughtered. But with gold, he might be able to hide away somewhere on a farm, he knew people who wouldn't give him away, though if they did, he would simply give the Germans his gold. And he would go alone, he didn't need his traitor of a daughter, and as for his wife, she'd never survive in a farm cellar. Anyway, what difference would it make where she died, here or there? But if he ran away, they'd shoot the *Judenrat*, still, they're going to be shot anyway, a day sooner or later, what difference does it make? He must first get the gold from Dina – she had it and she should have told him – then he'd get rid of her, he didn't want any witnesses.

I knew Yosif well enough to be sure that that's how his mind worked. He was of course aware that Dina offered to return the gold because she wanted to repair the blunder she had made in naming the people who were going to go and join the partisans. She had to rescue the list, but the one thing she was not going to get was that list.

Yosif put his gun down on top of the list and, in a quiet, practical voice, said, 'I can't show these people as dead. If they got caught, I'd be shot. But if you get me back my gold, I promise I'll destroy the list and forget I ever saw it.'

'Give me the list and I'll bring you your gold,' Dina said.

'No,' he retorted. 'You bring the gold, and I'll burn the list, here in front of you.'

Dina stretched out her hand, but Yosif was on guard and pressed the list down under his palm. But it wasn't the piece of paper that Dina grabbed, it was the gun.

'Put down that pistol, you fool!' Yosif screamed.

Yosif may have been a villain, but he was no coward, he was, after all, a Rakhlenko. Also, the safety-catch was on. What he didn't know, was that Dina could handle a gun. Dina heard the door behind her open and someone enter the room. Yosif reached across the desk and tried to grab the gun from her, and she shot him in the head. She turned round, with the gun still raised, in the doorway stood Khonya Bruk, Yosif's assistant, who quickly slammed the door on her. Dina snatched up the list of names, screwed it up into a ball and swallowed it. She heard the sound of boots, the door opened, she fired. Having no experience she couldn't guess that they would be expecting her to shoot, and she fired into an empty space, there was nobody behind the door. They shot at her through the window, but the poor girl wasn't killed, only wounded. If only they had killed her straight off, how happy she would have been, what luck!

Stalbe didn't give a damn about Yosif Rakhlenko. Nevertheless, he had been an official, appointed by the German authorities as chairman of the *Judenrat*, and he had carried out his duties loyally. Consequently, this had been an act of retribution, sabotage, resistance. Who had inspired it, who were the organizers and accomplices? The murderess was the daughter of the half-breed Yakov Ivanovsky, who had been freed from the ghetto, thanks to the efforts of Captain Le Court. His son had been caught stealing, and now his daughter had been caught in the act of murder. The girl wasn't saying anything, in spite of the extreme degree of interrogation. Her mother, Rachel Ivanovsky, says Yosif Rakhlenko was molesting her daughter and that, in self-defence, she grabbed his gun and shot him. The pistol had indeed been issued to him as chairman of the *Judenrat* by Commandant Stalbe himself, but he didn't like this explanation.

Stalbe himself interrogated Rachel Ivanovsky. According to one of the local ethnic Germans, an engineer at the depot, the grey-haired Jewess standing before Stalbe had been an object of romantic love for that scoundrel Ivanovsky, who was supposed to have come from Switzerland to Russia for her, and to have gone into the ghetto for her, and then refused to leave the ghetto, all for her.

This tale struck Stalbe as a personal insult. The Jews didn't have love, they only multiplied and by multiplying they preserved themselves as a race. For ages, they had exploited the myths in the Bible and other fables in order to dull the vigilance of mankind and hide their urge to take over the world. For the sake of strawberry filling, this woman had sent her son to his death, and looked on calmly as he hung on the fence. Now, she isn't willing to spare her daughter from torture, by telling them who had sent the girl to murder the chairman of the *Judenrat*. The way she held herself! The hatred in her eyes! How she could lie and fabricate! She took him for a fool, they took everyone for fools, these arrogant nobodies!

The inhabitants of the ghetto were all lined up on the square, where a cross had been erected. They brought Dina out, naked, beaten, covered in blood, her face a bluish colour.

They tied her to the cross, then Stalbe said to mother, 'There's your daughter. Tell me who sent her to murder the chairman of the *Judenrat*, and we'll just hang her. If you won't say, we'll make her confess.'

Mother answered, 'She has nothing to confess. Nobody sent her, and she didn't plan to kill anybody. It was he who meant to kill her. She was defending herself.'

At a sign from Stalbe, the executioner hammered the first nail into Dina's hand. Dina fainted and Stalbe ordered water to be thrown over her. She came to.

Stalbe said, 'Are you going to talk?'

Dina was silent.

'Maybe you'll sing us something?'

Dina was silent.

He struck her with his lash. 'Maybe you'll sing, all the same?'

And Dina started to sing. No, it wasn't singing. A wheeze came from her chest and blood came from her throat. They had damaged her lungs. She choked, wheezed something, then wheezed something again, all the time getting quieter and quieter. I couldn't say what it was she was trying to sing, maybe a Jewish song, or a Ukrainian or Russian song, or perhaps the 'Internationale', the hymn of our youth and our hopes.

She went on mumbling disconnectedly, too quietly to be heard, even in that deathly hush. The executioner hammered a nail into her right hand, then her left, and still she mumbled something, until she fell silent and died away, hanging crucified. Everyone stood still, looking, mother stood and looked at her daughter, crucified, and little Olya looked, and little Igor.

I think at that moment, all the boys and girls who had learned to use a weapon, would have used them then to avenge Dina, and to die alongside her, if necessary. But they hadn't been ordered to, they were already fighters and wouldn't act until ordered.

Dina hung dead on the cross for three days.

Khonya Bruk, Yosif's former assistant, was appointed chairman of the *Judenrat*. He would sign anything my mother asked him to, he was afraid of her, and maybe he sympathized. The ten men registered by Khonya as dead went to the forest. They left in twos and threes, guided by little Igor, who knew the way.

So died our Dina. Long live the memory of her bravery and daring! May her executioners burn forever in hell!

23 ▨

Did father know about the death of Sasha and Dina? The Germans had isolated the ghetto, severed all ties with the local population, but still, it was a small town and the people knew what was going on in the ghetto. They knew in general terms that there were shootings every day, executions, killings, but on that scale of mass destruction it made no difference who in particular had been killed. The people father had dealings with at the station probably didn't know, either. Also, father lived alone. After the war, I met quite a few people who were witnesses to his time at the station, far more than witnesses of my mother's life, but I know far less about his life then. 'He worked in the stores', that's as much as any of the railway workers could tell me about him. He worked and slept in the stores, he handed out spare parts, and outside work he saw nobody.

Nevertheless, I think father knew about the death of his children. Uncle Grisha wouldn't have kept it from him, it wasn't his nature. Father was in contact with Uncle Grisha through Andrey Stashenok, a signalman and eldest son of Afanasi Prokopyevich. Andrey, his wife Ksana, and their daughter Marya and son Kostya, lived in the railway settlement, they worked in the depot and supplied Sidorov's partisans with information on the situation at the station, on convoys passing through, and anything our command needed to know, and from Sidorov they received assignments for father.

The plan had been changed, there was no time left to buy

weapons. The action could take place any day, and it was likely to be the last, the clearing in the forest could easily accommodate three to four thousand people, in other places they were coping with tens of thousands at a time. There was no time to buy weapons, they must be seized.

The Germans were not allowed to store their weapons in goods-sheds, railway stations were bombing targets. Just like us, as a matter of fact, they had to unload their convoys some way off at branch-line halts and sidings. But order is one thing, war is another, war is a great disorder in human life. Convoys were unloaded in the goods-yard, wagons stood right on the main lines, weapons lay in goods-sheds for several days, sometimes a week. But the station was guarded by special units, it was surrounded by machine-gun towers, all approaches to it were closed off. To raid the station was an impossibility. A different sort of operation was a possibility.

The rear units of an infantry division arrived at the station, and the ammunition officer's equipment was not housed at the goods-yard, but in one of the depot stores. They cleared out some of father's state property, fenced themselves off and arranged a sort of stores-cum-workshop, where they unpacked the boxes, checked the weapons, to see if they were damaged, or if the sights had moved, changed the factory grease for regular oil, pulled through the barrels. A little way off, in a hollow, they even set up a small firing range, where they adjusted sights, and in general got the weaponry ready for battle, as there's no time to do this under battle conditions, you realize.

The stores, or workshop, call it what you like, was guarded by ordinary troops from the rear units of the division, and it was easier to find a common language with them, than with the SS. The armourers who tested the weapons would borrow tools from father, and this and that, they weren't at all wary of him, they took him for a local ethnic German. And the stores opened, not on to the town side, but on to the railway settlement, where there was no commandant's office and no soldiers. There was a small, surfaced road leading to the stores. In other words, the conditions were right. And they must hurry; at any moment, the rear units, together with their stores, could be relocated elsewhere. Would such a chance come again?

The officer in charge of the workshops, the clerks, storemen and armourers all lived in private quarters. At night there was only a patrol of six men, plus a guard-commander, and the sentry room was on the second floor, in the administration offices. Drivers who came to collect weapons slept in the settlement and left their trucks next to the stores, where there was an outside sentry-post. There was another one inside the building, in the corridor at the entrance to the stores. The guard changed every four hours.

I can tell you, the whole thing had been beautifully thought out. Have you ever been inside a large railway depot? No, but you've seen one from the outside, driving past? It has big buildings for locomotive bays and turntables, it's a major enterprise, covering a vast area, and employing large numbers of workers; engines are continually arriving and departing, crews constantly changing, so it wouldn't be too difficult to bring in five men, dressed like mechanics, particularly if the store manager is one of your own men. First one came, then two, with knives and pistols under their overalls, and father showed them where to hide in the stores. The last pair hid in Andrey Stashenok's house close by, in order to deal with the outside sentry.

As you will see for yourself, and as I've already said, the operation was beautifully thought out, thoroughly gone over, and the first half of it had now been successfully carried out: armed men had penetrated the depot and were ready for the raid. But, as you know, you can't think of everything, nobody is guaranteed against accidents.

Two policemen turned up and told father to come with

them. Where to? To the commandant's. What for? They'll tell you what for when you get there. In fact, father knew what for, they were always dragging him over there, it was nothing new, but he hadn't expected it just that day.

Imagine the situation. They are taking father away, and when he'll return, or even if he'll return, is unknown, and there, hidden in the stores, are Grisha and his men, who will all be shot if they are discovered.

Father tried to talk himself out of it: he had to issue spares to the second shift, it was impossible to lock up the stores, couldn't he go tomorrow? He spoke in a loud voice, so Grisha should hear, but the police wouldn't have any of it, they'd been ordered to deliver Ivanovsky to the commandant, and that was that!

There was nothing for it but to lock up the stores and go, leaving Grisha and his men there.

Circumstances had taken a turn for the worse, but luck was still on their side. Around midnight, father came back.

The Nazi German security system was complicated, it consisted of the Gestapo, the SS, the SD, various kinds of police, and army intelligence and counter-intelligence. When new army units arrived, their security service went over everything again from scratch, and above all they wanted to clarify the position of persons of mixed origins, which naturally included father. And, of course, some scoundrels would have written denunciations, alleging that father was not a person of mixed origins, but actually of purely Jewish extraction, and every such denunciation had to be looked into. Something of this sort had happened on this occasion. Some military top brass had arrived in town, with a new Gestapo or SD outfit (who the hell could tell the difference?), they kept father the whole evening, questioning him, and finally let him go. But father asked to be escorted back by the police, as the curfew was already in force. So the police accompanied him all the way back to the depot, they were seen by the patrols in town and the sentries at the station, and with the police right there, father unlocked the gates of the stores, went in and locked them after him. Everything was in order, Grisha and his men were there.

The guard changed at midnight, including the one in the corridor. There was a door into this corridor from father's stores, which he used when he went through to the offices. They were counting on the sentry dropping in on father, which they often did, as it was a lot cosier there than out in the empty, long, dark corridor. The sentries chatted with father, leaving the door open so they could watch their post, which was as good as being at it, they could always say they'd just popped inside for a smoke. Anyway nobody ever checked up on the inside sentries at night, everything was locked up, the guard commander was asleep, and he didn't even wake up the next shift, they got up on their own, or were woken up by the sentries coming off duty.

After he got back, father sat down at the table, lit the lamp, and began filling in dispatch notes. And the sentry, who had been kicking his heels for a while outside in the corridor, came in in due course, sat on a stool, and started up a conversation with father, though what it was about I have no idea, as I wasn't there, and those who were didn't understand German.

The hardest thing for me to visualize about the entire operation is father himself. After all, I had known him as a completely different person. I can perfectly well imagine Uncle Grisha and his boys, and I've taken a few German sentries myself. I can see the whole operation distinctly and I say again, it was brilliant in its simplicity. But father in the role of a decoy, and on top of that, in the role of someone who had to chat amiably with the sentry to distract his attention and blunt his alertness, knowing all the time that the sentry was going to be grabbed, gagged, and throttled, and to look him in the eye right up to the last moment – for that job, father must have become a different person.

They killed the sentry and cut the telephone and signalling wires, then, as one of them stood at the foot of the staircase with a sub-machine-gun, the other four went upstairs with father. They had taken off their shoes, some had socks on, the rest were barefoot.

The guards were housed in four rooms. The guard commander slept in one, and the rest two to a room. The room belonging to the two guards on duty was empty. Only the commander locked his room on the inside.

You probably know that in the early days of the war the Germans liked to set themselves up comfortably, and where the conditions were right they treated themselves to all the creature comforts. Here the conditions were right. This was no slit-trench or dugout, nor even a village hut. Here they had large, light offices with requisitioned furniture, big, comfortable beds with clean linen, and a warm lavatory, shower and kitchen near by. Even in shelters and dugouts they slept in their underclothes. Here, in these conditions, far from the front, on enemy territory, true, but at a large, well-guarded station, in a large, populated place, with troops and police, the only thing they had to worry about was air raids. In addition, as I mentioned earlier, some of their top brass were in town, and in the presence of top brass, the German feels much more secure, it's part of his mentality; the German soldier has devout faith in the omnipotence of his commandders – at any rate, he certainly did in 1942. They hadn't had Stalingrad, yet, the myth of the war as an afternoon stroll still hadn't been dispelled.

Well, the boys got them as they slept, they knifed them before they could make a sound.

With the guards out of the way, father knocked on the guard commander's door.

'Hans, open up!'

Half-awake, the guard commander had no idea who was knocking, he probably thought it must be one of his men, and he got up and opened the door. Uncle Grisha got him with a single stroke. Then, as they had planned, they moved the blackout curtain at the window very slightly as a signal to the partisans hiding in Andrey Stashenok's house, who now took the outside sentry, also without firing a single shot.

They went back downstairs, opened the doors of the stores, which were on a simple catch, and then opened the gates on to the yard. Close by were trucks that had been loaded during the day, ready to go. Yevsey Kuznetsov and the second driver, a boy from Sosnitsy, started up two of them straight away. They loaded boxes of sub-machine-guns, rifles, ammunition, grenades. Father showed them a cupboard where a box of detonators was kept under lock and key, they broke the lock and loaded the box. They also loaded six MG 42 light machine-guns and boxes of ammunition-belts, four mortars, and several boxes of canned meat, which happened to be in the stores, and then they got into the trucks and sped away. I was told later that the whole operation, from the moment they killed the guard in the corridor to the moment when both trucks left, took no more than fifteen to twenty minutes. You'll say it's a fantasy. No, it was a fact.

So, the trucks raced off and father stayed behind. Grisha had suggested he should leave with them, but he had refused· If he ran away it would prove that he had been part of the raid, they would have seized mother and tortured and tormented her, and vented their anger on her. They would have got their own back on her, and not only on her, but on Olya and Igor, the whole family, the whole ghetto. Grisha obviously understood and didn't insist, though father was bound to be a primary suspect, as he was closest to the scene of the incident, but the whole operation had been executed so neatly and precisely, that no evidence had been left behind. And the nightshift of repair mechanics had been working downstairs in the depot, but they knew nothing of what was happening, and heard nothing. Speaking as an intelligence officer, I say again, they did the whole thing superbly. They hid the body of the outside sentry behind a wall, out of sight of the passing patrol, and they put the body of the inside sentry in the store-room itself, not in the corridor, and the Germans only stumbled on them in the morning, at five or six o'clock.

Once they realized what had happened, the whole station and all the army and police units in the town were put on full alert. Seven soldiers had been killed and two truckloads of arms had been stolen! You can imagine what happened!

A company turned up from divisional headquarters, which had been informed, and was sent in pursuit. By evening, they found the trucks, burnt out, in the forest about twenty-five miles from the station. The dogs charged off into the forest, but the troops weren't eager to go deeper themselves, and they returned to base empty-handed.

As soon as the Germans had discovered the raid in the morning, they cordoned off the station and the depot, and they detained everyone who had been working there the night before; then they arrested all the depot workers in general. They searched all the houses in the railway settlement, detained suspects and put them together with those arrested, and in all they scraped together about one hundred or more men. They knew perfectly well that the raid would have been impossible without the inside help of depot workers, and not just one, but many, in fact a whole organization. The men were dragged off for interrogation, the Germans tortured and tormented them, trying to get out of them the names of participants and accomplices.

They also brought father in, but he had his alibi: the Gestapo had been questioning him that evening until midnight, and there were the policemen who had brought him in, taken him back to the depot and seen him go off to bed in his cubicle, they had watched him unlock and re-lock the door of the stores. And, as a person of mixed origins, he was under police surveillance the whole time, anyway. What an irony!

Father was the first person to be released, as having nothing to do with the raid!

And here's another irony: no shadow of suspicion fell on the ghetto. The Germans knew that Sidorov was active in the district, but there was no way they could connect him with the ghetto. The ghetto was in the town, on the other side of the railway, far from the depot, where there weren't any Jews working, anyway, but more than anything else, the Germans simply couldn't admit the idea that the Jews were capable of anything like this. So, a lot of police were transferred to guard duty at the station and the railway settlement as a place 'infected by partisans' and, as a result, security in the ghetto was weakened, so the ghetto gained a short but valuable breathing space. The action was not far away. The electric saws had arrived, and also German labour detachments for procuring timber. The ghetto was on the threshold of destruction, the fateful moment was approaching.

The Germans found the burnt-out trucks in the forest, twenty-five miles from the station. But the weapons for the ghetto had been unloaded right near the station, not more than a mile or so away. Venya Rakhlenko and his friends had been waiting for the trucks at an agreed spot, where Uncle Grisha gave them thirty sub-machine-guns with ammunition, a dozen pistols, a box of grenades, and detonators. The boys carried it all back over the permanent way to the fruit and vegetable depot, then through the underground passage, and safely into the cellars at grandfather's yard.

The Gestapo went on the rampage at the station in their efforts to find the accomplices. The people were tortured by butchers who had been brought in specially, real masters of their craft. They beat people half to death, tortured them with electric shock, scorched them with blow-lamps, put out their eyes with needles, held their heads under cold water until they suffocated, then gave them artificial respiration and repeated the treatment, they hung them up with hundred-pound weights tied to each foot, they twisted and broke their arms and legs, hung women up by their hair, men upside down, or by their hands tied behind, they tore out fingernails with pliers. Naturally, not everyone could take that kind of torture, they betrayed others, they betrayed themselves, and they weren't to blame, it was the butchers who were to blame. But the butchers were practised, they could distinguish truth from invention, they didn't want any faked confessions, what they wanted was to find the real accomplices. The accusations and confessions only confused and obscured matters, and the wretched people who had accused themselves and others wrongly, in order to spare themselves further suffering, were tortured all the more savagely because of it.

Nevertheless, the Gestapo managed to pick up the scent. Under interrogation and torture, someone mentioned Andrey Stashenok. How or why or in what connection, I don't know, but his name came up. Immediately, Andrey, his wife, Ksana, and their children, Vera and Kostya, were arrested and, of course, tortured, but they stood firm: they knew nothing, they hadn't seen anything, they weren't at the depot on that shift, in fact, they never worked the night shift.

There was no evidence, only suspicion. They already suspected that old man Stashenok had links with the ghetto, and the police had looked in on him, though they'd never found anything. But even to be suspected was to be guilty. They were exterminating millions of people they didn't even suspect of anything. They had decided they would find the accomplices of the raid, whatever it took to do it, and it could only be done by means of terror. They arrested all the Stashenoks and then announced that, if the inhabitants of the settlement didn't give away the other accomplices, all those being held under arrest, over one hundred of them, would be shot. If after that they still wouldn't give them away, the settlement would be burned to the ground and its inhabitants exterminated. The partisans should know the cost of their raids, and the population should know the price of collaboration with the partisans.

Now try and imagine my father's state of mind, and take his character into account, otherwise you won't understand what he did. He knew they were torturing and tormenting people, he knew about the arrest of the Stashenoks, he knew what awaited hundreds of innocent people. Of course, killing hostages, exterminating a peaceful population, and destroying towns and villages was lawless and barbaric, and to cease resistance would mean the enemy had achieved his aim and had conquered. Father understood that. On the other hand, he also knew that the lives of one hundred men depended on him. To save them, to spare them from torture and suffering and death, only one thing was necessary, and that was to name the man who had helped the partisans. He was that man, and he alone. If he confessed, they would kill him, but he would die with a clear conscience. They would kill his wife, his grandson and granddaughter, but the other hundred men also had wives and children and grandchildren.

That's how I imagine father's mind worked. He went to the commandant's office and declared that he had led the partisans to the depot, hidden them in the stores, helped them eliminate the guards and seize the weapons.

They didn't believe him at first, his alibi was established, but perhaps he was taking the blame himself in order to shield the real culprits? If that was so, he must have come to the commandant's on the instructions of the saboteurs, in order to save them, and not the hostages. That meant he knew who they were, and he was going to have to name them!

What they did to my father! My God, what they did to him, while he was tied down on a table in their torture chamber! Three days and nights without end, like the story of human suffering itself. Father named no names, he gave nobody away, and he betrayed nobody. Some men had come, dressed as workers, they ordered him to hide them in the stores, he hid them, then, when he got back from the commandant's office that night, he opened the door into the corridor for them, they killed the sentry, wiped out the rest of the guard and made off with the weapons. He was the only person who knew and the only one who saw it happen.

They took him to the depot, beaten and bloody, and he showed them what had happened, where the telephone and signalling wires had been cut, exactly where the weapons were taken from, and roughly what was taken, including the boxes of canned meat. It all tallied.

The Gestapo were convinced. Yes, he had helped in the raid, but he hadn't been alone! Who were the others?

Again three appalling days and three appalling nights of such torture as I doubt anyone has ever undergone anywhere in the world.

On the seventh day, a procession came out of the gates of the commandant's compound. It was led by the Gestapo chiefs, followed by SS men with sub-machine-guns and a cart, on which lay the stump of a man, the stump of a man who was still alive, my father was still alive and breathing. They dragged him to the gallows, unable to stand on his broken, scorched legs. And they hanged him in the square in front of the ghetto, not in the ghetto itself, but so that everyone should see, and on his chest hung a label, saying 'Partisan'.

So died my father, Yakov Ivanovsky, aged fifty-two, born in the city of Basel, Switzerland.

◆

Unfortunately, his confessions and his death helped nobody.

Another gallows was set up on Market Square, with ten nooses hanging from crossbeams, all the inhabitants of the town and the railway settlement were herded there and all the Stashenoks were brought out, Afanasi Prokopyevich, his wife, his son Andrey, his daughters-in-law, Ksana and Irina, his grandson, Kostya, his granddaughters, Marya, Vera, Nina and Tanya. Afanasi Prokopyevich was seventy-two, Tanya was ten. With their hands tied behind their backs, and a label hung round their necks, saying 'They helped the partisans', they were all made to stand on stools under the gallows.

Do you know what our sadistic police did? They arranged the Stashenoks under the gallows in the same order they used to stand in when they sang their Byelorussian songs at the cooperative club, with Afanasi Prokopyevich at one end and his wife next to him, then Andrey, Ksana, Irina and their children, all of them fair-haired, barefoot, and wearing white shirts. Then they knocked away the stools from under them in turn, pausing between each one, until they had knocked away the stool from under the ten-year-old Tanya.

Long live their memory! Eternal glory to those brave sons and daughters of the Byelorussian nation!

24 ❈

Mother saw father's corpse hanging. For three days he hung there – that was the Nazi norm, the Nazi standard. In that respect, he shared the lot of others who had been publicly hanged. Those three days were the last three days of the ghetto.

The Germans were great masters of camouflage. Above the gates at Auschwitz was a sign that read: *Arbeit macht frei* – 'Labour makes you free'. There was only one kind of labour, and that was to labour for breath in the gas chambers, and the only kind of freedom was to be freed from that terrible life. But it wasn't September 1941 any more – by September 1942 people knew the true meaning of those words.

And then in a small town everything is so close. Right next to the ghetto was an 'Aryan' street, right next door to decent people were the police, and whatever the policeman's wife knew, a decent man's wife would often know, too. In many houses lived officers of the *Wirtschaftskommando*, units for organizing the economic exploitation of the district, and ordinary soldiers, and either of them might accidentally, or not so accidentally, let things slip out which made it easy to guess what was happening. Then the *Judenrat* was in contact with the city council where, believe it or not, decent people also dropped in. And more and more, they were taking work-cards away from those working in the factories, which meant, if they could still work, that they would be working next day in the forest, and if they couldn't, then they would just have to wait till they were sent to the ditch in the clearing. In the way that birds sense the approach of a storm, or animals the first tremors of an earthquake, these people knew their hour was approaching, they knew the last and final action was being prepared.

On the thirteenth of September, twenty women were sent to tidy up the old sports centre. They washed and scrubbed it out, cleaned up the lavatories, carried in beds, sheets, tables, chairs and cupboards, that were taken out of store, and put out wash-basins. They were getting billets ready, but who for? Those in the know said they were for *Sonderkommando A*, from Chernigov. This 'Special Unit' spelled the destruction of the ghetto.

Mother sent word of this to Uncle Grisha straight away. But how?

After the raid on the station, the Germans again tightened up their regime, they intensified security, there were patrols, cordons, streets were closed off, they stopped everyone. Grisha was wary of coming to the ghetto himself, or of sending any of his men in, so for a short time there was no contact. But he had to be told about the forthcoming action, at all costs. The question was, who to send? And not even into the forest, which was impossible in those circumstances, but at least to the next village, where mother apparently knew one of Sidorov's men. But even to get to the next village was impossible, all roads and paths were blocked. The only person who might get through was little Igor. Until then, all his runs had been successful, but, as I said, conditions had changed, they were picking up everyone who wasn't where he was supposed to be, including children.

Of all the decisions mother had made, this was the most terrible, as she knew the danger Igor would be in. But there was nothing else she could do. She sent him at night. He got to the village and passed on his grandmother's message to the proper person.

He had almost reached the town on the way back, when he was stopped by a patrol.

'You seem to know the way to the partisans,' the police said.

'I don't know any partisans,' Igor replied.

'Where have you been?'

'To a village.'

'What for?'

'I asked them for something to eat.'

'Did they give you anything?'

'Yes.'

'Who?'

'A woman.'

'Come on, you can show us this village, and this woman.'

'I won't go. She gave me some bread, and you're going to kill her for it.'

'We're not going to kill her. Just show us who she is, then we'll believe you haven't been to the partisans.'

'No, I won't, I know you'll kill her.'

They hit him with their sticks and whips, but he stood firm: she'd given him bread, and they were going to kill her, so he wouldn't show them, and that was that.

A little boy of eight, yet he made up his story and just kept repeating, 'She gave me bread, and you're going to kill her.'

So, once again, it was the public square, once again the emaciated creatures resembling human beings, and once again my mother, now only with Olya. In the middle of the square Igor was kneeling down, with his hands tied behind his back. Behind him stood an SS man holding a pole-axe. Where they had got hold of it, I can't imagine. It was an ancient one, with a crescent-shaped head. I only know the SS used it to amuse themselves in the yard outside the commandant's office. They would make a child kneel down, with its hands tied behind its back, then they would order it to bend its head and they would then strike with the pole-axe. They bet each other to see who could split a child exactly in half with one blow. That's how they amused themselves in the commandant's yard; now the entertainment was for everyone.

Stalbe said to mother, 'Your grandson has been to the partisans. If he shows us the way, he'll live. If he won't, he'll die.'

'He doesn't know the way to the partisans,' mother replied.

Igor cried out, 'Granny, I'm frightened!'

'Don't be afraid,' she said. 'They won't do anything to you. Put down your head and shut your eyes.'

Igor bent his head and screwed up his eyes. The executioner, a real master, raised the pole-axe and split Igor exactly in half. The blood spurted out, but a leather apron protected the executioner from getting splashed.

Former schoolteacher Stalbe then announced, 'That's how we shall deal with any child found outside the ghetto. Remember that!'

Then he said to mother, 'Pick up your grandson, nobody else will do it for you.'

Mother took off some of her rags, wrapped Igor's bloody remains in them, and took them home. The same day, the burial team collected him and buried him at the cemetery.

Uncle Grisha was now faced with the question of what to do? To say that this was a serious question, and a serious problem, is to say nothing. The question was insoluble, so was the problem.

An uprising? In the entire ghetto, there were no more than a couple of dozen people who knew how to handle a gun, a handful of youths against regular troops. Where would they defend themselves? On two streets? In wooden houses? It only needed one house to be set on fire for the whole ghetto to go up, with all its inhabitants.

Make a break for the forest? A caravan of three thousand people, a crowd of fugitives, to break through cordons and barriers and cross open ground? Even supposing the fantastic possibility that they managed to get out of the ghetto and broke through into the forest, what then? How would you feed them, keep them together, defend them? Autumn was coming, soon it would be winter.

The alternative was to resign yourself to your fate, to lie down in the ditch next to your son or daughter, and expose the back of your neck to a German bullet, without putting up any righteous resistance, however hopeless, without raising your hand against your murderers. This was the least acceptable of all the options. They all offered death, only resistance offered death with honour.

So it was to be an uprising and escape to the forest. It was an unreal aim, but with no aim, there could be no activity. The rising would take place next morning, before the arrival of the *Sonderkommando*. As a diversion, Sidorov would launch an attack on the railway bridge, the same one, incidentally, I used to dive off to impress Sonya Vishnevsky. Le Court would send help to the bridge and, in order to reinforce the station, he would withdraw forces from the town.

It was a fantastic, desperate plan, but nothing else could be done. It was planned death, but death with dignity, it was the cost which the inhabitants of the ghetto would demand, and for which the Nazis would pay with their own lives.

That evening, Grisha and sixteen of his men mingled with the work columns. The sentries weren't checking them any more, they weren't counting or searching them, they were getting themselves ready for another, more important, action, and they were building up their hatred and hardness in preparation for that. They watched the people coming into the ghetto with the coldness of murderers; for them these people were already dead.

At midnight, in the cellar at grandfather's yard, Grisha gathered the twenty people with most authority, people others would follow.

But Grisha had grossly miscalculated. He had reasoned like a soldier, a fighter, and he hadn't reckoned that these people weren't soldiers and fighters. A year of unprecedented slavery and humiliation had killed their will to resist and instilled in them an animal fear of the Germans. So some of them had lost their nerve.

Well, yes, they were ready to resist, if they were taken out to be shot. But so far nobody was taking them out, maybe the barracks hadn't been got ready for a *Sonderkommando*, maybe there wasn't going to be any action. If they were to revolt, every single one of them would be slaughtered. People can resist when they're being murdered, but when nobody was trying to kill them, why should they throw themselves, unarmed, on to armed guards and armed troops, and run off into the forest where they would die anyway?

This was the feeling, mind you, of some of the people with most authority, and it reflected the mood of the ghetto, or at any rate a significant part of it. Grisha's plan was collapsing before his eyes.

Grisha was a bold man and he'd brought bold men with him. They were willing to take the desperate step of leading three thousand unarmed people into an attack on an enemy who was armed to the teeth. Whatever happened, it would at least be an attempt, it would be an act, it would be a fight. They had come for a fight and if they had to die, they would die fighting, like soldiers. To die without a fight, to go to their deaths out of solidarity, that they couldn't do, they hadn't the right, their lives weren't their own, they belonged to the struggle.

Grisha put the question this way: either they revolt right away, at four o'clock that morning, while the columns were forming up for work, or he and his men would leave right then and there. 'So, now, you decide, I can't force you!'

My mother, who had been listening in silence to the discussion, the way grandfather used to do, said, 'You're not men, you're mice! The Germans are right, you should be exterminated! You want to crawl away and hide in a corner, but there aren't any corners, they'll find you wherever you are! You say, there won't be an action? Then where are the eight hundred people from Cross Street? Don't you know the way to the ditch? They'll show you tomorrow, you'll walk along it for the last time. You say the people won't rise? In my house there are forty-six people who'll rise up as one man, the weak will follow the strong, the unarmed will follow the armed. We're going to fight, we're bound to die, but we'll die in our own house, not in the ditch.'

She said this to those who were against an uprising. To Grisha and his men, she said, 'If you want to leave, leave. If you want to leave your wives and children to die here, leave them. We'll fight on our own, we've got what we need, our children have got guns, and we've got axes, hammers, crow-bars, spades, stakes, fingernails, teeth, we'll tear their throats out!'

She turned to Venya Rakhlenko, Grisha's son.

'Venya, are you going with your father, or are you going to stay and defend us?'

And Venya replied, 'I'm going to stay here and fight.'

Grisha and his men realized they couldn't leave, as there was going to be an uprising, anyway. Those who were hesitant realized it, too.

During the night, mother went round the other houses and told everyone that next morning they were all going to be taken away and shot, so they must be prepared to resist, and to make a run for the forest. She was full of calm, powerful determination, which must have been transmitted to many of the others, especially as she spoke and acted quite openly, going from house to house openly, while the guard paid no attention to her.

At four o'clock in the morning, with the police still drowsy, the people started coming out on to the street and forming up in columns, many of them, as arranged, with axes, hammers, knives, and crowbars under their clothes, while the fighters had their pistols and sub-machine-guns.

But there were many houses from which nobody at all emerged, even those who should have come out to go to work in the forest. They had locked themselves in, barricaded their doors and windows, they had been seized by fear and were afraid to go out on to the street where death awaited them. We mustn't judge them, they were unarmed and terrified, and the fact that they didn't come out, but barricaded themselves in, was itself an act of resistance, it was the first time they had allowed themselves to break the rules.

That was the beginning of the uprising. The police started to break into the barricaded houses, and the chaos served as a signal. The first to fire at the police was Venya Rakhlenko, then the other youths started firing, and when the people saw that police had been shot, they threw themselves at the rest of them. It was like a detonator going off: when the snipers heard the pistol shots, they began picking off the sentries on the watch-towers, grenades were lobbed into the guard-house and as the S S ran out they were gunned down by machine-gun fire. Some attacked the police station next to the town hall, while others broke into the house where Stalbe lived and killed him, and another group broke into Commandant Reinhardt's house and killed his orderly, though Reinhardt himself managed to jump out of the window and there was no time to chase after him. Finally, there was a deafening roar, and the water-tower at the railway station flew into the air – that was the work of Sidorov's partisans. And during all the explosions, the shooting, the cries and moans and curses, the people moved out of the ghetto.

Some of the police managed to escape, however, and fire back, killing and injuring some of our people, and many S S also got away and fired back, as they ran towards the station. A sentry on one of the watch-towers managed to open up with his machine-gun on the crowd, and Commandant Le Court put the railway troops on full alert and mobilized soldiers who were either going on leave or returning from it. He called them all to arms, not to go in pursuit of the fugitives, but to defend the station. He had immediately radioed to the proper place, and S S units and *Sonderkommando* soon arrived in trucks.

While all this was happening, the path lay open and mother, holding Olya by the hand, led the people out of the ghetto, not by way of the main gates, which led towards the station, where the Germans were, but from the other end of Sand Street. They broke through the fence at grandfather's house, cut through the barbed wire, went round the edge of the town, then past the cemetery on to the road that led into the distant forest.

Six hundred people left the ghetto, the rest stayed behind. Those who had barricaded themselves in remained behind, as well as many who had come out but had fled back inside when the machine-gun on the watch-tower opened up and the streets ran with blood. And, of course, cripples and invalids stayed behind, and the sick, the feeble, old men and women, and anyone who was unable to move, as there were no stretchers to carry them on.

Grisha urged the people to move fast, the Germans would quickly collect themselves, their units would arrive, they would organize the pursuit, it was essential to get to the forest, to a particular place where two men were waiting with a machine-gun, and where it would be possible to organize some defence to hold off the enemy, though, as a matter of fact, it was nearly eight miles to that point. Now, Grisha hadn't expected that, while his men were assembling to leave, many of the young people wouldn't come out of their positions, but would go on firing from cover, in order to kill as many S S and police as possible. What did they know, these boys and girls ? They had enough courage to attack, but they didn't have the know-how to get out in time, they thought they were holding up the Germans, but in fact they were no longer doing any good where they were, it was all over. They were needed on the march, but they had stayed behind, and now they couldn't get out, either they were killed, or they joined the others in the barricaded houses.

Every fighter was important to Grisha – six hundred people make a long column, not a military column, a column of fugitives, seized with terror. He needed a large defence force for so many people, but what he had was a dozen partisans and a few boys and girls with guns.

Nevertheless, Grisha posted escorts ahead, on the flank, and in the rear, in the regular way. He left their first covering force at the cemetery, and a second one two miles further on, each of them to meet the pursuing forces on its own ridge. Of course, they would be slaughtered, of course, it was a death sentence, but, still, they would delay the enemy for a few precious minutes. Grisha couldn't spare extra men for the covering positions, it was necessary to protect the helpless, terrified people, who were heading for the unknown, with death behind them and in front of them, each one thinking only of his own salvation. At the first sign of panic, they would run in all directions, or rather shuffle – they were far too weak to run. The stronger of them were walking faster, hurrying to reach the forest. The weaker ones tried to keep up with them, but they hadn't the strength. They sat down at the side of the path, or they fell down and had to be picked up and pulled along, because to leave them for the enemy to defile would mean to turn the column into a herd of animals – animals don't carry their wounded with them, only human beings do that, as long as they remain human beings. They left behind only those who were already dead. There was no time to bury the dead and not enough strength to carry them. What strength there was was needed by the living. The column stretched out further and further, a long line of shuffling skeletons, falling down and getting up again, or not getting up, each one shuffling along on his own.

Suddenly, the people stopped. They heard shooting behind them and they saw tongues of flame leaping up into the sky. It was the ghetto burning and being destroyed.

Of course, the Germans could have waited to deal with it later, the ghetto wasn't going to fly away, they ought to have flung themselves into the pursuit. But fury and the thirst for revenge overcame them and they vented their rage on those who had stayed behind. The S S platoon that had come in by truck surrounded the rebellious ghetto and set about exterminating it right there, on the spot, in the streets. The S S tried to break into the barricaded houses where shots were being fired; they tossed in grenades, and when the people came running out, they mowed them down with machine-guns, and Sand Street and Hospital Street ran with blood. Yet people still tried to break through the cordon with whatever weapons they could find, but not one of them succeeded. When the resistance was broken and the fighters ran out of ammunition and were all killed, and the sound of shooting was no longer drowned by the cries and screams of the wounded, the avengers burst into the houses and finished off the cripples, the sick and the old; the dogs sniffed round the yards and the S S picked off the children who had hidden there. It was all over in a few hours, the ghetto was liquidated and nearly two thousand people found their graves in the ditch in the forest clearing. But they hadn't gone there themselves, they hadn't lain down in the ditch! Their corpses had been loaded on to trucks, driven into the forest, and thrown into the ditch. It had been necessary to exterminate the inhabitants of the ghetto in their own houses, the ghetto had put up resistance, it had exacted a price for its life, and it was wiped off the face of the earth. The Nazis never mentioned it, this shame and defeat of theirs, it is not even in the list of the fifty ghettoes we know about. But it did exist, it did fight, and it perished with honour.

Once they had finished with the ghetto, the Germans set off in pursuit of the fugitives, who were already getting close to the forest. The two covering forces had left their ambush and rejoined the main force, where they took up defence positions at the edge of the forest. They now had a machine-gun. The soldiers soon arrived, too, as they had no need to look for the path, which was marked out for them with corpses. But when they approached the forest, they were met by machine-gun, sub-machine-gun, and rifle fire.

Meanwhile, the fugitives went deeper into the forest. They were led by two partisans, Yevsey Kuznetsov and Kolya Gorodetsky, who were supposed to take them further, to the dense forest of Bryansk, where Sidorov's partisans were waiting, and where the Germans wouldn't dare to poke their noses. There were not more than four hundred of them left; the fighters stayed behind at the edge of the forest, and the others, who hadn't been able to survive the march, littered the melancholy scene with their bodies. But the forest, which they had to get through, was also big, over six miles across, and these people had already come eight and could go no further, especially as they had now left the open ground and so felt safe to a certain extent. They'd been told, 'The forest, we must get to the forest,' and now they'd got there, they were told they mustn't stop.

Mother said to Yevsey Kuznetsov, 'The people must rest. They can't go on.'

'No,' Yevsey replied. 'Grisha won't wait for long. And if they sit down, they won't get up.'

So they carried on, but more and more people kept falling down on the forest path, or stopping to lean against the trees.

So then mother said to Yevsey, 'You go on with those who can, and I'll stay with those who need at least a short break.

Leave Kolya to show us the way, and in half an hour I'll get them going again.'

Those who still had the strength went on with Yevsey, the rest sat down in a clearing, and mother went back for those who had fallen behind and brought them to the clearing.

◆

Then, in the presence of Kolya Gorodetsky, mother said to Olya, 'Ask Uncle Sidorov to send you to Chernigov, to a lawyer called Tereshchenko. Tell Tereshchenko that you're Rachel Rakhlenko's granddaughter. Kolya, will you tell Sidorov?'

'We'll tell him,' Kolya replied.

Mother then said to the people, 'Come on, get up, we can't stay here any longer, we must go on.' A few of them got up, but most of them hadn't the strength.

Then mother said, 'You hear those shots? That's your children dying to save you! You're not slaves any more, you're free, you're going to revenge the blood of your families and friends, you're going to make these monsters pay for your suffering, you're going to destroy them, like the mad dogs they are, because that's what you have to do with mad dogs. Find the strength to go on, come! Kolya, lead them!'

And the people found the strength in themselves to get up and shuffle along further. But mother didn't move, they shuffled past her, while she stood there and inspired strength in every one of them. It was hard to recognize the earlier Rachel Rakhlenko in this woman, though she was only forty-nine. Only the height and bearing of the original Rachel remained. Tall and straight, she stood without moving or leaving her place, but she was receding deeper into the forest for each person who went by her, her image faded, and she seemed to melt into the air and gradually disappear. And when the people looked back, she was no longer there. Nobody heard the sound of her footsteps or the crunch of twigs under her feet, she simply dissolved into the forest amid the motionless pines, she melted into the air, that was saturated with the sharp scent of resin, just as it had been when, as a girl of sixteen, she had sat in the forest with her Jakob, a boy with blue eyes, from Basel, Switzerland.

You think it's fantasy, or mysticism? Maybe. But, even so, nobody ever saw my mother again, alive or dead. She vanished, melted, dissolved into thin air in the pine forest, near the little town where she was born, where she'd lived her life, where she had loved and been loved, where, in spite of all the misfortunes, she'd been happy, where she'd brought up her children, raised her grandchildren and watched their terrible deaths, where she had endured more than any human heart can endure. But her heart did endure, and in the last minutes of her life she was able to be a mother to those wretched and unfortunate people, and to put them on the path of struggle and a dignified death.

Meanwhile, the battle at the edge of the forest continued. The Germans had no idea of their enemy's strength, so they took cover, fired off some shots at intervals, and waited for reinforcements. After an hour, Grisha sent on ten men and had twenty fighters left, then an hour later, he sent on another twelve, and that left him with eight.

When the SS arrived, the troops rose to the attack. The SS men were tall and strong. They were drunk, had no hats, and were wearing black shirts with rolled-up sleeves, bearing the skull and cross-bones. They ran at full height, and the machine-gun massacred the first rank. The second rank stepped over the dead, the third rank stepped over the second, and reached our boys, who went into hand-to-hand fighting with them. There were many Germans and police, and Grisha had all of eight men. They all died in the unequal battle. But the SS lost more than half their contingent and didn't go any further into the forest. Trucks came and carted off their dead and wounded, but the bodies of Grisha, his sons, Venya and Tolya, and of five other fighters, remained in the clearing. Next morning, the partisans collected them and took them away to the distant forest, where they buried them to a salute of twenty rifle salvoes.

About four hundred people arrived at Sidorov's. For many of them the dreadful march had been their last effort, their last hope had been fulfilled, and many were buried in the first week. Those who survived were either attached to Sidorov's partisan unit, or sent to join others, and the old and the sick were hidden away on farms by people who could be trusted, and there they lived out their last days. As mother had wanted, Olya was sent to Tereshchenko in Chernigov, and Tereshchenko took her in and became her father, she bears his name, Olga Tereshchenko. She now has two children of her own and, like her adoptive father, she is a lawyer, too. It was from Olya that I learned so much about the life and death of our family. She is the only witness left out of all of them.

The ghetto ceased to exist in September 1942, and the war ended in May 1945. Very few of those who got out of the ghetto are still alive; they either died in partisan battles, or later on in the army, when the partisans merged with our regular units, and those who survived have settled all over the country, scattered throughout the land; practically nobody went home, there was no home to go to.

Still, I did manage to discover a few partisans who were able to add some details to Olya's account, which she couldn't have known about. And these tough, brave men, who had been through just about everything a man can go through, confirmed that, before their eyes, my mother really did dissolve in the forest, she had simply melted away into thin air. They swore they had seen it with their own eyes. Maybe they didn't see it happen with their own eyes, maybe this legend arose like a hallucination in the minds of people who had reached their limit. The exodus from the ghetto had been a miracle, and when one miracle has been performed, another can occur, so the legend became rooted in people's minds as though it were reality, a fact.

But even Sidorov, who is still alive and whom I often see, even an old Communist like him, a man of sober mind and free of any superstition, when I asked him about mother, was not definite.

'I didn't see it myself, as your mother didn't reach us, but people say that's how it happened.' And he lowered his eyes. You see, as an old member of the Communist Party, the commander of a partisan detachment, a man who doesn't believe in God or the Devil, he didn't like to admit that he believed in mother's mysterious disappearance, so he gave an indefinite reply and looked away.

Before the war, there were several thousand Jews living in our town, now there are no more than two hundred. You already know what happened to those who remained under the Germans, and those who didn't either died in other battles or left with the evacuation and settled down in new places. It was mainly old people who came back, among them our barber, Bernard Semyonovich, still cheerful, grey-haired, but neat and fine-looking.

For many days, the old men wandered around the yards, the wasteland, along the roads, and through the woods and fields, collecting the remains of the dead in sacks. The corpses had decomposed, but Bernard Semyonovich could identify some of them by the hair – it seems the hair doesn't fall out after death. They also identified the remains of my sister, Dina. The S S had tied her to the cross with some old electric wire, which had remained on her bones, and that's how they knew it was Dina. They buried the remains of those they could identify at the cemetery, and the others they buried in a communal grave, the one the Nazis had dug in the forest. The old men wanted to move the communal grave to the cemetery, but it was impossible, several thousands had been killed, and in fact the cemetery no longer existed as, on the commandant's orders, the headstones had been pulled away, and the whole area ploughed over.

The remains of all ten Stashenoks were found, lying together, the way they had hanged together. I cabled Olesya, that is, Alexandrina Afanasyevna Stashenok, and she came, Maxim, her nephew, Andrey Stashenok's son, came, and we buried the remains of their family. Petrus, Stashenok's second son, couldn't attend the mournful ceremony, as he had been killed, fighting on the northern Donets.

We didn't find the remains of my father, Yakov Ivanovsky, though the neighbours pointed out exactly where he had been buried, a wasteland not far from our street, on the way to the river. I even found the man the police had ordered to dig the grave. But there was no grave to be found, only clean sand. We dug over the whole wasteland, and found nothing but sand, clean, dry, heavy sand. My father's remains had vanished without trace. Strange, isn't it?

I made frequent visits to the town, nearly every time I had time off, and I helped as much as I could. There was quite a bit to do, you know, to restore the old cemetery, to put the communal grave in order, to collect money for a memorial, to rebuild the fences. Alexandrina Afanasyevna Stashenok would come over, too, and we went together to the district committee of the Party and to the town soviet, where, of course, they were sympathetic, but had enough problems of their own. They had to rehabilitate the town and the factories, and get the agriculture going again, as everything had been smashed and destroyed. It is important to consider the living, that's true, but we cannot forget the dead, either, they won't be resurrected, they will live on only in our memories, and we have no right to deny them that, or to deprive them of it. I'd come, walk around, try and get something done, and when I got back to Moscow, I would write to

Sidorov. He had retired by then, he had time and he also did what he could to help – he had lived and worked and made war together with these people.

Then, I must admit, I started to go less often. My sons were growing up and demanding more of my attention, and at my age I had to have medical treatment from time to time, and my wife needed a rest. The last time I was there was 1972, September, the thirtieth anniversary of the uprising and destruction of the ghetto.

Sidorov came with me to the cemetery. The fields all round were turning into autumn gold, we went by the path, along which they used to carry the dead from the ghetto, and along which my mother, Rachel, and my Uncle Grisha had led the living. They had rehabilitated the cemetery and fenced it off and, where the graves had been, they had planted young silver birches, which had already grown tall, standing in straight lines and rustling their leaves above the unnamed graves. Inside the fence was space for new graves, where they would bury those who would die in their own time.

It was a sad picture, the deserted cemetery, almost without headstones, without monuments, without inscriptions, without flowers. Where were the graves of my forefathers? Where lay grandmother, Uncle Lazar, my brother Sasha, my little nephew Igor?

Sidorov and I stood for a while in silence, then we went to the communal grave, in the pine-wood, near Oryol's old veranda, where he used to sell *kefir* and ice-cream, where people used to relax in their hammocks, and where, once upon a time, my young father and mother had sat and tried to speak to each other in different languages, and where they were able to understand each other in only one language, the great language of love.

There were some other people at the communal grave, a few locals, some old men, some middle-aged, and some young people who had grown up here since the war. Some of them knew my mother Rachel, my father Yakov, my brave grandfather Rakhlenko, some of them didn't. But their grandmothers and grandfathers, and their fathers and mothers and sisters and brothers, were lying here, too, lying in this vast ditch where, unarmed and helpless, they had been massacred by machine-guns.

A large slab of black granite had been erected above the grave, and on it was engraved, in Russian: 'To the eternal memory of the victims of the German Fascist invaders.' Below it was an inscription in Hebrew.

Next to me stood Sidorov, an ex-miner, then manager of the shoe factory, then a partisan commander, and now a pensioner. He had been born in the Donbass, but he'd lived here a long time, he knew everything, understood everything through and through.

He pointed to the inscription in Russian and Hebrew and asked me, quietly, 'Tell me, Boris, did they translate the Russian text right?'

As a child, probably until I was eight or nine, I had gone to *kheder*, then I transferred to a Russian school and I'd long ago forgotten the Hebrew characters.

Yet, nearly sixty years later, those letters and those words came back to me from the unknown and eternal depths of my memory, I remembered them, and I read:

'*Venikoisi domom loi nikoisi.*'

The meaning of those words is 'Everything is forgiven, but those who have spilled innocent blood shall never be forgiven.'

Seeing that I was slow to reply, Sidorov gave me a look, he understood, the old fox, and again he asked,

'Well, did they get it right?'

'Yes,' I said. 'It's right, it's exact.'

Yalta – Peredelkino
1975–7